ANOTHER NUMBER FOR THE ROAD

a Cory Goodwin Mystery

ANOTHER NUMBER FOR THE ROAD

a Cory Goodwin Mystery

C J Verburg

When rock-protest guitarist Dan Quasi
reappears after 20 years to play for an
upscale exchange program, journalist
Cory Goodwin wants to know why.
A free trip to Paris? A new revolution?
Or a cover for murder?

https://boom-books.com

For Everybody Who Helped

That's too many people to list here, so
Special thanks to Big Sixteen, who made this book possible:
Jeremy Brown (keyboards, vocals)
Billy Conway (drums & percussion, vocals)
Joel Gramolini (guitar, vocals)
Evan Harriman (keyboards, vocals)
Rhandy Simmons (bass)
John Kwasie (sound)
Also to Neil Young for an inspired title, song,
and lifetime of music.
Thanks also to JoAnn Verburg, Bonnie Verburg, Ira Ingber (guitar
& production), Gregg McBride, Mitch Throop, Sara Neustadtl,
and Brenda Reinertson.
And three who passed on too soon: Howard Boyer,
Mark Sandman, and Jim Spellmeyer.

Music links and credits are at the end of this book.
A QR code reader also gives you the option of listening to four live
original songs at the point when you read about them.

If you enjoy the book, please tell your friends and post a review!

Intro

We do on stage the things that are supposed to happen off.
Which is a kind of integrity, if you look on every exit
being an entrance somewhere else.

—Tom Stoppard

Two nights ago I stayed up till dawn singing rock-&-roll, gospel, and blues with old friends and strangers in a bar near the Rio Grande. We'd come here across many miles and years to celebrate a life most of us didn't quite believe was over. *Paul della Costa, musician, age 67. On his Texas ranch, following a brief illness.*

How could a man with so much lust for life be plucked out of it by a brief illness?

Endings leave you standing on a cliff edge, but also at a crossroads. Now what? Which path should I take from here?

This death has opened a path I blocked off twenty years ago.

That was before the information age took hold. The media were still plural. Cell phones and the Internet hadn't yet turned the world global. News was as precious and elusive as truffles. You had to sniff it out. Dig for it. Track down rumors. Stick close to people who stirred things up. When an ordinary moment blew up into a headline, the only way to know was to be there.

And if you were there, you could decide what to say about it.

Twenty years ago, a harsher death than this one dumped me at a much more dangerous crossroads. I had to choose on the spot: agree to bury some key facts, or report the whole truth and risk several lives?

I chose the cover-up.

Being a detective's daughter, I got the whole story anyway. And being a journalist, I wrote it down.

Now that agreement has expired.

Now I can tell you what really happened.

Contents

Chapter 1: Magical Mystery Tour

The swan boats in the Public Garden were tied up for the night, and the Goodyear blimp was nosing toward Fenway Park, when I walked between two seven-foot gold lions into the Faneuil Plaza Hotel.

Across the street behind me stood a glass tower topped by the notorious penthouse where my onetime idol Mickey Ascher died. Past that was the river-view condo where I'd been holed up since January.

Two provocations had brought me here on this balmy spring evening. One was the invitation in my purse: *Please join Hands Across the Sea, 7 PM Friday, June 3. An Adventure in International Good Will!* A handwritten note added: *Hope to see you J.O.* The ink was blurred by a damp rust-colored stain. Blood? Pizza sauce, more likely. I'd fished it out of the trash after provocation #2.

"Hey, Cory."

Three syllables and I had to set down my teacup. "Rik?"

"Long time. How's the teaching biz? Done for the summer?"

"Fine. How's the media biz?"

"Busy busy, same as ever. You ready to have some fun?"

Not the question I'd braced for.

His voice lowered. "Your mission, if you choose to accept it, is to infiltrate Hands Across the Sea's kickoff bash and find out if their so-called Mystery Band is a scoop or a crock."

Was this a threat? *Help me out here or read about your not-officially-a-separation in "Names and Phases"?*

"I thought Hands Across the Sea's gimmick was a Mystery Destination. Pay your plane fare and you might wake up in an igloo or a grass hut."

"Yeah. Peace Corps for the fast track." Rik blew out cigarette smoke. "Sponsored by the Commonwealth of Massachusetts and the Greater Boston Chamber of Commerce. Can you see Jerry

Leroy and John Otis dropping a planeload of socially conscious, upwardly mobile professionals anyplace without fresh-ground coffee and the Sunday Times?"

"I don't have to. I quit, remember?"

Remember? Walking off the bus into Rik Green's office at Phases; handing him my first story. I and a hundred other grungy, sleep-deprived college students from Western Mass had spent the previous weekend protesting the Vietnam war in D.C., where I'd interviewed lead singer Mickey Ascher and guitarist Dan Quasi of The Rind. I was a nineteen-year-old English major. And Rik waved his blue pencil and turned me into a journalist.

"I'm not asking you to cover it. Just find out what the Silver Fox has got up his sleeve."

"Why? Come on, Rik. You can't believe Aerosmith or Pat Metheny would spend five days in some Mystery Destination with a bunch of yuppies."

"Cory. *Plausible* doesn't make news. But if it's *true*, we could be talking Fourth of July cover."

That shut me up. As Rik knew very damn well, there was a time when I'd gladly have woken up in an igloo or a grass hut for a cover story in Phases.

But July 4 was also the deadline Larry Thorne and I had set for deciding, like King George III and the American colonists, whether to reunite or declare independence.

I turned over my sodden tea tag as if it might hold a clue.

Darjeeling. *You are about to embark on a journey.*

The Faneuil Plaza's matchboxes call it "Boston's most accommodating institution." While corporate executives plot America's future in the Revere Room, you can lounge beside a palm tree in the Plaza Court, watch water splashing from a dolphin's mouth, and nibble triangular sandwiches from a tiered silver tray.

I discovered this oasis during my first Thorne Cosmetics sales conference two years ago. After we'd all toasted my husband's decision to join the family firm, I slipped out of the Grand Ballroom and commemorated the event privately by scratching my initials on one of the Plaza Court's marble tabletops with his great-grandmother's diamond.

CGT. Cordelia Goodwin Thorne. Named for King Lear's daughter by my godfather, a New York private detective; nick-named Cory by my socialite mother. My father stayed out of it, since he worked for the one and adored the other. My parents were married but didn't live together—the same arrangement in which, for different reasons, I now found myself.

Waves of cocktail chatter lapped at the twin cupids on the rococo barometer by the front desk. Those must be Hands Across the Sea's upscale professionals milling around the name-tag tables: Hosts and Ambassadors. A pair of paunchy polyester sales types at check-in were ogling the women in their summer dresses.

Sales types, we used to call them in Paris . . .

A red-jacketed waiter wedged past me with a tray of champagne balanced on his shoulder. Through the ballroom doors . . . and he was gone, vanished in a flurry of grabbing hands.

Piranhas. My fingers closed around my evening bag, where my notebook nestled like a pearl-handled revolver.

But that was where I'd find John Otis.

Inside the Grand Ballroom I scanned the hors d'oeuvres tables. Any clues to the Mystery Destination? Skewers of tandoori chicken and teriyaki beef, mini-quiches, finger-sized egg rolls . . . A secretive devil, the Silver Fox.

For our wedding reception he'd served Gulf shrimp and Oysters Rockefeller. And Mumm's Cordon Rouge—homage to our whirlwind French courtship. We'd been married in the eyes of the law before we left Paris, but it took the massive Episcopal pageant mounted by Elizabeth Thorne to sanctify us in the eyes of Boston. I didn't want it; Larry didn't want it. What deal our parents cut, I never found out. Mine showed up long enough for Archie to walk me down the aisle and Lily to fly us to her Montana ranch for a week's honeymoon. Knowing that this time tomorrow I'd be riding a horse up Sandy Spring Trail got me through a halluci-natory day. Standing under a crystal chandelier for what felt like hours, one white glove peeled back from my wrist, a champagne glass in my hand where my notebook should have been . . .

Someone bumped my elbow and I clutched my evening bag. Then let it swing back on its gold chain: socially conscious, upwardly mobile professionals don't purse-snatch.

"Cory!" said a hearty voice. "So glad you made it. What a dress! And those earrings!"

We exchanged air-kisses. "Lovely party, John."

He did look like a fox—wavy silver hair, gray silk suit, sharp nose, inscrutable smile. "Where's your glass? Here, wait. Pierre! Open a bottle of the Mumm's for Mrs. Thorne."

I pretended to adjust my hair, secured in a figure-eight by a gold barrette. What was I doing here? If I'd learned anything in the past five months, it was that Larry's and my friends, like our wedding presents, fell into two piles: His and Hers.

"Needless to say, you and I aren't drinking anything bottled in New York State." John handed me a tulip glass. "School's done for the year? How'd you like it? Teaching literature to young ladies?"

"Fine. Easier than writing feature stories."

"That's just what Larry said to me last week about being a VP at TC. 'Hell of a lot easier than writing a novel.'"

I clung to my smile.

"We had lunch. A short one—he had to get back for a new product meeting."

"I guess when you're dealing with eye shadow, timing is crucial."

John set down his glass. "Cory, the first time I met you, you told me writing was the most important thing in your life. Larry, too. The core of your relationship."

I thought: He can't have talked to Larry about this, or he'd know what a rotten core it turned out to be.

"Don't you miss it? Seeing your name in print? Chasing wherever your story leads till you track it down?"

"Spending the night in a snowbound airport? Scrounging a bag of pretzels from a hotel vending machine at two AM because the plane was late and they didn't hold the rental car and room service closed hours ago?"

"You didn't mind when you were doing it."

"Maybe I've grown up."

I reached into my purse. John's eyes followed my hand: not the right one, pulling out cigarettes, but the left one with its empty finger where Larry's great-grandmother's diamond used to be.

"So, I hear every Hands Across the Sea exchange includes a Mystery Band."

"That's right." John flicked his lighter. "New Orleans sent a Dixieland combo. Munich's nuts about jazz; who knew? Dallas sent country western. Lot of dancing. New York sent a string quartet, not a big hit."

"And Boston?"

"I'm mum. Like the champagne."

"Why? Isn't this the night when mysteries get solved?"

"Not that one. I tell you, Cory—"

A burst of static drowned him out. A short blonde woman on the ballroom stage was blowing into a microphone.

"Ladies and gentlemen! I'm delighted to welcome you to Hands Across the Sea's gala kickoff party. At last, the moment we've all been waiting for! Are you excited?"

"Sheila Bailey," John murmured. "Gordon's wife? Bank of Boston?"

"Now, in just a moment, I'm going to introduce our our Mystery Guest, who'll give us clues so we can guess our host city. But first I'd like to thank just a few of the many many people—"

"Host *city?*" I sipped champagne. "What happened to the grass hut?"

"Metaphorical. This is all about networking. Opening new doors for the technology and products created by our partners in the Greater Boston area. You saw the logo? A globe with a keyboard."

"Ah. And what is the Mystery Destination?"

"Paris."

The string of bubbles rising from the bottom of my glass scattered like pearls.

"Nice, eh? If I was thirty years younger— Oh, wait." A man

in a red jacket was waving from the doorway. "That'll be the governor. Want to come say hi?"

Spotlights, cameras, aides patting down Jerry Leroy's too-brown hair, turning his sagging profile best side out. "No thanks."

"If I'm not back in ten, come to my office and we'll have a drink at the Plaza Court."

He strode across the gold and blue carpet, purposeful as a bullet.

Paris. John Otis, you bastard.

In my head Joni Mitchell sang the song Larry and I used to play in our flat near the Place St. Augustin. *I was a free man in Paris: I felt unfettered and alive!* No demands to satisfy but our own. Nobody to please but each other.

"And now," Sheila Bailey blinked out at us, "I'm thrilled to introduce this gentleman, whose name I can't tell you because it might give away the surprise! So listen carefully and see if you can guess our Mystery Destination!"

I'd met him the very first night of my summer assignment. Standing on a balcony where I'd fled for a cigarette break, eager to go explore that rooftop landscape, dizzy from jet-lag and Bordeaux and chatting with people I didn't know in a language I'd half forgotten; when a breezy American voice inquired, "Hey, are you the Cory Goodwin who writes for Phases?"

Since Larry and I (so he said) were probably the last two writers in Montparnasse, we left the party for our own moveable feast. Aperitifs at the Café Sélect, where we scanned the bar for Hemingway look-alikes. Supper at the Restaurant aux Artistes: walls like a tattooed lady which Larry assured me really were painted by starving artists in trade for meals. Then onward to the Boul' Mich', to toast *la vie en rose* with a Pernod and watch the sidewalk parade of tourists, vendors, and bohemians. The Pernod, which struck both of us at the time as a poor substitute for cognac, took on a glow of nostalgia back home over Courvoisier on Chestnut Street.

My mother's friend who'd hosted the party called to warn me off. Thorne Cosmetics. Loads of money. A committed bachelor. Hard-nosed, hard-headed, and too damn charming for his own good. A trail of broken hearts from California to the Côte d'Azur.

But who could believe such a string of clichés? Not Cory Goodwin, international journalist. Anyway, it wasn't like I planned to marry the guy. Marriage to me was the Emerald City, a happy ending miles and miles down the Yellow Brick Road.

Onstage the nameless gentleman was tossing out clues. Famous monuments! Museums! Monarchs! The crowd leaped on each tidbit as avidly as it had devoured the hors d'oeuvres.

Harrison and Elizabeth Thorne apologized in advance for not meeting us at Logan Airport. The fall sales conference, Elizabeth explained—her voice a tinny buzz from the antique receiver pressed to Larry's ear. Harrison's keynote address on Retail Strategies for the Twenty-First Century. I'd guessed her first question from Larry's answer: "Of course it was legal, Mother. The man at the registry said my only requirement was to obtain the lady's consent." Then, his smile fading: "He didn't ask for yours. Just Cory's."

"Rome! Athens!" A hysterical young woman stood on her chair waving both arms at the stage. All over the ballroom people were shrieking, thumping each other on the back, splashing champagne on John Otis's carpet. The tables were littered with forgotten dolma and Swedish meatballs.

I yanked my notebook out of my evening bag. Enough! One circuit to look for the Mystery Band, then find John and get the hell out of here.

My high heels teetered on the soft carpet, forcing me to slow down. A familiar *frisson* of panic prickled the back of my neck. I reminded myself that I wasn't Mrs. Thorne Cosmetics tonight, nobody was watching me, there was no reason to be so edgy—

A slant of light from the chandelier glittered off the sequins on a pink satin shirt.

There were two of them. The young man in the pink shirt had hair so short it looked like iron filings. He stood with his arms folded, staring at the stage. His friend, in a white poodle jacket and sprayed-on black pants, shifted and glanced around as if she couldn't figure out what was taking these people so long. Her mop of brown hair was pinned up haphazardly with little plastic bows. One curl had gotten loose and tickled her neck. She scratched absently.

No way could those two be ambassadors for Hands Across the Sea.

I started to go ask them and stopped. If I were in a Mystery Band, would I spill it to a lady in a silk dress and gold designer jewelry?

Too late. He muttered something to her and stalked off, head down, thumbs in his studded leather belt. I knew that slouch: half hoping nobody will recognize you and half disappointed that nobody does.

"Hey, and Niko? Bring me some more shrimps," she called after him.

I sidled up beside her. "Aren't you Lacey Sky? The keyboard player?"

She looked at me, surprised and pleased. Her eyes were black-rimmed, smudged with purple above and below. "Yeah."

"Cory Thorne. We met at the homeless benefit concert last fall. My husband's company was a sponsor."

"Oh, sure." Lacey grinned apologetically. I could see she didn't remember.

"That was a great set you did with Magic Fingers."

"Wow. Thanks."

"Are you involved with—?"

"This? Yeah."

"Five days in Paris? Not bad."

She grinned. "When we've never even played in public. Bizarro, huh? Terry said these guys are rolling." Her arms waved, taking in bars, buffet, and chandeliers. "Too bad I hate champagne."

My heart thumped. How many Terrys could there be in Boston's music scene?

"Terry Morrissey?"

Lacey frowned and ran a finger across her mouth: Lips sealed.

"What, it's a secret? Like the Mystery Destination?" A wary

nod. "Then won't they announce it tonight?"

"Not till the plane leaves. Everybody'll know then because we're on it."

"You and Niko and Terry? And who else?"

She stared at me, stricken. "I can't talk about it."

"Only till Wednesday, right? So . . .?"

"That's the deal. Zero publicity." Shaking her frizzy head. "What are you, a reporter?"

"Me? No. Not exactly." I felt my cheeks heating. "Not lately."

"Oh." Lacey looked at me as though she didn't know how to take that—fair enough, given that I didn't either. "What'd you say your name was?"

"Cory Goodwin. I used to— I sometimes write for magazines. In fact the first piece I ever published was an interview in *Phases* with The Rind."

"Oh yeah?"

"When I was in college. Their free concert at the demonstration in D.C. over Nixon's bombing of Cambodia."

I could see she'd never heard of it. "Right after *Outta Sight, Out of Rind* came out."

"Oh, wow! Awesome, huh? That album's why I'm in this band. I hardly even ever *heard* The Rind until a couple months ago. But when Roach and me moved out here, he kept going, 'Lacey, you won't fucking believe this!' And I'm going, 'But who *are* these guys?' So he plays me *Outta Sight, Out of Rind*. Both disks." She sighed. "Wicked hot! The first night we went over there, I was shaking. I thought Dan would be seven feet high and glowing, like Darth Vader."

But I was thinking: The Rind is reuniting. Dan Quasi's re-emerged from wherever he's been hiding for the past twenty years. He's brought back Terry and Roach, and hired two kids to replace Mickey Ascher. And they're going to Paris on Wednesday night with Hands Across the Sea.

I must be hallucinating.

"So you met Roach, huh?" said Lacey. "I always wondered. What was he like back then?"

"I only talked to Dan Quasi and Mickey Ascher. And their manager."

"Oh." Lacey thought this over. "You'll probably still recognize Dan. Roach says he's changed, though. Terry, too."

"They're not *here*?"

"Nah. They OD'd on this kind of deal. Not me, man. Yo! Room service! Big silver bucket of Jack Daniel's!"

"Does Hands Across the Sea have room service?"

Lacey's nose wrinkled. "They better! Terry's working on it. *They* wanted to put us in all different houses, like the ambassadors."

I shook my head sympathetically, less for the band than for those five unsuspecting French host families.

A wave from the doorway: Niko, shrimpless, beckoning to Lacey.

"Gotta go."

I remembered John Otis waiting for me in his office. "Me too."

We walked together toward the lobby. In her theatrical eye make-up, her fluffy white jacket, shiny black pants, and spike-heeled boots, Lacey drew stares. If they only knew.

I opened my purse to find change for the phone. Behind us a shout rose, as a taped brass band struck up "I Love Paris."

I looked at Lacey, she looked at me, and we both laughed.

"To Paris!" I raised my champagne glass.

She picked up a half-full plastic cup from under a potted palm. "Room service!" She sniffed it, then downed it in a gulp. "See you Wednesday."

No! Should I tell her? On Wednesday I was meeting my mother in New York. I'd be listening to a young friend of hers play Bartok and Brahms when Phases' potential July 4 cover boarded their plane for Paris.

I shut my purse. Rik Green could wait. I needed to talk to John Otis.

Chapter 2: I Can See for Miles

Whose hotel room I was walking into I didn't know. Graham Douglas, The Rind's manager, had given me only the number on the phone, and the time: noon. Early for musicians.

The king-sized bed was unmade—sheets twisted, pillows and blankets spilling onto the floor. Half-empty plates, beer bottles, and coffee cups littered the furniture. From the bathroom came the hiss of a shower. A leftover groupie?

"This is Cory Goodwin," said Graham Douglas as he led me to a window alcove.

He didn't need to tell me who they were. Dan Quasi cradled a cup of coffee in his hands—those long flat fingers that could pull such heart-wrenching music from a guitar. Mickey Ascher sprawled in his chair gazing at nothing, a faraway sparkle in his eyes.

Mad Mick, the fan magazines called him. Dominating the stage with fringe and feathers and blond hair that gleamed in the spotlight, and the voice of a fallen angel luring souls to Hell. While Dan Quasi paced through the shadows like a panther, lean and intense, his guitar cord trailing behind him, dark hair curling with sweat.

"And what were they like?" John Otis prompted.

He regarded me across his smoked-glass desk. Half an inch of shirt cuff made a neat margin between his wrist and his gray silk sleeve. His fingertips clicked noiselessly, impatiently, over the buttons on his phone.

I smiled. "Terrifying."

"Oh, Christ."

"They were rock musicians!" How to convey what that meant in those days? "Arrogant, sexy as hell, charming when they felt like it, rude when they didn't. Furious about Kent State and the Cambodia bombing—but so were we all."

"Were they involved in the protest?"

"Sure. Music and politics were intertwined then, remember. And everybody under thirty opposed the war."

Clutching my notebook and my Instamatic camera in clammy hands, my throat dry. "Dan, Mickey, you've talked a lot about the role of rock music—and musicians—in the antiwar movement. What's your role at this demonstration?"

And Dan Quasi, staring me down through cold blue eyes: "Nixon says he represents the American people. We've had more people come to our concerts and buy our records than Richard Nixon got votes. We're here to speak for our people. Stop the bombing! Stop the goddam war!"

Leaning forward for emphasis; while I struggled to focus on what he was saying and not on the glint of gold in the V of his shirt. A good luck charm? A love token?

Then Mickey, half a beat late, with a bright artificial smile that chilled my heart: "Our people want to make *love*, not war!"

John Otis's fingers interlocked on his desk. "Did The Rind stay mixed up in politics after Vietnam?"

"I don't know. They broke up around the time Nixon resigned."

"Then what?"

His foxlike features, the way he was looming at me across the smoked glass, made me reluctant to answer. I found myself choosing my words, as if The Rind were not a thing to be dissected so casually. "You know what happened to Mickey Ascher."

"Beaten to death with a champagne bottle by an unknown assailant. Right over there," John pointed at the window. "I spoke to the detective in charge. He says, a welcome-home party that went off the rails. Ascher'd just got out of rehab. His manager found him. Doug something? Could've been anybody—thirty or forty people in and out of there—except he'd kicked them all out at midnight. So definitely Ascher let in his killer. The cops jumped on the manager first, only other key, then the band. Dan Quasi claimed he was out of town, couldn't prove it. But why would he want to kill his partner and best friend?"

"He offered a reward."

"Fifty K," John affirmed. "Lot of money back then. Didn't

stop the media circus. Every news outlet on the East Coast had a crew here. I could've got three hundred a night for a broom closet. Quasi was in and out of HQ like a revolving door, but in the end he was released without charge."

"So was *Grind*," I said. "Instant platinum. But The Rind was over."

"And Dan Quasi . . . ?"

"Disappeared. Nobody's heard from him in twenty years. Congratulations, John."

"Yeah. We're betting, twenty years, no arrests, cold case, sixties revival, there's more up side than down side PR-wise." He flexed his fingers. "I'll tell you, though, Cory. I'd rest easier if I had somebody going to Paris with them. Just to keep an eye out."

His eyes were on the pair of chairs across from his desk. I've never sat in one. With their gray pin-striped upholstery, they look too much like executives who've been shot and stuffed.

"What about Sheila Bailey?"

"Sheila's a mother hen, not a journalist."

"I thought your deal with the band was no media."

"Not up front. But when they get back . . ." His eyes met mine. "Didn't you say you talked to Rik Green?"

"Didn't you say the governor's office is sending a PR guy?"

"Hah! Some crony of Jerry's from a radio—"

The door slammed open with a bang like a gunshot.

I froze.

The Governor of Massachusetts strode to John's desk, halted, and clamped one hand on each of the former executives.

"Dammit, John! Who the hell picked these criminals for Hands Across the Sea?"

His eyes were flashing. On his cheeks glowed crimson spots —and not, I judged, the work of his make-up department.

"What criminals would that be, Jerry?"

"Murder suspects! Known ringleaders of the New England antiwar movement! Burned their draft cards right here on Boston Common! And we're sending them to Paris to represent our business community?"

John eyed the governor as if wishing he were shot and

stuffed. "If you're talking about the Mystery Band—"

"Damn right!"

"—we've been over this. The French committee requested them, because back in the day of burning draft cards—and may I remind you, that was twenty years ago?—they drew bigger crowds than the Red Sox."

"Unsolved Mysteries wasn't twenty years ago. It's airing in three weeks. I just saw the trailer. Their leader, slaughtered like an animal! Bludgeoned to death! Found half naked on a polar-bear rug after an orgy in his penthouse, drenched with blood and champagne! Is this the image we're out to project? Accused killers? Rabble-rousers who led a thousand kids on a rampage through Washington, D.C.? Who had to be dispersed by riot police with tear gas?"

The way he spluttered you'd have thought The Rind was whipping up a mob in the Faneuil Plaza lobby. I kept still, though I'd have liked to ask Jerry Leroy if he'd ever dodged police clubs and choked his lungs out on tear gas.

"Governor?" A red-faced young man poked his head in. "GBH is ready for you in the Adams Room."

"Jerry," said John. "Eighty-two percent name recognition. No other Hands Across the Sea exchange comes close."

"One minute," said Jerry Leroy. "Dammit, John, I will not send a bunch of goddam subversives to Paris!"

Subversives. Dan, Mickey, Roach, and Terry. My roommate Penny and me and our busload of comrades from Mount Holyoke, Amherst, Smith, and UMass. A hundred thousand young Americans gathered in our nation's capital, high on Spring, outraged by the Kent State massacre and the Cambodia bombing, wound up from the tension of finals, jubilant at finally getting the chance to tell Richard Nixon what to do with his war. The mood all over the city was heady. It's our turn now! You could feel it in the crowd that filled the Ellipse for the speeches and the music. Jackets and shirts off, pale skin open to the sun after a long winter. Joints passing from hand to hand: peace pipes on the eve of battle.

And from those four specks on the makeshift stage thundered "Government Man," The Rind's explosive hit from the

'68 Chicago convention. Anger and comradeship swept the crowd. People were finding space to dance, linking arms, waving fists, shouting. When the song ended a thousand warriors surged into the street. Look out, you bastards, here we come!

The cops were ready. In minutes the ragged army was on the run, fleeing tear gas that seemed to come from everywhere, so that you ran and choked and didn't know if you were getting away or in deeper, and fuck! here came some more cops, and you didn't know where you were going but you kept running, the asphalt hot and hard under your feet, till suddenly you were panting in some unfamiliar street and it was all over. An eight-foot cast-iron fence toppled, the papers said later, and three dozen arrests.

"What do I tell Monsieur Tréville?" The governor brushed off an aide straightening his tie. "Not a problem? These troublemakers we're sending you are a media magnet?"

"They're not troublemakers, for god's sake." John was exasperated. "So they burned their draft cards. Played rock music at a few demonstrations. So what? You're talking kid stuff. Wild oats. Nothing *dangerous*."

Nothing dangerous. We took over the streets of our nation's capital, fought with police, helped to oust the President of the United States; and now John Otis could sit here behind a smoked-glass desk and say The Rind had done nothing dangerous.

"I'm telling you, Jerry. When word gets out about this band? The press'll be on you like cabbage on corned beef. And I don't mean WGBH. I'm talking Barbara Walters. Johnny Carson."

"I don't care if—" The governor halted in mid-sentence. "What?"

"Front page of the Globe *and* the Herald. Now, *go*, will you? Don't keep your public waiting."

For a moment Jerry Leroy teetered. He frowned. He shrugged. Then he wheeled and marched down the hall.

Of course, I unclenched my fists, John's right. Who's into revolution nowadays? If a Rind reunion is news, it's as the soundtrack for a nostalgia trip, not a new assault on the system. We *are* the system. With Eldridge Cleaver out stumping the lecture circuit, with Bobby Seale marketing barbecue, what's Hands

Across the Sea got to fear from a couple of old rock musicians?

Yet in my heart I couldn't accept it. Lou Reed might pitch motorcycles; Eric Clapton might sell beer; but that Dan Quasi would play "Government Man" and "Tear It Up" for two hundred upwardly mobile, socially conscious professionals—

"I need a drink," said John. "Shall we?"

"Who's Monsieur Tréville?"

He grimaced. "One of our French supporters who's got a bug up his butt about The Rind. Or, I should say, Quasi & Company. New age, new identity, they tell us, and it damn well better be true. Your father-in-law calls Victor Tréville a conservative crusader— Reagan with a dash of Ross Perot. He's some kind of honcho in a big public-private development zone outside Paris. Marne-la-Vallée?"

Aha. "Thorne Cosmetics and EuroDisney."

John nodded. "Harrison said he was instrumental with the TC siting in '80-'81. They met ten years earlier, when Tréville was at the French consulate here in Boston."

"Is that where he got spooked by The Rind?"

"Could be. The thing is, why jump on us? It was their committee who asked for this band."

"You said that before. Who asked for them? The Rind broke up twenty years ago. Rik Green didn't even know if Dan Quasi was alive."

"Search me." John rose. "You interviewed them. What do you think? Is this Quasi & Company a front to go over and blow up Paris with the Weathermen?"

I laughed. "Like Errol Flynn left Hollywood to go rob the rich in Sherwood Forest?"

But as John and I stepped into the foyer, an old pulse was quickening in my blood.

Gonna lighten up my load!

Gonna leave this road behind me!

A hundred thousand joyful voices joining those four silhouettes on the stage and their backup choir from a D.C. church. Penny and I singing till our throats were ragged, clapping the beat, craning past love beads and ponytails, hands waving in the V sign of peace. Surely a nation that's landed a man on the moon can end war!

> *Got to get back to the time*
> *when my mind was full of wonder,*
> *And this burden that I'm under,*
> *It won't weigh me down no more!*

Our childhood dreams cast aside—no more going to the chapel to get married when your boyfriend was hiding out from the draft in Canada or holed up in the psych library devising a 4-F. Our destiny was ambitious but clear: We would forge a new era, the Age of Aquarius, when bombers would turn into butterflies and Richard Nixon would drown in music, love, and flowers.

"Cory?"

"Tell you what," I said. "If you can change a ticket to New York for a seat on that plane, you've got yourself a journalist."

Chapter 3: 2000 Light Years from Home

Sheila Bailey, her blonde curls squashed on one side, led us off the plane into the surreal brightness of l'Aéroport Roissy-Charles de Gaulle.

I still didn't see my photographer, Wendy Peres. Since I wasn't meeting a host family, I'd hoped we could catch up and make plans before I headed for the village of Fraises-des-Bois. John Otis had granted my wish to stay outside the city with a room at his friend Gaston Vlaemenck's country inn, halfway between tonight's opening banquet in Paris and Sunday night's farewell party at EuroDisney.

I hadn't seen the band yet, either, beyond a glimpse of denim and black leather, an acid-green sleeve (Lacey?), and a tall tangle of hair (Roach?). They'd boarded last, sat up front, and shut the curtain after takeoff.

Rik Green had chortled at the news. So Quasi's pulling a Rip vanWinkle! High time. Best guitar player who ever came out of Boston.

"Phases' Fourth of July cover?"

Silence.

What about Unsolved Mysteries? Ringleaders of the New England protest movement? Sex, drugs, revolution, and murder? Project sponsors on both sides of the Atlantic up in arms?

"Smoke." He was succinct. "I'm seeing page six here. You want the cover, find me a fire."

"Such as?"

"Will Quasi bomb the Eiffel Tower? Did he whack Mickey Ascher?"

"I'm not a detective, Rik, I'm a journalist."

I could hear his grin over the phone. "Two days ago you were a schoolteacher."

Now I was Hands Across the Sea's official media consultant. John Otis gave me one order: "Any fire you find? Put it out!"

I waited till I got to Logan Airport to phone Larry's answering machine. He'd left for the Island, to help Harrison and Elizabeth open their summer house. I pictured them half a mile below our plane as we rose toward cruising altitude: chatting on the porch about tennis and the Dow and waterproof mascara, over gin-and-tonics that got stronger as the sky above the Sound darkened to purple.

Through the roar of the engines, a tinny orchestra clamored for my attention. *Da-de da dom-dom . . .*

Baby, don't waste it! Come on and taste it, taste it!

I craned up in my seat.

No reaction from the band. They must be used to this—kick-ass rock-&-roll turned into kiss-ass background music. "Taste It" sounded grotesque with horns playing the bass part and violins where the lyrics used to be.

Was Dan Quasi listening? Writhing in his seat belt?

More likely counting his royalties. Dreaming of limousines and groupies, gold records and silver buckets of Jack Daniels.

Come on and taste it, taste it!

There'll be a party tonight after the march, he'd told me at the door. Come back if you feel like it. Blue eyes suddenly not so cold; wide lopsided mouth turned up in almost a smile. Holding onto my hand a moment longer than necessary. I'd examined his fingers and tried to sound clinical: I'd've thought you'd have calluses. No, see?—hard but not callused. They're used to it. So close I could make out every link in the gold chain inside his shirt. That half-smile again: Catch you later.

I'm not going, I told Penny loftily. I'm here to cover a demonstration, not group onto a rock star. My hand still tingling from the pressure of his uncallused fingertips. But you've *got* to! she wailed. Dan *Quasi?* Are you *kidding?*

She nudged me when he walked onstage. I frowned and shushed her. That wasn't a man you could party with, that tiny figure floating on a sea of waving hands and bobbing heads. I couldn't even see his face, only listen for him in the amplified roar from the speakers.

"Baby, don't waste it!" Behind Mickey's voice, the sweet sharp bite of Dan's guitar. "Come on and taste it, taste it!"

We'd gotten supper in a church basement: munching salad and spaghetti and counting up the missing. Somebody had the handout with phone numbers for legal and medical aid. Should we call the police station to see if they arrested Mark and Eric? No, don't us deal with the pigs, man, leave that to the lawyers. At the other end of the table, a hushed discussion about four people who'd been caught last week carrying a homemade bomb into a New York bank. Seventy or eighty of us, all slated to sleep here, with four sleeping bags and a dozen Army blankets to go around.

"Come on," Penny punched me in the shoulder. "Let's do it."

We pushed each other out of the hotel elevator into a hall thick with smoke, girls, beer, and noise. A hand grabbed the seat of my jeans. Three girls were screaming with laughter, pouring beer over the head of a roadie in a Rind T-shirt. Another hand thrust a joint at Penny. She took a toke and passed it to me. I shook my head: Where was Dan Quasi?

We found the room. A TV was blaring, not quite loud enough to cover the heaves and moans of a girl in the bathroom. Someone was snorting coke off the shiny surface of a bass guitar. Through the smoke, long hair, grinning bearded faces, and dilated eyes, I saw Mickey Ascher, a cashmere-sweatered arm around his shoulder, crimson-tipped fingers stroking his ear.

A party. Penny and I had expected a celebration of our battle that day to end the war. We'd pictured ourselves linking arms with the band, singing "We Shall Overcome." And afterwards Dan would hold my hand again, only this time instead of making some stupid remark about calluses I'd give him a silent smile . . . I'd thought a lot about losing my virginity, and on the bus coming over it had seemed to me that to spend the night with Dan Quasi would be not only thrilling but politically responsible.

I looked in again at Mickey Ascher. "Let's go back to the church."

But Penny's eyes were glowing. "What are you, nuts? When will we ever get another chance like this?"

I didn't follow her inside. I wandered up and down the hall

for maybe five minutes, wondering if I'd get mugged if I took the bus and if anybody at the church would have money to pay a taxi, till a door opened and I saw Dan Quasi. He was sitting propped up in the pillows of a king-sized bed, watching the demonstration on the news. The rest of the bed was occupied by four people playing cards and a girl who sat cross-legged beside Dan's feet, tickling his toes with her long hair.

He saw me and waved: Come on in!

I stood awkwardly beside the bed and told him how much I'd liked the concert. Nobody else even looked up. I asked him if the police had done any damage. Not much, he said, and pointed at the TV. They're just getting to that.

From the far side of the room came cheers and hisses. Hey, you guys, there's us! I looked at the screen, where tiny police in gas masks were advancing on an even tinier stage. I couldn't relate to it. My eyes went back to his feet. Thin, brown, bony, long-toed. Dan Quasi's feet.

When the news ended I turned to leave. "Stick around if you want," he said, without turning his head.

I found Penny up the hall. "What happened with Mickey?"

"Stoned out of his gourd." She grimaced. "Come on, let's get out of here."

But we'd done it: We'd marched in Washington against the United States government, and we'd gone to a party with The Rind. When we got back to Mount Holyoke we were heroes. Penny signed up for the student strike committee. I wrote up my notes for the campus paper. The next weekend, still fired with revolutionary zeal, I stormed Rik Green's office in Boston and badgered him into buying my story for Phases.

Domp-dom, dum-de dum domp-dom . . .

I should send Penny a postcard. She'd married a history teacher in Minneapolis during graduate school. Every Christmas I got a picture of them with two different kids since last year. Dear Penny, guess who I'm in France with!

Da-de da domp-dom, domp-dom . . .

We're here for the cherry blossoms, Mickey had winked at

me. Graham Douglas cut in smoothly: in Washington to mobilize support, protest Nixon's unconscionable, forced to reschedule two major West Coast, news media unfortunately misinterpreted, grateful to the hotel management for their excellent, sole concern is peace and quiet. And Dan pushed abruptly out of his chair: Peace or quiet, take your pick.

Bienvenu à Paris! Though the flight crew served coffee and croissants as cheerfully as if it were really morning, nobody was fooled. Getting off the plane, I looked again for Wendy Peres. No luck. There was Niko, skinny as a teenager in a black leather jacket, and Lacey's acid-green blouse. I elbowed through the crowd after them.

Could that broad back in a plaid flannel shirt be Terry Morrissey? Yes: still the same old moon face and walrus mustache, but now with a bald patch on top. The Rind's drummer and lowest-key member. When Penny used to lay out her cards during afternoon tea at school—King of Hearts for Mickey, King of Spades for Dan, King of Diamonds for the bass player (not Roach then but his predecessor, a mystical Afro-Asian known as Turbo) —it was always a letdown if you drew a club.

Roach loomed above the ambassadors like King Kong in New York. In 1973, when he'd pushed through my ticket line at Harvard Stadium, all wild hair and beard, I'd thought he was the scariest human being I'd ever seen. Now he looked historic, like a waxwork or a picture off an old album cover.

I caught up with him as he and Niko stepped onto the moving belt that carries passengers from the outer satellites to the airport's central core.

"Hi. Cory Goodwin. I'm doing a piece for Phases on your band."

Roach grunted and inclined his head a fraction of an inch. Niko eyed me as one inspects an insect before brushing it off one's sleeve.

"Niko Marx," he conceded. "With an X." Then, to Roach:

"Who's that with Lacey?"

He pointed up ahead at a rainbow-striped Guatemalan shirt. I'd noticed the same man taking pictures on the plane. Curly dark blond hair, aviator glasses, strong jaw, cleft chin: hip but slick. Unlike Hands Across the Sea's other male ambassadors, who'd opted for a buttoned-down look to meet their host families, this one wore jeans and snakeskin boots.

"Beats me," growled Roach.

Before he could go find out, our moving belt emerged into sunlight. Suddenly we were gliding through the air in a giant tube of transparent plastic, one of several that crisscrossed above an open courtyard. Down below a fountain tossed up curling jets of water. Businessmen and families sat at tables with brioches and coffee, oblivious of their fellow travelers overhead.

"Walt Disney in Airportland," Niko grinned.

Ahead of us Lacey—alone now—pounded on the plastic and waved at people in the other tubes. I thought: Walt Disney called it Tomorrowland. Not the high-tech glitz of Star Wars and Captain Eo, but a stirring future when men would fly rocket ships to the moon. Walt's kind mustached face smiling at me from our black-and-white TV: "Each week, as you enter this timeless land . . ."

"Cory Goodwin?"

I whirled around.

A dark-haired man in a mocha linen shirt. A fine gold chain around his neck. Blue eyes.

Dan Quasi.

The greeting I'd rehearsed on the plane evaporated. All I could do was stare and hope he'd shift back into proportion. Ignore the scrapbook in my head, the TV clips, magazine photos, and record jackets, and grasp that this man riding beside me in a plastic tube through l'Aéroport Roissy-Charles de Gaulle expected me to say something.

"Yes," I managed. "Hi."

Lacey was right—he'd changed. Not the overall impression but the fine points. Chiseled features not so angular . . . Lines between his eyebrows, around his mouth. Threads of gray . . . and surely his hair had been longer in The Rind. Did he have a beard back then? A mustache? I couldn't remember. It was like trying to recall an old song with a new one blaring in your ears.

"How's your French?"

"Not bad," I gulped.

Dan Quasi still loomed two sizes bigger than life, but that wasn't what made me want to step back. This was the man I remembered from D.C., who could stride onto a stage and transform a hundred thousand spectators into a demonstration.

"I have a problem." He extended one hand in front of me to the rail.

What incredible eyes! With black lashes that turned up at the tips—the kind of lashes Larry's father used to say women would endure torture for, if only the R&D people could find the right rack.

"Hands is supposed to provide us with a French road manager and a crew. They haven't shown up. Most of our equipment we're renting here, but we've got luggage and guitars and all that. I've left messages—"

His shirt was open at the top, making his skin look tawny and showing off the sinews of his neck. A fine brushing of black hair curled just below the hollow of his throat.

"So what I need is help explaining that to Customs. What do you think?"

What *could* I think? "Sure. I'll try."

We walked together up the moving belt into the central terminal. Sheila Bailey, at the head of the line, was looking harried. Now she and her volunteers had to pilot a planeload of curious Americans past postcard racks, money-changing booths, and food stands into the baggage-claim area.

Tough luck, Sheila. I cruised past her with Dan Quasi.

We commandeered an airport official. "He says they've got a truck waiting for you outside," I told Dan.

"A truck? What about the car?"

The official didn't know.

"I've got to find Terry." Dan slung his dark head around impatiently.

"Do you have the forms you filled out on the plane?"

"There he is. Hang on."

The official shook his head: Americans! I apologized and looked to see where Dan had gone.

The embarkation area was crowded. Some other big flight must have just come in—a girls' school on holiday, judging from all the designer T-shirts and jeans. And the excited way they were chattering . . .

Then I noticed the video cameras. And the purposeful glint in the eyes scanning incoming passengers.

They spotted Roach and let out a shriek.

Roach realized what was happening just in time to duck back into the crowd. A flock of teenagers ran after him.

The airport guards weren't prepared for this. They cut off some of the group, but two or three dozen were already through.

Roach's bushy head slipped between Hands Across the Sea's ambassadors like a beaver swimming through a logjam. Somehow he'd managed to grab Lacey. He dragged her along by the hand, with Niko loping after them.

Where was Dan?

I found him four seconds before the kids did, standing beside a luggage van with Terry Morrissey.

I started running.

Dan saw me and the approaching horde at the same instant.

"Over here!" I waved at a stairway entrance.

Dan and Terry reached it right behind me and we went flying down the stairs. "This way!" I felt surprisingly exhilarated. The airport's layout was coming back to me—mostly restaurants on this level, a good place to lose pursuers.

We skidded around a coffee shop through a maze of tables and chairs and thundered past a cafeteria. Startled customers scattered in front of us like pigeons. Another coffee shop. Then a mini-mall: souvenirs, a bar, pizza and pasta . . .

Dan, in the lead, swerved into a newsstand.

We stood panting in the corner. The stout woman at the cash register glared ferociously, clearly convinced we were fugitives. As soon as I got my breath I stammered an explanation. I backed off again as a patrol of teenagers came running past. They glanced in—but Dan was hidden behind a folding panel of paperbacks, and Terry had flattened himself between the wall and a revolving map display.

As the footsteps died away, Terry stepped into the aisle. "Looks like we lost 'em. Dan, you OK?"

Dan was emerging with some difficulty from the paperback section. "Goddam ridiculous," he muttered.

Watching him disentangle first his shoulders, then his long legs, I squelched an impulse to offer a hand.

"Fifteen-year-old kids! Who do they think we are?"

"Madame?" The woman at the cash register beckoned to me.

"That should be airport security." I moved to the counter to take the phone.

"And another thing," said Terry. "How did they *know?*"

As I picked up the receiver, I noticed a Japanese couple who must have watched this whole incident from the magazine section. With a wary eye on Dan and Terry, they resumed browsing.

"They're sending down some guards," I told Dan. "Your truck is right outside the door upstairs."

"What about Roach and Lacey and Niko? And our stuff?"

But I had already hung up.

"Dammit, we've got to get back up there!" Dan slammed a hand down on a stack of Herald Tribunes.

The *smack!* and the exasperation in his voice sent the Japanese couple backing hastily away. Madame the proprietor, alarmed, let loose a rapid torrent of French.

I calmed her down. "Listen," I said to Dan, surprised by the authority in my voice. "The airport people should be here any minute. Why don't you wait here for them, and I'll go back upstairs and see what I can find out."

Dan didn't look enthusiastic, but Terry nodded, "Good idea." He turned back to Dan. "Just to make sure everything's under control."

I could see from Dan's face what he thought of entrusting a job like that to a journalist. All he said, though, was, "We might have to do the switch. Go out in a cab and have the truck meet us."

"Yeah," Terry sighed. "Shit, I hope Roach and them got

through OK."

"Watch out." Dan pulled Terry back into the corner as another band of teenagers came prowling up to the window.

Hide-and-seek has never been my game. I nodded to the woman behind the counter and headed for the stairs.

Chapter 4: Sunny Afternoon

The airport staff assured me the band's belongings were even now on their way to the truck. Madame could be confident that both luggage and instruments would be handled with the greatest of care. That was cute. One thing no one had ever mistaken me for before was a roadie.

Outside the airport's sliding glass doors the world was strangely quiet. A distant shriek of planes landing and taking off, a rumble of bus and car engines, an occasional shout from a porter —in spite of the exhaust fumes, I felt released. And tired. I leaned against the sun-warmed side of a bus, glad for a moment by myself.

Above the concrete wall one airplane was cocked so that its wing and tail made a V. I watched it rise like a butterfly toward the sun.

Then I jumped. Over by the airport door a row of rock-&-roll fans eyed me hopefully.

Now, when they weren't moving, they looked like any harmless group of high-school kids. I framed Terry's question: *Comment avez-vous découverte . . . ?*

The glass doors slid open silently. Out came Dan Quasi, with a guard on each side.

The kids moved up. No screams this time, only giggles and murmurs. One of them called boldly, "Bienvenu à Paris!"

Dan grinned at them. "Merci."

That drew a squeal or two. The guards tensed; but the mood here was friendly. Several camcorders aimed at Dan, but their owners stayed back, and the rest seemed content to watch him.

I stayed back, too. Between the stolid uniformed guards Dan Quasi was a star, shining and confident. I felt suddenly shy of him.

As he passed he tossed me a smile. "So how's it going?"

His offhand tone shrugged off both the goggling teenagers and the two men who had stopped when he stopped. "Good." For me it wasn't so easy to ignore all those intent faces. "Your stuff's supposedly on its way to the truck. I haven't seen the rest of the band."

"They're inside."

"Are they OK?"

Dan nodded. "Roach lost most of his shirt. Otherwise, no damage. Except now we can't move without—" He jerked his head to either side.

"Too bad." I heard myself holding him with conversation, angling to keep him from ending our shared adventure. "Does this blow your no-publicity plan?"

Dan shrugged. "I doubt it. We're not that famous." He reached into his shirt pocket for cigarettes. "We'll know better when we know why they're here—who leaked what to who. You got any ideas?"

"I'll see what I can find out."

He offered me the pack: Marlboros. I took one. "Are there people waiting for you?" he asked. "A host family?"

"No." I told him about the Hôtel des Fraises.

"You should come to sound check, then. Get a sense of the band."

Sound check? "Thanks," I said. "I will."

Dan cupped his hands around a match and held it toward me. "Three things. One, this is a new band, not a reunion. Ask whatever you want about Quasi & Company, but stay off The Rind and Mickey Ascher."

I couldn't help asking: "Do you think that's realistic?"

"That's the deal." He lit his own cigarette. "Two, no reviewing the music. We aren't far along enough. And three, no taping, audio or video. I don't care if you tape interviews, in fact I'd rather you do, but absolutely no taping of gigs or rehearsals."

"OK."

"The truck's over here someplace, according to these guys. You want to interpret for me?"

I could tell as I translated Dan's questions that the driver didn't like the idea of chauffeuring a bunch of American rock musicians. When I asked him if this truck would be at the band's disposal all weekend, he refused to commit. "Aujourd'hui, oui. Demain, je ne sais pas. Vous devrez parler à Madame." He jabbed a thumb at the airport door. "Moi, je ne suis que conducteur."

"I can guess," said Dan. "Don't ask me, I'm just the driver! So who is this Madame and where do we find her?"

"Comment s'appelle Madame?" I asked.

The driver was scornful of our ignorance. "Madame Tréville."

Tréville! I glanced instantly at Dan. He gave no visible sign of recognition; but it seemed to me that something changed. As if someone had hit his Pause button, and for just a fraction of a second he went still.

Before I could be sure, though, he was saying, "She must be on the committee. I'll go see if I can find her."

As Dan and his retinue bustled off again, I wandered back toward the truck. This was disturbing. According to John Otis, Victor Tréville might very well remember The Rind from when he worked for the French consulate in Boston. It hadn't occurred to me—nor, I was sure, to John—that The Rind might remember Victor Tréville.

"Excuse me."

I looked up.

"Are you Cordelia Thorne?"

Standing beside the truck was Lacey's sandy-haired friend in the Guatemalan shirt. Now what?

"Steve Connelly." He smiled, put down his flight bag and held out a hand. "Bonjour, neighbor. I'm also staying in Fraises-des-Bois."

I tried not to look startled as we shook hands. "Are you sure?"

He pulled a yellow Hands Across the Sea card out of his pocket. "Here's the address. Max and Judith Croft, Rue de Clos Chardin, Fraises-des-Bois."

He was right. Two large coincidences in five minutes. I didn't like it.

"Oh!" Steve grinned apologetically. "I forgot to mention, I'm your photographer. You were expecting Wendy Peres, right? She couldn't make it. Came down with the flu."

I didn't smile back. The Paris airport was no place to be finding out that the images for everything I wrote would come from someone whose work I'd never seen. Nor did I relish sharing my seclusion with Mr. Hip-But-Slick.

"Are the Crofts picking you up, then?"

"Unfortunately they couldn't make it. Sheila—Mrs. Bailey—suggested I hitch into Paris with you and the band, and then we can share a cab to Fraises-des-Bois."

That sounded to me like a most unlikely suggestion to have come from Sheila Bailey. "Sorry," I said, "but I'm going to sound check."

"Sound check?" Steve raised his eyebrows. "Hey. Great. I'll come with you."

How he talked the band into it I couldn't imagine, but Steve Connelly did ride with us into Paris. The truck was a small white enclosed U-Haul. With Quasi & Company's instruments loaded along the back and the suitcases in the middle where we could sit on them, there was still room to dance, had anyone cared to. The contract specified both a truck and a limousine, according to Terry, but nobody was about to hang around waiting for the car. Roach said he guessed the French crew had picked it up and were halfway to Monte Carlo.

He and Lacey sat in a semicircle with Terry, Niko, and Steve around the truck's open end. I stood behind them, where I could just make out Dan Quasi in the back, hunched over a guitar.

"Well, shee-it!" Roach slapped Lacey's knee. "What do you think? We're going to have to schlep our own stuff like some two-bit bar band?"

"Your shirt's buttoned wrong." Lacey reached inside his jacket.

"Where was goddam Neil? Hey, cut it out."

"What I want to know," Terry interposed, "is why were those kids after us?"

"Yeah," said Niko. "What happened to zero publicity?"

"I can tell you that." I shrank inside as five pairs of eyes focused on me. "They said a TV station in Paris has been talking up the American Mystery Band. Offering a prize to the first person who brings in proof of who it is."

"Well, shee-it!" said Roach again, this time in wonder.

"A TV station?" Terry was shaking his head. "Dan, did you hear that?" He looked toward the back of the truck, where from the sound of it Dan was fitting a new string to a guitar.

"We could maybe get some big crowds if they let in people who aren't in Hands Across the Sea," Lacey said hopefully.

"Fat chance," drawled Roach. From a pocket of his jeans he pulled out a half-squashed cigarette pack. "Anybody want some Rooftop Red?"

"You hippies," said Niko. "Dope, dope, dope."

"Roach, I wouldn't if I were you," I blurted. "Drugs are highly illegal here."

"Drugs?" Roach scowled at me. "This is *marijuana.*"

"She's right, though," said Terry. "We had a roadie on our first tour who got locked up for half an ounce of hash. Even Dougie couldn't get him out."

"And he never returned," Niko added solemnly, "and his fate is still unlearned."

"So, what?" said Roach. "We're supposed to play for four days straight?"

"Pretend you're back in Texas," advised Niko.

Lacey patted Roach's arm. "Roach used to deal in Texas."

Roach, sensing he was about to acquire an audience, stretched out his legs. "Yes sirree." He looked around at all of us with a wicked grin. "Drive down across the border with a couple of bows and arrows. Buy us a key, chop it up, tape it in baggies. Tape the baggies on the arrows. Then shoot 'em across this narrow stretch of the Rio Grande into Texas. Drive back home, pick 'em up, and yee-ha!"

Steve Connelly stared at him with mixed shock and admiration.

"You know, there's a metal wall between us and the driver,"

said Terry. "And nobody's watching the tailgate."

"Gentlemen," Niko intoned, "start your engines."

I looked back to where Dan was sitting. He was still working on his guitar string. He didn't look up even as marijuana smoke began to fill the truck.

As the joint went around, the mood grew more expansive. Roach and Terry started recalling their favorite French hangouts from past tours, which segued into wild nights with The Rind. Some tales I'd heard years ago—the time Mickey and Turbo stole a statue from the Tuileries and dragged it down into the Métro, and that party on the Bateau Mouche that ended with four nightclub dancers and Mickey and Dan stripping off their clothes to swim across the Seine. What staggered me now was Terry's nonchalance. This amiable, balding fellow leading the French police on an all-night chase through the gravestones of Montparnasse?

Steve Connelly had been taking his turn when the joint came by. Now he made his first plunge into the conversation.

"If you could be any musician who's ever played, who would you be?" he asked Terry.

Terry shrugged; took a hit from the joint Steve handed him.

"Come on, Terry," said Lacey.

Dan had the string on his guitar. Its low rising *twang* as he tightened it gave a thin bass line to the discussion.

"Who'd you want to be?" Lacey persisted.

"Shit, I don't know." Terry let out a stoned giggle. "Me is good. If this band takes off?"

"Boooo!" Lacey reached over to swat him on the shoulder.

"Boo yourself! You weren't around in the old days. Lot of people wanted to be us."

"I sure did," Roach agreed.

"Where were you then?" Steve asked him.

Roach was mellow enough to be obliging. "I was with Brass Knuckles for a while."

"Then Pynk Pyg," said Lacey.

"But I always wanted to get in The Rind. The first time Turbo split—remember, Terry? Looked like it was going to work out. But then he came back." Roach shook his head sadly.

"Turbo," said Lacey, "like the engine?"

"Like the fish," said Terry.

"The *fish?*"

Niko said, "You brought back the lost energy."

"That was mostly Mick," said Terry. "Why Turbo quit."

"Nodding out, or else bouncing off the walls," Roach agreed. "Even when he was straight, you never knew if he'd make it through the set."

I pressed my forehead against the truck wall. That thousand-watt sparkle in Mickey's eyes the day I met him: a rough night, I'd told myself. Film clips of Mad Mick in fringe and beads, feathers in his hair, chanting cryptic revelations into a mic; dancing at the edge of the stage while the band rocked on without him. All part of the mystique, right?

"Was that where The Rind's energy came from?" Steve asked. "From Mickey Ascher? Is that why you didn't try to re-form the band without him?"

There was a long pause.

"I'd be Janis Joplin," Lacey declared. "Or you know who else? Billie Holiday! She wasn't a rocker, but I love how she sings —kind of growly, but not, like, *rough*—more sweet, and sad—"

"Babble babble!" Niko mocked.

"Shit, Lacey, everybody you want to be's dead," said Roach.

She fixed him with a lofty stare. "You gotta suffer if you want to sing the blues."

"You gotta suffer if you want to play the drums," said Terry. "Highest mortality rate outside of organized crime."

"I wouldn't mind being Michael Jackson," Niko said reflectively. "Talk about a truly gross income."

From behind them came a flat metallic *twang!*

"Capitalist!" said Roach.

Steve turned toward the sound of the guitar. "Dan!" he called boldly. "What about you? You've played with the best. Who'd you want to be?"

They all swiveled expectantly.

Dan didn't even look up. "Jesus fucking Christ."

Silence. Roach took a slow hit off the last half-inch of joint and passed it to Niko. Lacey peered out the back of the truck, as if she'd just noticed we were coming into Paris.

At last Dan lifted his head. "Terry. You got the schedule?"

"In my suitcase. You want it?"

Dan shook his head and stood up. There was a quiet stirring all around the truck.

"We've got one set tonight at this banquet." He leaned his guitar against a suitcase. "Roach. Is the list done?"

"Almost."

"We need it by sound check. I want to run through 'Time' again, and a couple other things if you're up."

Evidently they were. Lacey and Terry were watching him with solemn concentration. Niko had slid around to face into the truck. Roach pinched out a newly lit joint.

"Neil and the crew should have everything set up." Dan stepped forward, in among the band. "Niko, you've got 73 keys tonight plus the DX-7. Lacey—"

Steve Connelly took his cue and walked over to me at the side of the truck.

"Round One to Quasi! What do you think? Am I off the guest list?"

I didn't know what he meant, nor care to. I wanted to listen to Dan until I figured out how he made every casual remark sound so important. But I could see from Steve's unfocused grin and puffy determined eyes I wasn't going to get the chance.

"I ask too many questions, right? That's what my mom's always telling me. 'Stop pushing, Steve!' That's what ticked him off. When I asked about Mickey Ascher and The Rind breaking up."

I shot him a quelling look meant to convey that if he wanted a sympathetic ear, he hadn't found one.

"Touchy, though, isn't he? Twenty years . . . but hey, no statute of limitations on murder. Means, opportunity— They just couldn't pin down a motive."

Or any evidence, I didn't add.

"Why kill the golden goose? Your front man's losing it— give rehab a chance. 'Course, looking back, the up side: album sales through the roof. Signed copies of *Grind* bootlegging for hundreds of bucks. Plus with Ascher dead, so was the court case. I never did hear that whole story. The big drug bust? Like where Quasi fit in, and why the cops hushed it up?"

"Steve, listen to your mom, OK?—and stop pushing."

"The whole thing doesn't add up. You know? Top of the charts, and where's The Rind? Gone! Poof!" His hands fluttered. "Where else but the wild and crazy world of rock music?"

"Everywhere else. Remember Richard Nixon, who used to be president? Remember the war in Vietnam?"

"And here they are, starting over." Steve was still staring intently at Quasi & Company. "Why *now*? Why Paris? Why Hands Across the Sea? If they want a reunion, do a benefit. Starving Africans! Rainforests! Rind type stuff. But this? A mickey-mouse networking trip to not even a third-world country?"

"Don't ask me," I said sincerely.

"Sure. That's why you're here, is to find out." Steve chuckled. "Be careful what rocks you turn over, though. You never know what might crawl out."

I looked past him at the band. Niko was scratching the back of his leg with a sneakered foot, listening to Dan and Terry. Lacey and Roach sat on their suitcases: Roach with one arm braced against the truck wall, Lacey with her head on his shoulder.

"That's what makes a story, Steve. Surprises."

As soon as I heard it come out of my mouth I knew I'd just issued Fate an invitation I was going to regret.

Chapter 5: Tales of Brave Ulysses

Paris looks quite different depending if you arrive in a topless MG or the back of a U-Haul. I'd finally figured out we were on the Périphérique, the highway that circles the city's outskirts. Now we cut in, and soon turned into a curved street where colored awnings jutted like banners from ancient façades and café chairs crowded the sidewalk.

Je reviens! Unexpectedly my heart felt light as my sleep-deprived head. I stretched my arms and legs as if shrugging off the weariness that had hung on me for weeks like a winter coat. This was the way to come back! Not tiptoeing through a minefield of memories. Not charging at my past like Don Quixote.

Watch. Listen. Find an angle. I'd done it before. I could do it again.

Steve Connelly's advice from his mom had brought back what my dad said when I called to break the news about skipping the Big Apple for *la ville lumière*. Since it was Lily who introduced me to Paris, through Babar and Madeline and then in person, and since Archie claims credit for my investigative tendencies, I expected no complaints.

What I didn't expect was his first question.

"What's the story on the Ascher murder?"

"You remember that?" Of course he did; he's a private detective. "No breakthroughs, far as I know." I told him about Unsolved Mysteries.

"Your Beantown police don't like to rush this kind of thing, do they. 1974 . . . I guess they're still sifting through the party debris looking for clues." Did I mention Archie's a Yankees fan? "Who do you think killed him?"

"Not a clue."

"Then that can't be why you're going to France with three of the top suspects."

"I'm a journalist, not a detective, *mio*." My version of Escamillo, Lily's pet nickname for him. "And they're professional musicians, not assassins."

"Do you know where they were when it happened?"

"I know where the cops say they were. The drummer, Terry Morrissey, stopped by to welcome Mickey home but left before the party. Roach, the bass player, stayed until it ended at midnight. Dan Quasi was expected but didn't show up. He'd been away since Mickey started rehab. Said he got stuck on the road and crashed with an old girlfriend. She backed him up, but . . ."

"Your governor's got cold feet."

"Yeah, well, his own fault. Should have done his homework. I followed these guys for years, I spent today scanning microfiches, and I don't share his concerns."

"It hit you hard when Mickey Ascher was killed."

"I was shattered. Not just the brutality of it, but the loss."

"What about them? His partners?"

That stopped me short. Nobody else had asked about the impact of Mickey's murder on the surviving Rind members. How shattered must they have been? By the loss, and by the brutality of being harassed for months by the press and the police, only to have the investigation dropped.

"Good question, *mio*. I'll have to find out."

"Cory. You're a pro, so I don't need to tell you. Cold case or not, this is an unsolved homicide."

"I'm not taking your Marley." Though he doesn't care much for guns, Archie always carries one on a murder investigation.

"Ha! No. You're a journalist, not a detective. If the cops couldn't close the Ascher murder twenty years ago, or the TV crew last month, what can you do in four days?"

I saw where he was going. "Open Pandora's box?"

"Watch what you step on. Toes. Chewing gum. Land mines."

I started to say Sure, of course. But this wasn't pat advice he was giving me, and I didn't want to give him a pat answer.

"You've been playing defense so far. Hitting back what gets thrown at you. Once you're in France, it's a different ball game."

So it was. For days I'd been juggling John Otis's agenda, Rik Green's, Quasi & Company's, even Larry's. Now the ball was in my court. And whatever I or anyone else might rather I focused on, I'd better not forget the elephant in the room.

"Hey!" Lacey jumped up. "Are we here?"

The truck had stopped at the foot of a wide stone staircase. Exhibition hall? Remodeled railroad station? The driver shot us a pointed look as we climbed out which suggested that we had indeed arrived, and not a minute too soon.

Roach craned back to take in arched windows, fluted columns, flashes of bronze and glass. "It ain't the Fillmore."

Inside was a large dim space empty except for rows of collapsible tables. Faint light filtered through skylights in the high ceiling. The only other light came from a platform at the far end, where two figures sat in front of a pyramid of bright blue metal-flake drums, dangling their feet over the edge, smoking cigarettes.

"Hey! Neil!" somebody yelled.

Both men jumped down. They met the band in an enthusiastic reunion: handshakes, hugs, slaps on the back. "Hey, man!" I got a kaleidoscope impression of wavy waist-length red hair, a denim jacket, jeans patched with an American flag, tattered running shoes. "You get lost or what?"

"Cory! Steve!" Lacey beckoned. "Come meet Neil!"

"This is François, who's running the French crew," Neil told the others.

The two of them could have been an ad for Hands Across the Sea. Neil representing America: gaunt and dreamy, with an air of being about to float off into space, and a narrow face overshadowed by his splendid curtain of hair—longer, curlier, and redder than mine. François, in contrast, moved with a contained grace that fit his tan slacks and black polo shirt. He was slender and fine-boned, with dark hair razor-cut to his shoulders. From the ceremonious way he shook hands with the band, we might have been meeting in the Grand Trianon at Versailles.

"So how come you weren't at the airport, asshole?" Roach poked Neil with his elbow.

"I lost the piece of paper with your flight on it. I figured, no sweat, we'll call the airport. So François gets this chick on the phone, and she goes, 'I'm sorry, I can't tell you that. I have customers to wait on.' And he's going, 'Well, jeez, lady, I'm a customer!' And she goes, 'You'll have to come to the airport for that information.' And hangs up on him."

"So we give up!" François finished with a grin.

Dan Quasi's mind was on practical matters. "Is everything set up?"

"All but the guitars and cymbals," said Neil. "The crew'll be back at 4:30. Hands wanted us out of here till then so they can do their chairs and shit."

Chairs? I glanced at Dan, braced for a blow-up. But it was Roach who growled, "*Chairs?* What is this, the fuckin' bar circuit? No rattling the glasses during happy hour?" He kicked a table. "How are we supposed to do a fuckin' sound check without a fuckin' crew?"

"We did a lot before they left," said Neil.

"We've done it before." Terry too was watching Dan.

"Springfield," Dan nodded. "Roach, you remember? When they switched the hall on us and the crew got locked in the gym?"

"Mickey swearing he wouldn't go on without somebody to carry his guitar," said Terry, "Dougie threatening to sue—"

"Hah!" crowed Roach. "And I picked up Mickey *and* his guitar, and I go, Listen, man, I joined this band to hear you squawk *on*stage, so go check your own fuckin' levels!"

"Who needs a crew?" Terry punched him in the shoulder.

"Fuck 'em!" Roach agreed.

"Neil," said Dan, "what kind of board have we got?"

They all moved forward to look at a large panel of knobs, dials, and levers sitting on a table about fifteen feet from the stage. Dan and Neil started discussing it in a language as foreign to me as French was to them: DB's, snake, reverb, flanger, patching in.

"Cory?" Steve Connelly spoke quietly in my ear. "This is about to get boring. Want to go find some coffee?"

I glanced up at the stage. Terry was stepping in among his drums. Niko was opening the lid of a wooden spinet piano with a smaller, sleeker keyboard on top. At the other end of the platform, Lacey ran her fingers noiselessly down the keys of a chrome-legged electric organ.

"No thanks."

I walked up front and pulled out my notebook.

"Neil!" Terry called. "Where's my Kotex?"

"Isn't it on the snare?"

"No."

Neil loped around the board to the edge of the platform.

It would help, I reflected, if I could tell what they're talking about, not to mention what (if anything) I should write down.

Journalists' Rule #2: *When in doubt, find out.*

But Dan Quasi was no longer at the board. Nor onstage, where two guitars stood upright in stands waiting for him. I didn't see him anywhere in the hall.

Thump! Thump! Thump! A drum boomed through the speaker. I moved closer. There were four: the big bass drum, with a sweatshirt stuffed behind its round transparent skin; a smaller drum riding above it on a chrome antenna; a medium-sized one on the floor to the left; and a flat drum suspended on the other side which I recognized as the snare. Terry was going around the floor drum with what looked like a roller-skate key, tightening bolts around the rim, tapping near each bolt with a drumstick.

He looked down at me. "Hi."

"Hi," I said. "Are you tuning that thing?"

"Yup."

"What's the Kotex for?"

"Muffles the snare. You'll see tonight. Neil's got a spare at the hotel."

"Are those rubber tips on your drumsticks?"

Terry winked. "They're really wood. They just paint 'em to look like rubber."

He put down his stick and skate key; picked up a cymbal and set it onto a second antenna sticking out of the bass drum.

All around the platform electrical cords snaked and coiled among microphone stands and those various-sized boxes I used to notice at rock concerts: single or stacked, black, red, or blue, some studded with knobs and dials, some trimmed with metal like an old trunk.

"What are all these?" I asked Lacey.

"These?" She pointed at a pair of speakers on the floor. "These are monitors. Those over there, too. And that little one on Niko's piano, only that's called a hot spot."

She sounded so matter-of-fact that I felt ashamed of my ignorance. "What's a monitor?"

"Oh." Lacey's mouth screwed up as she considered. "Well, we have to hear ourselves onstage so we know how we're sounding out there. The monitors play what's coming from the different mikes and instruments to us up here, like those big speakers on the sides do for the house."

"Hey!" Roach called from a metal folding chair. "What are you guys doing?"

"I'm playing rock-&-roll," said Niko. "Somebody told me you can make money at this."

"What are *you* doing?" countered Lacey.

"We've got a bass rack here going to waste." Terry twirled a drumstick. "Want to try her out?"

Roach shrugged and picked up his guitar case.

I withdrew to the sound board.

Lacey swung into a Motown rhythm: *bomp, de bomp! bomp, de bomp!* The curve of her back behind the organ turned her oddly serious. How did she ever learn all this? You surely couldn't get into Quasi & Company without knowing what you were doing, even if you were the bass player's girlfriend. But where would Lacey have picked it up? The same thing I used to wonder in high school about boys and cars: How does a guy who's spaced out the entire curriculum become an expert on fuel-injected engines?

"Neil, can we have some more light?"

"Lights!" Neil shouted from behind the board.

Colors splashed across the platform: red, yellow, blue, green. The lights were mounted on a long horizontal pole hanging from the ceiling. They looked too heavy to be safe up there, clunky black cans with bright snouts.

The Motown sound shifted to French horns. Not an organ—a

synthesizer. Lacey's face and her fuzzy hair were burnished with red. Her eyes were intent with listening. Her fingers made decisions every fraction of a second which spilled out of the speakers stacked beside the stage and fluttered through the hall like moths.

Neil, behind the sound board, was watching her too, anticipating what she'd play next. François walked around the back of the hall, a silent silhouette sliding in and out between tables.

"Niko, how's that piano for you?" Neil called.

Niko rolled his eyes and pranced his hands down the keyboard in a showy double scale. "I've seen so many pianos in my life and time!" he wailed soulfully. "This one, she rates about five-point-nine!"

Lacey laughed. A rumble of bass notes came from Roach, hunched crowlike around his guitar.

Terry flipped a drumstick in the air and caught it. "Anybody want to try 'Marinda'? Roach?"

"Where's Dan?" asked Lacey.

Shrugs. "Men's room?" said Niko.

"'Marinda!' Let's do it!" Roach shifted his bass on its strap: a whole snakeskin.

Terry tapped with his stick. "One, two, three, four."

And suddenly I was in the front seat of Penny's Buick, heading for the lake. Unseasonably warm—April? May? The DJ on the radio was babbling about finally having got the new Rind album. I grinned at Penny and turned it up.

We'd expected a rocker like "One More Hit to Wonderland," the single we'd bought last week. Instead came slow hot blues:

"Oh, Marinda,

Won't you leave this man alone?

Your mouth's like fire,

But your heart is cold as stone!"

Not a car radio now, or Penny's and my third-hand stereo with the speakers under the turntable. That lazy beat was Roach's fingers moving up and down the neck of his bass, and Terry stroking a cymbal with a brush.

It didn't sound the same. I stopped filling in lyrics and listened. Instead of guitars, Niko's barroom piano tinkled at the ends of lines.

Dan Quasi walked up the steps to the stage.

Lacey's synthesizer rose under the missing melody, piling chord on chord till the song seemed to be heaving toward a resolution—

Dan slipped his guitar strap over his shoulder; fiddled with the dials on his amplifier.

Ar-ar-ar-arrrr! One note, slicing through the chords.

The strap had hiked up his shirt so that a patch of skin showed above his jeans. Five steps and I could have touched him. Would no doubt have ached to touch him if he'd been a distant gleam on a stage and I one of 5000 fans in the bleachers. Not here. Not in this empty hall with no one watching that bare patch but me.

I glanced around. Terry, half hidden by the drums, was laying out the beat with grave concentration. Lacey's shoulders slumped over her keyboard. Her curly hair veiled her face. Roach stared at the floor, head bowed. Niko gazed into space.

Da, da, da, dee-eee . . .

Dan's head was tilted back. The cords of his throat and wrists were taut as guitar strings.

Da-da-da BAM!

Whew! I let out a sigh of awe and relief.

"Not bad," said Roach. "You could have come in stronger, though, Lacey."

Niko shook his head. "I liked it how she did it."

"Was I too heavy?" asked Terry.

"Sounded good to me," said Dan. "You want to run through it again, with vocals?"

My eyes stayed on Dan as he and Roach and Terry started the intro. That silver-gray guitar . . . part of the Rind legend. What did he call it? Old Smoky?

But they were coming to the verse. My insides tightened. Who could possibly sing "Marinda" but Mickey Ascher?

Dan leaned forward to his mic.

"Well, I couldn't sleep last night, babe,
I was wonderin' where you'd gone."

His voice was jarring: plain, a little sardonic, not at all like Mickey's anguished tenor. Dan sang the words as if they were coming to him as he stood there.

And why not? I reminded myself. He wrote it, didn't he?

"Oh, I didn't get to sleep at *all* last night, baby—"

Dan threw in a Chuck Berry quaver on his guitar. Lacey giggled. Terry wiggled his eyebrows.

"Just a-lay there wonderin' where the hell you'd gone!"

A guffaw from Roach as he slid in a bass riff.

I wished they'd stop fooling around so I could concentrate on the music. It wasn't just Dan's vocals—the whole song seemed to have shifted not forward but backward in time.

"OK!" grinned Roach as they finished.

"Marinda." Niko was shaking his head. "Where'd you dig that up?"

Dan groped at his pockets as if hoping to find cigarettes. "I wrote it as 'Marcella.' We were just getting ready to tape it when the Beach Boys came out with theirs."

"Oh, Marcella!" said Terry. "Prettiest bartender in the state of Maine. Roach, do you remember her? What an ass!—sweeter than a ripe peach." His hands shaped a descriptive curve.

"Before my time." Roach plucked a regretful bass note.

"We all had the hots for her," Terry said reminiscently. "Who finally got her, Dan, you or Mickey?"

Dan was laughing. "Both of us."

"One at a time or together?" inquired Niko.

"Hey!" Lacey drowned them out with an impatient chord. "Can we finish sound check?"

Amen, I seconded silently. Not that Phases' readership wouldn't love to know the inside story on 'Marinda,' but some of us aren't quite through hanging onto our illusions.

"Floor drum," called Neil.

Thump. Thump. Thump. Thump.

"Dan, you were right about me coming in later," Lacey said.

Dan moved into place behind his mic. "We can use that on

'Time.' You know where you come in right after the break? If you let Roach carry it up to the verse."

"Yeah," Roach approved.

"OK," said Neil. "Snare."

"Why don't we just use it on 'Marinda'?" Lacey folded her arms. "It's such a good song!"

Terry beat out a rapid rat-ta-tat on the snare. "This isn't a blues gig, Lacey."

Roach leaned over and ruffled her hair and added, "You must've got switched when you were a baby. Little white girl hot to play the blues."

"Good," said Neil. "Riding tom?"

The way they talked to each other was making me dizzy. Like a basketball team—passing a topic, catching it, dribbling it a few steps, and snapping it off again.

"So are we doing the Rat tonight?" Niko asked.

"Roach?" asked Dan.

"Nope."

"How come?" asked Lacey.

"Doesn't fit."

"What do you mean, 'doesn't fit'?" Niko asked. "Doesn't fit with what? Isn't that what we're here for?"

"Tonight's their opening banquet. We play after they eat."

"So?" Lacey spun her stool around to face him.

"So Dan and me figured we'd start with standards—'One,' maybe 'Night'—"

"You mean they want The Rind, so let's give it to them?" Niko interrupted.

"Who are we playing for?" Lacey demanded. "Us or them?"

"Lacey—" Roach began.

Terry cut in. "Both." He stood up, revealing a red-topped wooden seat like the ones elephants put their feet on in circuses. "There's no point hitting 'em with the Rat when they're all jet-lagged, and we're getting our shit together, and it's about boozing and schmoozing anyways more than listening."

He didn't look at me, and neither did the others, but I got the impression Terry was signaling everybody to cool it in front of the press.

Roach ignored him. "Why do you think they hired us instead of some bar band? It ain't for 'Mr. Rat.' If you think we're getting offstage without playing 'Government Man' and 'I'm the One,' you got your head up your ass."

"That sucks."

"You knew that, Niko." Terry glanced at Dan. "Occupational hazard."

"And you know I didn't join this band to play kiss-ass rock for a bunch of retro hippies."

"Yeah! Me neither!" said Lacey.

Dan pivoted to face Niko. "We all joined this band to play rock-&-roll, and that's what we're doing." His thumb flicked a string as if for punctuation. "So let's do it, OK?"

End of discussion. The band moved back into place. They didn't play any more songs, though—just fragments, as Neil called the name of one instrument or another. François moved around the hall listening, for what I wasn't sure.

They were on keyboards when things fell apart.

"Neil!" yelled Lacey. "I've got a bad wire."

Neil came up, calling, "François!"

François jogged toward the stage. "One of the speakers is out."

"Well, fuck!" Roach slid off his guitar strap. "Let in the assholes with their chairs."

Dan asked, "Neil, are we checked into the hotel?"

"No." Neil was crouched on the floor, wiggling a wire on the back of Lacey's synthesizer.

"I'll do it," said Roach. "I need a shower anyway."

"A nap, you mean," said Lacey. "Mr. Snooze!"

"Anybody who wants to might as well go," said Dan.

Lacey voted to stay with her sinking ship. Terry asked me to come with him and Roach as interpreter.

We were on the Left Bank, west of the Latin Quarter. My spirits rose as we walked up the chilly, sunny street: yes, I still knew Paris! This way would be ambassadors' residences and the Rodin museum; that way, the Seine. I gazed at everything—long beige façades with their massive wooden garage doors, cobbled courtyards, balconies, small neat gardens—and stoked up my tired soul with familiarity.

The hotel had no reservations for Quasi & Company.

Terry and Roach and I looked at each other in weary dismay. The woman at the desk waited without expression for us to decide what to do. I took in her glossy blonde hair, the careful detail of her makeup, the pastel earth tones of her clothes, and I wondered if the problem was these two unshaven men who'd been up all night on an airplane, whose faded jeans and leather jackets were better suited to setting up equipment than ornamenting a hotel lobby.

They looked like musicians, all right. Did she think they were going to trash the place?

"This was confirmed three days ago by phone from Boston," said Terry. "Can we speak to the manager, please?"

The woman at the desk said, "Certainly, if he is here," and went off to find him.

Terry leaned his elbows on the desk with a sigh. Behind us, Roach was shambling around the little lobby like a woolly mammoth.

The woman returned without the manager and assured us she was helpless: There were no reservations, there were no rooms, what could one do? For the young man who had stayed last night there was still a single room; but for five others, impossible!

Terry gave me a look which moved me to ask if Madame had a telephone number for Hands Across the Sea. Alas, she did not.

I glanced around at Roach. He was slumped in a chair, asleep.

It's all yours, Cory.

"May I use your telephone?" I asked Madame in French.

I called my hotel in Fraises-des-Bois. "Monsieur Vlaemenck, s'il vous plait." Rallying the helpless female manner that had often been useful to me in France before, I explained that five guests of his friend Monsieur Otis found themselves stranded in Paris. No doubt his inn, with its excellent reputation, was very busy at this time of year; but could he, by any chance . . . ?

Monsieur Vlaemenck hesitated, then capitulated. Of course. Somehow, rooms would be found.

"OK," I told Terry and Roach. "It's no Holiday Inn, but you've got a place to sleep."

As we stepped outside, Terry kissed me on the cheek. "You win a free ride to your hotel."

His walrus mustache tickled my ear. My eyes watered unexpectedly. How long since I'd been kissed by a man with a mustache? And with no other motive than to say thanks. I felt an absurd urge to hug him.

The band's limousine was waiting at the banquet hall, conjured up by François. It was agreed that Neil and François would deal with the broken synthesizer and speaker, while the band headed out to Fraises-des-Bois. "Sleep, eat, shower, and change," said Niko. "Choose one from column A and one from column B."

Steve Connelly and I rode up front with the driver. I was so glad of the big window that I didn't mind being stuck between him and another cynical French chauffeur. I watched the scenery greedily as we drove toward Fraises-des-Bois—or Thursday Blah, as Lacey called it.

We'd already left behind the ring of skyscrapers that encircles the city like galactic sentries. Out here in the suburbs the horizon was lower: industrial parks and shopping malls, flat glass islands in a sea of cars.

But it was the towns I coveted. They're never close to the road; you have to look for them, tucked behind a hill or flashing into sight when a river makes a sudden space among the trees. First would come a glimpse of slate roof, and then a street would open up, a thread of silver shining through a canyon of warm stone shops and houses. Sometimes I could make out a wrought-iron balcony, and above it a row of shutters latched against the midday sun.

When we left the highway my hopes soared. We turned onto

a narrow road that ducked under a railroad bridge and wound past fields of corn, meadows dotted with sheep or cows . . . then the concrete gave way to asphalt, and the farmhouses to stucco cottages aproned with Monet gardens of roses, iris, poppies, and lupines. Here and there a stucco wall or wrought-iron fence hung with climbing roses screened out nosy passers-by.

The Hôtel des Fraises fronted on a cobbled square. You could tell it had stood here since long before Holiday Inns began, and expected to remain long after they were plowed under. At some point during the past century someone had yielded to modernity enough to hang boxes of geraniums under the windows, and a wagon wheel—also planted with geraniums—beside the front door. The hotel's only identification swung from its red tiled roof: a wooden shield painted with three strawberries.

And that stout gentleman on the stoop must be Monsieur Vlaemenck. I went to say hello, knowing he would expect us to introduce ourselves and doubting this would occur to the band.

Meanwhile, half a dozen curious housewives and children had interrupted their errands to see what visitors had come to Fraises-des-Bois in such a fancy car. One middle-aged couple held up a placard. Fans? No: *Welcome Stephen Connelly.*

Dan, Terry, and Roach headed straight from the limo to the front door. Lacey and Niko trailed behind, fascinated, nudging each other and staring as if they'd landed on a strange planet.

I lagged at the rear. Steve Connelly was shaking hands with his hosts. Too late for me to run over and meet them. As they walked off together down the hill, resistance tightened in my chest. I wasn't ready to go inside with Quasi & Company. This was France! I needed time to savor this town, this blessed ordinary afternoon. Like that woman with a string bag and baby stroller, heading down the cobbled street toward the shops. When I lived in Paris I too did my marketing every day. I could follow her—pick up a croissant at the bakery. Or sit on that bench across from the two old men in tweed coats and admire how the sun was dappling the cobblestones and streaking the archway of the town hall.

I looked up into the linden tree over my head. Dark heart-shaped leaves, rustling when a breeze came by . . . and on the tip of each branch the paler, thinner leaves the French pluck off and dry for tilleul. I used to drink tilleul most mornings when I was working in the apartment near the Place St. Augustin, when my nerves would start jangling from too much caffeine. Larry always brewed a big pot of dark-roast coffee as soon as he got up . . .

But I was not going to think about Larry.

The Hôtel des Fraises' tiny lobby was a jumble of luggage, noise, and musicians. I pieced together enough fragments to deduce that Quasi & Company had decided to eat first, leave the suitcases in a heap for the bellman, and hit the showers and/or beds after lunch.

The clerk handed me my key. Was I with them or on my own? My stomach rumbled. I reminded myself of Phases and followed the band in to lunch.

Windows along both sides made the dining room look spacious, though it held only eight square tables. Three of these had been pulled together in the center for Quasi & Company. A girl of about sixteen in a black dress and white apron greeted us with a formal nod. "Bonjour, mesdames, messieurs."

"Enchantée!" Lacey grinned.

Monsieur Vlaemenck's staff had laid out a feast: platters of cold roast beef and ham, carafes of wine, a bowl of fruit, baskets of fresh French bread, a splendid cheese board.

"Oh, super! Cole slaw!" Lacey gave a pleased little bounce.

"Yech!" said Roach. "How can you eat that crap? It always smells like a fish died in it."

"I don't think it is cole slaw, anyway." Lacey was peering into the dish. "Cory, what's this white stuff?"

"Celery root," I told her with a wave of déja vu.

Niko, inspecting the cheeses, asked the waitress, "What are they all?"

"Camembert, Brie, Caprice des Dieux." The names rolled out like cathedral bells. "Chèvre, Roquefort, Gruyère, Pyrenées."

Across the table Roach fingered a fruit knife curiously. Lacey slid in beside him and poured herself a glass of red wine. I sat down opposite and helped myself to the celery root.

Dan and Terry stood by the windows talking business. "Hey,

you guys want to stuff it?" Roach let out a loud belch. "I'm trying to eat."

"Here comes the landlord," said Terry.

Monsieur Vlaemenck was smiling nervously. "Good afternoon, good afternoon! Is everything to your satisfaction?"

For a few seconds nobody answered.

"Yeah," said Niko.

Terry said, "You got any beer?"

Roach said, "I'm in the mood for a double cheeseburger. Rare."

I grimaced. Monsieur Vlaemenck, however, far from being offended, seemed pleased to be of service. "I shall have made for you a cheeseburger," he declared. "And for you, beer!" he told Terry. "What beer will you like?"

Terry and Niko both put in for Heineken. Roach wanted a Beck's, preferably two. Dan had sat down next to Lacey and was pouring himself coffee. Monsieur Vlaemenck gave orders to the waitress for *quatre biers et un cheeseburger.*

Terry, meanwhile, filled a glass of wine and offered our host a seat at the end of the table. Lacey and Niko passed him meat, cheese, and bread. Under all this attention, the innkeeper soon was chatting with his unusual guests as if he'd known them for days.

"You have picked a fortunate weekend to come to Fraises-des-Bois! You have heard of our Fête des Fraises?"

No, they hadn't, but Lacey at least was eager to be informed.

"Well! It begins Saturday night, with the *Retraite aux Flambeaux.* That is a sort of parade. The children carry—what do you call them?" He sketched a shape in the air. "Flambeaux?"

"Torches," I translated, puzzled, and then, "Oh! Japanese lanterns!"

"Ah, yes! And afterward, in the large field where the schools have their games, there is the *feu d'artifice.*"

"Fireworks."

"Wow! Super!" said Lacey.

"It will be very fine," Monsieur Vlaemenck agreed complacently. "People come from all the towns around, and some even from Paris. There will be many important visitors—the *maire,* the *sous-préfet*, perhaps the *préfet de Paris*."

Dan shot a swift look at Terry. "What about music?"

"Bien sur, music, of course," nodded Monsieur Vlaemenck. "For the *retraite* we have bands from the high schools, and then rock music from a tape for the *feu d'artifice*. Our young people in France, just as yours in America, they like very much the rock music." He smiled graciously around the table.

Dan smiled back. "Maybe you'd like to have live rock music, then, instead of a tape."

Lacey paused in the middle of a chew. Terry reached across Niko to refill Monsieur Vlaemenck's wine glass.

"Live rock music?" he echoed, nonplussed. "We have never done such a thing." He glanced from Dan to Lacey to Roach. "Your band would play for our Fête des Fraises?"

"Why not?" said Dan. "You're giving us a place to stay."

"We'd like to return the favor," said Terry. "Right?"

"Oui! You bet," grinned Lacey. "Fireworks and rock-&-roll!"

Roach lifted his beer bottle and attempted to sound nonchalant. "Tray B.N."

I watched the overhead fan turning in the bowl of my spoon like a tiny propeller. Thinking: Jerry Leroy's going to guillotine you guys, unless Victor Tréville beats him to it.

"Well," said Monsieur Vlaemenck. He appeared flustered but pleased. "You are most generous to make this offer. I will telephone right now to *le maire*, Monsieur d'Aumont, to learn if we can arrange it."

"Tell him we've got a crew," said Roach.

"And sound equipment," Lacey added.

"All you need to arrange is a stage and lighting," said Terry.

As soon as Monsieur Vlaemenck had bowed and departed I turned to Dan. He was daubing mustard on a chunk of bread.

"Pardonnez-moi, Dan," said Niko. "Not to rain on your parade or anything, but what about Hands Across the Sea?"

"No problem." Terry popped a grape into his mouth. "They've got a museum tour Saturday."

"So they won't care if we use their sound system, crew, truck, drums, synthesizers, et cetera, for an outside gig?"

"No." Dan stuffed roast beef into his sandwich.

I stared at him. He meant it.

"International good will," Terry told Niko. "We play at this fête thing, Hands gets the publicity. That's our job, is PR. Right, Cory?"

"Right," I conceded.

But that's not why Dan is so sure they won't care, I thought, and you know it.

Monsieur Vlaemenck came back beaming: On behalf of the mayor and citizens of Fraises-des-Bois, he was pleased to accept Quasi & Company's kind offer. The band clinked glasses and voted to go catch some Z's. Though Monsieur Vlaemenck looked perplexed, they didn't explain. Nor did they speak to me. Most likely they lumped us both with the waitress: useful for certain functions, but not significant.

I left them waiting for the ancient wrought-iron elevator to chug back down the middle of the spiral staircase. There was a phone booth in the lobby—probably the only public outside line.

But John Otis wasn't in. I told his secretary about Quasi & Company's change of hotels. Would she be amused? Shocked? Impressed? No. She said she would have Mr. Otis call me, and hung up with a brutal click.

My back sagged against the glass. I'd forgotten about this part of being on the road: how you get so tired you can't think, and the one thing you crave, more than sleep or food or a stiff drink or even getting the job done, is to connect with somebody. That line some English poet wrote four centuries before Bob Dylan was born: *Christ, that my love were in my arms, and I in my bed again!*

I looked down and saw that my address book was open to a number I once knew better than my own.

Luckily I'd anticipated this question back in Boston and decided not to call Marian Thorne. She belonged in Larry's pile, not mine. Though, ironically, she of all his Paris connections had welcomed us into her home as if I were the last, rather than merely the latest, of his lovers. With her regal bearing, her love of ceremony, her disdain for anything canned, plastic, or disposable, Great-Aunt Marian had swept through our Hemingwayesque summer like a gust of Henry James. We spent most Sundays in her flat near la Madeleine . . . measuring out our lives in coffee spoons, as Marian liked to observe. Larry mounting the steep steps with Le Monde and the London Times, while I carried the pâtisseries in their twists of paper; and at the top, the rich aroma of French coffee. That coffee, Larry told me teasingly, was the main thing he and Marian agreed on until I came along.

I stared at the number. *And should I then presume?*

Then I could hear the phone ringing on the other end, and I realized I must have dialed it.

"Allo?" The aged, quavery voice I remembered so well.

My heart thumped. "Marian? It's Cory."

"Well, for heaven's sake! Where are you, chérie? Are you in Paris?"

"Almost." I decribed my situation.

She chuckled. "Leave it to you to come to France with *des mecs américains!* But surely you can get away for a visit. When may I expect you? For tea this afternoon, perhaps? I have a dinner engagement at seven, I'm afraid."

Her autocratic tone made me want to call a taxi immediately. "Give me time for a nap and a shower and I'll be on my way."

"Good! Fivish, then? I'll look out for you. And take care, chérie. I remember all too well from my youth what musicians can be like."

I smiled. "You'll have to tell me about it."

I walked up the carpeted stairs feeling buoyant. Who needed the *mecs américains*? Paris was my turf. With my notebook and my tape recorder, a new job and an old friend, I was home free.

I swung down the hall to my room humming that tune from D.C.:

"Got to get back to the time
when my mind was full of wonder,
And this burden that I'm under,
It won't weigh me down no more!"

Chapter 6: Break on Through (to the Other Side)

My lecture on T.S. Eliot wasn't getting through to my tenth graders. Somebody at the back of the long, dim hall was playing a radio, distracting the whole class—including me. Rock-&-roll? I should make her turn it off . . . but if I could figure out who the band was . . .

My eyes opened. The classroom dissolved into the white walls of my hotel room, but the music didn't stop.

As consciousness ruthlessly invaded my brain, I realized (a) it wasn't Quasi & Company, and (b) it was coming from next door.

If you can't beat 'em, join 'em. I slipped into jeans and a T-shirt and padded down the hall.

Monsieur Vlaemenck, bless his old-fashioned heart, had put Lacey and me on the first floor—that is, the first above the ground floor—and the gentlemen (his term) on the second. What Lacey and Roach intended to do about this I didn't know. Given that the Hôtel des Fraises had only one bathroom per floor, I'd find out soon enough.

Lacey's door was open. She sat cross-legged on the bed, her blouse a splash of tropical green against the white tufted bedspread. Her bare feet were tucked under her knees, and she was toking on a joint.

"Hi!" she said with obvious accuracy.

"Lacey," I said, hoping I didn't sound like a tenth-grade teacher, "you're nuts to do that here. Especially without shutting your door."

She ducked her shoulders apologetically. "I thought if it's so illegal I better keep the air moving."

"Then open the windows!"

"Would you?" Lacey waved a vague hand. "I couldn't deal with those shutters and cranks and shit."

Hopeless. "What's this?" I nodded at the tape deck on the dresser, where a female vocalist was singing loudly about love.

Lacey misinterpreted. "Oh, Dan's new boom box. I borrowed it. Prick-o Mr. Snooze kicked me out so he could sleep." She inhaled another hit and talked over held breath. "I wanted to go to Paris. Couldn't get anybody to go with me."

I turned down the music. "Aren't you tired?"

Lacey shook her frizzy head. "You should never sleep right after a long plane flight. Bad for jet lag."

I could just see her back in Boston, determined not to be pushed around by the guys, memorizing useful facts from a guidebook.

"Anyhow, shit, man!" She rested the joint in the ashtray on her knee. "We're in France! I want to get out there! Go see all that stuff they were talking about in the truck. What's that place with the bars and artists?"

"Montmartre."

"That first. Then the Eiffel Tower." She ticked them off on her fingers. "Then coffee and French pastries in an outdoor café, with the umbrellas, and maybe walk along the Seine and look at the old men in berets. And then shopping—I bet you can get some amazing clothes in this town! Paris is where all the designers live, you know? They must have outlets."

So jubilantly earnest I didn't dare laugh. "Sounds like a busy weekend."

"Doesn't it?" Lacey nodded. "Can you believe those zombies are wasting the whole fucking day? Jeez! Should've taken their Geritol."

She toked again at her joint, but it was out.

"So I guess I'll go tomorrow. You coming to sound check?"

I shook my head. "I have to visit an old friend in Paris. Do you think I could get a ride in with you all?"

"No problem," said Lacey. She slid toward the edge of the bed. "Who's the friend?"

From the way she didn't look at me, I realized she was sniffing for a romance. "A woman I used to know." I wondered what she'd think if I told her the whole story. Whatever Lacey Sky had to say about my foundering marriage, it was bound to be different from any view I'd heard.

"Is that why you came on this thing?" asked Lacey, lighting a match. "To see your friend? Or was it us?"

"You," I admitted.

"You were a Rind fan, huh?"

There was a note of reverence in the question that filled me with sudden empathy for my father when I'd asked him if he listened to Duke Ellington and Count Basie before I was born. "Well, sure," I said. *Garçon! Un Geritol, s'il vous plait!* "It was partly the political thing—they were a focal point for the antiwar movement."

Lacey nodded. "Roach said they were the only band that played protest songs you could boogie to." She offered me the joint. I declined. "Who was your favorite? Mickey?"

"Mickey before I met them. Then Dan."

"He's pretty amazing, huh?" A puff of smoke came out with the words. "I used to wish, when we started this band— But I'd never do that. Hard enough keeping it together with Roach. I should meet Stevie Nicks sometime and find out how she and Lindsay worked it out for so long."

Lacey and Dan Quasi? I covered my shock: "Who's Stevie Nicks?"

"Fleetwood Mac? Aren't you a music writer?"

I explained about freelancing and feature stories. "Even that piece I did on The Rind was more why they were at the demonstration than about the band."

"But you were *in* the sixties, right?" Lacey sounded disappointed. "You must have known like the Beatles and the Stones, didn't you?"

Again she held out the joint. This time I took it. Her fingertips were hard, her nails short and unpolished. A musician's hand.

"Depends what you mean by know them." Drawing smoke carefully into my lungs; remembering when I used to relish this acrid prickling at the back of my throat. "I danced to the Stones at parties—everybody did. And the Beatles—I probably still have *Revolver, Sergeant Pepper*—"

"I'm a Stones person," Lacey said. "Terry says you had to be either Beatles or Stones back then."

"We used to say it was which Beatle you liked." Trying not to sound old. "Like horoscopes or something."

"I like George. He did those neat things with Indian music. Who'd you like?"

"George at the beginning, then John."

"Yeah. My favorite Beatles song of all time is 'Norwegian Wood.' That's one of the nice things about Dan. He's been catching me up on who did everything."

Dan again: leitmotif of my fantasies. My brain was floating. I couldn't think of anything to say.

"Is he always like this?" I asked finally. "So—intense?"

"Dan? Nah. Everybody's pretty weird right now. Roach too. As soon as we start playing it'll be different."

I would have liked to ask how it would be different, but I was having trouble framing the question. The last thing I wanted was for Lacey to tell Dan—

"How did you get involved with these guys?" I asked instead. "How'd you meet Roach?"

Lacey grinned and rolled her eyes. "After a gig in San Francisco. I thought he was crazy! I dug how he played bass—you know, sort of winking at you, like ain't this a gas, and at the same time turning out these incredible licks. Then the next time I saw him, it was at this loft party in Oakland, all kinds of speakers and a couple of strobes and a slide show on the wall, and there was this big tent in the middle"—she sketched it in the air—"full of pillows, made out of a parachute—" Her hands fell. "Babble babble! Anyhow, me and Roach were both totally wasted, and we wound up in the tent around four in the morning, and when we woke up I moved in with him."

Not quite what I'd expected. Is that how it always works with musicians? I wondered, faintly repelled. They go home with whoever's left when the party's over?

"So what's your deal?" Lacey asked. "They're all trying to figure it out."

I blushed. "What? Who?"

"The guys. Are you married or divorced or what?"

Immediately I tightened. "Married." The box I always checked on forms. Spoken, though, it sounded dishonest. "Sort of," I amended with a familiar sense of shame. "We're living apart."

"Huh." Lacey cocked her head. "How come?"

Nobody in Boston would have asked me such a question. What was she doing, this mop-headed kid who hardly knew me, nosing into the private corners of my life?

"Irreconcilable differences."

"Like what?" Lacey persisted.

I walked over to the window. I was shivering, probably from the dope. "Like we both wanted to be writers."

"Oh. Gotcha." Lacey nodded sagely. "I had that problem with a singer last year. Joey Domini from Magic Fingers, as a matter of fact." She reached for matches. "How'd you meet him?"

My hands gripped the windowsill. Down in the square, two little boys in shorts were playing tag around a linden tree. Sun sparkled in the leaves, bright as Lacey's blouse. Obla-dee, obla-da!

"At a party in Paris. He was working on a magazine piece on drug smuggling, which he later decided would make a better novel, and he took me out for dinner and told me stories about informers and cocaine deals and underwater reconnaissance, and"—I hesitated—"a week later we moved in together."

Lacey was lighting another joint. "Did he ever finish it? The novel?"

I shook my head.

"So you split?"

I wanted to tell her it wasn't that simple, I'd just endured three years of counseling to testify that nothing involving marriage could ever be that simple; but the dope was fuzzing my sentences. "Right," I said.

Lacey held out the joint sympathetically. "Love stinks, huh?"

I had to laugh. "Yeah. It's a bitch."

"Men!" With an expressive grimace she swung her feet onto the floor. "Who would've ever picked them for an opposite sex?"

I was gazing into my closet, contemplating my clothes, romance, and existence, when the intercom on the wall buzzed. Lacey saving me a seat in the limo? No. The desk clerk's tinny voice: Telephone call in the lobby for Mrs. Thorne.

Oh, god, I thought, Marian. I never should have smoked that joint.

"Allo?"

The voice that answered was distant, think and crackly. "Cory! Thank god."

"Well, John! What a surprise! Did you get my message?"

"Yes. I've talked with Gaston Vlaemenck. Thanks for trying to straighten things out."

"You don't sound happy."

"I'm not," John replied curtly. "I told Gaston I'd have the band out of there by tomorrow and he won't hear of it. Says they're playing at the Strawberry Festival. Christ! What is this, French Woodstock?"

"What's wrong with that? They play at the Fête des Fraises, Hands Across the Sea gets the publicity."

"Cory," said John, "I want you to move to the Ritz in Paris. Tonight."

"Why?"

"You remember that French politician who asked us not to send over The Rind?"

"Victor Tréville." My grip on the receiver tightened.

"Well, Jerry Leroy just called me, foaming at the mouth. Tréville phoned again. He had to evacuate his office an hour ago due to a bomb threat which he says came from this band."

A hundred questions swarmed into my brain. "Why does he think that? What kind of threat? Where was this? Paris?"

"Brière. Five miles from Fraises-des-Bois."

Uh-oh.

"A local messenger service hand-delivered a note while Tréville was out at lunch. I quote: 'The day of judgment is here. We will blow you sky-high.' The police took that literally and cleared the building. Sent in a squad to search. Didn't find anything."

"This was in English?"

"Right."

"Who gave it to the messenger service?"

"They can't say. Their books show an over-the-counter cash transaction. One of hundreds they handle every day."

"French cash?"

"Yes. We gave the band a thousand francs for immediate expenses, if that's what you're wondering."

I had my notebook out and was scribbling furiously. "Any fingerprints on the note or envelope? Watermarks? Other distinguishing features?"

"They're checking."

"What makes Tréville think it came from Quasi & Company?"

"The last line. 'We don't forget, government man. Now it's your turn to die.' I understand," John added caustically, "'Government Man' is a song of theirs."

There was a short but expensive pause.

"Good thing I'm here. I'll ask—"

"No!" John's voice spluttered explosively. "You're not to mention this, Cory, not to anyone. Officially you don't even know about it. Their security forces are adamant about that, and so is Tréville. Whoever sent him that threat could be—well, god knows! If Larry—" He stopped.

"If Larry what?"

"He called me this morning. He's not pleased I sent you over there."

"I hope you told him you didn't send me over here. And it's not his business anyway."

"I'm putting this wrong," John said. "He's concerned about you. He doesn't want you running around with a bunch of—who knows what."

Across the lobby the sun was outlining the hotel's shuttered windows in neon. A thin beam of light striped Monsieur Vlaemenck's chintz sofa and slanted across the red and gray carpet, blunting itself against a chair.

"Let's get this straight," I said. "A, when I'm on a job I run around with whoever I need to, as Larry of all people should know. B, this threat thing is absurd. I've been with Quasi & Company all day, and I can assure you, they're no more dangerous than I am."

John's reply was lost in static. All I got was, "—about Larry. I'm the one who's asking you—out of there! This is no joking—"

"It damn well is a joking matter!" I interrupted heatedly. "It's ridiculous."

"Well, Jerry Leroy, —police, and Monsieur Tréville aren't laughing. Listen, Cory. Maybe it's just some—, or a publicity stunt, I don't know. All I can say is—"

"A publicity stunt?"

"—I'll rest a hell of—easier when you're out of there. Forget Larry. If anything were to—I'd never forgive myself."

"I forgive you in advance," I told him, and hung up.

Lacey and I rode to Paris in the back seat of the limo. I'd expected the guys to kick us out, or at least kick me out, but evidently dibs went to whoever got there first.

There wasn't much conversation as we headed toward the highway. Everybody seemed tired but OK. Nobody made any cryptic remarks or darted any meaningful glances suggesting a secret plan to blow Victor Tréville sky-high.

I should have told John how unAmerican that note sounded. Formal. Stilted. Not like Quasi & Company.

But then, if one of them did want to kill Victor Tréville, or scare him, wouldn't he/she disguise his/her voice?

I should have pointed out that you don't just walk off a plane and find a commercial messenger service in a country whose language you can't speak. How many hours from our arrival in France to our arrival at the Hôtel des Fraises? Four at most. No chance for anyone from the band to sneak off from the airport or sound check or lunch to Brière and back.

Unless he/she took the limo after the rest of us went upstairs. Or the truck, or a taxi. Or bribed one of the French crew to do it, or a hotel employee.

What I should have asked John was: Is Monsieur Tréville married, or otherwise related, to Madame Tréville of Hands Across the Sea's French committee?

Merde! Was I so touchy now about Larry that just hearing his name knocked me from offense back to defense?

Roach reached up to poke Niko in the front seat. "Hey, dude, you got any more of that nose chili?"

"Wait till we get there," said Terry. He sniffed discreetly, as if he'd caught a cold since lunch and didn't want us to catch it.

Double merde!

"When's our day off?" asked Roach.

"Do we get a day off?" asked Lacey.

"Off?" Dan echoed as if he hadn't heard the word before. "You mean our day to rehearse?"

"All we get off is daytimes," said Terry. "We've got a gig every night."

Lacey made a face. "Rehearse phooey! Man, I'm going to Paris!"

Roach folded his arms around her. "Lacey's going to be a dancing girl. What do they call 'em? The Folies Bergère."

Lacey twisted in his enveloping hug. "And you can sit in the audience and drool! If you get a haircut. Otherwise they'll drag you onstage to be the dancing bear."

"Don't get uppity, kiddo! I've got me a big old empty bed back there, and all those little girls from the airport looking to get in it."

"Hah!" They were tussling now, Roach trying to tickle Lacey, Lacey fighting back with fists and elbows. "They don't want your creaky old body! They just wanted your shirt!"

I squeezed farther into my corner, away from flailing arms and unwelcome suspicions.

"Hey!" said Niko, who had been staring out the window. "Is that the Seine?"

Roach and Lacey stopped wrestling to look. There it was,

silvery and glittering in the late afternoon sun, the river people had been writing songs about since long before rock-&-roll.

"So, Cory, where's the Eiffel Tower?" Lacey tucked in her blouse.

"Twenty minutes or so from here. Not far from where we're going."

Hold it. We?

"Let's go see it!" said Lacey. "Is there time?"

"Sure," said Dan.

Their limousine, or our limousine, pulled up at the Place du Trocadéro, just across the river from Paris's most famous landmark. On our left was the grassy circle of the Place with its statue of Marshal Foch. On the right curved the long white-columned pavilions of the Palais de Chaillot, and rising behind them the iron lacework spire of la Tour Eiffel.

"I'm getting out!" announced Lacey.

They all wanted to get out. I stayed behind to make sure the car would wait.

The driver watched them wander off across the pavement with an expression of amused tolerance. "Ce sont des gosses, eh?"

"Oui!" I agreed with the expected chuckle. Evidently he hadn't picked up on where they got that childlike exuberance.

I caught up with Lacey at the top of the wide steps at the end of the terrace. Her arms were spread out as if to hug the whole panorama in front of her: the Eiffel Tower across the river, and beyond it the green lawns and rectangular pools of the Champ de Mars.

"Wow!" she crowed. "France! I love it!"

Dan and Terry had gone down the steps for a closer look at the tower. Niko stood inspecting a huge gilded statue behind one of the Palais pavilions. Roach was talking to an African hawking beads and statuettes from a blanket spread on the pavement.

How could any of those gosses, I asked myself, possibly want to kill Victor Tréville?

✈

The limo dropped me at the Place de la Concorde. I needed a few blocks' walk before climbing out on the Paris limb of my erstwhile family tree.

What news had reached Marian Thorne about Larry's and my separation I had no idea. I'd tried writing to her, but what could I say? *Stand by, please, we are experiencing technical difficulties.*

The last time I'd stood on this spot I was holding a bottle of Dom Perignon Larry and I had brought back from Reims to toast our marriage.

Triple merde!

I pressed the bell.

Marian stood waiting at the top of the stairs: a small commanding figure in a dressing gown of pale blue Chinese silk that set off her silver hair. We kissed each other on both cheeks. Her skin was limp and soft, her shoulder thin as a bird's wing in my hand.

"But do come in, chérie. My, you're looking fit! This adventure must agree with you."

She moved across the mirrored foyer with an air of preparing to clap her hands and summon an army of footmen. I followed her into the salon.

Nothing had changed. There was the red-and-white striped recamier, my favorite seat in this apartment; the oriental rugs, the polished parquet floor, the french windows half open, drapes tied back. I could have been stopping by on my way home from the Beaubourg.

"The kettle's on, but I haven't made the tea," said Marian. "What would you prefer? Darjeeling? Tilleul? Or sherry?"

"Tilleul is perfect." Was it too soon to ask if I could smoke? "May I help?"

"Oh, it won't take a minute."

I sat. Marian's ideas about hospitality are firm: the guest offers, the host refuses. As far as I knew, only Berthe, her housekeeper, had ever set foot in her kitchen. Larry used to tease her about that—at least she should let him in, if only so as to brag someday that the famous novelist Lawrence Thorne once washed her dishes. And Marian would retort that it was quite enough having him in the salon, thank you, given his cavalier way with her teacups.

My eyes prickled treacherously. I was too tired for this. I wished I'd asked for sherry.

Marian came in with a silver tray of tea things. "We'll let it steep a bit longer."

"Is Berthe still with you?"

"Oh, yes. Bien sur." She seated herself on a needlepoint chair. "But tell me, chérie, about this band."

My gaze moved over the tea set to the windows behind her. *For I have known them all already, known them all.* The mahogany desk with its quill pen and crystal inkwell. Twin chairs —Louis Quinze? On the wall over the marble fireplace, Larry's favorite painting: a small Delacroix of a tiger tearing at an antelope.

And Marian wanted to know about the band.

I temporized. "Have you heard of this exchange program, Hands Across the Sea?"

"Yes," said Marian. "Isn't that the one Marie Tréville is running?"

"You know her?" I sat up straight.

"Mais oui. They used to live in Boston, you know. Now they're in Brière, where her husband is sous-préfet."

"I thought he was a development official in Marne-la-Vallée."

"That too. France's bureaucracy allows a good deal of overlap." She handed me a cup, fragile as an eggshell. "You've met them?"

"Not yet. Probably tonight."

"Marie really is a sweet girl," said Marian. "This Hands Across the Sea ought to be just the thing for her."

She might have been approving a friend's sending an errant child to military school. "Why is that?"

"Well," she considered, "Marie Tréville has always been rather—how to put it?—high-spirited. Now that her two boys are off at school . . . and Victor not the domestic sort . . . A daughter might have kept her busier—sewing, dolls, and whatnot."

"I'm not following."

"She is attractive," Marian stated. "In the literal sense. Marie Tréville is the kind of woman who draws things to her."

"Men?"

"Men, of course, but more than that." Marian's hand was as translucent as her china cup. "It's an idea, or perhaps legend is a better word, as old as France itself: that there are certain women who cause events. Carmen. Lulu. Marguerite Gautier, la dame aux camelias. Women who through no particular design of their own are forever at the vortex."

"And that's Marie Tréville?"

"Well, I do think the melodramas that have swirled around les Tréville owe as much to Victor's intransigence as cherchez la femme. But there is a quality about her . . . You'll see."

"Victor's intransigence?" I didn't want her to stop. "What do you mean? What kind of man is he?"

If Marian wondered why I was so nosy, she was polite enough not to ask. Victor Tréville had come into public service from the Army on Charles deGaulle's coattails. He irked his colleagues from the start: got into hot water during the Algerian crisis, and worse with the students in '68. DeGaulle finally shipped him to Boston to get him out of the way.

"Were he and Marie married then?"

"Oh, no. Oddly enough, they met in Boston. Their families were old friends back in Brière. Marie had been badgering her parents to let her go to America, and Victor got her a job at the consulate. Where he found the time to fall in love with her I can't imagine, because he was no less difficult there than here. Hanged in effigy by students outside the Bibliothèque Française on Marlborough Street! He was recalled when Richard Nixon resigned the presidency. Then he married Marie, and with a little string-pulling, landed a sous-préfecture."

"She went back to France with him?"

"Yes. To the immense relief of her parents."

"Do you happen to know if either of them ever ran into a rock band in Boston called The Rind?"

"I shouldn't think so. They're more the Fauré sort. But who knows? If I had to guess," said Marian, implying she was glad she didn't, "I'd say Victor would have tried whatever it took to win her. It was he who fell for her, tu comprends—she'd have nothing to do with him at first. Even after convent school, Marie was quite a headstrong girl."

"Headstrong enough to take up with an American?"

"Only within the bounds of decorum."

"An affair?"

"No." Marian was positive. "If she'd had an affair, he wouldn't have married her."

I let out a long breath. There was a key in here somewhere . . . but to what, exactly?

"But here I am wasting our little time with gossip! Enough of Marie and Victor. What about you, chérie?" Marian smiled at me over her teacup. "Such a surprise to hear you'd gone into teaching! You were sweet to send me your stories about the Beaubourg—I enjoyed them enormously."

So long ago I didn't even remember what I'd written.

"How is it that you find yourself in France with Hands Across the Sea and their band?"

My fingers tightened around the plushy curve of the recamier. Speaking of bad company, you mean? No need to be tactful, Marian. I've already been reminded it's bad form for a Thorne, even a fallen-away Thorne, to turn up in Paris with a bunch of—who knows what.

I heard myself repeating what I'd told my friends: no security in freelancing, no stability, but with the summer off from school, John Otis, media coverage, international good will . . . My voice pleasantly reasonable; my heart as full and hollow as a cactus tree. Cordelia Goodwin Thorne, ladies and gentlemen, reprising the role she created at her wedding reception.

Marian, can you hear me? What are we doing in this verbal game of lawn tennis? You know why I've come back to Paris, and it's not for Hands Across the Sea.

"More tea, chérie?"

The eyes that fix you in a formulated phrase,

> *And when I am formulated, sprawling on a pin,*
> *. . . Then how should I begin?*

Her thin translucent hands tipped the pot, a fortune-teller pouring out tea leaves. What will it be, Marian? You ran away, yet here you are presiding over silver and tradition as if you never left Beacon Hill. Will you speak of me to your dinner companions tonight as lightly, as ruefully, as you spoke of Marie Tréville? Will you say that Larry and I should have had children? Or that he's better off without me?

My eyes moved up the curve of the fireplace to her small Delacroix. Seven years, and still the same tiger was tearing the throat of the same antelope.

"Almost out," said Marian. "Shall I make some more?"

Erect in her pale blue dressing gown, she might have been carved in ice.

"Tilleul," I said. "It's been so long. All it needs is a madeleine."

There was the slightest pause; then Marian said, "Have you seen Kilmartin's *À la recherche du temps perdu*?"

Not the response I wanted. "Only from the outside."

"I hear it's not so different from the Moncrieff. A word here, a phrase there, but still Proust, all the same." She emptied the teapot into my cup. "Is that why you admire this Quasi & Company, chérie? For coming back after so long in search of lost time?"

Quasi & Company! What about Larry and me?

"Admire them?" I stared past her at the treetops outside. "I suppose that's why they interest me."

"You'll hear them play tonight?"

"Yes."

"You must come back and tell me all about it."

I stood up. "Marian, thank you. It's lovely to see you."

"And you, too, Cordelia."

Our eyes met, and for an instant I thought maybe, enfin—

But her gaze went opaque: "Do call and let me know how you're getting on. Will you?"

"Of course." I kissed her cheek. "Goodbye, Marian."

I walked through the golden evening light like fallen leaves. I'd intended to take the Métro, but now I felt a need to stay on my feet, to clear my head, or at least tire myself out.

Green hedges across the Rue de Rivoli marked the Jardin des Tuileries. Don't think. There will be time, there will be time. Focus on the banquet. Quasi & Company. Dan Quasi.

Once we start playing it'll be different. Yes! The old crush will kick in again. Isn't that why I'm here? To get back—yes!—to when my mind was full of wonder. Listening to The Rind as I drove toward my next assignment. Crawling into my motel bed wishing Dan Quasi were beside me for real instead of on tape.

No sailboats in the Bassin Rond. It was suppertime in Paris. Only a few children still bounced on the bright painted horses-on-springs under the trees. Twenty yards away, live ponies at the pony ride drowsed in a late shaft of sunlight.

Not blue eyes but hazel ones smiling at me: Let's stay home tonight. Home! Our salon with its twin Smith-Coronas; our chambre hardly big enough for the great sagging four-poster some ancestral Thorne bought at a chateau sale. We always lit the oil lamp before we made love. Larry said the glow on my skin brought tears to his eyes.

I blinked back my own tears. Get back? To what, Cory? The sixties? Music, love, and flowers? A nice place to visit, but you can't live there.

Where can you live when you reach the end of the yellow brick road and find you're not cut out for the Emerald City?

The flowers at my feet were blurred splotches of color in a field of dust. Gradually they reorganized themselves: geraniums and begonias, rosebushes, statues, benches, outdoor cafés. Everything the same as seven years ago . . . except me.

That summer I'd never asked where I was going. Simple: home for a night with my lover, then back to work. Cory Goodwin of Phases!—who can change the course of mighty paragraphs, bend clauses with her bare hands! Scuffing my sandals in these dusty paths, my mind seething with active verbs; while an interview with a gallery guard matched up with a tourist's comment, and a page of notes linked magically into a story.

Right now Hands Across the Sea's ambassadors were mustering for their welcoming banquet. Soon my notebook and tape recorder and I would march up the steps, to take risks and take charge.

I raised my fist at the pony man. Sancho! My horse!

Chapter 7: White Rabbit

The giant stone goddesses reclining in the arch over the doorway dwarfed Sheila Bailey in her beige polyester suit and heels.

Her eyebrows went up—no host family? no husband?—and then down as she recognized me. Cory Thorne. Just in time; dinner should be starting any minute. Yes, Marie Tréville was inside.

"Where would I find her? Is Monsieur Tréville here, too?"

But Sheila was beaming her warm American welcome at a new group of arrivals. "Head table," she called over her shoulder. "Red dress."

I'd come to an important conclusion while I walked. Whatever John Otis might say, I owed it to him to investigate the link (if any) between Quasi & Company and Victor Tréville's bomb threat (if that's what it was). Who else had my access and expertise? Nobody, including Steve Connelly. However eager he was to bag the elephant in the room, Steve was no journalist, and he hadn't spent the day with the band.

Three points piqued my curiosity. First: Victor Tréville's odd reaction to the message. Say you're such a dedicated politician that you hold not one but two government jobs. An anonymous note threatens to blow you sky high. You call a bomb squad to evacuate and search your office. What next? Rush home to make sure your wife is safe? Help the police with their inquiries? Or telephone the Governor of Massachusetts and throw fits about a visiting rock-&-roll band?

Second: Was it Victor Tréville who identified 'Government Man' as a Rind song? If so, did that confirm that he'd crossed paths—or swords—with them in Boston? If not, why go ballistic the minute he heard they were coming to France?

Third, and most intriguing: Why did Tréville take the note so seriously?

OK, sure, a bomb threat, best to err on the side of caution.

But this threat was also an accusation. *The day of judgment is here. We don't forget. Now it's your turn to die.* What sin had Victor Tréville committed that cried out for vengeance? And why did Tréville jump straight to defense, without pausing at surprise and denial, unless he knew the answer?

When in doubt, find out.

The head table was empty. I scanned the crowd and didn't see a magnetic woman in a red dress, nor anyone from Quasi & Company.

So I joined the hosts and ambassadors lining up for the buffet-style banquet.

I must be hungry. It was hours since lunch.

Something about this scene, though, made me itchy. All these jovial Americans joking with their new French friends. I used to take the same detour around the language barrier when I lived here. *Ah, c'est drôle, n'est-ce pas?* Sharing a chuckle at the whirling water sculptures at the Centre Pompidou, or the green elephant-machine vacuuming up litter with its trunk. Here it was this gargantuan hall, lit up like a basketball court with hanging lights in wire cages. The tablecloths were so white they seemed to vibrate. Faces shone with the effort of being humorous. Even the vegetables gleamed: mounds of shredded carrots and shiny purple beets, a hilly landscape of peas, rows of soft red tomates provençales.

Someone was waving at me. Steve Connelly.

In a tan sport coat that matched his blow-dried hair, smiling his TV-commercial smile, Steve looked healthy and uncomplicated. I mimed that I'd be right over.

He was sitting between the couple who'd met him in the square. Six hours ago!—it felt like days. Max Croft rose to to shake my hand. He was English, stout and sleek as a badger, with gray hair slicked back from his sloping forehead. Judith Croft, plump, blonde, and energetic, clasped my hand in both of hers and confessed that she hailed from Milwaukee.

"We feel a little guilty even being in Hands Across the Sea. It's too bad for Steve not to stay with real French people."

"Not at all. Au contraire!" Evidently for Max and Judith,

Steve was gallant and charming rather than hip but slick. "They've been marvelous, Cory. Showed me all over Paris on our way here. I'm very lucky."

He and Judith beamed at each other. It reminded me how French Larry and I always felt when we were entertaining Americans.

"So how's the band doing?" Steve speared a chunk of boeuf bourguignon.

"Oh, yes! How exciting that you're staying at the same hotel!" Judith's pink knit dress bulged at the seams when she leaned in to speak. "You know, our daughter used to be crazy about Dan Quasi. She had a life-size poster on her closet door. What's he like? I want to hear everything! Steve said you all rode here from the airport in a truck?"

I nodded, boggled by the image of Dan Quasi on a closet door in Fraises-des-Bois.

"We're not rock fans ourselves," said Max, "but Judith insists Susan will expect a full report. Never mind that she's forty-seven years old and the mother of three teenagers."

"I brought my camera." Judith patted her purse.

"How about some more wine?" Steve stood up. "Judith? Max? Cory?"

"I'll help you carry it," I said quickly.

But as we neared the bar, Steve surprised me by asking, "What *is* he like?"

I held the glasses, and the tip of his tie, while he poured. "You're asking me?"

"The more I think about it, the more I wonder if he didn't mean what he said. Who would you want to be? Jesus Christ? You heard how he talks to them—like the Sermon on the Mount."

"That sounds like a stoned insight."

"Maybe." He set down the carafe. "But, you know, this whole deal doesn't compute. What's Lacey Sky doing with three guys from The Rind? Or Niko, either? Like I said in the truck: There's got to be a connection with Ascher's murder, the drug bust, and Quasi breaking up The Rind."

"Maybe."

"Or why the new band? Why Paris? Why Hands Across the Sea?"

Pretty much the same questions I'd been asking. The set to Steve's jaw, though, and the glint in his eyes, made me wonder why he felt so intensely about it.

A flurry of action on the stage: two workmen were pushing back microphones, setting up a podium.

Steve followed my glance. "We'd better hurry or they'll be making speeches before we get our dessert."

I handed him a glass. "Can you manage this?"

"Sure. But what—?"

"I just found somebody I've been looking for."

"Madame Tréville?"

The lady in the red dress stopped and turned. "Oui?"

Of course I was watching for signs that this was a woman at the vortex; but in any case Marie Tréville would have struck me as no ordinary bureaucrat's wife. She had the kind of large, long-lashed brown eyes men write songs about, in a triangular face which also included sculptured cheekbones and a full pouty mouth. Her dark hair, almost black, was skinned back in a chignon —not from demureness, I guessed, but to keep it from cascading in voluptuous waves over her shoulders.

"Cory Thorne." I held out a hand, and told her in French that I was here to cover Hands Across the Sea's publicity for the American end.

She smiled—quick and bright, like a flashbulb—and said in English that she was happy to meet me.

"I'd like to ask you a few questions about the French view of this exchange program," I said.

"Certainly."

As we chatted, I thought: Red is not the word for that dress. Cabernet, possibly, or Chateauneuf-du-Pape. It was cut from some silky fabric which didn't so much cling to her curves as tell you where to look for them. I was beginning to wonder not why she'd had a hard time settling down, but why she'd bothered.

"Boston is such a pleasant city," she said. "I'm sure our ambassadors will enjoy their visit."

"You used to live in Boston, didn't you?"

"Briefly," she nodded. "A long time ago. And you, Mrs. Thorne?"

"Cory."

"Cory. Have you been to Paris before?"

"With my mother as a girl. And then I spent a summer working here seven years ago. I liked it very much."

"Ah." Again that quick smile. "So you are pleased to be back again?"

"Yes." And, hearing myself say it, realized it was true.

"Who is your host?"

"I'm staying in Fraises-des-Bois, actually. At the Hôtel des Fraises."

Wrong answer. Marie Tréville's eyes were on me like a pair of FBI agents. "You—?"

Of course: the band; the note. I hastily explained that I wasn't with Quasi & Company. There'd been a mix-up . . . Her alarmed expression didn't change. I might as well have declared myself a *plastiqueur*.

I tried another tack. "Can we sit down for a moment? I'd love a cup of coffee."

"Unfortunately I haven't time."

"Later, then? After the banquet?"

"Not tonight. I'm sorry."

So much for international good will. The obvious next step was to pull strings: mention Marian, or my connection with Thorne Cosmetics. I had reasons for not caring to do either.

"Is your husband here?" I asked instead. "I understand he used to be with the French consulate in Boston. I hoped to meet him tonight."

"Unfortunately he had to work late."

That figured. Like Lacey and her synthesizer, Victor Tréville would stay with his sinking ship.

"But he's involved with Hands Across the Sea?"

"Oh, yes. Very enthusiastic." She was darting glances around the hall, planning her escape.

"Tomorrow, then?"

"Perhaps. I can't say. Now, if you—"

I stepped into her path. "I was interested to hear that Quasi & Company were picked for Hands Across the Sea by your committee. Can you tell me who asked for them?"

Her surprise and alarm were unmistakable. "No. I— That can't be— No. Certainly not." She fluttered, poising for flight. "Please excuse me. I must find Sheila Bailey."

Her dress swirled around the backs of her legs as she hurried toward the head table.

If the rest of them are this eager to talk, I mused, it's going to be slim pickings come publicity time.

Unless . . .

You're not to mention this to anyone, John had insisted. But it wasn't his voice I heard as I strolled past waiters setting out trays of tartes and éclairs, gateaux and Napoleons. It was Rik Green's: *Find me a fire.*

Along with a plate of pastries, Steve Connelly had picked up a dark curly-haired ambassador. She was one I planned to interview—Latina and/or South Asian at a guess, in a mauve-and-green shirt and chunky jewelry. She'd taken over my seat and was hand-feeding Steve a petit-four.

Fraternizing with the subjects instead of shooting photos! Well, then, I would just step outside for a cigarette break.

From the top step I watched other guests passing through the circle of light under the street lamp, smoking and talking, heads and shoulders popping in and out of sight like targets in a shooting gallery.

"You're not leaving?"

The flash of a lighter revealed Niko's gargoyle shape in the darkness beyond the doorway.

"Just taking a break."

"Smoke?" He held out a pack of Gauloises.

"Thanks."

Again Niko flicked his thumb. Light from the street glinted off the silver case and the massive ruby ring on his finger.

"Interesting ring."

He showed it off: the band heavy, ornate gold, the large stone black except when a flash of light turned it red.

"I got it in Italy. Handy for foreign travel." He touched a hidden spring with his thumb, and the stone popped up to reveal a small compartment—empty at the moment.

"Doesn't it get in the way when you play?"

"I take it off."

Now that I could see better, his shadowy face looked intent, almost grimacing—as if this conversation were a game which, though amusing, required concentration.

Of course: Niko was high.

I drew on my cigarette. "Where's the rest of the band?"

"Inside." An abrupt laugh. "With the crew shortage, Dan's turning us all into drudges. You included." He tipped back his head and puffed out a smoke ring.

"So why did you come on this trip?"

The floating circle rose, expanded, and dissipated in the air. "What bizarre twist of fate led Niko Marx, who secretly admires pop punk and hip-hop, into the company of Dan Quasi?" He gazed at me through half-closed eyes—slits, like a cat's eyes. "Stay tuned for the following messages."

"You mean, the music?"

"Right on. See, I know a few hippie words."

"From what you said at sound check, I'm surprised."

"Anything said at sound check is not for the record."

"What is for the record?"

He giggled. "If you were in a band, what would you put on a record?"

With an inward sigh, I tried another approach. "If you don't want to play warmed-over Rind songs for yuppies, why hook up with these guys?"

Niko blew out another smoke ring. "Why did Eric Clapton

play with Howlin' Wolf? Why did Michael Jackson play with Paul McCartney? Those are legends in there. They know they're not The Rind anymore. The Rind died with Mickey Ascher, and he died with the sixties. Not murder—suffocation. They stopped making his kind of air."

"Why like this, though? Paris with Hands Across the Sea."

"Why not?"

"No money? No exposure? No filming or recording?"

"To see how it goes. That way"—he pointed up at the doorway—"or that way." Below us, a group of scruffy young men in leather jackets stood around a street lamp. "They came to check out the band. Hear the music. So should you, Lois Lane. You won't get it from talking."

"How about the several million music fans who read Phases? If listening to the music were the whole story—"

"Your boss wouldn't have flown you to France to ask questions like, 'Niko, why did you join this band?'"

He released another smoke ring. I thought about which way I wanted to go, and how to get there.

"What about the Rat?"

Niko grinned. "I don't do words," he told me with a smirk. "I only do windows."

Windows. Right.

"Then I'll wait for a window."

I walked down the steps. On the sidewalk I tossed my cigarette butt and squashed it with my shoe till nothing was left but shreds of paper and tobacco.

Mickey Ascher, Mickey Rat, and EuroDisney. Coincidence? Not a chance. The band would have known about Hands Across the Sea's farewell party when they signed on.

Had Niko given me a straight answer to the $64,000 question? They'd come to Paris to perform their new piece *in situ*?

If only! Not for any secret agenda involving Mad Mick or Victor Tréville. For the music.

But then why France? Why not California or Florida? Why fly three thousand miles to launch the Rat with rented equipment, a small and indifferent audience, no scenery, no special effects, no publicity—

The Rind never would have done this. Even in an Arizona desert, the *Gone with the Rind* tour used a film backdrop. As for press— Mickey beaming me that loony smile, hardly able to get the words out but glad to try.

He suffocated, Niko said. What did that imply for Dan, Terry, and Roach, who'd kept breathing? Or didn't Niko think they had? Legends—like those old jazz musicians who wind up appearing nightly in piano bars.

How could you score points for playing with legends if no one was watching?

I sat on a stone step and gazed at the hosts and ambassadors under the street light. With their contours flattened, their colors bleached to black-and-white, they looked like cartoons. In contrast, the leather-jacketed teenagers around the lamppost were solidly three-dimensional.

They'd come to check out the band, said Niko. Like the kids in the old joke who didn't know Paul McCartney had another band before Wings.

They were nudging each other, glancing at the open door. No Sheila Bailey to check yellow cards. They slipped up the stairs behind a group of official guests and were in.

Was that the answer? Stop pushing and wait for a window?

Steve Connelly's mom would have said yes. Maybe my dad would, too.

Mickey Ascher gave me the same advice twenty years ago. *Hang loose. Go with the flow.* It had sounded true and right then— not just because the phrases were still fresh but because everything going down that spring in D.C. was fluid, resistant to structure.

When logic and proportion have fallen sloppy dead . . . How did the Jefferson Airplane put it? *When the White Knight is talking backwards—*

"Niko!"

It was Lacey, dodging the people in the doorway. "I've been looking all over the place! Come on! We're late!"

"Do I care?" Niko unfolded himself from the wall. "Ask me if I care."

I started up the stairs.

"Cory! Oh, good." Lacey was breathless. "Come on! Dan's having fits."

What she meant by these non sequiturs I wasn't sure, but I went after her as she ran back inside.

Just past the main doorway a smaller door stood open on the left. Lacey darted through it and down a dark narrow staircase. I followed, groping for a banister, guessing from her fluffy white jacket which way the stairs turned. Down, down . . . and then we were in a hall, and toward the end a light appeared which became a doorway, and leaning in the doorway was Dan Quasi.

He was frowning as a young man in a Fruit of the Loom T-shirt and baggy overalls gesticulated at him in French. When he saw Lacey and me, Dan swiveled. "Cory. What's he saying?"

I had to force myself to tune in. Dan Quasi with his tousled dark hair and half-buttoned tan corduroy shirt had an irritated, restless look that made it hard to focus on anything else.

Then a burst of giggles floated out from the dressing room like balloons. Female voices.

My cheeks heated. This particular aspect of life on the road I'd forgotten about. But of course—girls are to rock-&-roll bands as cockroaches are to Boston apartments.

I wrenched my attention back to the Frenchman. Or kid: he looked younger than François, and much less sophisticated. He was trying to speak English, I realized, but in such a heavy accent I couldn't understand him. Something about microphones . . . .

Lacey pushed in past Dan. "Cripes, Roach! You can't keep your hands to yourself for five minutes?"

"Am I touching her? Look! No bodily contact."

"Whatever he told you, don't believe him," said Lacey.

Dan leaned in. "You mind keeping it down? I'm trying to find out what's up with our sound system."

A female voice, not Lacey's, answered something I couldn't make out.

"Look," Lacey said, "if you guys are gonna fill this place with girls, I'm going back upstairs and get some boys."

"Fill it?" Roach sounded aggrieved. "There's only two of

'em."

Dan swung around again into the dressing room.

"They were just leaving," said Terry.

In the hall, Niko was just arriving. "Well, goodness me!" He jumped back in mock astonishment as a redhead in a ruffled Victorian blouse ducked out between Dan and the crewman. Behind her came a tall thin model type with sculpted brown hair. "Don't go on my account."

"See you later." The redhead flickered three fingers.

"Come back after the show," called Terry.

"And bring a friend," added Niko. "Several friends."

Wishing to establish that I was here not as a girl but as a fellow professional, I moved into the doorway.

Lacey sat at a dressing table in the corner, scowling into the mirror as she dabbed mascara on her eyelashes. Roach slouched in an armchair across the room. He had one hand wrapped around the neck of a beer bottle and a cigarette dangling from the other.

"Hi, Cory." Terry smiled up at me from the beer cooler.

"Cory," said Dan, as if it had taken the sound of my name to remind him I was standing beside him. "Tell him that's OK. Neil can check those two mics again afterward."

"Dan," asked Niko, "how long is this set tonight?"

"He wants to know if he can go," I told Dan.

"Yeah. Fine. What? I don't know. An hour?" Dan stepped inside, running a hand through his already disheveled hair.

"Terry. She sure was looking good, huh?" Roach spoke louder than necessary. "Man, I can't believe she's in fuckin' Hands Across the Sea!"

Lacey snapped without turning, "I can't believe you're still talking about her."

"Aw, give me a break. I haven't seen her in twenty years. Shit, she sure don't show it, though." He winked at Terry, and I wondered in surprise which girl he was talking about. "Legs won't quit. She used to wear her skirts up to here—"

A crash suggested that Lacey's patience had run out.

"Cory," said Terry, "want a beer?"

"Sure. Thanks." I stepped inside.

Roach had put down his beer to light a second cigarette from the end of his first. "You're gonna look like somebody punched you in the face if you put any more of that crap on your eyes," he told Lacey.

"Fuck you."

"Would you two knock it off?" said Dan.

Niko was rummaging through the cooler. He didn't look mystical now, or even high, just thirsty. "Well, shit alors!" He stood up with an indignant clinking of bottles. "Tell me there's no more Heineken."

"You jivin' me?" said Roach. "Jesus! What's the point of being an ex-famous band if you can't get enough fuckin' beer to make it to the show?"

"Roach, you're such a pig!" Lacey tilted her head disdainfully. "There's six other kinds in there."

I crossed to the other side of the door. Even without girls, the dressing room was crowded and cluttered. Yellow walls dingy from years of smoke; chairs tattered from all the people and paraphernalia that had sat in them. Even the unshaded light bulb overhead looked dusty.

"If I knew we were gonna get jerked around like a bunch of amateurs—"

"Why don't you just shove it?"

"Up yours!" He jabbed his cigarette at her.

"Roach," said Dan, "what's our third number?"

Roach fished the list out of his jeans pocket. "'Sizzle,' 'Do What,' then 'Night.'"

"Did we pull 'Checkout'?"

"Dum . . . dum . . ." Roach ran a finger down the list. "Yup. Gonzo."

"Let's put it back in. Instead of 'Night.'"

"Shit, Dan!"

"No big deal."

"You and your third number." Roach crossed out and penciled in. "What is it, some kind of superstition?"

Lacey's arm was across the back of her chair, her chin on her arm. "You know what you could arrange for me, Dan, is 'Fine and

Mellow.'" She turned back to the mirror, singing to herself: "My man don't love me, he treats me oh so mean . . ."

"Dammit, Lacey, would you cut the—"

"Why don't you?"

"Why don't both of you?" Dan put in. "We've got a decision to make about tomorrow. Have you thought about that?"

He ambled into the middle of the room; and without any change I could put a finger on, their five separate preoccupations converged into one: Quasi & Company.

"Yeah." Niko lifted his beer bottle. "I bid a club."

"Why?" asked Terry.

"Better for our purposes in every way."

"I second that emotion," said Roach.

"Well, I don't," said Terry. "Like I said before, we could mess up the rest of this trip, plus wind up in legal trouble back in the U.S."

"What are they gonna do, sue our ass?" Roach lit another cigarette. "They could care less. Those turkeys don't know shit from shinola, man. Give 'em some dude in a monkey suit and they'd probably dig it."

"They would not!" Lacey glared at him through enormous black-rimmed eyes. "Turkey yourself."

I wondered uneasily what they were talking about. Whatever the question was, I suspected John Otis wasn't going to like the answer.

"Dan, what do you think?" asked Terry.

"Wait," said Niko. "Somebody's coming."

Dan moved to the door. "Can I help you?"

The visitor was a short man in a gray suit. He spoke with a strong French accent: "Mees-tair Qua-see?"

Dan stepped into the hall and shut the door behind him.

"I vote with Terry," said Lacey. "I don't think we should break the law."

"You just don't want to miss playing at the Eiffel Tower," said Niko.

"Well, I don't! Cripes, Niko! It's one of the most famous places in the whole world! I mean, you guys talk about Winterland

and the Fillmore, when fifty other bands are bragging about the same thing. Who'd you ever hear of getting to play the Eiffel Tower besides us?"

"Yeah," grunted Roach. "Who'd play the Eiffel Tower besides us?"

Dan slid back inside. "Roach? Let's keep the set how you had it. 'Night' third, and skip 'Checkout.'"

For a moment Roach stared at him. Then he took the set list out of his pocket and shredded it into a small white mound on the floor.

Dan looked at me. "You mind coming back later?"

Chapter 8: So You Want to Be a Rock 'n' Roll Star

The girls were lurking outside the door. They pounced when it opened and backed off, disappointed, when they saw it was only me.

"Are they coming out?" the tall thin one demanded.

The redhead was too busy craning for a glimpse of Quasi & Company to say anything.

To call them girls was to classify them by function, not age. The tawny brown-haired one looked around thirty, with a greyhound edginess you see more in New York than Boston. The other one seemed younger, though that might have been the ruffled blouse. Her hair was more carroty than mine but less vivid than Neil's, and her eyes reminded me immediately, if unfairly, of Bambi.

"Are you with them?" the first one persisted.

I explained. She introduced herself and her friend: Rachel, Mary Ann.

I wanted to ask which of them knew Roach, but we were interrupted by a man with a short sandy beard and wire-rimmed glasses who came padding up in suede running shoes—ready, evidently, to jump in whatever direction the situation called for.

"Gary Laporte." He thrust a hand at me. "You're with Quasi & Company?"

I explained again.

"Associate professor of sociology, Boston College." His eyes skimmed Rachel and Mary Ann; decided I was a better prospect. "I teach a course on the sixties, and it would be terrific if I could talk to Dan Quasi."

"I can't help you."

"He might remember me from the Boston Tea Party. Don Law's club? I realize, now's not the best time, but I'd like to make an appointment. Sometime tomorrow?"

Wondering if I should try French, I said, "I'm not with Quasi & Company. You'll have to ask them."

"Talk to Terry," Rachel advised. "He's handling road manager kind of things."

"Terry Morrissey? The drummer?" Gary Laporte stared at her as if she'd referred to Beethoven as Ludwig.

"Which was the one who died?" Mary Ann asked.

"Mickey Ascher. Beaten to death with a champagne bottle. June 26, 1974."

"He was a Scorpio," Rachel said, "wouldn't you know."

"They never solved it," said Gary Laporte. "The police report claimed they found no conclusive evidence at the crime scene, if you can believe that. Thanks to Ascher's welcome-back-from-rehab party plus some clumsy EMTs. My opinion? You've got forty people leaving fingerprints, cigarette butts, vomit, and pieces of clothing, you've got a damn good—"

He stopped, and pivoted in unison with the girls, as footsteps approached behind them.

"François," I said.

The head of Quasi & Company's French crew still wore the black slacks he'd had on this afternoon, with a flowered silk shirt open far enough to show off the planes of his chest. He shot me a look: Do I know you?

"Cory Goodwin," I said. "We met upstairs this afternoon."

"Oh, yes." A courteous nod.

"Are you with the band?" Gary Laporte stepped around me to hold out his hand. "I teach a sociology course on the sixties—"

François, however, was smiling at Mary Ann. "You are a fan of Quasi & Company? I am François."

She giggled. "I'm Mary Ann."

"Marianne! That is a French name, you know?"

"We were just talking to them in the dressing room," interjected Rachel, who didn't look too pleased at the way François was sidling up to her friend. "They told us to come back after the show."

"I want to set up a meeting with Dan Quasi," said Gary

Laporte. "I've been into The Rind since their first concert with Don Law. I own every record they ever released. If you'd just give him my card—"

"Me, I am also in a band," François told Mary Ann. "You like the New Music?"

I left them to slug it out. Me, I was supposed to be covering this performance for Phases; and that meant I'd better set up a meeting with my photographer.

Come back after the show. Like that night in D.C. Was that what I had to look forward to at the Hôtel des Fraises?

It doesn't matter, I reminded myself. You're not a student now, you're a journalist. If that's what they want, put it in the story.

Upstairs at the buffet tables, what everybody wanted was coffee. I found Steve near the stage shooting pictures of the banquet. François's crew had dragged away the speakers' podium and rolled out Niko's piano. Except for the kids who'd sneaked in and were now leaning against the back wall, nobody seemed to be in a hurry for Quasi & Company's historic debut.

François stepped onto the platform. *Tock tock tock!* One mic working, anyhow. He was all pro now, gesturing at the crew, moving a monitor, playing chords on the piano.

Maybe they were still fighting over the set list. Maybe Rachel and Mary Ann had rejoined them and Lacey had brained Roach or his ex-girlfriend or both with a beer bottle. Maybe—but no. Sheila Bailey was taking the stage.

I opened my notebook.

"Ladies and gentlemen." She raised her hands for silence. "Please put away your video cameras, because no recording of any kind is allowed during the musical portion of our evening. It's time to put on your dancing shoes! Hands Across the Sea is pleased to present our Mystery Band, Quasi & Company."

Polite applause as Niko walked onstage and squeezed behind his keyboards. Then Lacey, who'd fluffed out her hair like Louis XIV. Why didn't somebody turn off the house lights? Hard for the audience to grasp this moment's significance with nary a smoke machine, laser, or giant inflatable in sight. I looked around and saw Gary Laporte sitting in a folding chair up front, and Marie Tréville with the other committee members farther back.

When Roach and Terry came out, a few old Rind fans cheered. Roach grinned at them. Terry waved at me. I waved back. My mouth felt dry. Any moment now . . .

There he was. Still in his corduroy shirt, though he'd buttoned more of it. A flicker of applause: At last, Dan Quasi!

The lights dimmed. He picked up his guitar and nodded: one-two-three-four!

What is it about rock-&-roll that jolts through your blood-stream like espresso? Fast piano chords, a guitar line bubbling like a brook— The pen I'd poised above my notebook tapped a cloud of dots on the page. *Daddla da-da-dah!* Dan's guitar riff swooped, dived for an instant under long strokes of organ, popped up again in a splash of cymbals. His mouth was moving—talking to himself? Neil? nobody? I didn't care. I was surfing on a cascade of music, my ears bobbing from guitar to synthesizer to bass, trying to catch it all.

Daddlah! Daddlah! A streak of guitar arched, then plunged into the rhythm underneath, and all the sounds gathered into a rush, and we were emerging into vocals.

I couldn't make out the words. There weren't many— something about partying, getting it together with rock-&-roll. Then drums and bass tumbled us out into the melody again.

A short solo from Roach. His huge frame curved around his bass, swayed with it. His eyes glinted under bushy brows; white teeth gleamed through his beard. I began to comprehend why Lacey liked this guy. Roach was a manic sorcerer, plucking spells from those four strings under his fingers.

"Turn it up, burn it up,

Come on and have a good time!"

Over to Lacey. She'd sprayed something on her hair that sparkled like rubies in the red light. Such great rolling chords for such a little body!

Niko's turn. He hammered on the piano, double-timing, high, low, all over the keyboard, vest flapping, head jerking with the frenetic notes he poured into the speakers.

"Come on and have a good time!"

Back to Dan. He'd swayed on the vocals, but now he barely moved, just stood with his fingers curled around that smoky silver guitar. Sliding his solo into the crowd as smooth as an arrow into a bullseye. And they were with him, radiating back at him the electric energy he was drawing from that guitar. Six double-A high heels, size eleven wing-tips, sandals, loafers, all through the front of the hall feet were tapping. Women leaned forward, elbows on the table. Men pushed back their chairs and loosened their ties.

I felt as though I were plugged into that tall still figure. As if I'd blow a fuse if he stopped.

He didn't stop, but pulled the rest of the band around him into another chorus. Terry flailing away in his yellow spotlight, cheerful as sunshine; Roach hunched over his bass; Lacey with red stars twinkling in her hair; Niko's thin shoulders heaving with the beat. And in the center Dan Quasi, shining like a hood ornament.

"Turn it up, burn it up,
Come on and have a good time!"
Wham!

Hands Across the Sea burst into applause. They *were* having a good time. Hosts and ambassadors grinned at each other over the remains of cream puffs and strawberry tarts, the language barrier melted away by the heat of the music.

"Thanks." Dan was grinning, too. "Merci."

I felt a nudge and turned my head reluctantly. Steve Connelly stood beside me watching the band over his half-raised camera. "So what do you think?"

What a question!

"You know what I think?" Steve squeezed off a shot of Dan, then lowered the camera and looked at me. "If I was them, I'd be filming this."

His face wasn't more than two feet from mine. When had he got rid of his jacket and tie? That narrow determined chin.

"Think about it. Why would a rock band come to Paris and play at a banquet, the Eiffel Tower, and EuroDisney, for Christ's sake, and not bring along even one guy with a camcorder?"

"The Eiffel Tower?" I felt a twinge of uneasiness. "When's

that?"

"Tomorrow night. Am I right? It doesn't make sense! No personal videos, hard on the ambassadors but OK, copyright, bootleg and all that. But to just throw it away—!"

Steve clapped his camera to his eye again. I looked up at the stage. The band was suspended in that motionless instant before Dan gave the signal and the hall blossomed into sound.

Don't do it, I urged them silently. Listen to Lacey. Stick with the Eiffel Tower.

Terry hit the cymbals.

This tune wasn't as hard-driving as the first one. Guitar and piano. . . synthesizer . . . Roach was playing, too, but it took my ear a few seconds to pick out his bass line. That's the odd thing about live music—traveling through all those wires and boxes, what you hear doesn't match what you see.

A voice, male. Not Dan, not Niko, not Roach. Terry?

"I checked," said Steve. "They never even asked."

"What?" I was listening to the song, which jumped into your lap like a farmhouse cat and kneaded your leg with its paws. Thinking: Dan Quasi wrote this?

"The Rind, I mean Quasi & Company, never asked Hands Across the Sea if they could film. Which has got to make you wonder—a band that's always been so big on multimedia, re-entering a market defined by MTV—"

I blocked him out.

"Nobody knows when it all comes dow-own," sang Terry.

"You make your plans and they turn out wro-ong,
I don't mind growin' old,
That's just the way things go—"

Steve had stopped talking and was shooting again. It occurred to me I should be taking notes. But notes about what?

"How come
A man do what he do, do what he do?"

First Dan and Niko, then Roach and Lacey wove into the last line, turning the words into sounds whose meaning was no longer what they said but only what you heard.

Steve started to speak. I held up a hand. "Listen."

After a few seconds he asked, "What? Doo-wacka-doo?"

I shook my head. The instruments had picked it up: no more voices, just guitar, synthesizer, piano, and bass singing those same syllables.

"Cory—"

They finished. "Steve," I said. "That is not The Rind."

Though he clapped along with me and Hands Across the Sea, Steve was frowning. "What?"

"Think of the Rind songs you remember. 'Government Man.' 'I'm the One.' This is a whole different—"

"That's just what I've been telling you," he interrupted. "No way would The Rind ever have done a trip like this in the first place, much less without a film crew; and second, Mickey Ascher must be flipping in his grave to hear a voice like that fronting his band."

I swiveled to answer, but the opening notes of the next song swiveled me back. A slow, lyrical piano solo. Then a cry from Dan's guitar; and my insides twisted. For an instant I didn't even know why. Then the sounds in my head dovetailed, and my brain brimmed with images: arms around me, lips brushing my ear, singing softly with the record.

"Thousands of faces in the dark,
Eyes that glitter like sparks
Watching the man
Who's clutching his heart in his hands—"

I felt dizzy. Where was Mickey? Whose voice was this? My ears struggled with the slower tempo, the wry piano where Dan's bitter, aching guitar used to be. I could see two men standing on a stage, a girl plunging her hands against a keyboard, cymbals like hammered gold in yellow light; but it was as if I were caught in a dream where nothing matched up.

"And I'm trapped
behind this microphone—"

I closed my eyes. I didn't want Quasi & Company, only the song. The staggering sensation of whirling like a leaf on a cataract of music: tile floor, pine-paneled walls, graduate students and their dates, all revolving around us, distant as constellations, while my lover's hand caressed my hair, his body pressed against mine.

It was falling into place now. Jeff, the aspiring art historian. My first major romance after college. The Rind's last album, released after Mickey had died and the band scattered.

"But it's you
I'll be waiting to find,
Shining and true,
My light at the end of the night."

When it ended there was a breathless hush. Then the whole hall opened up into applause.

"Thanks," said Dan, wiping his forehead. "That was 'The End of the Night,' as I guess some of you recognized."

Over the clapping someone yelled, 'I'm the One!'"

"We're going to play a new one for you, called 'Give Me Some Time.'"

They swung into a fast rhythm-and-blues number with a dance beat. The ambassadors were right in there: feet tapping, a few of the bolder ones clapping along.

At the head table, a woman in a dark red dress stood up. Marie Tréville touched the man next to her on the shoulder; nodded to the other committee members as she passed behind them toward the aisle.

Was she coming up front? I stepped back to where I could see better. No; turning, she walked quickly toward the door.

I stuffed my notebook into my purse and headed after her.

But when I pushed through the padded doors, Marie had vanished. If she'd left the building, she must have stepped right into a waiting car—nothing was moving in the street. Downstairs? Unlikely. Not much there but the band's dressing room, probably locked.

I checked the ladies' room: empty.

Back into the banquet hall. There were the kids in leather jackets, not drumming fingers or wagging feet but watching intently. From here, Quasi & Company looked so small I wondered if they could tell who was who.

"Give Me Some Time" ended in a crash of bass and cymbals. Applause rippled across the room, noisy and cheerful as bacon crackling in a pan. Like this noisy, cheerful music.

"I'm the One!" a voice called out again. And another voice yelled, "Tear It Up!"

"Wonderland!" hollered somebody up front.

Dan glanced around the stage and nodded to Terry.

"You want sixties?" he shouted back at them.

Cheers from the crowd. Roach started off: a hollow pipeline bass, followed by Lacey on synthesizer.

But when she sang, it wasn't a Rind song. This was Motown: hot summer nights, drinking, laughing, having fun . . . "Dancing in the Street."

The audience didn't mind the bait-and-switch. Music, sweet music! They were stepping into the aisles, swaying with the beat. A few started dancing, then a few more . . . .

Dan's guitar gave a long shudder. The synthesizer's bouncy organ sound went tinny. Terry's drumming tightened to the beat of a pounding heart.

"Everywhere I hear the sound of marching charging feet, boy!"

Scattered Rolling Stones fans clapped as the band swerved into "Street Fighting Man."

I walked toward the stage. A camera flashed behind me. Steve Connelly? As I turned, a patch of red in the doorway caught my eye: Marie Tréville.

For no reason I could identify, my stomach tensed. She stood with her arms folded, watching the stage; watching her hosts and ambassadors pair off, drop jackets onto chairs, kick high heels under tables, boogie onto the dance floor, as the band proclaimed a palace revolution.

The front half of the hall was going up like popcorn. People dragged tables and chairs aside to make more room. I saw Rachel tossing her hair at a chunky man in a striped shirt, and François twirling Mary Ann under his arm.

Is that all they hear? Dance music?

The beat quickened. Sticks on drum rims . . . and a throbbing bass line which even after twenty years I recognized instantly, sinkingly.

I peered through the dim light at Marie Tréville, but I couldn't see her face.

"You're smokin' down the highway," chanted Niko,

"Your baby there beside you,

Better empty out your ashtray

Cause he's comin' up behind you!"

You want sixties? This was it, all right. The anthem of the protest generation blasting from the speakers; while on the floor women twirled their skirts and men rolled up their sleeves, flaunting international good will as if neither France nor America had ever heard of Vietnam.

"Watch out, friend,

When you're in the hands

Of the Government Man!"

Chapter 9: Mr. Soul

I didn't see the fight break out. They'd reached the second chorus when I heard yelling, and heads started to turn, and a woman shrieked.

Not being attached to a host family, I got there quick. In the hall between *Dames* and *Hommes*, a fracas was turning into a melee. Most of the yelling was in French, from the leather-and-denim gate-crashers and two young men in crew T-shirts, and a security guard waving his baton at them. The English yelling was mainly *Hey! Stop!* and *Call the police!*

Steve Connelly was right in there, shouting for calm, pulling on the combatants but getting in a punch or two. Another guard showed up, and soon the forces of order outnumbered the fighters.

Nobody seemed to know what it was about. A shaky American told me the gate-crashers had assaulted someone in the ladies' room. Her hostess said no, they'd swiped a few bottles of wine from the bar and got drunk and rowdy in the hallway. Her husband said he'd heard an ambassador started it by ordering the intruders to leave.

They were leaving now, wrestled out the fire door by two security guards. The other guard shooed the rest of us back to the banquet. Quasi & Company had moved on to "I'm the One." Apparently they, along with the other hosts and ambassadors, Sheila Bailey, and Marie Tréville, had missed the whole thing.

I grabbed a skinny mop-haired crewman and asked if he knew what the fight was about. His answer was a Gallic shrug, pursed lips, and a nod at the band: "C'est ça."

Meaning, I gathered, *That's what happens when you bring mecs Américains to Paris.*

When Hands Across the Sea drained out of the banquet hall an hour later, it left a damp ring of rock-&-roll fans. The hosts and ambassadors simply drifted off, murmuring like a movie audience who'd come for *Fiddler on the Roof* and got *Pink Floyd: The Wall.* Marie Tréville disappeared before I remembered I was looking for her. But twenty or thirty people hung around glowing, as if they'd just gotten back something they were glad not to lose.

Steve Connelly circled the room shooting pictures. Most of the others swarmed around Dan and Roach. They were the first to come back upstairs, and the only ones who stayed on the floor. Terry went onstage to collect his cymbals. Lacey and Niko sat on the edge chatting with the fans who gathered around their swinging feet. Lacey had a towel around her neck from the Hôtel des Fraises.

I of course had lingered so as to interview the band and representative audience members. No, Sheila Bailey didn't know there'd been a fight. Absolutely she would look into it. She would speak to the French committee tonight and make sure security kept a better watch on the doors. She hoped she could count on me not to discuss this with any of the program participants.

Two hosts and three ambassadors said they'd had a great time, enjoyed the dancing, thought Boston was brilliant to send a rock-&-roll band, and couldn't wait to see more of Paris tomorrow.

Then I walked up front, clutching my notebook like a back-stage pass.

All I could see of Dan was his shoulder. The line he'd cast from that stage had hooked quite a catch. I skirted him—them—and made for the platform. Better to miss him than come off as what I felt like, one more wriggling fish.

A dolly stacked with black boxes trundled into my path. The crewman pushing it glared around balefully, as if willing all these happy people to go home.

"You OK?"

He gave me a blank stare. I asked in French if he'd been hurt in the scuffle.

This time, a snort. "Hurt? No. Only bored. A fight is more

amusing than this."

Except for the language difference, he could have been an American kid hanging out at a shopping mall. I figured him for maybe 19. He had short blond hair and an indoor pallor which, coupled with round ears and a receding chin, suggested a truculent white mouse.

"Don't you like this band?"

He shrugged.

"Why did you take the job?"

Words erupted from him. I didn't know most of them, but evidently what he liked was high-tech equipment. "After they go," he jerked his head at the stage, "I'll have a real job at EuroDisney."

He maneuvered his dolly around me. I spoke English to his departing back: "If the Seven Dwarfs need a Grumpy!"

It wasn't just his manners. Didn't France have enough fledgling engineers for Hands Across the Sea to hire a music fan?

I was assessing possible pathways through the crowd when Gary Laporte came padding over. His shirt looked damp and his glasses were hanging off one ear. His step had a healthy spring, though, for a man who'd flown all night and danced off a big French dinner.

"Hi. Cory Goodwin, is it?"

"Professor Laporte. Enjoying yourself?"

At some point I should interview him. Not right now.

"Gary. Please." He adjusted his glasses. "Un fucking believable, huh? Twenty years and it still works! I might have to change my class outline."

That caught my attention. "What still works?"

"The curse! You remember, don't you?"

Sure I remembered. I'd been hoping I was the only one who did.

"The Stones had 'Sympathy for the Devil' and The Rind had 'Government Man.' The song they had to quit playing in public, because every time? Big trouble."

"Gary, you know that was just PR."

"The '68 Chicago convention?" He was offended. "The

Cambodia demonstration in D.C.?"

"Those were *about* trouble. That was the point."

"Not Nashville. Were you there? The *Gone with the Rind* concert in '73? God, I'll never forget it. The air was crackling with electricity. Hot and humid, thick clouds but no rain. One roll of thunder when they started 'Government Man.' Then they hit the lead break, and up goes Mickey Ascher's fist, and *zap!* A lightning bolt blows up the speaker tower. Sparks shooting out like fireworks all over the crowd. Nobody killed, but eight people hospitalized."

His arms were folded, his chin up, defying argument.

"OK," I said. "Put it this way. Curse or no curse, Hands Across the Sea would deeply appreciate your keeping that memory to yourself until we get back to Boston."

Up on the platform, Terry had the snare drum on his lap.

"What are you doing?" I asked him.

"Changing heads."

In his hands was a large round piece of skin or plastic: the drumhead. "Mind if I watch?"

"Sure." He flashed me a brief smile. "It's not very interesting. Like changing a tire." Terry loosened the chrome bolts around the drum rim with his skate key. "Hold this."

I took the drumhead gingerly by its metal frame. It looked like a large flattened diaphragm.

"Was the sound awful where you were?"

"No! You sounded great."

He wiped his forehead on the arm of his already damp flannel shirt and took back the drumhead, which he fitted onto the rim. "Wait till you hear us with decent sound, then. Jesus, this place is the pits."

"Did you see that fight at the end?"

He nodded, retightening bolts. "I don't blame them. I couldn't hear anybody but me."

Twenty feet away Dan and Roach were surrounded by fans,

most of them female, all of them eager to make contact. Dan radiated that flirtatious heat I recalled vividly from the airport. I fought a surge of jealousy: What's so special about a bunch of starstruck yuppies?

"You coming to Montmartre with us?"

I was startled. Then I was touched. "Thanks, but I can't. Places to go, things to do."

Terry picked up a drumstick and tapped around the new head, listening. What did he hear? To me, every tap sounded alike.

Rachel and Mary Ann had closed in on Roach. I glanced at Lacey. If she cared, or even noticed, she didn't show it.

"Which girl was Roach talking about in the dressing room?" I asked. "Who he knew a long time ago?"

Bom-bom, bom-bom. "Ask Roach."

OK. Fair enough. "About the music, then. That medley in the middle—'Street Fighting Man,' 'Government Man'—why those particular songs?"

He tightened a bolt. "They wanted sixties, they got it."

"You didn't care how they took it? As dance music?"

"I don't care if they dance, as long as they listen." Terry lifted the end of a web of tiny beads hanging from the drum; laid it carefully across the new head.

I gazed thoughtfully at his bald spot, at his sweat-stringy dark hair and mustache. There must be a way to tune into Terry like he was tuned into that drum.

"You didn't feel they missed the point?"

He glanced up as if I were deliberately being difficult. "All you see is what meets the eye."

A line from an early Rind song. I had the uncomfortable suspicion I was losing this conversation.

"But to play a song with that much history—?"

Terry grinned, and tossed me another line. "Tell me what you heard and you'll hear what I told you."

"Thanks. Circular, like a record."

He laughed.

"So are you saying Quasi & Company's music has no message? It's whatever anybody wants to make of it?"

"There's not that many things you *can* make of it." He set the drum back on its stand. "Like, you'll never hear 'Government Man' playing behind a Pepsi commercial."

"But as a warning, a threat— You know what people used to say about it."

He stood up, wiggled his shoulders, stretched out his arms.

"Could 'Government Man' be what sparked that fight?"

He didn't answer. I squelched an impulse to shout "Victor Tréville!" and see if he jumped.

"You want to know about 'Government Man,' ask Dan. He wrote it," Terry said, and walked over to the steps.

Yes! My heart lifted absurdly. That's what I should do. Ask Dan!

But Dan was still three deep in fans. I watched, impressed and demoralized by his easy way with all those people swarming around wanting something from him. A handshake, a smile, a chance to comment on the show, an autograph; whatever they asked him for, they got.

Just like in D.C., when I'd sat across a coffee table trying to think up questions he hadn't heard a thousand times. Yes, I write songs on the road. "Taste It" started on an airplane, some woman yelling at her kid. Turning to thank the roadie who'd brought sandwiches and wanted to talk about tomorrow's schedule; signing a stack of albums Graham Douglas dropped in his lap; till I understood that to him we were all the same: outstretched hands.

I slid onto the stage next to Lacey.

"Cory!" She threw a sweaty arm around my shoulder. "So what'd you think? The sound sucked, right?"

"That's what Terry said. It sounded fine to me. I was so glad to hear you—"

"It'll be better tomorrow. And we'll have more time, and no ladies getting their cooties on the mics. Niko, you got a cigarette?"

Niko was listening to a chubby American who kept emphasizing points with her elbows. "Niko!" Lacey pounded his shoulder. "Cigarette emergency!"

He pulled his pack of Gauloises out of his vest pocket and passed it to her without missing a beat.

"You want one?" Lacey offered.

"No thanks. I'm heading back to the hotel."

I leaned behind her and tapped Niko on his leather vest. "Good show."

He clasped my hand, pulled me forward, and kissed me lightly on the mouth. "Thanks."

It didn't seem strange at all. Just one more flash of the energy crackling through everybody here.

I hopped down to the floor with warmth spreading inside me. "Have fun in Montmartre," I patted Lacey's knee.

"I will!" She grinned. "I can't wait!"

Say good-night and go, Take Two. The longer I lingered the harder it got. Now I really did want to talk to Dan. Not just to ask him about 'Government Man,' but to tell him—to see his blue eyes recognize me, to bask in that smile he'd been shining on Hands Across the Sea—

I flipped open my notebook and sat on the steps.

A shadow fell over my pen: Steve Connelly. "Don't you ever stop working?"

I let him pull me to my feet. We traded notes as we walked toward the group around Dan and Roach. The fight? A couple of gate-crashers over a girl, was what the security guards said. Not worth calling the police.

Good. If Steve hadn't connected it with the so-called curse, maybe nobody else would.

"Yeah," he said, seeing me notice the large wet patch on his shirt, "I need a shower. How come you weren't dancing?"

I held up my notebook. "I was listening."

"Well, you missed a good time." Steve shot me a no-offense grin. "But then you don't let loose much, do you?"

I was startled, then annoyed. "Lena!" Steve was reaching into the crowd. "Lena Michel, meet Cory Thorne. The writer I was telling you about."

The woman he pulled out was the ambassador who'd fed him dessert before the concert. I was prepared to force a few pleasantries and escape; but Lena looked so exhilarated that I found myself smiling back, instant friends, bound by our rush from the music and our crush on the band.

"They're all right, huh?"

And as we shared an insiders' grin, I realized something that hadn't hit me until this moment: It was for us, the women, that rock-&-roll existed. For us—Lena and me, Rachel and Mary Ann, even Sheila Bailey and Marie Tréville. We were the ones the bands wrote songs about, who inspired their hottest licks onstage and off. Steve Connelly was nobody's light at the end of the night, nobody's Ruby baby, foxy lady, teen angel or devil woman. He could listen to rock-&-roll and dance to it, but Quasi & Company didn't play it for him. They played it for us.

"Oh, god!" I laughed. "I feel like I'm back at the junior high prom reeling from my first kiss."

"Good thing they're playing tomorrow, that's all I can say," Lena agreed. "Withdrawal city!"

"Tomorrow's the Eiffel Tower," said Steve. "Hard to imagine, isn't it?—a band like Quasi & Company at the Eiffel Tower? Should be great material," he clapped me on the shoulder, "right, Cory?"

"Right," I said. Thinking: It may be harder to imagine than you think. And then: There's another question for Dan.

I hoped they wouldn't back out. I didn't need any more clashes with John Otis, not with Larry *en garde* and a room holding for me at the Ritz. I wanted everything to go on how it was tonight: the band onstage doing their job, me on the floor doing mine.

"Then Saturday's the Strawberry Festival in Fraises-des-Bois," Steve was saying. "Sheila didn't want to announce it till they work out transportation, but Hands Across the Sea's adding it as an optional event. I told her—"

His mouth kept moving, but nothing of interest was coming out. I glanced at the knot of fans behind Lena. Damn you, Dan Quasi, how did you know? Whose arm did you twist? What strings did you pull?

"Fireworks and rock-&-roll!" Lena chortled. "Hallucinatory!"

"Speaking of Quasi & Company," said Steve, attempting to

tighten his grip on the conversation, "you two should come to Montmartre with us."

Lena let out a wail. "I can't! I'm an ambassador! I have to go back with Louis and Hélène." She gave Steve a not entirely friendly poke in the stomach with one bronze-ringed finger. "Where did you stow your host family that you can go paint the town?"

He shrugged. "Judith's American, Max is British. They give me plenty of space."

He was being cool, master of the situation, but something didn't ring true. I suddenly recalled how he'd turned up with housing in Fraises-des-Bois and no ride out there except with Quasi & Company. I'd have to ask John, if I ever spoke to him again, to check out this dude.

"Cory, are you joining us?"

I told him I was too tired.

"That's the other thing," nodded Lena. "I'm ready to pass out on my feet. We walked here, can you believe? God knows how many hours it's been since I last saw a bed."

"Stick with the band—" Steve began.

Lena's eyes and mine met for a second. Both of us were glad he didn't finish that sentence.

Possibly realizing he'd become *de trop*, Steve excused himself to go congratulate Lacey.

Lena sighed as he walked away. "I wouldn't mind. Would you?"

"What?"

She grinned. "Going home with Dan Quasi."

"No," I said. "But I don't think it works that way."

"Let's go talk to him, anyhow."

We moved in. The outer layer had the atmosphere of a waiting room: people striking up acquaintances as you might leaf through magazines, ready to drop them the minute the door opened. I heard a female voice saying something about software.

"I never even *heard* of him before the concert," another woman said. "And they start playing, and it's like *insane!*"

" . . . island in the Caribbean," said a man's voice. "Security up the wazoo."

"I mean, I'm not a rock fan. I'm an ordinary person! But there's like ten thousand people screaming and jumping on their seats, and next thing I know I'm running up the aisle yelling "Mickey! Mickey!" And this cop grabs me—"

Lena elbowed past Gary Laporte, who reached for his glasses. I gathered he hadn't gotten a chance yet to explain about his course on the sixties.

Bare shoulders pressing against mine, warm and lightly sticky; smells of perfume, damp hair, cigarette smoke; till at last I could hear Dan Quasi. "It's kind of a relief doing a slow song," he was saying. "You can think about what you want to play before you play it. The fast ones, it comes right from your head out your fingers."

I craned around a pin-striped shirt and there he was. Dionysus, I thought. All he needs is grapes.

"Hi, Cory." Smiling as if we'd run into each other on the street.

"Hi." I glanced at the circle of faces, the glittering eyes. "How about an interview?"

"Get me out of here and I'm all yours."

He tossed it at me like a message in a bottle. I wondered how many women had read his autograph on their album covers with this same absurd brightening inside, while Dan scrawled the same thing for the next one in line.

Lena pushed in and kissed his cheek. "Great show."

"Thanks," he said. "The sound was for shit."

It was impossible. I could no more ask him about 'Government Man' or the Eiffel Tower than I could conjure up a helicopter to fly us through the skylight.

"Dan!" The hefty ambassador who'd been talking to Niko was waving. "Annie Axelrod! I'm a patient of Dr. Richie's." An expectant pause. "You and Mickey's old dentist?" She wedged between Lena and me, beaming, confident of her welcome.

"Tomorrow," Dan told me, with Lena's hand still on his arm. "What? Oh, sure. Dr. Richie. How is the old sadist?"

Annie Axelrod guffawed as if Dan were a stand-up comic.

Sadistic as ever, with those creepy animal skins still hanging on the walls, and did Dan remember how he rushed through Saturday morning appointments to go duck hunting?

Eyebrows arched around the inner circle. Who was this twit who thought rock stars spent Saturday morning at the dentist?

"He used to tell me, 'Annie, they might be famous, they might even be good musicians, I don't know, but as far as dental hygiene—!'" She interrupted herself with another snort of laughter. "He said to me, 'You'd think their musicians' union would warn them heroin rots your teeth!'"

I stared at her, yukking away as if anything she could think up to prove her connection with Dan Quasi was reason enough to say it. While the other women crowding around him rolled their eyes, each dying to come up with the witticism that would show Dan—

I couldn't stand it. As I squirmed away I thought: If this is being famous, no wonder he quit.

The bus trip back to Fraises-des-Bois cooled me off. Out of Quasi & Company's electric aura, my feet hurt, my shoulders ached, my eyes itched, and my mind was crackling like an untuned radio. Lena had the word—hallucinatory! Chased by teenagers at the airport; trucked into Paris amid wild stories and marijuana smoke; rescued by Monsieur Vlaemenck, confused by John Otis, daunted by Marian Thorne . . .

There my mind stuck. After seven years, after all our Sundays together, why didn't Marian say something—anything!—about Larry?

Why didn't I ask her? Some journalist, dropping allusions to Proust! And why didn't I ask Marie Tréville more aggressive questions about her husband? Or Dan Quasi about "Government Man"? Why hadn't I known what to ask anybody all day?

No one was awake at the Hôtel des Fraises but the desk clerk. I refused his offer of cocoa and sandwiches and plodded upstairs to my room.

My room. Groping through my suitcase, carrying my cosmetics bag down the hall to the bathroom. And this cursed bed with its saggy mattress and musty sheets . . . just like our four-poster in the Place St. Augustin . . . .

I turned the light back on and blinked away a guerrilla attack of tears. Dammit, Cory, get hold of yourself! You think Larry's lying awake right now missing you? If he walked through that door, you think it'd be any better than three months ago?

We'd be in Paris! My eyes hotly overflowing. Why for god's sake didn't we have the sense to stay here? What did we need with Beacon Hill, the house, the Jaguar, his mother's fancy wedding, his father's corporate job? Why didn't I stand my ground and say no?

Fucking hindsight, recognizing Eden as it vanished in the rearview mirror.

I found my purse and lit a cigarette.

The familiar disgusting taste gave me a foothold. All right; so I was alone again in a rented room. So what? Things would look clearer in the morning. I would buckle down to work. Take risks. Take charge.

I rubbed my cigarette against the glass wall of M. Vlae-menck's ashtray until its tip glowed round and red. Comforting to indulge in a vice Larry and I had given up together. I would make lists tomorrow. I would schedule interviews. I would . . .

Hours later, noise outside the window jolted me awake.

Slits of light instead of print curtains; a strange soft bed. The Hôtel des Fraises. Hands Across the Sea. Oh, hell!

Though my shutters were closed, the window was open. I heard a door slam, and an argument—in English—down the street. The loudest voice I recognized: Steve Connelly.

"You've got to keep her on her feet. You can't let her go to sleep."

"Would you stuff it?" That sounded like Niko.

Steve was past listening. "You guys should know this. You've got to make her walk—"

He was cut off by a voice I couldn't make out. Then another car door slammed, and the motor started up again and faded away across the square.

Under my window, mutters, and the sound of something heavy being dragged across cobblestones.

When the hotel's front door creaked, and the night clerk's startled tenor drifted up to my room, I grabbed my clothes.

Soon a series of thuds and scuffs outside in the hall suggested the party was arriving at Lacey's room. Though the voices were muffled, I caught a few curses. If they didn't keep it down they'd wake everybody on this floor. I opened my door.

Terry Morrissey was holding up Lacey, who drooped as if the air had been let out of her. One of her arms was draped around his neck, more to keep it out of his way than for support. Niko, who had the other arm, was fumbling with her room key.

"Want some help?"

"Yeah."

I got the door open. Lacey wasn't entirely unconscious; once her eyes fluttered open and she tried to speak, but she only managed a few syllables. Her acid-green blouse was rumpled, and her curly brown hair half-covered her face.

"What happened?"

They dragged her inside to the bed. "Too much Jack," Terry said tersely.

"And a Brand X chaser," added Niko.

"What do you mean?" No answer. I scrutinized their faces, trying to gauge how serious this was. "Should she be kept awake?"

"Oh, honey!" Niko grimaced. "Trust us. She's been up and down a mountain and round the bloody Taj Mahal."

"She puked up most of it," Terry said. "The rest she can sleep off."

We stood around the bed. Lacey was already asleep, her mouth half open, a strand of hair bobbling across her lips as she breathed. I brushed it back from her face.

"Where's Roach? And the others?"

"I'm off. Good night, all." Niko bent down and kissed Lacey. "Sweet dreams, kid."

He closed the door behind him.

Terry stretched his arms and wriggled his shoulders,

preparing to follow. Oh, no you don't, I thought. And tossed a question at him like a grappling hook: "Terry, what else did she have besides Jack Daniel's?"

He shook his head. His eyes were still on Lacey. "You don't know?" I persisted. "Then how can you be sure? Shouldn't we have Monsieur Vlaemenck call a doctor?"

This time he looked at me. "No need." And the weary matter-of-factness in his eyes and his voice reminded me this was one of Terry's areas of expertise.

"The guy downstairs is getting me a sandwich," he said. "You want some cocoa?"

I thought fleetingly of my empty bed, and of all the places I'd planned to visit tomorrow in Paris. "Sure."

In the lobby we sat at opposite ends of the plump chintz-covered sofa. The desk clerk brought out a pot of cocoa and a chunk of baguette stuffed with meat and cheese. Terry started eating as soon as the tray hit the coffee table. I poured.

"How did Lacey—" How to phrase this so he wouldn't stonewall me? "What happened in Montmartre?"

"Not much." He swallowed. "She was doing a number with that dude Steve from Hands Across the Sea. Roach got pissed and took off, and then Lacey got pissed and drank maybe half a pint of J.D., plus whatever. So Niko and I decided to call it a night."

"Half a— Why didn't you stop her?"

Terry shrugged, as if it were a meaningless question.

"Where was everybody else?" In the back of my mind was an irrational conviction that Dan at least couldn't have been so callous.

"Neil and François were still boogieing when we left. They'd picked up some girls." That thin smile again. "They'll be back in time to set up tomorrow."

"And Dan?"

"Never showed."

My heart thumped. "You mean he didn't go with you?"

"He stuck around to help the crew pack up. He might have come back here after that. He was pretty wiped."

"Is that like Dan? To just not show up?"

Terry shrugged, his mouth full. "Who knows?"

Feeling unbearably transparent, I returned to my cocoa.

"You've got to realize—" He swallowed and cleared his throat. "It's been a long time since we traveled together. With The Rind, things were always kinda crazy. This—Quasi & Company—it's a different trip."

"Other than the joints, coke, J.D., and Brand X chaser?"

"There's always drugs around a band. Occupational hazard. Like flies around a garbage truck."

"Even here? With Hands Across the Sea?"

"It's like, we're the excuse. They figure, if we do it, it's cool if they do it."

"Are you saying . . . Somebody just handed Lacey something in a bar, and she took it? No questions asked? Just to get high, or because she's pissed off, or that's what bands do?"

There was a pause, as if Terry were figuring out how to translate for this pushy American. "You do what gets you through. Cigarettes, coffee, booze, whatever. Did you ever play a show after a short night on a plane? There's what gets you up for the gig, or down after, and then there's what flies you over the moon. Sometimes they get mixed up, especially if you're not used to it." Terry refilled my cup. "Lacey's OK. As long as nobody turns this into a media opportunity."

Aha, I thought. So that's why you invited me down here. "Meaning me?"

"Or your pal Steve."

"Steve's not—" But two decades' experience stopped me in time. "I'll speak to him."

Terry nodded appreciation.

"But, you know, he and I do have a job to do. Obviously, since we're all working for Hands Across the Sea, I can make a case against negative publicity. Still, we've got to come out with a story. Ideally, for the cover of Phases."

I sipped cocoa, to give Terry time to digest his sandwich and the deal I was tacitly proposing. After a minute I decided to take his silence for consent. I'd have loved to run back upstairs for my tape recorder, but that would be pushing it.

Now to find the right questions.

"So, how is Quasi & Company a different trip from The Rind? If drugs are still an occupational hazard— Wasn't that what destroyed The Rind?"

Terry nodded, but he didn't speak. He picked up a piece of cheese that had fallen onto his plate and stuffed it back into the baguette.

Should I try again? Change tacks? No. Wait for a window.

"A lot's different," he said finally. "Stuff you wouldn't . . . Like, we're running our own show. That hasn't happened since way back. With The Rind we had agents, assistants, A&R people, plus two trucks full of roadies. And, of course, Dougie."

"Graham Douglas?"

"Our manager." Terry bit off a chunk of baguette. "Roach used to say Dan ran the music-making, Mickey ran the hell-raising, but Dougie and the crew ran The Rind."

I couldn't tell, as he chewed, how Terry felt about that.

"What about you?" I asked him.

He tapped a quick syncopated *rat-a-tat* with his fingers on the edge of the coffee table. "I keep the beat."

At first I took it he was ducking the question. Then I understood it wasn't just drumming he meant.

And all these years I'd thought I met The Rind in 1970, on the strength of half an hour in a D.C. hotel room with Mickey Ascher, Dan Quasi, and Graham Douglas.

"Do you think he'll manage Quasi & Company if things work out?" Where was Terry that afternoon? Asleep next door?

"Dougie? Shit no. Jesus."

"Why?" I scanned my mental files: had I missed a link between Graham Douglas and The Rind's breakup, or the speculations and accusations surrounding Mickey's murder?

"He was Mick's man all the way. Mickey brought him in, and Dougie never forgot it. He married Mick's sister Gail, you know?"

I nodded. Thinking: And picked him up at McLean the day they let him out. And the next morning, after no answer to his phone calls—

But Terry was on another track. "You talk about drugs— One time, the night before we're supposed to finish taping something or other, we're all smashed, out at my place, it's like five AM. Turbo's crashed on the floor, Mickey's snuggled with some chick on the couch, and in walks Dougie with a tray, big glasses of milk and a bottle of aspirin, going, 'OK, everybody, drink up, session in four hours!' Kind of cute. Except Mick starts freebasing, snorting heroin, and Dougie's still giving him aspirin and milk. Drag him in the studio and he'd pass out on the floor. Don't worry, Mick just had a bad night. That's what got to Turbo. The Rind wasn't the four of us playing together anymore. It was Turbo and me, and Dan overdubbing two guitars, plus all the writing, and Dougie pretending like everything's cool."

Terry wiped a streak of mayonnaise off his mustache with his sleeve and took a drink of cocoa. "So Turbo left," I said, "and then . . .?"

"Then things got messy. Dougie wanted to bring in this kid he was managing, and Dan and me wanted Roach. We had a tour starting in like three weeks. Finally Dan told Roach to come on over. We'd played with him before, so we knew it would work. But Dougie just about pissed his pants. He'd been stringing this kid along, telling him he and Mickey had it fixed. He threatened to sue. I had to walk him around the pond at my place for an hour to cool him out. Luckily Dick Field, our A&R guy at Optimum, convinced Dougie to shut the fuck up. But it was never good after that. All Dougie cared about was Mickey getting everything Dougie thought we owed him. Dan quit talking to him. And then, when Mick got killed— Fuck! You'd think it'd bring them back together, but just the opposite."

Terry bit off another hunk of bread.

I recalled mud-slinging in the media. "They blamed each other? Dougie and Dan?"

"Well . . . Dougie said some things he shouldn't of. But I guess we all did. It was a bad time. Anyways," Terry lifted an eyebrow, "it's history."

While he finished his sandwich, I pondered. So much he'd told me; and so much I still needed to find out.

"What did you do after The Rind? And what made you decide to get back together after so long?"

Terry laughed. "You want my life story? Let's just take what I did last year. Producing, mostly. Some writing. Surfing with my kids in Hawaii. Building a new deck on my house. What about you?"

I'd been rephrasing my question to steer him back to the critical segue between The Rind's flaming crash and Quasi & Company's rise from the ashes. "Me? What do you mean?"

"What do you do when you're not grilling people?"

I could feel myself coiling up like a spring. I'm the interviewer! What business is it of yours what I do?

"Well . . . Last year, teaching school, mostly."

"I thought you were a reporter."

"Freelance journalist. Like, magazine features. I don't ever do reporting, like news." My mind scrambled for a way to change the subject. "What about everybody else? Is this all they do? The band, I mean. Do you all have other jobs?"

As I finished this awkward dodge I could see Terry's reply coming. But instead he said, "It's all Dan and me'll probably do for a while. Roach was doing session work on the West Coast before we started Quasi & Company. Niko was in another band— still is. I don't know about Lacey."

I was going to ask how Niko could be in another band, but the image of Lacey once again overshadowed everything else. Spending her first night in France passed out on a hotel bed.

"What did Roach— When he left you all, did he go with that woman he was talking about earlier?"

Terry swung his feet off the coffee table onto the floor. "Ask Roach."

"Off the record! I like Lacey, OK? I care what happens to her. You don't have to act like I'm some kind of—"

"Magazine writer."

"FBI agent."

"Same thing."

"How do you figure that?"

"Don't ever say anything to anybody with a notebook that you don't want J. Edgar's crew reading tomorrow." Terry held out a hand and helped me up.

"You know, journalists are human beings, too," I said stiffly.

"Tell me about it." He licked cocoa off his mustache. "You weren't the one they were chasing through the airport."

We were standing closer than I was used to being with a man I'd only known a few hours. I dropped his hand to collect our cups; then realized that keeping a safe distance meant letting go of something more essential.

Terry's head was turned toward the stairs. On his ear was a tiny dimple that might once have held an earring; and above it, an inch of gray in his brown hair.

"Is it always like this?" I asked him.

"Is what always like what?"

"Being on the road. Is it always this crazy?"

Terry laughed. "This? Shit, this isn't crazy. This isn't even being on the road."

And suddenly I didn't want to hear any more tonight about what it was like to be a rock musician.

"Are you going to check on Lacey?"

He shook his head. "She'll be OK. Anyways"—his round shoulders went up—"that's Roach's department."

We walked toward the elevator. I glanced at the clock over the desk: four-thirty.

"Another hour and we could watch the sun come up."

Terry smiled. "If I was ten years younger and less married, I'd invite you to watch it come up in my room." He stretched his large chunky body and yawned.

I was too surprised to answer. Finally I stammered, "Good night."

"See you tomorrow." He kissed me on the cheek.

I started up the stairs, but Terry didn't follow. Waiting for the elevator? At the top of the first curve I looked down. He was in the phone booth, his bald spot shiny under the light.

Chapter 10: Somethin' Goin' On

When I woke up again my room was still dark. The luminous dial of my watch said 12:46.

Past noon? How . . . ?

With a shudder I lowered my feet onto the cold wooden floor and pushed open the shutters. A light rain was coming down. The linden leaves brushing my window were dark and wet; rivulets ran between the cobblestones in the square. A dismal day for splashing around Paris. And half gone already.

For a moment I stood shivering by the window, watching raindrops roll off the geraniums, listening to the soft pattering sound like applause on the eaves. What had Terry and I talked about so late? Images trailed wispily into my brain: his plaid flannel shirt, cocoa cups on a tray . . .

Lacey, passed out on her bed.

That cleared my head. OK. A warm sweater and jeans. Figure out my angle of approach for l'affaire Tréville. Thick-soled walking shoes. Then, Roach or not, go see if Lacey's all right.

I found socks. Would the Hôtel des Fraises have a Paris newspaper? But with Victor et al. keeping a lid on the bomb threat, that wouldn't tell me anything unless someone did blow him up. In which case I could expect a hysterical call from John Otis . . .

No messages at the desk. I phoned Sheila Bailey. Yes, she had the Trévilles' home number in Brière. She'd spoken with Marie there an hour ago. No, she didn't know Victor's office number or where he worked. If I waited, I could talk with him tonight at the Eiffel Tower. Yes, Quasi & Company would be there, too. Sheila hoped their repertoire included some nice dinner music.

So when nobody answered the Trévilles' phone I hardly minded. With Victor intact, and on a collision course with the band, we might get our fireworks a day early.

Lacey lay where Terry and I had left her, on top of the bed, half covered by a lightweight blue blanket. Her face was deathly pale behind her purple-smudged, black-rimmed eyes.

"Are you OK?" I asked her.

"Do I look OK?"

"You look miserable."

"Well, I feel miserable."

That made us both laugh. "Do you want coffee? Or food?"

"Yeah." Lacey heaved a sigh and moved her feet up under the blanket. "A huge white coffee, no sugar. And some toast or something."

I lifted the antique intercom by the bed off its wall hook. Along with Lacey's coffee, I asked for a pot of tea for me and croissants for both of us.

"So Hands Across the Sea does have room service," Lacey said weakly. She was half-sitting now. "Can you get me some aspirin, too? Like about twenty?"

That order I went and filled from my suitcase. Handing her the bottle and a glass of water, I asked, "What did you do last night that gave you a twenty-aspirin headache?"

"It wasn't my fault! If Roach wasn't such a prick—" She swallowed three. "Well, the Jack was kind of my fault because I made François get it for us. Did you know French bars don't serve Jack Daniel's? Can you believe?"

She subsided into her pillows. I prodded: "And after the Jack Daniel's?"

"Huh. Good question." Frowning, Lacey shook her head, slowly and carefully. "I remember up to dancing with Steve in this bizarro bar. Then—nada."

"Is that unusual for you?"

"Blanking out? Yeah. I mean, not with Jack. This is more like—"

"What?"

"Downers. Only I didn't do any. Far as I know," she added.

"Far as you—?"

"I can't remember," she cut me off. "How long's it gonna to take for the coffee?"

It only took a few minutes. I sat on the edge of the bed, holding the tray, and Lacey drank coffee till the color started coming back into her face. A couple more questions about Montmartre didn't produce any useful answers. For the first time I sympathized with the cops who'd investigated Mickey Ascher's murder.

"Where's Roach?" I asked her, daubing strawberry jam on a croissant.

"Search me. I don't think he was here. I don't know if he came back or got it together with his ex-chick or what."

"What ex-chick?"

"It's no wonder he never wants to play 'Mr. Rat,'" she went on vehemently. "His theme song!"

"Lacey, what ex-chick and what's 'Mr. Rat'?"

"Oh." She looked surprised. "Wow, that's right. We haven't done any of the Rat yet. Our biggest thing! Nobody told you?"

She was losing me faster and faster. "Niko told me a little about the beginning—"

"Where Big Walt catches them in the Tiki Room? That's his favorite part," Lacey nodded. "I like the next scene, where they get kicked out of the fifties. All those cartoon creeps sneering at them"—she jabbed an accusing finger—"Beat it! Scram! We don't want you here! Which really sucks, since that's like their whole life. So Mickey's trying to cheer up Annette till they get out of town, and they climb on the choo-choo and he starts singing, 'When yoo-oo-oo wish, upon a sta-a-ar'—only it's like a dirge. So they're chugging down Main Street, and the wheels are going *when you, when you, when you, when you,* faster and faster, and Snow White and Minnie and everybody's jeering at them—" Lacey paused for a gulp of coffee. "And they get out the gate, and all the ticket-takers come jumping out of their booths. They're black, like Mickey, with these big curly Afros like Annette. And whammo!" Lacey's hands flew open. "Wall of sound!"

I thought: I should have brought my tape recorder. "Amazing."

"Wait till you see it." She grinned and nibbled at the tip of a croissant. "It's gonna be awesome when we get it all together with video and lights and shit."

"This is, what? A rock opera?"

Lacey said she guessed so, sort of, but more multimedia than like *Tommy*, or anyway they figured it would be when they finished it.

"Is that why you came here with Hands Across the Sea?" The $64,000 question again. "To play the Rat?"

"Oh. Well, we can't, since we've only got a couple of songs done. But, definitely, we're playing those."

"When? At EuroDisney on Sunday?"

"Sure. That's like the ultimate. But I hope tonight, too. At least 'Mr. Rat.' That's my favorite."

Roach's theme song. "Mr. Rat, like Mr. Right?"

"You got it." Lacey bit the tail off her croissant.

She didn't look upset, though. Maybe if you were involved with a musician you learned to take ex-chicks in stride. The Pynk Pyg fans, the Brass Knuckles fans, the Rind fans, each one with a gig and a party and a hotel room to remember him by. But when show time came, the only woman in Roach's life was his keyboard player.

"Like we were talking about yesterday," said Lacey. "Wasn't that what happened with your husband? The one who wanted to be a writer?"

"I've only had one," I said drily. And wished with a flash of envy it were that easy with computer keyboards.

But Lacey was waiting for me to answer.

"It wasn't that he turned out to be a rat." Remembering our marriage counselor's warnings about blame. "He just didn't—we didn't turn out to be as good at being married as we hoped."

Lacey looked skeptical. "What was he, real straight?"

"Not when I met him." How to explain Larry Thorne to this girl whose romances seemed so black-and-white? "I guess he had a hidden straight streak that came out after the wedding."

"Terry says it does that to you," Lacey nodded. "He got straight when he got married. Now he's trying to get weird again."

Once again I felt turned around. Was that what I'd represented to Terry last night?—a shot at unstraightening?

The idea charmed me. I told Lacey about our encounter— most of it—and what Terry said about keeping the beat. She smiled. Plainly in her mind I'd performed a valuable service by giving him a helping hand on the road back to rock-&-roll.

While I'd been imagining myself the recorder of events and Terry part of the force that made them happen.

"It's good you're here," said Lacey. "For all of us. We can't talk about it much ourselves, so it's good we can talk about it to you."

"What do you mean?"

"Oh, you know. When you get into analyzing what you're doing with who else is doing it, it screws it up." She shrugged. "You get mixed up in the concept and it's like looking in a mirror. You're so busy watching that you lose your energy for doing it."

No, I thought. That's not right. Our counselor could explain how it's only through talking about your interactions that you understand the choices you make, the wrong turns, the breakdowns in communication.

"But you can't be sure what it is you're doing unless you discuss it," I said.

Lacey shook her head positively. "Uh-uh. As soon as you discuss it, it changes. Then you really don't know where you're at."

"I don't agree. That's what got my husband and me into trouble—we never talked about our relationship. If we had—"

I stopped. If we had, then what? Would talking have pried Larry loose from his family? or synchronized him with mine? Would it have kept us together longer, or split us up sooner? We'd sat in French cafés joking about Rue Mass and the Jardin Publique till we'd convinced ourselves we were ready for the quantum jump across the Atlantic, but it beat us all the same.

"Like that song of Terry's," said Lacey. "I asked him once how I'd ever get through; he looked me in the eye and said, Do what you do."

"Terry wrote that?" Remembering how it had intrigued me last night. "I thought Dan did all the writing."

Her head went back and forth in the pillows. "Not for us. He did for The Rind, but this is different. In this band you get to do what you want. Like, I'm a singer, but I play keyboards, too."

"Do what you do," I repeated musingly.

"It's *about* The Rind, you know." I looked up from my tea. "It's the story of what happened to them all after they split up. Terry sent it to Dan for Christmas, and that's how he knew it was time to come back. At least that's what Roach told me."

I thought: I definitely should be taping this.

"Will you play it again tonight?" I asked. "I was so caught up in the sound of it last night that I didn't hear all the words."

Lacey's nose was hidden in her coffee cup. "Probably not. This thing tonight's pretty short. We need a whole show," she added. "One good solid night where the sound's right and we're hot and the people are really into it. You won't believe how much happier everybody gets!"

What I needed, after chasing around like the Mad Hatter's tea party since the plane landed, was time alone. Top on my list was the Musée d'Orsay. All my favorite Impressionist painters in a spectacularly rehabbed railway station—what better way to spend a rainy afternoon?

But when I reached the lobby, I turned down the hall to the dining room.

Dan wasn't there, nor Niko. Roach was, sitting with Terry at a window table on the courtyard side. Terry saw me and beckoned.

"Sit down. Roach thinks he saw a waitress, but I think he's still asleep. Anyways, we haven't ordered yet."

I took the chair facing the windows.

"So the crew's bringing everything out here?" Roach asked Terry. It sounded like a new conversation, not a return to whatever I'd interrupted.

"Yeah."

The same girl who'd waited on us yesterday approached the table. From her wariness, I guessed she hadn't had the job long. Or maybe these were the first rock musicians she'd seen up close. They both looked harmless to me—Terry quite ordinary, really, in a plaid flannel shirt and jeans, and Roach too sleepy or hung over to be threatening.

"Hi there," Terry said to her. "Bonjour." He pronounced it with such a strong American accent that she nearly giggled. "What's your name?"

"Denise."

"Duh-neez," Terry repeated. "Do you speak English, Denise?"

She still wasn't sure how to take him, or what to make of all three of us. But Terry was working to win her over; and she was too young and too shy not to succumb. "A little," she said with a small Gallic toss of her head. "I know coffee."

"Coffee!" echoed Roach, coming alive at last.

"Will you like coffee?" Denise asked Terry.

"I sure will."

Roach seconded, then sagged back into somnolence, head in his hands, eyes closed. I ordered a café crème. Denise offered us menus. I shook my head.

"Aren't you hungry?" asked Terry.

"I had croissants upstairs with Lacey."

That roused Roach. "She's up?"

"She's awake. Or was. She's not feeling too well—"

"I'm going. Order me a couple of eggs with sausages and toast." He pushed back his chair and lumbered toward the door.

With a demure glance at Terry, Denise served our coffee.

As soon as she moved out of earshot, I started to ask him again about last night.

"Coffee!" came a voice behind me. "Don't let that pot get away!"

Niko reached us too late to catch Denise. He dropped into Roach's chair. "Well, old Neil never made it back." He picked up Roach's untouched cup, sniffed it, and took a long swig of black coffee. "You think we'll see him today?"

His eyes briefly acknowledged me, of more interest than the sugar bowl but less than the coffee pot.

"We better," said Terry. "They're supposed to bring our stuff out here."

"Maybe he slept on the stage, like a watchdog," said Niko.

"God, what dreadful sound! What a dreadful place!" He picked up a menu but didn't open it.

"Niko—"

"Were you horrified, Cory? Did you fax home that Quasi & Company sound like a lizard blowing on a comb inside a brown paper bag?"

"It didn't sound so bad in the audience," I said, wondering if this branded me a philistine. "Can I ask you—"

"No bass at all, and the high end like a dime-store harmonica. I kept thinking, somebody pinch me, this has got to be a nightmare."

I tried again. "Niko!"

His head swiveled an inch.

"About Lacey."

"She's up. Roach—"

"Yes. I talked to her. What did you mean last night when you said she had a Brand X chaser besides the Jack Daniel's?"

The question seemed to surprise him. "Well, you saw her."

"Did you see her take anything?"

"Like an illegal substance? Certainly not. Why?"

"Then why did you think—?"

Denise chose that moment to reappear with the coffee pot. She stood watching Niko fan himself with his menu as if she expected him to sprout horns and a tail.

"One omelet with sausage," Terry told her firmly but kindly.

"Why did you think it wasn't just Jack?"

"Elementary, my dear Watson. She and Jack have an intimate long-term relationship, and that wasn't it."

"One omelet with ham and cheese."

"No staggering, no babbling, no analysis of the universe. She went down like a TV station going off the air. One minute there's the flag waving above the Mormon Tabernacle Choir, *da-da-dum, dum, dum, zot!* Snow and nothingness."

"Got that, Denise?"

"Oui oui!" She scribbled on her pad.

"You mean she suddenly passed out?"

"She suddenly went fuzzy," Niko corrected, "then she passed

out."

"Cory?" Terry nudged me. "Food?"

I passed. "You should try the croissants, though."

"And some croissants."

"I don't suppose there are bagels. Do they have French toast in France? No? Well, let me see." Niko ran a finger down the menu. "This. Whatever it is. Surprise me." He handed the menu to Denise. "Has anyone seen Mr. Q this morning?"

Terry nodded at the door. "Right on cue."

I glanced around and forgot my next question. Dan Quasi was walking toward us.

He looked as tired as the others, but even so he stirred my corpuscles. He had on a dark green T-shirt with a plaid flannel shirt over it (Terry's?) and worn jeans. His hair was wet, as if he'd just gotten out of the shower.

"I was about to leave," I told him.

"No need." Dan angled a chair in next to Terry's. "Coffee?" It seemed to be the Quasi & Company password.

"She'll be right back," said Terry.

"I talked to Neil." Dan picked up Terry's cup, made a face at the cream in it, and took a sip from Niko's. "They're on their way. Half an hour."

Is it caffeine deprivation, I wondered, or a good night's sleep, or is he always this relaxed first thing in the morning? I let his voice flow over me like music as he and Terry and Niko discussed whether this room was big enough to rehearse in, whether to find Monsieur Vlaemenck first or go ahead and set up. Thinking: Nothing to distinguish this man from anyone else waiting for breakfast in a hotel dining room. Yet later I'll write in my notebook *Dan Quasi likes his coffee black*, knowing that hundreds, maybe thousands of women will read it and remember it.

"Denise," Terry called. Already he'd slipped into the American pronunciation. "We need more cups."

Denise waved and nodded and went back into the kitchen. What did she care about Dan Quasi?

"I ordered the car for seven," said Terry. "I called, François called, but that's the best they'll do for us."

Dan stretched and sighed. "Just like the good old days. No car, no studio, no crew . . ."

"No hotel reservations," Terry said.

"No sound check till they set up the chairs," Niko contributed.

"Déja vu all over again." Terry grinned. "When she comes back, Dan, you should ask for peanuts."

"Peanuts?"

"You remember the peanuts. When we first started The Rind? All four of us crashing at my place in Somerville, one room with a bathroom down the hall—"

"I remember that," said Dan. "Trolling for girls so we could spend the night in a bed."

"Summer of '67. You and Mick just got back from the West Coast."

"Monterey Pop." Dan was shaking his head. "What a trip! Music like nobody ever heard before"—he turned to Niko and me —"Gracie Slick and the Airplane, Janis Joplin belting her heart out, Otis Redding, incredible, the Animals. . . . The Who smashing up the stage, Hendrix humping and torching his guitar— We were so blown away, we hitched up to San Francisco to start our own band."

"I thought you guys had a band before that, in Boston," Niko interjected. "High school?"

"Junior high," said Dan. "The Alley Cats, which is what we sounded like. A true garage band—we could only practice when my mother took the car out."

"Mickey Ascher on guitar and Dan Quasi on keyboards," said Terry.

"Keyboards! Caramba!" said Niko. "What did you play?"

"School dances. We copied licks off the radio, made our own mix. Picture Little Richard, Elvis, Dylan, and Phil Spector put through a food processor."

"Cuisinart rock," said Terry.

"And then you went to Monterey," said Niko, "and in San Francisco you met Roach?"

"He'd just joined Brass Knuckles," Terry said.

"We couldn't find anybody else we liked, and we were flat broke. I think we made maybe four bucks playing pawn-shop mandolin for the tourists down at Fisherman's Wharf. Our best day, some girls gave us a loaf of sourdough bread, took us home and cooked us a spaghetti dinner."

Dan was performing now, not even half-throttle but reflexively. I wondered if I dared take notes. Why, though? How likely was I to forget Dan Quasi and Mickey Ascher passing the hat on a San Francisco street corner?

"So you hitched back home to Boston and showed up on my doorstep." Terry accepted two coffee cups from Denise.

"And you, dumb shit, let us in."

"Hey." Terry poured. "Nobody else was beating down my door to be a rock-&-roll drummer."

"Then Mick found Turbo playing stand-up bass at a jazz club in Allston," Dan hoisted his cup, "and that was the Rind."

"The Rind!"

We all raised our cups. "So what about the peanuts?" Niko asked.

"Ah!" said Dan. "The peanuts."

"You have to understand," Terry interjected, "our money level was below zero. I stole most of our food from this dive in Union Square where I was bussing tables."

"So one day Terry and me are walking up Comm Ave," said Dan, "and this nice little old lady comes around sticking peanuts in the barks of trees for the squirrels. The minute she left, we ran around and ate all the peanuts."

"Well, shit alors!" Niko reached for the coffeepot. "Poverty and starvation? That's not how I pictured it at all."

"Yeah," Terry nodded. "Me neither."

Niko refilled his cup and then mine. "Cory wants to hear the part where you get famous."

I did, actually. "How long did it take?"

"Not long." Dan ran a hand through his hair, mostly dry now. "We played the bar circuit for about six months, and then Mickey talked Don Law into putting us in one of those concerts on the Common. That'd be, what? Spring '68? Then we cut 'Government

Man'—"

"Bye bye peanuts," said Terry, "hello White Castles."

"Then Mick brought Dougie in as our manager—"

"Ha!" said Niko. "Bye bye White Castles, hello filet mignon."

"Hello breakfast." Terry moved the coffeepot so Denise could deliver it.

Damn! As she set down plates, unconcerned with the revelations she'd interrupted, I persisted: "Dougie was into fame and fortune?"

But they were through talking. For two or three minutes they ate, while I weighed whether to miss the next reminiscences or the next bus. Then Niko said, "Dan, any news on the you-know-what?"

Terry raised a cautionary fork.

"Hi!" Steve Connelly's cheerful voice echoed in the empty room. "Mind if I pull up a chair?"

Niko shuddered eloquently.

"Coffee." Steve slid in between Niko and me. "Boy, I could use some of that."

He didn't look hung over, though, or even tired. His blue shirt was crisp, his curly hair combed. Even his jeans were abnormally unwrinkled.

Dan and Terry exchanged looks.

"What are you doing here?" Dan asked.

Steve hesitated, glancing at me. "I hoped you'd have a few minutes to talk."

"What about?"

"It's sort of—" He paused. "Maybe later, when you're not busy?"

He meant me, not the food; but I wasn't about to leave now.

"This is as not busy as we're going to be for a while," said Dan.

Steve inclined his head. "OK."

He poured himself a cup of coffee with an assertive confidence that made my jaw clench.

"I'd planned to tell you this yesterday, but I never got a

chance. You know Hands Across the Sea hired me as a photographer. My other gig, and why I took this job, is director of arts programming for a Boston radio station. They've asked me, with Hands Across the Sea's approval, to tape a special on your— about Quasi & Company," he amended.

Well, well!

"You're right." Terry laid down his fork. "You should have told us that yesterday."

"You should have told us two days ago, before you came all this way for nothing," said Dan.

Their eyes met. For an instant it looked as though Steve meant to stare Dan down. If so, he thought better of it.

"It's not for nothing," he replied, still pleasant. "But obviously I could do a better piece with your cooperation than without it. Wouldn't you agree?"

"Our deal with Hands is we control our own publicity."

Steve gave a little laugh. "You're sitting here having breakfast with Cory Goodwin."

He shot me that no-offense smile I was beginning to yearn to slap. I glared at him.

"That's got nothing to do with you," Terry said.

Dan didn't say anything, but his expression made me think maybe it was time to leave after all.

Steve looked at Terry, then Niko, then Dan again. "I guess I don't understand your position."

"It's not that complicated." Dan propped his elbows on the table. "We know Cory. You I've never heard of. What's your name? Steve Connelly? What station are you with? What else have you done?"

"What kind of piece are you talking about?" Terry added.

Steve folded his arms defensively. "Mainly human interest. My observations about the trip, some of your music, plus quotes from you on what it's like to come back after all these years, pulling your old band together without Mickey Ascher."

"We are not fucking pulling together our old band!" Dan slammed a fist on the table, rattling plates and silverware and spilling Steve's coffee.

"This isn't a good time," Terry confided to Steve. "Maybe later."

Steve didn't like it, but he didn't have much choice. As he retreated out the French doors I turned to Dan, waiting for him to dismiss all possibility of cooperating—

"You know what?" said Niko. "I bet we're on Boston time. When did we go to bed? Four AM? And now it's, what?—one-thirty? Subtract six hours . . ." He started counting on his fingers.

I looked at my watch. Ten minutes till the bus left. "I've got to be going."

No reaction from Dan.

"Yup!" said Niko. "Seven-thirty AM in Boston!"

Walking away, I heard Terry say, "And when were you ever up at seven-thirty AM in Boston?"

Chapter 11: Across the Great Divide

In the lobby I stripped the cover off my collapsible umbrella with a vindictive thrust. So Steve Connelly planned to tape a radio show about Quasi & Company! And tell me about it when?

Bless Dan and Terry for busting his treacherous ass!

Did John Otis know about this?—that Jerry Leroy's crony from a radio station had bumped my photographer and gone rogue?

Did the governor know? Was Steve just a snake, or was he also a mole?

And what (if anything) did this mickey-mouse cloak-and-dagger have to do with Victor Tréville's bomb threat?

I punched the button. My umbrella shot open with a satisfying *thwt!* The linden trees were drooping. The hotel and its geraniums looked bedraggled, the square sodden and gloomy: hedges dripping, cobblestones slick with rain. A wretched day for sightseeing.

Maybe Steve was improvising. He could have ramped up his radio plan after that skirmish at the airport, when we learned Quasi & Company's publicity wall was already breached.

Maybe I should improvise, too. With a Paris TV station spreading the word about Hands Across the Sea's Mystery Band—not to mention two hundred ambassadors and their hosts, François and his crew, whoever Neil spent the night with, and the bar patrons of Montmartre—Fraises-des-Bois could be swarming with sleuths by the time I got back.

OK, Cory. Are you on the bus or off the bus?

The truck lurched up to the front door as I shook off my umbrella. Neil jumped out of the back, his long red hair in a ponytail, a black beret on his head. Then two figures in hooded plastic slickers. Someone inside passed boxes and instrument cases out to them. François? It figured he wouldn't care to get wet.

The dining room had turned into the OK Corral at shoot-out

time. The tables were laid for tomorrow's breakfast, but they were bunched near the door, like cattle in a pen, shying away from the equipment piling up at the other end.

Here came the piano. Then several giant hatboxes: drums! Tops were unclipped from black boxes which became speakers. François screwed chrome legs onto a long flat box and turned it into Lacey's synthesizer. A pile of black frisbees were bases for microphone stands.

Since it clearly was going to take a while before all this was ready to make music, I went back upstairs to find Quasi & Company.

Nobody home chez Lacey. On the next landing I heard the faint sound of a harmonica. I listened at doors until I tracked it down.

"Yeah!" Dan's voice answered my knock.

He was sitting on the edge of the bed with an acoustic guitar, leaning forward to look at a notebook on the floor. Terry sat cross-legged on the floor on the other side of the notebook. Niko knelt beside him with a blues harp.

"Da-da-da home all right," sang Terry. He glanced up briefly as I came in. "Or should I stay on the same note? What are you doing there?"

It was a bigger room than mine or Lacey's, and more American: a double bed, a TV, shag carpet, chairs with arms and cushions, a sink. No clues to who was staying here—just two suitcases on the dresser. I sat inconspicuously on the floor behind Niko.

Dan sang back the melody to Terry's harmony: "Well, I hope you get home all right!"

"What do you think?" said Terry.

"Stay on the same note for now, till we see what Roach and Lacey want to do."

"Can we run through it from the beginning?" said Niko. "I need to hear the verse again."

"Sure."

Dan plucked a low ascending introduction on his guitar. Terry, who had drumsticks but no drums, tapped out a rhythm on the open notebook. The tune was slow and meditative, almost a minuet, nothing like the rock-&-roll they'd played last night.

He repeated it, with Niko playing quietly behind him on harp. A love song? I leaned forward hopefully.

"Be sure to walk where there's plenty of light—

"I"—Dan held it—"hope you get home all right."

From the last note, his guitar rose again into the baroque opening chords. It was a distinctly odd combination: Dan plucking a line that could have graced an eighteenth-century drawing room, while Niko's harp quavered like a lonely cowboy and Terry laid out his slow beat on a notebook.

They stopped. "What do you think?" Dan asked.

"I like it," said Terry.

"Niko?"

"Yeah. Do it again?"

I realized: It's a new song. Coming out of that notebook and Dan's head like a chick pecking its way out of an egg.

Dan started to sing the second verse. He got as far as "I hope you—" and then the door opened and Lacey came in, followed by Roach.

"Just in time!" Lacey tossed her wet jacket on the bed.

"Is this that 'Hope You Get Home' thing you were talking about?" Roach asked Dan. He set down a brown paper bag on the dresser.

"You seen any glasses?" Lacey asked Niko. She started poking around, opening doors and drawers. Though she wasn't moving as fast as usual, and her face was still pale under her make-up, Lacey looked remarkably fit for someone who'd been flat out with a hangover an hour ago.

Dan had resumed plucking chords. "I'll jes' go an' get mah bass," said Roach.

"Aha!" Lacey held up two glasses. "Roach, bring ice."

Niko pulled a bottle of Jack Daniel's out of the paper bag. "Good work, you guys. Lacey, you got a snort here for me?"

"Yeah," mocked Terry. "Snort a little J.D." He made loud sniffing noises.

"Let's finish the song, can we?" Dan played an impatient run on his guitar.

Terry and Niko immediately settled back into place. I was struck once again by how readily Quasi & Company separated into individuals and how quickly they re-coalesced as soon as anyone mentioned music.

They started from the beginning. I wished they'd play the whole thing—I felt sure the song's real thrust was still to come. What would it be? In their set last night there hadn't been one new love song. With The Rind, Dan hardly ever wrote anything that let you see through the band's tough surface into his heart. What secrets was he ready to tell now, twenty years later, twenty years older?

"I hope you get home, all right, tonight," Dan sang.

Lacey, hovering behind Terry, harmonized on the next line in a sweet high soprano. It sounded terrific. They all grinned at each other, except for Niko who could only wiggle his eyebrows over his harp.

Roach came back as they were finishing the verse. After he took out his bass, he set the open case on end. Half of one side was a speaker.

"Handy gadget," said Niko.

"Best appliance Sears ever made." Roach plucked an experimental note. It resonated with amplification.

"From the top," said Dan.

Still the same song; but this time it had a soprano and a baritone harmony on the vocals and a bass line all the way through. The difference was stunning: as if the new parts were always there and just needed to be uncovered.

They wound it off triumphantly, if a bit raggedly. "All right!" crowed Lacey.

"Let's take it downstairs," said Dan. "You haven't even heard the bridge yet."

And suddenly everybody was packing up: bass and speaker, notebook, harp, drumsticks.

Neil had the board set up on the garden side of the dining room. Dan plugged in his silver Stratocaster. Lacey chopped out chords on her synthesizer—"96 Tears," it sounded like. Niko played "Chopsticks" at the same beat. As usual, there was so much going on that I could only catch a fraction of it.

"Are we ready?" asked Dan.

"Too many chopsticks!" sang Niko. "Yeah. Let's go."

Even in this small space, with no lighting but the overhead fixtures, the five of them among their instruments, amps, and speakers melded visibly into a band. Still, what came from the speakers startled me: Music! The intro was seamless: Niko on piano, Dan harmonizing on guitar. Hard to believe this was the same song I'd just watched them build line by line, layer by layer.

"I hope you get home all right, tonight," sang Niko.

I walked around the room, listening.

"Be sure to walk where there's plenty of light . . ."

Niko's voice was harsher than Dan's; I wasn't sure I liked that. He gave the words a cynical tone that blunted the lyricism of the melody—made it more ominous.

A clatter at the door. Dan and Terry went on playing for a few seconds, but everyone else stopped.

"Here come de judge!" said Roach. "Whaddya wanna bet they kick us out?"

"Madame Thorne?" The desk clerk glanced around warily, Stanley searching a cannibal tribe for Livingston. "Ah. Téléphone, Madame."

"Merci."

If it's Marian, I thought, I'll ask if I can call back. If it's John, I'll tell him to stop blowing his budget on transatlantic—

"Cory?"

My blood chilled from my scalp to my feet. "Larry?"

"Who were you expecting?" His voice was playful—hinting at jealousy, affection, husbandly possessiveness. Against Niko's faint piano chords it sounded dissonant.

"Nobody." I didn't want to mention Marian. "John Otis?"

"John sends his regards. And a message. Why aren't you at the Ritz?"

Why are you asking me this? Forget John! What about you, Larry?

"Not to be pushy, he said, but you can appreciate. He's responsible for your safety as well as Hands Across the Sea if anything goes wrong."

"Tell him nothing's going wrong. There was no bomb. That threat to Victor Tréville is looking like a bad publicity stunt. And not by Quasi & Company. They don't need it or want it. Everybody here wants a piece of them."

In the dining room they were starting over. I shut the phone booth door.

"And why's that?" said Larry. "Because this is the first time they've shown their faces since they lost their leader. Because a lot of people think Dan Quasi and his pals dodged a bullet twenty years ago, and now the truth's about to come out. Don't be blasé about this, Cory. I spent some serious time in the under-culture when I was researching my novel, and I can tell you—"

"Blasé? I'm a journalist, for god's sake. I've been—" Oh, hell. Screw it up, why don't you? "Listen. You know from experience, Larry, things look different from the inside. You and John are three thousand miles away. I'm here, eyes wide open, and I can tell you, nothing sinister is going on with Quasi & Company."

So stop wasting our first conversation in six weeks! What's your stake in this, anyhow? What do you want? Why did you call me?

"John tells me they blew off their contract with Hands Across the Sea as soon as they hit Paris. And I remember enough about the Ascher murder to see a pattern. Promise one thing and do another. Whether that's show up at your friend's party or play where you're supposed to play."

"Meaning what?" Hoping he wasn't about to blame me for the band's Strawberry Festival gig.

"Their contract includes a dinner-dance at the Eiffel Tower. John just heard from the coordinator over there, Gordon Bailey's wife, they've hired some chanteuse to take their place."

"Is that a problem?"

"Is that a problem? Cory!"

"You've got to admit, dinner at the Eiffel Tower isn't the ideal venue for a rock band."

"France isn't the ideal venue for a rock band. Not with Hands Across the Sea."

"How can you know that? If you could have seen them last night— The hosts and ambassadors were so nervous, and then Quasi & Company came on and everybody loosened up. Dancing together—"

I could hear Larry's skepticism in his silence. How could he understand, when he hadn't heard the music?

I nudged open the door with my foot. Niko's voice floated down the hall: *Be sure to walk where there's plenty of light . . .*

"Can you hear that? They're putting together a new song. A love song—the most beautiful thing— It's magical, Larry. Like watching a Polaroid picture develop."

"Cory."

"What does John want me to do? Tell the band that Hands Across the Sea insists on rock music with their dinner instead of dinner music?"

"They didn't even ask Sheila Bailey! Can't you—?" He reined himself in. "No. At this point, we'll just have to hope this chanteuse gets through the night all right."

I stifled a giggle.

"John also said, Since you are still at the same hotel as the band, will you please remind them they're under contract to Hands Across the Sea, not Phases or some record company or whatever they're thinking."

I pictured myself walking back into the dining room and delivering this message.

"If you can't get them to the Eiffel Tower, he said, make sure the dinner tonight gets enough coverage so nobody will notice."

In other words, forget about going wherever they're going instead.

"Sure," I said. "But ask John this for me. Who sponsored a TV contest to identify Hands Across the Sea's mystery band?"

"Oh. That was the French committee. They've apologized. Somebody who didn't know about the publicity blackout thought it would give the program a boost."

I resisted pointing out the injustice of this double standard. Enough secondhand arguments! Why didn't John Otis call me and deliver his own messages? Why turn it over to the man I met and married seven years ago in Paris?

"Are you OK with that?" Larry answered as if I'd asked him out loud. "John dumping all this in your lap? I mean, media, that's one thing, but an unsolved murder, a bomb threat, and a rogue rock band?"

I took a deep breath. "If you're concerned, why don't you come over here yourself and check it out?"

Silence. That's it, I recognized. That's why he called me. But now that it's out there on the table, he's backing off.

"You'd love it, Larry. The Hôtel des Fraises . . . Or stay at the Ritz if you'd rather. Or we both could."

Don't you remember? Our own *recherche du temps perdu*: Blue twilight from the Pont Neuf. The Arc de Triomphe shining like a half moon down the Champs-Elysées. Rain pattering on linden leaves outside our mullioned windows while we snuggled, warm and dry, in our four-poster bed.

"I can't." He said it so softly I wasn't sure I heard him. "I've got a director flying in Monday, meetings Tuesday—"

"You'd come back here tomorrow but for the work you've taken on?"

"I'm not the one behind the star-maker machinery."

"That's not what this is. Didn't John give you his Hands Across the Sea speech? The band's job, and mine too, is connecting people."

God help us, half a world apart, and all I've got to bring us back together is words! I felt like a fisherman, reeling inch by inch, playing that mouth on the other end of the line.

"Well, my job is here." He spoke fast, his decision made. "I've got a full plate, Cory. Besides, honestly— We made a plan; let's stick to it."

Right. We made a plan not to rock the boat till Independence Day. But, dammit, Larry, whose boat is it? Ours or our marriage counselor's?

He'd shifted into placatory mode: wishing me the best, assuring me he trusted my judgment, he'd tell John Otis what I'd said, just be careful, that's all. Up the hall Quasi & Company finished the first verse again.

I slammed down the phone and shoved open the door. Let me out of here! Let me go back to work I can do, solving problems that have nothing to do with me.

"I hope you get through the day, OK," sang Niko.

I stepped between tables. Dan was staring at the floor; Roach gazed out the windows. The scalloped pegs on his bass looked like ginkgo leaves.

"Watch where you go and what you say . . ."

This is where I belong, I thought with a rush of gratitude. Right here.

"I"—Niko saw me and smiled—"hope you get through OK!"

I smiled back: Thanks!

At last, the bridge. I folded my arms in anticipation.

Roach's bass sliced down like a machete. The synthesizer shuddered. Niko's voice went hard.

"Cause Johnny went down in the street last week,
And we lost Angel on the cloverleaf—"

I pressed my arms tight against my chest. A love song? Hah! Guitar snarling, cymbals slashing across keyboards and bass—this was a horror story, a cold tale of violence in a world gone out of control.

"And nobody knows," Niko added grimly,
"What happened to Ros-alie."

I felt as if I'd been punched in the stomach. While Quasi & Company glided back into the melody as if nothing had changed.

"Well, I hope you get home all right." Niko didn't sound optimistic.

"Well, I hope you get home all right," the others echoed softly.

Behind the voices, footsteps: plucked guitar chords and drumbeats following at just enough distance that you couldn't be sure . . .

"Cause you know Johnny went down in the street," Niko whispered. "Seems like it was just last week."

The drums louder now, the guitar like harsh laughter. I shrank inside, trying to shut it out, but the song closed around me

—taunting chords grabbing my shoulders, drums and bass pummeling me, synthesizer jeering at my helplessness.

Then gradually they let up. A tinkle of cymbals. A few piano notes. I was shivering, alone in an empty street.

For a long moment, silence.

"OK!" It was Neil calling from the sound board.

"Not bad, huh?" said Niko.

The band was disengaging. They moved back from their mikes, flexed their fingers. I stared at them: five strangers who no longer seemed either harmless or friendly.

"Lacey!" Terry thumped his bass drum. "What'd you do with that Jack?"

"Can we run through it again?" said Dan. "The last part was a little sloppy."

I fled out the door.

Chapter 12: Travelin' Band

In my room I lit a cigarette and took out my file on The Rind.

Seeing them summed up by the Rock Encyclopedia restored my sense of proportion. **THE RIND: Mickey Ascher (rhythm guitar, vocals), Dan Quasi (lead guitar), Paul "Roach" della Costa (bass, replacing Thabo "Turbo" Ebihara), Terry Morrissey, drums.** Just another band. A scoop for Rik Green, a PR hook for Hands Across the Sea. Two pages of ten-point type between The Righteous Brothers and Rock Revival.

The Rind's story is a sad one because of its premature ending. Their last album, GRIND, showed four talented musicians who seemed to have hit their stride as a tight, innovative, multifaceted band. A week before its release, vocalist Ascher was found murdered in his Boston penthouse, an advance pressing of GRIND playing beside him. The crime was never solved, and The Rind disbanded.

After that came their early history. *The Rind's first single, Government Man, released on the eve of the 1968 Democratic convention in Chicago, became an anthem for antiwar and antigovernment demonstrators nationwide.* That was us!—me, Penny, Bev and Jill from down the hall, and Karen our house president with her obnoxious boyfriend who wrote slogans on the bus windows with Karen's lipstick, and those two cute Amherst guys who unfortunately weren't staying at the church . . . *The subsequent album THE RIND did well despite hasty production and a fragmented focus, with Ascher's lyrical vocal style sometimes meshing and sometimes clashing with songwriter/ guitarist Quasi's hard-edged political rock. Musical and personal tensions between the two increased with success, leading to a second impressive single, Dynamite Wheels, and another spotty album, RIND OR REASON.*

Spotty? Bullshit! That was a great album!

I skimmed ahead, through *Outta Sight, Out of Rind* and the Cambodia demonstration.

Ascher, always the group's most visible member, escalated his off-and-on drug use as his flashy personal style attracted growing media attention. Quasi became reclusive, turning out tunes increasingly reflective of his mounting cynicism with the music business.

More bullshit. Mickey and Dan had flamed through the *Outta Sight* tour like a pair of Roman candles. And Dan's cynicism had more to do with Nixon and the Vietnam war than the music business.

Quasi's disenchantment may have been partly due to manager Graham Douglas—Ascher's brother-in-law—taking over The Rind's financial affairs and piloting the band into two marginally successful films. BEINGS OF LIGHT, released in late 1971, was a disappointing throwback to the group's earlier stylistic and thematic vacillations.

That I had to agree with. I'd never understood why they put in all those horns and strings.

In May 1972 Turbo, fed up with intragroup tensions, left the band. The effort to find a replacement became a struggle which pitted Ascher and Douglas against Quasi and Morrissey. When the latter pair succeeded in bringing in Pynk Pyg bassist Roach, a power trio was established which would dominate The Rind's musical direction in 1973's GONE WITH THE RIND and onward, pushing Ascher to the sidelines.

It sounded so succinct. Hardly a hint of the anguished infighting and disillusion Terry had described last night.

Shortly after the completion of GRIND in the spring of 1974, Ascher was arrested on drug charges. Released following mandatory treatment, he was found dead in his Back Bay penthouse on June 26, his skull smashed and numerous other bones broken by blows from a champagne bottle. Despite a prolonged investigation and a $50,000 reward offered by Quasi, the murder was never solved.

Suitably terse. But then any Rind fan knew the rest: Graham

Douglas phoning Mickey all morning, no answer; letting himself into the penthouse with the key he'd promised never to use. The singer's battered corpse sprawled beside his black marble fireplace on a polar-bear rug, soaked with blood and champagne. His own voice blasting him from four new Bose speakers: "Baby, don't waste it! Come on and taste it, taste it!" The empty bottle bobbing upside down in a silver bucket of melted ice.

My pre-trip research filled in a few more gaps: The rage that must have impelled the killer to slam that heavy glass weapon into Mickey Ascher's left temple, and then club his naked torso at least twelve more times, splintering his skull, right collarbone, both jaws, upper and lower arm, and four ribs. The homicide squad's frustration when their search through the rose-tinted water turned up no frozen clots of skin or hair, and their examination of the bottle found no fingerprints, and their analysis of the bodily fluids on the victim and the polar-bear rug revealed that, yes, Mickey Ascher had sex during the evening, but no, this wasn't where he was beaten to death. The media's endless speculations about what kind of monster could slaughter a man in a hot frenzy and then coldly carry his still-bleeding corpse to the fireplace, douse it with champagne, clean up the real murder site, and bury the weapon (wiped clean) among the hundred other bottles strewn around his home.

'Cause Johnny went down in the street last week . . .

How could anyone who knew Mickey Ascher—least of all one of his bandmates—do that to him?

And nobody knows—

I shut out Quasi & Company and read to the end.

Though GRIND went platinum, The Rind was finished. Roach joined the short-lived Rosie and the Riveters, then reunited with Pynk Pyg guitarist Jim Clark to form the San Francisco group Suisun. Morrissey retreated into session work, later producing several Boston bands including Big 16 and Magic Fingers. Quasi left the music industry and as yet has not returned.

No answers there. Only questions. The same old standbys— where did Dan Quasi go, and why? Plus a minor surprise or two:

did Terry's producing Magic Fingers mean he knew Lacey before she met Roach? Did it matter?

More surprising was what the Rock Encyclopedia didn't ask. Larry's question, for instance: why didn't Dan Quasi show up at Mickey Ascher's party?

I hadn't asked him which party he was referring to: the *Grind* celebration that ended in a drug bust that dragged Mickey through court into rehab, or the welcome-home celebration that ended in his murder? I didn't wanted to encourage Larry's back-seat driving by admitting it, but he did have a point. Once was suspicious. Twice was tragic. Three times started to look like a pattern.

Not that I cared. I was in France to cover Hands Across the Sea, not psychoanalyze a rock star. Any views I might have about Mickey Ascher's murder were as irrelevant now as they had been twenty years ago.

There at least I had to give Steve Connelly credit. Whatever his flaws as a human being, as a professional he was pragmatic. To him Quasi & Company were just a job. Whereas I kept getting entangled in their music, their personal lives—

There was a knock on my door.

I put the sheet back in its folder. "Come in."

"Hi," said Dan Quasi.

He leaned one arm against the door frame. His flannel sleeve slipped down around his elbow, leaving his forearm bare and brown as a branch against the white sill. He seemed altogether too vivid and too three-dimensional to fit in this prim little room. I had a sharp unwelcome flash of D.C. twenty years ago, and wished he would go away.

"Mind if I . . . ?"

"Sure. No." I got up off the bed. Pragmatic. Professional.

My sweater and tape recorder were on the chair. "Here, let me—"

"No need."

Dan Quasi sat on a corner of the bed. I stayed where I was, standing by the window.

"You asked me about an interview."

"You mean . . . Right now?"

"Why not?"

I wished I hadn't left my cigarettes on the bedside table. "OK. Great."

I set my tape recorder next to him on the bed; dropped in a tape. Dan tipped his head back to look up at me. His hair was longer in The Rind, I noted professionally. You never used to be able to see his ears.

"What'd you think of our new song?"

As if he didn't know. I pressed Record and went back to the window. "Very effective."

"You took off out of there like somebody hit you."

"Wasn't that the idea?"

For a moment he didn't answer. Then he said, "Why don't you come sit down?"

"I'm fine."

"You look cold."

I was. I was shivering. I crossed to the head of the bed, pulling up one leg under me so that I half-faced Dan across a yard of bleached cotton.

He rose and walked around behind me. I tensed: What . . . ? His hands came down on my shoulders and rubbed to warm me up. His palms chafed my arms; his thumbs massaged the knots at the base of my neck. I could feel his breath in my hair. I knew he must know how it unnerved me to have him touch me like this, and that he was doing it as consciously as he'd decided which song to teach the band this afternoon.

"Thanks," I said, wishing he'd stop and hoping he wouldn't.

"What didn't you like about it?"

"For that I need a cigarette."

Dan picked up my Merits and returned to his seat on the bed. He took one from the pack, lit it, and handed it to me; then lit another one for himself.

"Well?"

My lips felt the moisture from his lips. "I wasn't expecting how it came out." Groping for reactions I could tell him. "I was hoping it was—more personal. You hardly ever write about your own feelings."

"What about 'End of the Night'?"

"That's always been one of my favorites. Why don't you write more like that? It's such a beautiful song!"

He blew out smoke. "I guess I don't feel like that very often."

Irrelevantly it struck me that my fantasy had come true. Here I was; there he was. Not exactly how I'd pictured . . . Still, I wished I could call back through time and tell Cory Goodwin of Phases that all those lonely nights in roadside motels would lead to this: sharing a bed (and a French hotel bed, at that!) with Dan Quasi.

"Why did you come here?" I blurted. And amended, blushing: "On this trip. To Paris. With Hands Across the Sea."

The blue eyes swung back to me. "I thought you knew that. We wanted to try out the band in front of an audience, without the hassles we would have run into at home."

"Like fallout from Unsolved Mysteries?"

"Like media hype in general. The nostalgia market. A reunion of The Rind! Save the dinosaurs! That's not what Quasi & Company's about."

"What is it about?"

"Rock-&-roll."

Pat and predictable. Was this going to be another game of hide-and-seek?—Ms. Journalist probing while Mr. Rock Star ducks behind glib answers?

"So you're saying this trip, five days in France with a yuppie exchange program, has nothing to do with Mickey Ascher's murder or the shitstorm it unleashed, and may again? It was just a way to launch Quasi & Company outside the system?"

"I wouldn't call this outside the system. Yes, outside the standard industry path. And yes, that's what I'm saying."

"Why?"

He didn't answer immediately. I said, "Was it strictly a professional choice, or did you have other reasons? Political? Personal?"

"Timing, mostly. We were ready to play out. Hands made us

an offer."

"You knew that offer came from Marie Tréville?"

"No. It didn't. Our contract is with Hands Across the Sea." Dan ticked ash off his cigarette. "They offered us a deal that we talked over and agreed would work for us."

"Then why start changing it as soon you got here? Adding the Strawberry Festival, copping out on the Eiffel Tower—"

"Copping out?" he interrupted sharply.

"What would you call it?"

"Finding a compromise. They get their marshmallow music, we get to play our stuff. We're not Lawrence fucking Welk."

"What are you? The Lone fucking Ranger? You knew Hands Across the Sea's agenda. If it didn't suit you, why sign the contract?"

"They signed the same contract. Hotel reservations in Paris. No advance publicity. And what do we get? A TV contest about the mystery band. Kids waiting at the airport to tear off our shirts."

"One shirt."

Even to me it sounded lame. Dan stretched out his blue-jeaned legs and ran his hands through his hair. He looked tired, and old.

"This isn't what we're here for. You wanted to do an interview. Ask me some other questions."

Ask me some other questions. Drop a quarter in the jukebox and hear the man sing it one more time.

I wouldn't get a scoop for Phases by lambasting Dan with other people's anxieties. If I wanted to learn anything useful, I needed to find his key and tune to it.

"OK." I stubbed out my cigarette. "What about Mickey Rat?"

A corner of Dan's mouth curved. "Good. Yes. If you can understand the Rat you've pretty much got the whole thing."

"Was that a reason for coming here? To play the Rat at EuroDisney?"

"To play the Rat, yes. EuroDisney was more of a sign than a reason. A confirmation."

"Of the trip? Of Quasi & Company? Of this particular

music?

That twitch of a smile again. "Yeah."

I recalled my descriptive phrase for him at the Cambodia demonstration: poetic-cryptic. "What *is* the Rat?"

"You could say it's America. Or the history of rock-&-roll."

"Starring Mickey and Annette?"

"Sure." He was nearly smiling now. "All this time the rest of the world's been going through disco, reggae, punk, rap, et cetera, they've been tap-dancing around Never Never Land. So when they get kicked out, they've got forty years to catch up on."

OK, I thought. I'll bite. "And what do they do?"

"What do they do?" he repeated meditatively. "Well, they start with the early sixties—Phil Spector, Motown—"

"The choo-choo and the ticket takers."

"Right." He looked pleased.

"That's all I know."

"In the parking lot they meet a bunch of surfers. These guys figure Mickey's a wimp, but they dig Annette. Which is cool with her after Goofy and the Three Little Pigs. So they jump on their Hondas and roar off yelling about beer, chicks, cars, and sun sun sun."

"Beach Boys?"

"In black leather," said Dan, "with a Laurie Anderson postcard video backdrop, waves licking the beach."

That nearly derailed me: Dan Quasi was into Laurie Anderson? But I righted myself. Phases; Hands Across the Sea; breaches of contract. Drugs, mayhem, and murder. "Then what?"

"Then . . ." He leaned back and stretched, as if fast-forwarding for highlights. "They go to New York. Mickey heard years ago from a tourist there's a big musical show where people sing about peace and love and hand out flowers, just like back home in Fantasyland."

"Hair?"

"Yup. But when they get to Greenwich Village—surprise! Everybody's soloing around in headphones."

I could see it: a giant mouse and a girl in black felt ears searching Washington Square in vain for hippies.

"So they decide to end it all. Jump off the 59th Street Bridge. They walk out—dark sky, dark river, strings of lights—*aaaahh!* But instead of water they hit a boat. People cheer! What is this, heaven? No. A new concept in theater: you cruise around Manhattan and whatever happens is the performance. Usually they get seagulls and garbage scows. Never anything as cool as this black-and-white dude with ears like an old movie camera and this chick with her name on her tits dropping from the sky.

"Well, Mickey and Annette are weirded out, because something about this is awfully familiar. The floor starts flashing colored lights, and it hits them: Anything Can Happen Day! So they tap out their old routine, trying to fit in. But the boat people don't want them to fit in. You guys are the show! More! More!"

I blushed. Was that what we did to him when we hollered for encores?

"The floor rises up under them like a pedestal. Behind it, a huge screen. Mickey's getting into this—he's a star again! Yah! The lights move faster, flickering onto the screen like static. A picture tunes in: Thirty-foot shadows dancing over them, twitching their fingers with the music."

Dan's fingers pranced as if pressing chords from an invisible keyboard; but it was his eyes that held me, urging me to see with him.

"Annette tries to stop but she can't. She and Mickey have turned into marionettes—live puppets controlled by video puppeteers."

I saw it so vividly I shuddered. And in Dan's urgent blue eyes glimpsed the true history of rock-&-roll, and possibly America.

"And then . . . ?"

His hands fell. "That's it so far."

What? I blinked as if the house lights had come up midway through the show. That's all?

"Then why— If you only—" I paused; tried again. "Why bring it to France with Hands Across the Sea while you're still figuring it out?"

"Ask Terry."

"Terry? Why?"

"He talked me into it." Then, seeing my puzzlement: "Not the Rat so much as the band."

"You mean . . . 'Do What You Do'?"

That surprised him. "Right. You caught that?"

"It's not an answer, though. 'How come a man do what he do?' It's a question."

"But that's all there is. That's the point of the song: You don't know why. You just know that's what you do. And if you talk it to death, you lose it." He shook out another cigarette. "You drain off the energy you need for the music."

"Was that why you blew off Unsolved Mysteries?"

His fingers paused with the matchbook half-open. "Did you see that?"

"No. It's not airing for three more weeks."

"They didn't talk to us. They interviewed Dougie and Gail, a couple of cops, a couple of techies, and some kids who were at the party. It's nothing about The Rind. Just the same old guessing-game crap: Who killed Mickey Ascher? Who was close to him enough to get in and drink champagne with him, but hated him enough to beat him to death with the bottle? Total fucking waste of time, same as the cops. Because they can't answer Question Number One: Why?"

Why do you think? The obvious interviewer response. The question Dan Quasi must have been asked a hundred times.

"Drugs?" I said. "That was the cops' first theory. A deal that went wrong? They dropped it when they found Mickey Ascher was clean. Nothing in his system but champagne. Nothing in his condo but a few flakes of marijuana and a smear of coke in the bathroom."

Dan was watching me curiously, but he didn't respond.

"Robbery? Another dead end. His wallet and his watch were gone, but that could have happened earlier, according to his sister." I reached for the Merits. "Whose airtight alibi means Mickey wasn't killed for his money. He didn't have a will. Everything went to Gail and the courts."

Dan lit a match and held it to my cigarette.

"Vengeance? A crazed girlfriend?" Inside I was cheering. "According to the autopsy report she'd have to be a body-builder —rare in 1974, and not Mickey's type. A girlfriend's jealous boyfriend? That could fit, except for one thing: the killer was somebody Mickey trusted enough to open his double-bolted door and let inside." I looked at Dan. "So . . .?"

"Don't ask me."

"You're launching a new band. People will keep asking, don't you think?"

"Why? when I've got nothing to tell them?"

I started to retort and stopped. *He isn't being flippant, Cory. He's asking you a question.*

"Because a lot of us were Rind fans, and Mickey's death kneecapped us. Who would kill a gifted musician? and a great band? We'll keep on asking you, because you knew him better than anybody, and if you can't make sense of this, what help is there for the rest of us? And how about you? We didn't just lose Mickey Ascher and The Rind, we lost you, too. Are you back now for real? Why'd it take you so long? And why start over from scratch, instead of surf the reunion wave like everybody else? Of all the venues on earth you could have picked, why Paris? Why Hands Across the Sea?"

Even to myself I sounded like those tourists who think if you just ask the same thing again, louder, he'll answer in English.

Dan didn't look annoyed, though. His head tipped back as if he were thinking about it.

"Born on a mountain top in Tennessee," he sang. "Something something, land of the free—"

"Davy Crockett?"

"Not the Lone Ranger. Mickey had a theory, that's why our generation turned out how we did. When Davy Crockett's wife died, first he fell apart, then he pulled it together and ran for Congress. 'Be sure you're right and then go ahead.' Remember?"

He was grinning, and so was I. "Sure."

"We used to sit in my grandmother's parlor, Mick and me on the rug and Gram in her armchair, when I was living with her after my dad—" He stopped himself. "She was a cool old lady. Dug the hell out of Walt Disney. And that other dude, who gave the sermonettes?"

"Jimmy." I was trying to picture Dan Quasi and Mickey Ascher six years old, watching TV with Dan's grandmother in their mouse ears.

"Jimmy. Right. Him too. All of them. Remember Spin and Marty?"

"Spin and Marty! My favorites." Suddenly it seemed important for Dan to know I too had a childhood, a family, a TV, that there was more to me than a notebook and tape recorder. "My cousin Dinah and I would make horses out of sofa cushions and pretend we were at the Triple R Ranch. One time I lassoed the living room lamp. My mother couldn't decide whether to shoot me or give me a prize."

Dan nodded approvingly. "Marty wanted to learn how to ride, so he took out his horse in the middle of the night."

"And broke his arm."

"You run into something you want to do, you do it. Bust your ass, or your arm, whatever it takes."

"And when you grow up you start a rock-&-roll band—"

"Or write for a magazine—"

"And turn it into a multimedia performance piece."

"Beats shootin' b'ars for a living, wouldn't you say?"

I stifled an impulse to hug him. "That's the answer to everything, is it?"

Dan chuckled. "Hand me my coonskin cap, mama, and call me the king of the wild frontier."

I blew smoke at him. "You're impossible."

"No I'm not." Dan stretched out his arms and opened and closed his fingers. "I just don't like interviews."

And this one, I thought with a rush of regret, is over.

A quick syncopated rat-ta-tat at the door. I stood up.

"Come in, Terry," called Dan.

Terry poked his head in, saw me and stopped. "She wants to talk to you," he told Dan.

"Did you tell her I'm busy?" Dan motioned at me to sit down. "Tell her I'm doing an interview."

I recognized that tone. The one Larry used when an old girlfriend would call and he wanted me to get rid of her. I'd say that at least he could pick up the phone long enough to say he was married but they'd have lunch sometime; and he'd retort that it wasn't lunch she wanted, and he wasn't going to talk to her.

"She's pissed," Terry said.

"Tell her if she wants to talk to me she can come down to the club."

Terry raised his eyebrows and closed the door.

I wished Dan had left sooner. Or I'd kept my mouth shut about Dinah and the sofa cushions. I wished he'd gone on dodging my questions, stonewalled me with the same dazzling smile he gave every fan who crowded around the rock star, rather than let me think he understood I was a human being. I wished—oh, crap. Whoever she was, she had my profound sympathy.

"Where were we?" asked Dan.

"Finished."

"No more questions?"

"I was going to ask you why you never write love songs, but you already told me." I opened the door. "You don't feel like that very often."

Chapter 13: Disney Girls

The Eiffel Tower. Built for the Paris Exposition of 1889, France's monument to the new age of technology. Five thousand blueprints, 15 million pounds of pig iron, two and a half million rivets, 37 tons of paint. Three hundred meters tall before the addition of television transmitters. Three hundred skyjacks put it up; three hundred outraged artists and writers petitioned to tear it down. Now it was the nation's highest-grossing landmark, if you counted souvenir paperweights.

Steve Connelly and the Crofts gave me a ride in. Steve had called with the offer and an apology: sorry if I sounded, no intention of undermining, committed to our ongoing . . . I asked him about Lacey and Montmartre. He said not on the phone. I said in that case I accepted his apology and would meet him and Max and Judith outside the hotel.

Pragmatic. Professional. You want to play king of the wild frontier, Dan Quasi, you can damn well do it at EuroDisney.

We waited in a long line for the elevator on the ground floor and another line for the restaurant on Level Two. I might have regretted my high heels except for the satisfying shock on Steve's face when he opened the car door and saw my legs.

What was holding us up here? Craning around heads, I caught glimpses of an elegant gallery with high ceilings, a wall of scenic watercolors, a grand piano . . . and Marie Tréville.

She stood blocking traffic beside Sheila Bailey, looking more poised than I'd have felt if I had to shake several hundred hands. Her shimmery pastel dress, pearl eardrops, and flawless makeup gave her an air of having emerged in porcelain perfection from a tissue-lined box.

I braced myself for a Snow Queen smile. Instead she greeted me cordially: Was I enjoying my visit to France? How nice that I'd met the Crofts. Were my accommodations satisfactory? I wondered why the thaw until I noticed the man behind her.

Could that be Victor Tréville?

Not the dashing right-wing rebel I'd envisioned. In his bespoke gray suit and dark patterned silk tie, this gentleman would have fit right in at the Faneuil Plaza. He was barely taller than his wife, with a clipped mustache and neat black hair combed over his bald spot. His deep-set eyes were sharp, his manner formal. For the price of his lizard-skin shoes, Ronald Reagan could have kept himself in cowboy boots till the next century.

When Judith Croft introduced us, Monsieur Tréville softened visibly. He made a graceful bow over my hand; murmured pleasantries similar to his wife's. If I hadn't witnessed his impact on the Governor of Massachusetts, I'd never have believed this man was once hanged in effigy by Boston's French students.

On the other hand, I still couldn't picture those manicured fingers ripping the hairpins from young Marie-Carmen-Lulu's chignon.

Steve commandeered a window table. The view was awesome, with Paris spread out around and under us. Pink linen, white rosebuds, crystal chandeliers, the muted chink of silver on china . . . I felt as if I'd been set floating like a water lily on a pastel pond.

We ate bisque d'homard; we drank sherry (not bad) and Vouvray (better). The ambassadors had settled in visibly: fewer jokes, more relaxed smiles. Even the chanteuse was getting through the night all right, though if I were singing at the Eiffel Tower I wouldn't have opened with "Ma Chérie Amour."

Halfway through dinner came a surprise: I was having fun. Without Quasi & Company roping us into a tug-of-war, Steve and I could argue about larger topics. The European Community. NATO. Nuclear power. Here at last was a realm—informed discussion with an intelligent, accomplished partner—where I felt at home. As the lights of Paris twinkled on through the blue dusk, rock-&-roll seemed long ago and far away.

We finished our second bottle of wine. The waiter brought cheese and cognac. The sky deepened to indigo. My brain felt wispy as a cloud. When Steve invited me to dance I decided this was my chance to ask him about Lacey. He led me onto the floor among couples box-stepping to an old Simon and Garfunkel tune.

Yes, said Steve, in his opinion Lacey had definitely taken drugs. No, he didn't know what, when, or how. But then it wasn't like he'd been keeping an eye on her. The nightclubs of Montmartre were full of, shall we say, diversions? And Quasi & Company had picked up a motley entourage, including a swarm of guys buzzing around Lacey.

Then why was he so sure . . . ?

Hm. Hard to say. You could just tell: that glaze in the eyes; that blur in the voice. No, he hadn't seen her do anything but Jack Daniel's. But, again, he hadn't been paying that much attention.

As I wasn't now, thanks to the music, my unaccustomed heels, Vouvray throbbing in my head, and other couples bumping us. Surely, though, Steve was stretching the truth? I distinctly remembered someone—Terry? Niko? Lacey herself?—telling me they'd flirted all night.

"I heard the two of you were more together than that."

"Oh, well, we danced." He gave my hand a reassuring squeeze. "Best thing about this job. You might have noticed, I've been asking you to dance ever since we landed."

"Not very professional."

"Sure it is. Why'd you think Hands Across the Sea always has a Mystery Band? Old club-owners' rule: The girls come for the band, the guys come for the girls. Bottom line? Everybody's happy."

"But the band's not here. I don't follow."

His hand went around my waist. "Then let's try another format."

I still couldn't follow. Too much wine, or too many years since dance class. After a moment we quit trying to match steps and moved closer together. Steve's body against mine felt warm and strangely familiar. There were, I mused, certain advantages to the chanteuse.

"Da dum-tee dum tee tum," he sang tunelessly. "So long . . ."

So long, echoed the piano as his hands caressed my back. So long since any man but my husband has held me like this. So long, so long, since I've smelled the clean cotton of someone's shirt collar and the faint tang of his aftershave, or appreciated the fit of my chin against his collarbone.

"So long, so long . . ."

Steve bent his head so that I couldn't keep his cheek from pressing mine. Should I pull away? Oh, who cares?

The sky outside the windows had darkened to purple by the time I got to talk with Victor Tréville. Steve, having left me for a duty dance with Judith Croft, invited Marie Tréville to take the floor. Her husband gallantly asked if I would care to join them. He piloted me at a careful distance that took me back to Fathers' Weekends in college.

Judith had introduced me to Victor Tréville as Cory Thorne. Now I told him I understood he knew my husband's father and great-aunt. I could see Thorne Cosmetics glittering in his eyes as we inched across the floor. Ah, yes!—such a delightful woman, Marian Thorne. Such a pleasure to do business with Harrison Thorne. And his fine corporation, such an asset to the French economy.

"Now you have EuroDisney in your district as well," I said. "Were you involved with that?"

"But of course," he said modestly. "Such an enormous project."

"One-fifth the size of Paris, isn't it?"

"Indeed. The park and the hotels, you understand, occupy only a portion so far. This is a grand work in the honored tradition of France—the Louvre, Versailles. Requiring, naturally, the historic expertise of our people as well as yours from America. Precisely the type of cooperation we wish to foster with Hands Across the Sea," he added graciously.

Peace Corps for the fast track indeed. "Will you stay involved as development continues?"

"Certainly. Massive though it is, EuroDisney is only one part of my government's plans for this area. Our success depends on a wide array of elements—transportation, education, utilities, housing—which all must move forward together."

"Very impressive. Very challenging, I should imagine."

"Oh, yes. That is the pleasure, of course. The greater the difficulty, the greater the reward."

His chin lifted. I still couldn't picture the neck in that Egyptian-cotton collar being strung up on Marlborough Street. But then (as John Otis had noted), that was twenty years ago. Kid stuff. Wild oats. The band had grown up, and so had the Government Man.

"And you, Cory? What brings you here with Hands Across the Sea?"

I summarized: Boston sponsors, media coverage, Phases, Quasi & Company.

Victor didn't flinch. "Aha."

"This isn't my normal line of work"; and I mentioned the Crownhill School and my summer as a journalist in Paris. "But living in Boston in the early seventies, I'm familiar with rock music. You were there, too, weren't you?"

"Briefly, yes."

"Was that where you got to know about The Rind?"

"The Rind? I don't— What is that?"

I'd have believed him if I hadn't known better. "Wasn't that why you didn't want Quasi & Company coming to France? Because three of them used to be in a Boston band called The Rind?"

"Oh. No, no. May I be frank? I was shocked that our Boston partners chose rock music for this exchange program. Such musicians are known for bad behavior, are they not? Drugs, promiscuity, destruction?"

Though my hackles were rising, I didn't intend to be distracted from the key point: this man steering me around the dance floor had just lied to me.

Why? To save face after his Boston partners overruled him? For fear of another death threat from their unsuitable musicians?

"Luckily Quasi & Company aren't like that," I said. "What a shame you missed them last night. Some trouble at the office, was it?"

"Oh, nothing of importance. I wear two hats, as you say in America. My own office is near my home, but often I must attend meetings some distance away. It is not easy for my wife, social engagements and the like, but as you see," he flourished the hand that had rested on my waist, "I make it up when I can."

Maybe he was just naturally evasive. Weren't politicians known for that?

"And Madame Tréville? Does she like rock music? Did she ever listen to it in Boston?"

"My wife likes French music. Ravel, Debussy."

"Then you don't know who on her committee asked for Quasi & Company to come to Paris with Hands Across the Sea?"

I felt Victor Tréville stiffen. "That was arranged in Boston."

"No. Someone here requested them. Any idea who it might have been?"

His shoulders went up a centimetre. "I do not know all the committee members. But I can assure you, none of them would make such a suggestion."

The song ended. We separated; clapped. For the umpteenth time I tried to compose a veiled question about the threatening note.

As we walked back to the Trévilles' table I inquired, "Did your wife enjoy Quasi & Company's performance?"

Victor was smiling at Sheila Bailey. "I don't know," he said. "We haven't discussed it." Perhaps thinking this sounded cold, he added, "She stayed in the city last night with her cousin. We have scarcely talked at all."

I glanced around and spotted her and Steve lingering on the dance floor.

So that the bomb squad could search their house in Brière? Or had the lady in red found herself another vortex?

"Victor—"

"Excuse me," he said at the same moment, and took off to recapture his wife.

Steve grabbed my hand for the last dance. I pleaded exhaustion but was overruled. On the floor I asked him if Marie Tréville had mentioned Quasi & Company. He said he'd raised the subject, but without success. He didn't blame her, after they insulted her committee by ditching this party. He hadn't pushed it.

We rode home in the Crofts' Fiat with considerably less space between us than on the way in. When Steve slid his arm around me I had to remind myself I didn't trust him to keep from nestling into his shoulder.

I woke to sun streaming through my shutters. Thanks to Graham Douglas's aspirin trick, I felt terrific. Rain over, the linden leaves in my window sparkling green and gold— I wouldn't have been surprised to look down into the square and find it magically transformed from gray cobblestone into Technicolor.

And I did, and it was.

Overnight an army of wooden carts had set up camp among the tree trunks. Vendors in aprons were arraying long green courgettes in rows, building pyramids of shiny purple aubergines, hefting bins of turnips, stacking crates of strawberries and cherries. Under a canopy a cheese merchant had spread out his bricks and wheels on a cloth-topped table. As I watched, shivering, a stout matron pointed at a Brie, and he sliced off a runny wedge, weighed it on a scale hung from a branch, and wrapped it in layers of paper.

The dining room was empty. Nine-fifteen—too early for musicians. To me it was so late I felt decadent. Denise looked as though she agreed. She brought my tea and croissants in silence, shy again without Terry to flirt her out of it.

When the bus's elderly silhouette lurched into view around the drugstore, I realized I was humming out loud. *Baby, don't waste it! Come on and taste it, taste it!*

Paris! Maps, prints, and books in bouquinistes' stalls along the Seine. The Musée Marmottan: glimpses of garden through the windows echoing the Impressionist paintings on the walls. Sidewalk vendors in Le Marais. At the Louvre my favorite marble Apollo stood serene in a shaft of sunlight.

You visit a city for a weekend and you come home with a head full of snapshots. Live there for a summer and you learn it from the inside: the quickest route to the bank, where to have your shoes, your teeth, your toaster fixed. But write about it for a magazine and you discover the Poster Museum, the skin-diving club, the miniature train in the Bois de Boulogne, the Mother Earth Lost & Found 33-1/3 Record Café. The woman at the Arts Collective shows you where her mother used to rendezvous with Sartre. A Chinese waiter tells you in pidgin French about his great-uncle who built the railroad in California. You learn how to paint roses on porcelain, make strawberry sherbet, buy an office building, swallow a sword, build your own bicycle. And you realize you'd rather live out of suitcases any day than give up this heady sense of starting fresh each morning on a new fork in the road.

What had I been thinking, to resist coming back to Paris? Why did I imagine Boston was the proper vantage point for untangling my life? Gazing at the sailboats on the Charles, waiting for things to settle. Well, things don't settle. Like the man said: Peace or quiet, take your pick.

And speaking of Dan Quasi, I had a strawberry festival to cover.

At the hotel I ran inside for my tape recorder, socks, and a sweater. No messages. Monsieur Vlaemenck, whom I met in the lobby, told me the band had already gone down to the soccer field where the fireworks would be.

"But you will not miss the *retraite aux flambeaux*?" he asked anxiously. "The children are gathering now at the school to receive their flambeaux." He pointed up the hill. "Very soon they will come down into the town, and we will have here the best place to see, right in the front of the Hôtel des Fraises."

Denise was waiting outside, looking even younger than usual in jeans and a blue-and-white American baseball jacket. Monsieur Vlaemenck put his arm around her; and I realized, as I should have done earlier, that she was his daughter.

Was Monsieur widowed, then? No Madame Vlaemenck I could picture would have let a rock-&-roll band this close to her child. I imagined a life for them: Madame passed away, God rest her soul; a son at hotel school; an older married daughter or two; and Denise, the baby, so like her mother as a young bride . . .

A light flickered at the end of the street. One yellow globe popped into sight, then another; and then paper lanterns were bubbling down the hill like a river of lava. Proud smiles on chubby faces—every child in town had a lantern, although some of the youngest had handed theirs over to their parents. The babies rode in strollers with their lanterns bouncing from the handlebars.

Denise waved to a mustached gentleman relighting his daughter's candle. "Voilà le maire," murmured M. Vlaemenck.

Being mayor in Fraises-des-Bois must be a full-time job. In addition to directing tonight's festivities, I learned, M. d'Aumont would sit on the strawberry judging panel tomorrow morning.

And then my heart thudded. Behind the mayor marched Marie Tréville, arm in arm with her husband.

But surely he wouldn't have come unless the police were satisfied he'd be safe.

Then again . . .

The jut of Victor Tréville's round chin, the tight set of his lips, and the alert gleam in his eyes suggested a man who scoffed at danger.

His wife's free hand rested on his arm linked through hers. Her face was expressionless.

Be sure to walk where there's plenty of light . . .

A firecracker popped. Marie Tréville gripped her husband's arm. Victor tensed. His eyes darted around the square, checking the upper windows of the hotel, sweeping the shadows under the linden trees.

If anyone did want to harm him, they couldn't ask for a better shot.

The flood of lanterns winked through the trees and snaked down the street toward the bakery. I edged into the parade, close behind the Trévilles.

We reached the town's lower square. The shimmering light revealed a butcher shop . . . clothing store . . . tavern . . . Above their dark plate-glass fronts, white faces watched from windows; white hands waved.

As the retraite wound into the narrow streets beyond the square, I was tracking every movement that might turn Victor

Tréville from a bureaucrat into a headline. Every time a shutter banged open, a sparkler whizzed into the air, a firecracker exploded, I was ready to lunge toward the shiny balding head that stood out so ironically tall in this crowd of children.

At last we reached the soccer field. The file of bobbing lights widened and dispersed.

I let out a long breath. OK, Victor! Nothing around you now but the starry sky.

The mayor turned his two small children over to his wife; smiled and nodded hello to the Trévilles. Mme. d'Aumont clucked over a shoe that had come untied. Marie Tréville asked the older child something about a float for the parade tomorrow.

I wished I could hear Victor and the mayor. It sounded as if they were discussing tonight's program—I caught "son et lumière," a sound-and-light show. Then M. d'Aumont mentioned a petit discours—

Marie Tréville straightened and turned. "But no!" she exclaimed to her husband in French. "You won't stay here."

Victor responded with a lofty look and a speech that sounded rehearsed. "I attend the Fête des Fraises every year, and I shall attend it tonight."

He sounded so deliberately pompous that I half expected him to thrust one hand into the breast of his trenchcoat.

"But, chéri, surely it isn't wise—"

"Wise?" Victor's thin lips pursed dangerously. "Wise? What was not wise was allowing this band to play at the Fête des Fraises! It is not I who have caused this dérangement." He tossed back his head. "Stay here with Marie-Yvonne if you like."

"I'm coming with you."

Victor gave a small shrug. He and the mayor moved off to the right, toward the band's platform.

Oh, great, I thought. He's making a speech!

The two men mounted the platform. Their wives and children waited on the ground. Marie Tréville's face was impassive.

Where were Quasi & Company?

Even thinking it made me feel like a traitor. I told myself I wasn't worried, just curious. And I scanned the field; and I didn't see anyone from the band.

Onstage the geometric silhouettes of monitors and microphones loomed like goblins from a space-age fairy tale. Behind them crouched the humped black shapes of drums. A tall acoustical panel at the back angled forward over the space, giving it a contained, theatrical look. One chrome rim—the snare?—betrayed itself with a wink as a spotlight shifted on a nearby tower.

Watch where you go and what you say . . .

Where were Quasi & Company?

Erector-set towers had been set up at this end of the field, their throats and bellies bulging with speakers. Around the perimeter, lampposts and trees cast spiked and shaggy profiles against the blue-black sky.

Tock! Tock! Mayor d'Aumont tapped a microphone.

There was the sound board, floating in a pool of light, and Neil behind it, his long red hair hiding his face. Beside him on a stool sat that young French crewman, AKA Grumpy.

But not Dan Quasi. No one from the band.

The field was crowded: parents and children on picnic blankets, babies in strollers, grandmothers in lawn chairs. No doubt they too attended the Fête des Fraises every year, and live rock-&-roll or not, they'd come to see the fireworks.

White light illuminated the stage. MM. d'Aumont and Tréville stood blinking and exposed.

I prowled around, looking for—what?

"Mesdames et messieurs!" The mayor's voice reverberated from the speakers. "Bienvenus à notre Fête des Fraises!"

Victor's bald spot and the rims of Terry's drums gleamed against the dark panel behind them. At the sound board, Grumpy —not in overalls tonight but Levis and a baggy green Rind sweatshirt—watched Neil make adjustments among the rows of colored knobs. Mayor d'Aumont introduced Monsieur Tréville. The soccer field rippled with polite applause.

Apparently Victor wasn't going to make a speech after all. In a few graceful words he announced that it was his pleasure to be here this evening, and his honor to introduce the marching band from his hometown of Brière, which after playing so admirably for the *retraite aux flambeaux* would now perform some additional selections.

The two men came down the stairs. I was close enough to see Marie Tréville welcome her husband, take his arm, all smiles. A bright flash: so the press were here! And a young policeman, holding a chain that must have blocked off the steps. I didn't see Steve. Several well-wishers surrounded the Trévilles, hands extended. Another flash.

As Marie Tréville turned toward the photographer, her eyes caught mine. I smiled back at her. "Bonsoir, Marie."

"Ah! Cory Thorne," Victor hailed me. "Will you join us for a glass of champagne?"

I replied that I would be delighted.

We followed Mayor d'Aumont behind the stage. I glanced back again at the crowd. They weren't all locals. That group with spiky haircuts and black sweaters looked like refugees from the Beaubourg. A cluster of kids in leather jackets stood smoking around a tree. Near the platform, fifteen or twenty blue-jeaned teenagers had spread out blankets like the older folks. I saw a Who T-shirt, and a Foreigner one.

Hah! In this motley crew, who wasn't a foreigner?

We came to a large white trailer parked beside the band's truck. Mayor d'Aumont unlocked the door and led us up narrow steps into a narrower hall. Imitation wood paneling . . . a tiny bathroom with a faux marble sink . . . an abstract print built into the wall . . .

Marijuana smoke.

In front of me, Marie Tréville stopped short.

Mayor d'Aumont spoke first, a shade too genially: "Good evening, mademoiselle, messieurs."

Against the trailer's gold asbestos curtains Quasi & Company glittered. Roach, on the sofa, had propped his booted feet on a coffee table. His purple satin shirt was open to the waist. Around his neck hung a shark's jaw, jagged white teeth gleaming amid the black hair on his chest.

A splash of electric blue: Niko, in a cowboy shirt, leafing

through a magazine.

But it was Lacey who was stopping traffic. She posed in the center of the room, her silver sequined top splintering the light from the table lamps. Her legs were sleek in black satin pants. She'd pinned her frizzy hair back over one ear with a crimson rose, like a splotch of blood, which matched her lips and fingernails.

The Trévilles in their trenchcoats looked suddenly dowdy, sparrows in a tropical jungle.

"Lacey, there's no ice."

Terry, at the bar, held up a bottle of Jack Daniel's. He'd switched from his standard flannel to a black T-shirt painted like a tuxedo.

"That's OK." Lacey moved away from the Trévilles with a theatrical toss of her head. "But make it a tall one."

Terry shot a wry glance at Roach. But Roach was smiling at the newcomers.

"Bonjour, Marie."

She smiled back, unruffled. "Bonsoir, Roach."

Chapter 14: One More Saturday Night

Silence, as pieces fell into place.

The first person I looked at was Lacey. Her hand was out to Terry for her Jack Daniel's. Not a tremor.

She already knew.

I could have smacked her. Dammit, Lacey, when did he tell you? Why didn't you tell me?

But Roach was swaggering around the coffee table, still grinning at the woman he knew twenty years ago in Boston, when she wore her skirts up to here.

Marie Tréville turned away. Whatever had happened then, she clearly didn't want it revived now.

Victor Tréville's face remained fixed in an unreadable smile.

"We have champagne arriving in a moment," Mayor d'Aumont said anxiously to Lacey. "Perhaps you will wait and join us in a toast to the Fête des Fraises?"

It wasn't Roach and Marie Tréville he was concerned about but the whiskey. Young women in France don't drink tall glasses of Jack Daniel's.

Roach chuckled. "Champagne, Lacey?"

She scowled at him.

"Sounds good to me," came a voice from behind the bar.

Victor Tréville's head swiveled as Dan Quasi stepped out of the kitchen.

Next to the rest of them Dan was dressed inconspicuously: jeans, a black V-neck sweater, a gray sport coat. He nodded to the mayor and to the Trévilles; then he leaned against the wall beside the bar. The implication was that he didn't want to interrupt their conversation. But his exaggeratedly casual pose and the faintly mocking expression in his blue eyes made it hard to look anywhere else.

Mayor d'Aumont attempted introductions. Nobody paid

much attention. He might as well have said: Dan Quasi, this is Victor Tréville and his wife. Victor, this is Dan Quasi and his band.

I guessed Dan had staged his entrance to divert Roach from Marie Tréville; but Roach didn't go for it. He resumed talking to her as if the two of them were alone in a hotel room. "So you couldn't stay away, huh, Marie?"

She gave him a look cold enough to have dry-iced anyone but Roach. Lacey held her glass up to her face and stared at them both through an amber window.

In my head fragments of information were tumbling around like unmatched socks in a clothes dryer. Roach and Marie. Mickey Ascher's murder. Victor finding a job in Boston for his neighbors' daughter. Champagne. The woman at the vortex.

Roach turned to Victor. "We're old friends, me and your wife." Then to Marie, conversationally: "How'd you find out we were putting a band together?"

Victor's shoulders squared inside his trenchcoat like a general ready to defend a fortified position. *If she'd had an affair,* Marian's voice echoed, *he wouldn't have married her.* It worked both ways. He had married her; therefore she couldn't have screwed some hippie bass player twenty years ago. And if Roach kept hinting otherwise—

"I was asked by our committee to recommend a band from Boston," Marie Tréville answered calmly. "I telephoned Terry to see if he knew of anyone suitable for this program."

"And he told you about us." Roach folded his arms.

"Naturally the committee was happy that a band as well known as The Rind would join Hands Across the Sea."

Victor Tréville's jaw was rigid.

"We're not The Rind anymore, Marie." Roach wasn't smiling either. "Not without Mickey."

I glanced at Lacey, then Dan, then Victor again. Nobody moved. We might have been playing Statues.

Marie Tréville slipped her arm through her husband's.

A note in English threatening to blow him sky-high. Warning him the day of judgment was here. A bomb threat, concluded the police, and searched his office. *We don't forget, Government Man. Now it's your turn to die.*

The door rattled. Beside me Mayor d'Aumont gave a nervous start.

Down the hall came Steve Connelly, bowed under the weight of a large cardboard box.

"Steve!" cried Lacey, with the relief of a beleaguered fort commander who's just sighted the cavalry.

"Hi," Steve grinned back at her. "Monsieur d'Aumont, where do you want this?"

With the arrival of Steve and the champagne, the atmosphere lightened a little. Roach ambled toward Lacey as if he'd just discovered she was here. Steve carried the box into the kitchen. Terry lined up plastic cups on the bar. Niko went back to flipping through his magazine.

I longed to take Steve aside and fill him in, but where could we go? The bathroom?

"Oh!" Steve had wrapped a towel around one bottle and was wiggling the cork. "Terry, we can't use those. This is real French champagne."

"Shut up and pour," Terry murmured.

As the champagne went around, everyone made an effort to be festive, even Victor and Lacey.

"To the Fête des Fraises!" proposed the mayor.

We raised our cups and clicked them together.

"Lacey," said Marie Tréville. "You don't care for our champagne?"

"Lacey doesn't care for any champagne," said Roach. "She's a Jack Daniel's girl."

And she's mine, he might have added. Roach hadn't missed the way Marie had taken her husband's arm.

"Dan," said Niko. "What happened to your girlfriend?"

Dan was still leaning beside the bar with the nonchalance of a riverboat gambler. "She had to go."

Roach laughed. I could tell what he was thinking: You mean you got rid of her.

Marie Tréville slipped off her trenchcoat. Victor slid it from her shoulders and folded it over a chair.

"So, Monsieur Quasi," she said pleasantly. "What are your hopes for this evening, if one may ask?"

Her voice carried an undertone of challenge that drew both Dan and Roach around to look at her. In her soft blue summer dress, you could hardly believe Marie Tréville was old enough to chair a committee.

"Our hopes?" Dan repeated the word with polite disdain.

"Play some rock-&-roll!" said Roach. "Whaddya think?"

Marie Tréville almost glanced at him, but she stopped herself. She raised her cup to her lips and sipped in quick little swallows like a bird, watching Dan over the rim, her gold earrings quivering.

Between her and Lacey there couldn't have been a more striking contrast: the demure lady in blue, the rock musician with her crimson lips and nails.

"Good question." Steve moved into the middle of the room. "I was wondering the same thing. You wouldn't play at the Eiffel Tower, but here you are at a small-town strawberry festival. Why?"

Oh, Christ, I thought. Who cares about that now?

Dan, gazing into his champagne cup, didn't respond.

"We came to play for Hands Across the Sea," said Terry from behind the bar. "Here we are, here you are."

"When it suits you."

Roach swaggered over and loomed an inch from Steve. The shark's jaw swung forward. Steve stepped back.

"You got any more bubbly in there?" Roach clamped a hairy hand around the bottle Steve was holding.

Across the room Victor Tréville refilled his wife's cup.

"I'm still curious." Steve spoke to Dan in the same man-to-man tone he'd used yesterday at breakfast. "Why'd you pick here to debut the band? Isn't the normal thing to record an album before you go on tour?"

"We're not on tour," said Dan. He held his cup under his hand, fingers splayed around the rim. Maverick, I thought: You want to settle this over tequila, Steve, or you want to step outside?

"You've been rehearsing for six months, right? That's a lot of effort for an exchange program."

"Jesus," Terry muttered under his breath.

"We didn't do it for them." As Lacey stepped toward Steve and Roach, light from the table lamp slid over the oily black of her legs. "We did it for us."

"Yeah," said Roach. "What's it to you, anyway?"

"I told you yesterday. I work for a radio station. Our listeners ask questions. Your listeners," he added pointedly.

Dan set his cup on the bar. "Time to get out there."

Steve looked from Niko to Dan, waiting for a response. His expectant expression darkened as he saw he wasn't going to get one. Niko tossed aside his magazine. Terry emerged from behind the bar. Lacey eyed Roach, who appeared to be considering what kind of goodbye to say to Marie Tréville.

But Marie was still watching Dan. As he walked past her she touched his sleeve. "And what will you play for your audience tonight?"

Dan barely glanced at her. "Listen and you'll see."

Victor Tréville's thin lips tightened to a double line. I knew from the twitching corner of his mouth that he was aching to string up all five of these foreign hoodlums. Not because they were rock musicians and therefore drug addicts and terrorists; but because he finally grasped why he'd been sent that note. It was no bomb threat. It was to get him out of the way so an aging hippie could relive the golden days of yesteryear with his wife.

I groped my way around the dark platform to the soccer field.

Be sure to walk where there's plenty of light . . .

What do you call a band that cuts a performance? Disconcerting. How about a bass player who shares a lurid past with a bureaucrat's wife? Demoralizing. And the gag order on media coverage? Depressing.

I bumped into a motorcycle under a tree and jumped back

superstitiously.

But that was silly. This was Fraises-des-Bois, not Altamont. No Hell's Angels here, just the townsfolk and a few dozen kids who'd come to hear some American rock-&-roll.

The Brière marching band must have finished its selections. The younger people in the crowd were moving forward, clustering around the speaker towers, pushing closer to the stage.

I should be finding a spot with enough light to take notes, not wondering if Lacey had finished her drink and whether the Trévilles would stay for the music and how Victor would vent his new grievance against Quasi & Company. Let them worry, not me. Whatever happened, I'd go home with a story.

A spattering of applause. Five silhouettes were stepping into place through a dark tangle of equipment.

They opened with a fast bass-and-synthesizer intro I didn't recognize. Roach rolled his eyes at the crowd; Lacey tossed her hair. Whom rock hath joined together . . .

The couples in lawn chairs watched with the detachment of TV viewers. A woman sitting on a blanket poured lemonade from a thermos. A little girl buttoned her sweater. I saw Steve shooting pictures, and Max Croft tucking Judith's shawl around her shoulders.

I'd better call John Otis ASAP. Tomorrow? Saturday—damn. Maybe later tonight. Important to relieve his worries (and Jerry Leroy's) about the band blowing up Victor Tréville—preferably without mentioning that the real threat lay in another direction.

The song ended. Polite applause. There was Gary Laporte, peering up from the edge of the stage through his wire-rims. And François, with his arm around that redhead . . . Mary Ann?

The second number was another rocker. I glanced at the rows of faces behind me. No reaction. Couldn't Quasi & Company see this was a crowd for fireworks, not dance music?

A uniformed flic—the guard of the stage stairs—spoke to Neil at the sound board. *Turn down the volume, please.* Neil gave him an impassive stare I remembered from concerts in the sixties. *Not a chance, man.* After a moment the flic shrugged and walked away.

They'd all told me the same thing: We're not The Rind! An artistic statement, I'd assumed when I heard it from Niko during the banquet, from Terry over cocoa, from Lacey in her room, from Dan at breakfast. Not this time. When Roach said it to Marie Tréville—*We're not The Rind anymore. Not without Mickey*—it wasn't music he was talking about.

So many crucial facts I didn't know. How involved were Roach and Marie in Boston? Why did she invite his new band to Paris? What had she told Victor, then and now?

One fact I did know: Whatever brought Quasi & Company to France, it originated with The Rind.

"E-e-eh!" The Rind. White letters on green. Grumpy the crewman blocked my view, grinning like a satyr. "Madame la journaliste!"

"Having fun?" I inquired drily in French.

In reply he flapped his elbows and capered, a Disney-animated pterodactyl. "You want a story for your newspaper? Talk to me!"

Showing off the sweatshirt. I got out my camera, wondering if it was the band's gift that had inflated his spirits, or the festivities, or what.

"I know the most of everybody!"

The flash lit the dark sockets of his eyes and the sharp points of his incisors.

"You like our Fête des Fraises?"

"You've been here before?"

He threw back his head, shrieking with laughter. "I live here!"

That startled me. "You live in Fraises-des-Bois?"

"But certainly!" His arms waved in the air, unfurling the sweatshirt like a spinnaker. "When I was a baby I marched in the Retraite aux Flambeaux. As a boy, the Défilé des Chars. Now I am a man, I work."

"Why aren't you working, then?"

"All the time I work! I set up, I break down." Pouting, he pirouetted. "I talk, I listen. Nobody see me, but I see everything, eh? The whole story, I know. Only me."

Jealousy? Patriotism? Intoxication? "What whole—?"

"Dead American dinosaurs!" he screeched, and flew away.

Dinosaurs. Et tu, brute?

Did the kid really have a story, or just an overdose of ambition? I wedged my camera back into my shoulder bag. I hoped music fans back home wouldn't share his attitude, or we'd all be screwed.

Waves of purple washed the stage. I watched Lacey's lithe hands flash over her keyboard, Roach's gnarled ones slide along his bass.

You were in the sixties, right? she'd asked me. As if the decade were a space capsule—my generation's cosmic trip that her generation could only relive on tape. Counting down on Ed Sullivan: The Beatles or the Stones? Blasting off in Monterey: the Airplane, the Who, Jimi, Janis, the Dead. Apollo moon landings. Big Pink. The draft. Watts, Newark, Detroit. Woodstock: stars overhead and mud underfoot, while the President sent thousands more of our brothers to fight in a country we'd barely heard of. Tapes shuttling from college dorms to state-of-the-art stereo equipment bought on R&R in Tokyo or Bangkok. Letters on airmail stationery thin as rolling papers: Today we mined a trail, tomorrow we take a village. Today we occupied the administration building, tomorrow they're sending the National Guard. Khe San, My Lai. Chicago, Kent State. *Watch out, friend, when you're in the hands of the Government Man!*

Oh, Lacey! Who told you it was ten years of music, love, and flowers? Ask your dinosaur boyfriend. Ask Professor Gary Laporte, clapping and pushing up his glasses. Ask those people dancing along the edge of the stage. Ask Steve Connelly, Jerry Leroy, Victor Tréville.

Ask Dan Quasi.

He stood in white light, head bowed, eyes half closed, lips moving. Not the icon I'd worshiped since D.C., but a man who earned his living playing rock-&-roll. His best friend dead, though we refused to bury him; his band dispersed, though we'd trekked to Fraises-des-Bois tonight to hear it.

Ask him, Lacey. The man who helped write the sound track.

Old Smoky shone like silver as Dan Quasi curled out a solo that twined around Roach's bass, twisted through Terry's drumming, wailed a counterpoint to Lacey's synthesizer; as T-shirts, leather jackets, and Calvin Kleins moved forward, rising from blankets, emerging from under trees, setting down beer cans and stubbing out cigarettes to clap along.

"Hey! Cory!"

Lena Michel grinned at me, breathless and happy. "They're hot tonight, huh?"

She looked hot herself in round striped earrings and mauve overalls. I felt a twinge of regret for my fisherman's sweater and jeans.

"I was talking to Dan in the trailer before the show. He said this could be the gig where they really got rocking. When are the fireworks?"

Gears grinding in my brain. "I don't know."

Where's your girlfriend, Dan?

"So what've you been up to?" Lena pushed her glossy black curls back behind her ear. "Dan said you've been staying away from the band?"

She had to go.

"What?" I echoed dumbly.

"Well, he said you were kind of pissed about them doing the club, and you didn't show up today at all."

"I—" My mind wasn't functioning. Dan thought I was avoiding the band? I was pissed about the club?

Dan Quasi noticed I hadn't been around?

A burst of applause. "Oop!" Lena poised like Cinderella at the stroke of midnight. "Got to get back. I promised Louis a dance."

Lacey was stepping up to the vocal mic in front. Stop! I wanted to shout at them. Give me a minute to think, will you?

It's kind of a relief doing a slow song. With the fast ones, it comes right from your head out your fingers.

No relief tonight. Dan's guitar neck went up, Terry's sticks came down.

Dam-dam! A double chord and a wild guitar tailspin.

Something clicked in my head: Mickey Ascher, blond hair shimmering, hands cupped around his mic.

Dam-dam! Recognition and applause rippled across the field. The hit single from *Rind or Reason*: "Dynamite Wheels."

"Well, I was walkin' through the dark," Lacey crooned,

"My baby by my side.

A car pulls up—

He wants to take me for a ride!"

The Rind had done it wall-of-sound. Lacey's cockier tone fit Dan's stripped-down guitar part and Terry's clipped drumming. No message here—this was dance music.

And people were dancing, springing up along the front of the stage. Families moved aside: fathers swung babies to their shoulders, mothers grabbed blankets. A few left, but most stayed to watch this year's twist on their Strawberry Festival.

"Now my baby's in the dark,

And he's feelin' all alone!"

Lacey strutted and flirted with the boys around her feet. Her sequined top shimmered like a fish's skin. Her mouth was a splotch of crimson.

Overhead the first firework flung a shower of gold across the sky. A pause; then *boom!*

"Dynamite wheels!"

Lacey twirled her mic. Niko hammered on his keyboard.

"Dynamite wheels!"

Now Dan took over, whipping out a solo that lit up the night. His right hand barely moved, while his left hand skittered up and down the neck of his guitar like a water spider. His dark hair was fringed with sweat, his eyes jubilant. When he kicked the cord out of his way a girl in front screamed. Ten yards closer and I'd have screamed with her.

Another firework exploded in a blizzard of white. Roach grabbed a bottle of champagne from behind the acoustical panel. He threw it in the air, loosing a plume of spray into the red light; took a swig.

I ached to dance. My whole body throbbed with the music,

craved to plunge into it as I'd done twenty years ago when every frat-party band ended the night with "Dynamite Wheels." Who could hear that wild wicked guitar and not answer it? I yearned for someone to run up and whirl me into the crowd. I wanted to be in there, not out here watching!

From Terry's maniacal drum finale they slammed into "I'm the One," welcomed with shouts from the front lines. This was a more spectacular version than The Rind ever played. Fireworks were sailing overhead like champagne bubbles—green, white, orange, pink.

Roach held up his bottle and poured champagne into his mouth, splashing a cascade of gold over his beard, into his hair. Niko—up front on vocals now—shook a tambourine at him till Roach threw him the bottle, and he too swigged champagne.

The fans along the stage were screaming, waving their arms. There was Grumpy the crewman, too, capering in and out of the crowd, wildly clapping his hands above his head.

Quasi & Company's concert was turning into a free-for-all. Niko had taken his mic off the stand and was singing and making faces at the front row as if they were a fun-house mirror. Roach threw back his bushy head like a satyr's; his eyes glittered with exhilaration, his beard with champagne.

Grumpy clambered onto the stage. Others followed: a girl with a purple T-shirt and long blonde hair, another with earrings like chandeliers, two boys in jeans and studded vests. Niko took a quick step back—but it wasn't him they were after. Grumpy snatched the bottle from Roach, tipped back his head and drank. One of the others grabbed for it and missed. Grumpy was gulping like mad, his eyes wild, his sweatshirt streaked with dust, bent apparently on getting high in a hurry. When the bottle was empty he tossed it to the blonde girl, who clutched it ecstatically to her chest.

More kids were climbing up from the side. An eruption of red and blue in the sky overhead lit up Steve Connelly, struggling to help a harried flic who'd chained off the steps and was trying to guard the perimeter. But Niko was shouting encouragement into his mic; and Dan, at the front edge, egged them on.

All over the stage revelers were dancing, swept along by the wild music and the weird fitful light.

Suddenly I realized Dan was beckoning to me.

"Come on up!" Niko's voice boomed over the speakers.

I scrambled up, helped by a hand from Dan. His jacket was gone. In his black V-necked sweater, his face and neck slick with sweat, his dark hair wet and tousled, he might have been Dionysus.

Up here it was full-tilt bacchanalia. Roach and his bass and the blonde girl were waltzing around the stage. Lacey, still at her keyboard, had kicked aside her chair and was doing a jig as she played. Grumpy danced between fans, monitors, instruments, and electrical cords with Niko's tambourine. From the erector-set towers beams of blue, yellow, green, and red played over the stage in a garish rainbow, while fireworks blossomed in the sky, huge explosions of colored light. Terry walloped the cymbals: *crash! crash! crash!*

Roach and the blonde girl whirled by. Grumpy was spinning madly with Ms. Chandelier-ears, clinging together as if they couldn't let go.

Dan looped his arm through mine and swung me around. Where was his guitar? He was hot and wet, his sweater soaked through. I swayed and struggled to keep in step.

His arm went around my back. Suddenly his mouth was on mine.

Someone stumbled into us and we staggered to keep our balance. I was pressed against Dan's chest, my arms around him, a roaring in my ears, my eyes shut against bright yellow light, his tongue urgently exploring my mouth.

Again someone bumped us, harder this time, and we were knocked apart. I was so dizzy I hardly knew where I was. I tripped, looked down—and there was Grumpy, crumpled at my feet.

The girl with the earrings was trying to haul him up, but he didn't seem to be able to move. His shoulders gave a spasmodic heave, rolled sideways and fell back on the floor. His legs twitched; one sneaker caught in an electrical cord. His open eyes were blank as glass.

Dan pushed at the people who were closest. "Get back."

"François!" Roach shouted into the blackness beyond the platform. "White spot!"

I fought off my vertigo. There was Victor Tréville, elbowing past the flic, unchaining the steps to the stage. Roach and Dan were pulling on Grumpy's legs, trying to straighten him out. Victor glowered at them as he hurried up the stairs.

Some of the fans jumped off the stage.

"Is he—?" began Victor, and stopped.

"Breathing," Dan nodded.

"Get him to the trailer." That was Steve, standing on the ground beside the platform.

Dan and Roach each hooked an arm under one of Grumpy's shoulders and dragged his unconscious body toward the edge. One hand trailed across the wooden planks of the stage. Victor snapped at them to be careful. They eased him down to Steve and Mayor d'Aumont. Victor jumped down, unexpectedly agile, and helped the other two carry Grumpy into the darkness. Dan followed them.

I glanced around the stage. Terry and Lacey hadn't stopped pounding out the song. Lacey's body was stiff with fear and Terry's face was grim. Almost through. I thought of those nine Boston musicians honored on a marble plaque at Symphony Hall for going down with the Titanic, still playing.

The platform was empty except for the band and half a dozen oblivious dancers.

François jumped up beside us. "What happened?" he asked Niko. "Did you see?"

Niko shook his head. "He was dancing and he fell. I don't know if he tripped or passed out or what."

Terry nodded to Lacey and the music ended.

From the applause, I realized most of the crowd in the field had missed the whole thing. Terry and Niko herded the remaining fans off the stage. François, with characteristic poise, grabbed a mic: Good night, mesdames et messieurs; thank you all for coming; the Fête des Fraises will continue tomorrow morning with the crowning of the Strawberry Queen and the Défilé des Chars.

Roach put his arm around Lacey's waist. "We're outta here."

We all moved toward the steps, leaving the field to François and his remaining crewman. Up ahead Dan stood with M. d'Aumont and a flic. The rest of us climbed into the band's limousine, which was waiting beside the truck.

"Home, James," said Niko.

Lacey said, "What about Dan?"

"He's cool," said Roach. "Let's blow this joint."

I glanced over at the trailer as we pulled out, but all I could see was lights in the curtained windows.

Chapter 15: Easy to Slip

Picnic baskets and folding chairs glided past my window, arms around waists, a baby's sleepy smile. Not the glitzy, giddy party-on wheels I used to picture when the limos left Boston Garden after concerts.

But the main picture in my mind was Grumpy: his thin legs and twisted torso in its Rind sweatshirt sprawled across the dusty planks; those horrible glassy eyes.

Lacey, staring out the other window, let out an audible sigh.

We all looked at her. "What?" she said defensively.

"What yourself?" Niko returned.

"I hope Bear's OK."

Bear. Grumpy. I hadn't asked what his real name was.

"Yeah," said Terry.

"Yeah," said Niko. "If he's not, guess who they're gonna land on like a ton of bricks."

At the Hôtel des Fraises, a flic was waiting for us. I girded to play interpreter and/or negotiator . . . but no. He was clearing us a path, pushing back the cluster of kids who surged around the car.

In the elevator Roach draped an arm around Lacey's sequined shoulder. "Hey, babe, your place or mine?"

She wriggled away. "Keep your teeth to yourself!"

Roach slipped the shark's jaw off over his head and set it on her hair like a crown.

"Where's the perks?" Niko asked Terry. "Like some good old U.S. of A. roast beast?"

"I'll ask," said Terry.

"My floor," Lacey announced.

Roach got out with her. So did I. Nothing much was likely to happen here until Dan came back.

I took a quick shower; put on my favorite linen shirt; brushed out my hair. How many nights on the road had I listened to The Rind while I wrote up my notes, pretending Dan Quasi was playing "The End of the Night" for me? Now half of me was impatient for whatever news he'd bring us, while the other half was still reverberating from his wet sweater against my chest, the planes and hollows of his back under my hands . . . waiting like a star-struck groupie to find out what he'd meant by kissing me onstage, and whether he'd try it again in private.

I grimaced at myself in the mirror. Some journalist!

Upstairs, the welcome sound of an acoustic guitar. I followed it to an open door: a small room, twin beds (one heaped with clothes and towels) and a dresser. No Dan, though. Niko sat on the empty bed strumming dissonant chords. Roach lolled behind him in the pillows, legs crossed, one foot bobbing in the air.

"And you tell meee!" Niko sang in greeting. "You don't believe they own the means of production!"

I laughed. Roach gave him a friendly kick in the back.

"Hey, you guys know any Led Zep?" said Terry from the doorway behind me.

"Love your sound!" Niko mocked. "You do any U-2? How about Genesis?"

"Dan had a good thing for that when we were on the club circuit." Terry had changed from his wet T-shirt into clean plaid flannel with a towel around his neck. "Some drunk'd yell for Rolling Stones. And Dan'd go, 'OK, here's a tune we picked up jamming with the Stones last week in Chicago.' And call one of ours, and they'd go nuts."

"We should've tried that tonight," said Niko. "One more nostalgia orgy and I could turn into Charles T. Berry."

Terry grinned. "You'd be worth a lot more."

He snapped his towel at Niko, and Niko looped it around his neck and pretended to strangle himself, eyes popping, tongue out.

"Is Mr. Snooze down for the count?" Terry asked.

"No," said Roach.

"Which reminds me," said Niko. "I'm up to here with 'I'm the One.' If we have to play it, at least let's strip it down, like 'Wheels.'"

"You don't fuck with 'I'm the One.'" Roach kicked him.

"You're talking historic landmark."

"*You're* talking historic landmark," Niko retorted. "I wasn't in The Rind."

For two seconds Roach glared at him; then he sank back again on the bed and patted his pockets for cigarettes.

Dan's gesture. Where was he? Still placating the honchos of Fraises-des-Bois? Standing by his fallen crewman in the trailer? Downstairs ordering our post-show feast? Two doors up the hall celebrating with Lena Michel?

"Where'd you lose Lacey?" Terry asked.

"OD'd on afterglow." Roach was lighting a joint.

Niko plucked aimless notes on his guitar. Roach sucked in smoke and passed the joint to Terry.

I could go downstairs and call Steve Connelly to see if he'd heard anything about Grumpy AKA Bear. Or phone the Fraises-des-Bois police . . .

"I hope you get home, all right, tonight," sang Niko sympathetically.

"Dum-da bum bum," Roach filled in the bass part.

Terry handed Niko the joint and harmonized: "I hope you get ho-o-ome all right, tonight."

It sounded lugubrious, like a record played at the wrong speed.

"You all are awfully quiet," I said.

Roach rolled his eyes wickedly. "I'm worn out!"

"I feel like I'm sleepwalking," said Niko. "Roach, what'd you put in that champagne?"

"Spanish fly, looks like," said Terry.

Down the hall a door slammed. Dan's back. My stomach tightened. I shifted my legs around so I could watch the door.

Long minutes went by. The joint made another circuit. Finally Lacey's voice inquired: "So what happened? Is he OK?"

Don't just tell her, Dan, tell all of us!

He walked in behind Lacey looking tired and preoccupied. Where will he sit? Near me?

Lacey sniffed the air and demanded: "Who's got the dope?"

"What's the word?" asked Terry.

"Come to my room." Dan had changed back into his tan corduroy shirt. "They're bringing food."

We moved to the big room where the band had created "I Hope You Get Home." It looked more lived-in than yesterday: Dan's sport coat crumpled on the floor, his black sweater balled up next to it. A boom box was edging out the suitcases on the dresser. In the middle of the shag carpet stood a tea-cart of beer, bread, cheese, cold cuts, and fruit. The band swarmed around hungrily.

"OK." Terry tossed Dan a beer. "Spill it."

"Yeah. How is he?" asked Roach through a mouthful.

Dan leaned against the window. "Bad. They called a doctor in to pump his stomach. Took him to the hospital, next town over. I went to the police station with Marie's husband and the mayor. The cops think he might've OD'd."

"Shit alors!" said Niko. "Seriously?"

"On what?" said Terry.

"Don't know. He was still out when the ambulance got there." Dan's voice was flat. He's furious, I realized—or scared. "From the questions, it sounds like whatever he took, they think he got it from us."

"Oh, fuck," Terry groaned.

Lacey huddled close to Roach and toked on the joint.

"He was high as a fuckin' kite onstage," Roach said. "Even before he chugged my bubbly."

Earlier, too, I realized belatedly. Poor arrogant, ignorant kid!

"But that wouldn't've . . .?" Lacey glanced anxiously from Dan to Terry to Niko. "Would it?"

"Electric kool-ade?" Niko's mouth curled. "Très passé."

"I don't know." Roach took the joint. "I'm kinda sleepy."

That drew hoots. Terry glanced at me and asked, "Roach, where'd you get that champagne, anyways?"

"Brought it out from the trailer. Why waste free booze?"

Lacey persisted: "That's not what I meant. If the champagne was spiked, you'd all be fucked up."

"I hardly got any," put in Niko.

"Me neither," said Roach. "Plus, if somebody dropped something in the bottle, most of it would've sunk to the bottom."

"What if Bear did, like, downers before the show? Could just plain champagne knock him out?"

"Maybe," said Terry.

Although I respected their expertise—which, after all, had pulled Lacey out of a similar hole two nights ago—I couldn't help cringing at their sangfroid. "Do the police— What are they saying?"

"They're pissed," said Dan. "They say French people don't do drugs."

"Jesus!" said Terry. "What do they think, we tied him down and shot him up?"

"Hah! You kidding?" Roach snorted. "A bunch of gringo rock-&-rollers?"

Niko exhaled marijuana smoke. "When everyone knows we never touch illegal substances!"

"So anything you're holding, use it or lose it," said Dan.

"That's what I was doing," Roach said virtuously. "Know where that J came from? Kid waltzes up to me onstage, sticks it in my pocket. French people don't do drugs my ass!"

Niko set down his guitar. "Party in my room!"

"Then Paris?" proposed Lacey, nudging Roach toward the door.

"Sure," said Dan. "Why not?"

"But if you—if Bear—if the police—" I started, and stopped.

Dan slung his arm around my shoulders. "Get it while you can."

"So we sailed off to the fun," sang Niko as we marched up the hall, "in our mellow limousine!"

Lacey joined him on the chorus: "We all live in a mellow limousine!"

"Venereal disease, venereal disease!" sang Roach.

Dan's arm still rested on my shoulders, where I was carrying it as carefully as a water jug. The weight of it pulled at my hair.

"Catchy tune," said Terry. "Who wrote it?"

"Don't ask Niko," Roach said nastily. "It's not his historic landmark."

"Or The Rind's either, or you wouldn't be fucking with it."

Niko unlocked his door. I didn't want to leave now; but even less did I want to stick around while the drug supply at the Hôtel des Fraises was smoked, snorted, popped, or flushed.

I touched Dan's hand. "See you all later."

And, stepping away from him, I headed for the lobby, where I got directions to the Fraises-des-Bois police station.

The square was so empty and silent it was hard to believe a flock of children had paraded through here two hours ago. I paused on the cobblestones to button my jacket. The shutters above the storefronts were closed, the lights out. Everybody in town must be asleep but me.

And the cops. And the family of poor fallen Bear/Grumpy.

Around the corner past the mairie stood a dark café with a red-and-white striped awning: Restaurant, Tabac, Stella Artois. In the street beyond it I spotted an official-looking motorcycle and sidecar. A sign by the door confirmed: POLICE. The building had a stucco front, like the rest of Fraises-des-Bois, with steel bars on the windows instead of shutters. Two cops about Niko's age, a man and a woman, stood talking in the doorway.

I told them in French I was Madame Thorne of Hands Across the Sea and I needed to speak with Monsieur d'Aumont or Monsieur Tréville.

The woman cop led me into a narrow hall. A coil of plastic wire like a telephone cord dangled from her blue polyester slacks, fastening her revolver to her bullet-studded leather belt.

The Fraises-des-Bois Commissariat de Police had the same down-at-the-heels, chip-on-the-shoulder air as every other police station I've ever been in. The hall opened into a hospital-green reception area with a brown linoleum floor. In the center a high L-shaped wooden bar walled off the desk. Behind it sat an older cop who glanced up at us from a chart spread out beside a stack of oversized books.

My escort told him what I'd told her. He looked me over, then disappeared through a door in the back wall. After a few minutes he returned with M. d'Aumont.

The mayor's face was tired and sad. A dark premonition stiffened my smile.

"Madame Thorne." He shook my hand, and spoke in French. "How can I help you?"

I told him (also in French) that as a representative of Hands Across the Sea's Boston sponsors, I wanted to report to my colleagues as soon as possible on this evening's unfortunate incident. And, of course, to know if there was anything we could do for the young man or his family.

He and the cop conferred. Then the mayor said, "Please come this way."

He took me down a hall to a corner office. A cluster of men rose as we entered: Victor Tréville, looking grimly serious; a uniformed officer whom M. d'Aumont introduced as Commissaire Guerin, the chief of police; and a younger cop with a steno pad.

"I regret to inform you, Madame Thorne," said the mayor, "that Albert Vaux is dead."

My first stunned thought was: Bear. Short for Al-bear. Of course.

My second was: Not to them. To these men he'd have his own identity, his own place in their town. They'd watched him grow up with the other neighbors' kids, and tonight they'd watched him struck down, on the stage he'd helped build for their American guests.

I told them how sorry I was for their loss. The young cop brought a chair. I recognized him as the one who'd directed traffic outside the Hôtel des Fraises.

"May I ask what happened?"

"The doctor was unable to revive him," said Commissaire Guerin. He was a tall, broad man with thick graying hair and a deep scar that twisted his left eyebrow like a cowlick. "He was rushed by ambulance to the hospital in Brière."

"His stomach was pumped," the mayor added.

"Anyone could see he was drugged!" Victor Tréville interjected. "At our Fête des Fraises!"

Commissaire Guerin continued in an unemotional baritone.

"Despite every measure, he never regained consciousness. The laboratory is running tests and will notify us of the results. It appears, as M. Tréville says, that a drug was involved."

He might as well have said: Never before, drugs at the Fête des Fraises. Never before, an American band.

"What kind of drug?" I asked. "Do you know? Or how he got it?"

"That we cannot tell until the report comes." M. d'Aumont hadn't forgotten I represented the press as well as Hands Across the Sea.

"The doctor suspects a narcotic," said Commissaire Guerin.

"Given to him by whom?" Victor Tréville leapt to his feet. "Can there be any doubt? Whose presence here I protested from the start!"

I looked around, expecting remonstrances or at least winces of embarrassment from the other men, and I didn't see any.

"This crime will not go unpunished, I promise you!"

"My friend," murmured M. d'Aumont. "Please do not distress yourself."

You either, Cory. This is France, not Boston. Passion is honored here, remember? It's expected. Don't let him get to you.

"Your compatriots have been very helpful, madame," the police chief assured me. "We spoke with Monsieur Connelly, Madame Bailey . . ." He paused for a fraction of a second. "And Monsieur Quasi. Of course, if drugs are confirmed by the laboratory report, further interviews will be necessary—"

"They will learn they cannot slaughter innocent citizens! Not here! Not while I have a breath in my body!" Victor pressed his fist to his chest. "In Boston perhaps, but not in Marne-la-Vallée!"

I shot him a look: Was he referring to Mickey Ascher? His face showed nothing but righteous anger. I wished his colleagues would tell him to shut up and sit down—not only because his histrionics were getting on my nerves, but because their silence alarmed me.

As if he understood, M. d'Aumont explained: "Perhaps you know, madame, that it was Monsieur Tréville who arranged for Albert Vaux to work for this band."

"Arranged—for Quasi & Company?" I was astonished.

"To my eternal regret!"

That I didn't doubt. "But why?"

M. d'Aumont answered for him. "Monsieur Tréville has been a friend and patron of les Vaux for many years. When Albert needed a job, they asked him to help."

"The boy was a student of electronics, but had no chance to use his training," said Victor tightly, resuming his seat. "With the growth of EuroDisney, there soon will be opportunities for young men with experience. So, when my wife told me her committee needed assistants for their visiting musicians—" He stopped as if choked by his own words. "I was an idiot! A criminal idiot! But who could think such a group as Hands Across the Sea would choose such a band as this Rind?"

"They're not—" I stopped. Only a criminal idiot would make the same point to M. Tréville that Roach had just made a few hours ago to his wife.

Anyway, who was he kidding? I knew as well as he did who'd chosen Quasi & Company, and so did the mayor.

"Surely you don't mean to condemn them without evidence," I started over. "If you—"

"Evidence?" he interrupted angrily.

"Yes," I snapped back. "If you, monsieur, or any of you gentlemen, know of any connection between the band and this young man's tragic death, I would be grateful to hear of it."

I looked at them. They looked at each other. The mayor put an admonitory hand on Victor's arm.

Commissaire Guerin spoke. "It is too soon for an investigation to have begun. Only an hour ago—" He shook his head. "As yet we have only a few statements. Your help will be welcome, madame. May I ask if you saw Albert Vaux before he came onto the stage with Quasi & Company?"

Fair enough. My only way to stay in this all-French, all-male game was as a witness. I wished I'd asked Dan back at the hotel what else he'd learned from these men—and what he'd told them.

Yes, I answered. I saw Albert Vaux before the show, and spoke with him, briefly. Yes, he appeared intoxicated. Yes, I watched him drink champagne onstage from the same bottle as Roach and Niko. No, I didn't see him eat or drink anything else.

Where might he have gotten drugs? Squelching Terry's quip about flies around a garbage truck, I asked where he might have gotten Lacey's bottle of Jack Daniel's. Shrugs: evidently in Fraises-des-Bois, supplying your guests with booze was hospitality, not drug-pushing.

"Did you see who gave the champagne bottle to Albert Vaux?" asked Commissaire Guerin.

"No one gave it to him. He grabbed it away from one of the band members."

"You yourself observed this?"

"Yes." And please don't ask what I was doing at the time.

He didn't. He merely lifted an eyebrow at M. d'Aumont. Meaning what? New information? Or my story matched Dan's?

"What became of the bottle?" Victor Tréville demanded.

"A girl with long blonde hair took it."

"Took an empty champagne bottle?"

"As a souvenir."

Victor shrugged eloquently: Who can believe such nonsense?

That did it. I'm all for helping the authorities, but I had questions, too. How many electronics students in Fraises-des-Bois? More than one? Why pick Albert Vaux—who despised their music —for a coveted job with the band?

Commissaire Guerin hadn't asked me what Bear and I said to each other before the show. The crewman's face and words leered in my mind: *Nobody see me, but I see everything, eh? The whole story, I know. Only me.*

Was that why Victor put his friends' son on Quasi & Company's crew? As a spy?

It fit the facts. Victor Tréville had lobbied like mad to keep the band out of France. Whatever neo-sixties chaos he feared, he couldn't have guessed what form it would take. He must have guessed that his wife had her own priorities, which she wasn't sharing.

Could Albert Vaux have discovered a secret that got him

killed?

I couldn't flat-out ask M. Tréville what mission (if any) he'd given his protégé. Drop one hint that his tale of noblesse oblige smacked of Fantasyland and he'd kick me out.

So I agreed with him. Ah, yes, how different are the ways of Fraises-des-Bois and Boston! No doubt a man of his experience, helping an unworldly boy, would take steps to protect him? Perhaps warn him against dangerous foreign customs?

"Indeed," Victor squared his shoulders. "Had not I myself witnessed the rock concerts? The drugs, the violence?" Fists clenched. "Smash the instruments! Wreck hotel rooms! Bite off the heads of chickens! Throw garbage at the audience!"

"Surely you don't suggest—?"

"Not at all," M. d'Aumont stepped in. "One has heard of such things. We are assured by Gaston Vlaemenck that Hands Across the Sea's musicians have been most agreeable guests."

"One of their own, brutally murdered! Beaten to death! And with what weapon? A champagne bottle!"

The young cop flipped a page of his notebook. His face, like Commissaire Guerin's, was blank.

"So you urged Albert Vaux to be watchful? And to inform you if . . . what?"

The police chief spoke. "We are grateful, madame, for your assistance."

Translation: Back off. You're a foreigner, a woman, a journalist—what business is this of yours?

I persisted: "Given your concerns, and your loyalty to your young friend, your associates, Hands Across the Sea—"

"I failed!" Victor Tréville flung up his hands, appealing to heaven. "I admit it! How can I ever forgive myself?"

Murmurs of *no, no* came from his friends.

"How can his poor mother ever forgive me?—who sent her beloved son to his doom!"

"No one can blame you for a generous heart," said Mayor d'Aumont.

"We will get to the bottom of this, I promise you," said Commissaire Guerin.

M. Tréville bowed his head. Under the fluorescent light, his bald spot was a halo.

How long did I have? Twenty seconds?

"Gentlemen, again, please accept my sympathy. My colleagues in Boston will be deeply saddened to hear of tonight's tragedy. May I offer them the comfort of knowing that an open, unbiased investigation is under way?"

"Absolutely," said M. d'Aumont.

"With the utmost discretion," Commissaire Guerin nodded.

"Monsieur Tréville?"

"Of course," he bristled. "Myself, any small privacy I have preserved as a public servant I would gladly sacrifice for the sake of this poor young man." He looked at each of us. "But shall I sacrifice my privacy, or my wife's, or my reputation in this district, for the sake of a criminal? No, by God! Elsewhere it may be said, All publicity is good publicity. Not here! Not in Marne-la-Vallée!"

The Disney corporation might have taken issue with that. Not me.

"I would be desolated to trespass on your privacy, monsieur. Is there any aspect of this matter that you specially wish to shield from the public eye? For your own sake, or Madame Tréville's, and her committee, who brought this band to France?"

A moment of strained silence; then M. d'Aumont spoke up. "Madame Thorne." Tardily checking his watch. "We have kept you here too long for such a late hour. Commissaire Guerin? Will you arrange . . .?"

That was fine. I wasn't looking for an answer, or to air anybody's dirty linen. I just wanted to remind Victor Tréville he had as much to lose as to gain from trying to pin Albert Vaux's death on Quasi & Company.

"Good night, madame." Victor held the door for me. "You may assure your colleagues of our diligence and discretion. To call attention to the role played by Hands Across the Sea in this sad affair could only tarnish the reputation of a worthy organization and embarrass its sponsors."

Touché.

And stalemate. Till tomorrow, gentlemen.

Chapter 16: Ramblin' Man

Three hours later I was jabbed awake by a legal point.

Not that I'd slept much. I'd left a message for John Otis, promising an update in the morning. Every time I dozed off, the elevator clanked and my ears pricked up. Someone from the front desk? Quasi & Company coming back from Paris? They couldn't have heard yet that Bear was dead. Maybe Lacey would knock on my door asking for news. Or Terry. Or Dan . . .

No footsteps outside. Maybe the elevator had taken the flics up to search Quasi & Company's rooms. Did French law require a warrant? Or just M. Vlaemenck's permission?

What were the rules here on habeas corpus? Extradition? Reasonable doubt? Capital punishment?

That was when I recalled the fax from my subconscious that had woken me. In France, suspects of a crime are considered guilty until proved innocent.

I threw back the covers, pulled my white cotton robe on over my head and slid my feet into slippers.

Lacey's door was shut. Pressing my ear to the wood, I could make out murmurs. Cops? More likely Lacey and Roach. Either way, I wasn't about to join them.

Upstairs I braced myself and tapped—lightly, in case he was asleep.

"Who is it?"

"Cory."

The door opened.

Dan Quasi stood there in only his faded jeans. His bare shoulders and chest looked so beautiful that I caught my breath. Heart-stopping guitar solos, a hundred songs in his head, and this too? I couldn't meet his eyes. Nor did I dare go on staring at the triangle of shadow contoured by the hollow beneath his collarbone, the silver threads in the curled dark hair between his breasts. I thought: I must have been out of my mind to come here.

He motioned me inside.

"I couldn't sleep," I explained defensively. "I started thinking— After you all left I went to the police station. Did you know—but how could you?—they'd only just found out, and you were going to Paris—"

Babble babble! Like a child with a nightmare. Ambulance. CPR. Autopsy. Investigation. Why hadn't I stayed downstairs with my insomnia instead of making a fool of myself to Dan Quasi?

His reaction answered me.

"Dead. Shit!" He scooped his sport coat off the floor and hurled it at a chair. "I can't fucking—" Visibly he stopped himself. Then he retrieved the jacket and felt the pockets. "Well, sit down." His voice flat, angry, frustrated. "Have a smoke."

"Did anybody at the police station say anything to you about . . . responsibility?"

He shook his head; mimed holding a poker hand an inch from his nose.

"Do you know if they searched the hotel?"

"No."

"They didn't, or you—?"

"They didn't. Local cops, I'd know." A short laugh as he lit a match. "Just like the good old days, huh? When you'd scout every room you stayed in for hiding places."

He inhaled; and I recognized with a jolt the comradely odor of marijuana.

Dan held out the joint. I stepped back in disbelief. "What are you doing?"

Dan laughed, which made him choke on the smoke. "Shit, Cory. It's four o'clock in the morning." He sat on the bed, coughing. "Anyhow, they won't bust us here. Not if they can help it. Too hard on the innkeeper."

I watched, immobilized, as he sucked in another hit.

"Come on, sit down. You said you can't sleep, right?"

Behind him the lamp beside the bed outlined his head and shoulders with a thin rim of gold. Smoke curled into the air like a silk scarf from a magician's fingers.

I brought over the chair and took the joint.

"Me neither. Not just because of Bear and all that. Any gig, you get so much adrenalin pumping, takes a couple hours to come down."

Over the smoke I was holding in my lungs I said, "You almost sound like you're used to it."

"I almost feel like I'm used to it."

I was starting to float. I handed him the joint, thinking: No more. I don't want to lose this conversation.

But I didn't ask him about Bear, or his interview with the flics. "What was it like for you? Being on the road."

"Manic-depressive," he said over a lungful of smoke. Then, after a moment, "Wherever you are, you're rushing or waiting. OK, must be a Holiday Inn because the lamp's here, the phone's there, but is this San Diego, Detroit, or Miami? You play the gig, then unwind till the sun comes up and you crash. Stuff like laundry and bills, the road manager does. You eat in restaurants, and you sleep in a bed that was somebody else's the night before —or that somebody else is sleeping in with you."

I reddened. Was this a tactic from the good old days? End the interview by embarrassing the interviewer?

But we're not in the sixties, Dan. Embarrassment is out. Rude personal questions are in, whether you like it or not. And whether I like it or not.

"Was that . . . disorienting? Sleeping with strangers?"

"No more than the rest of it." He shrugged. "The chicks amazed me, though. Where do they come from? I used to imagine there was this machine in Holiday Inns, like the ice machine, clunking out chicks. What do they do when we're not there? Mick and I got in a thing for a while of asking. 'If you weren't in this hotel room with your clothes off, where would you be?' We never found out. They didn't know."

I could see my next question forming, and it made my heart pound so hard I could hear it. "Was that how Roach met Marie Tréville?"

Dan's eyes swung around to meet mine. For an instant I was afraid— But he didn't move; and I didn't look away.

"No," he said at last. "Some kind of street festival. I don't know about all French people, but she didn't do drugs. Or anything else. Roach couldn't figure her out. Drove him nuts. He was crazy about her."

"How involved were they?"

"Ask Roach." The corner of his mouth twitched. "Or Marie."

"Were they lovers?"

Dan took a toke off the joint and didn't answer.

I tried a different tack. "Why do you think she invited your band to come to Paris with Hands Across the Sea?"

"Ask her."

Useless to get mad; and useless to remind him Marie had already answered that question in the trailer.

"Roach said people give you stuff. That joint he was smoking? And Terry told me drugs around a band are like flies around a garbage truck. Like the sixties—your little old lady on Comm Ave with the peanuts. Does that get to be—"

"The peanuts!" Dan laughed. "Christ! Are you going to print that?"

Not funny. Was that why he kept stonewalling me? Did he think—could he possibly think—I was using Albert Vaux's death and my visit to the police station to scrounge juicy tidbits for *Phases*?

Outrage was evaporating the mist from my brain. But Dan spoke first. "Not just drugs. Every kind of stuff. T-shirts, teddy bears, jewelry, chocolate chip cookies, their pet kitten they named after you. Pictures they drew of you. Videotapes. Explanations of your music. Poems they wrote about you, songs you should record, pages and pages about your childhood or who you were in previous lives. Astrology charts, love letters, hate letters, death threats. Room keys. House keys." The tip of the joint glowed as he inhaled. "Weird, huh?—some kid you never met, writing his term paper about a song you knocked off in an hour."

I had to agree. Nothing in my life came close. As a journalist, my road was always solo. And Larry's hangers-on offered us more conventional bribes for access to power: martinis, party invitations, skyboxes. But to be idolized by strangers, deluged with such bizarre and intimate gifts, only to connect?

"Like they don't get it. That for us it's how you put it together, not take it apart."

"There's a thing in T.S. Eliot," I said. "'And would it have been worth it, after all, To have squeezed the universe into a ball; To say: I am Lazarus, come from the dead, Come back to tell you all— If one, settling a pillow by her head, Should say: That is not what I meant at all.'"

Dan was watching me as if I might expect him to clap or set it to music.

"No big deal." I took the joint. "No reply necessary."

"Say it again."

"That actually was an abridged version—"

"Say it again."

I did.

"I like it. T. S. Eliot?"

"Right." Holding smoke in my lungs. "His biggest hit. Aside from Cats."

"Dude knows how to write."

I smiled as I exhaled. "So do you."

"So do you," said Dan. "I looked up that piece you did on us at the Cambodia demonstration. 'Dan Quasi plays guitar like Fred Astaire dances.'" He grinned. "You can have the peanuts."

I blushed; and wondered how badly my Phases piece would be compromised if I kept letting my own yearning to connect fog my professional objectivity.

"About Roach and Marie—"

"No."

"Whatever kind of relationship they—"

"No," he repeated. "Let it alone."

"Dan. It's not just me."

"Right now it is." He stretched out his legs. "The cops can make their own mistakes tomorrow."

"But maybe they don't have to." Fixing my gaze on the faded knees of his jeans: DMZ between his bare chest and bare feet.

"Maybe they do. They're coming at it the same way as you

—looking for connections between a bunch of things that aren't connected. The reality is: Roach is with Lacey. Marie's married to Victor, and they have been for a long time. Anything that happened before doesn't matter."

"But if—"

"Reality number two," he overrode me. "None of us gave drugs to that kid. If he OD'd, he did it on his own."

"Oh, I see. And the cops, me, Hands Across the Sea, everybody should take your word for it? Sorry, accident, nobody's fault, let's all go home now? Is that reality?"

Dan turned his head away. For a long time he stared at the lamp on the bedside table. I didn't speak either. You get to a point where you're just not in the mood to keep struggling for ways to row, row, row the boat without rocking it.

Finally he said, "If you haven't been through this before, you don't know what you're talking about."

Retorts popped into my head: Oh yeah? How do you know what I've been through? Have you read anything I've written that wasn't about you? or asked me one question about my work or my life?

I took a long slow breath and let it out again. "Then maybe you could tell me."

We waited—for what, I wasn't sure. After what seemed like a very long time, Dan addressed the bedside lamp.

"I had nothing to do with Mickey Ascher getting killed. None of us did. The tabloids didn't care. They wanted a story, so they made one up. OK. Water under the bridge, right? Twenty years, it's history. Then last winter I get a call from my lawyer. Unsolved Mysteries is doing a—what's their word?— dramatization. Fucking déjà vu." He faced me. "My lawyer said I should sue. If I didn't, I was asking for it. Not just that TV show, but who else picked up the idea. 'You're leaving a vacuum' was how he put it. Talk to them or not, you're letting the media—and not just tabloids anymore; everything from Time magazine to talk shows—you're leaving them free to invent some fantasy bullshit version of The Rind. Which would frame how people saw Quasi & Company, and limit what we could do even before we started. I told him, no fucking way. If I once get sucked into this, no matter how, then I lose. If it's a no-win situation, at least I can stick with the music till my time's up."

Be sure you're right and then go ahead. Did the ethics of Davy Crockett apply in the twentieth-century entertainment industry?

"How much time do you think you'll have?"

"Four days, to start." Dan reached toward the night table for cigarettes.

My eyes traced the lamplit curve of his arm. With dope-sharpened vision I watched him tap the pack on the edge of the table. Real cigarettes this time—Camels, like Roach's.

"To get back to the time when my mind was full of wonder," I murmured.

A corner of Dan's mouth curved. He took the cigarette from his lips and handed it to me. "Back before the Holiday Inns. When it was just the five of us and a sound man and a truck, playing the New England circuit." Smiling as he lit another match. "Drive all day, sleep on cots in the attic over the bar, play in some moldy basement with water dripping on the board and pinball machines in the corners."

I tried to picture Dan Quasi and Mickey Ascher sleeping on cots, hauling equipment out of a truck, competing with pinball machines for drinkers' attention. More than twenty years ago—Dan thinner then, probably, the angles of his body sharper. By now I'd lost the image of him I'd carried in my head since D.C. Reaching for it, all I found was this man in front of me.

"You enjoyed that?"

"There was a—hmm. Not purity, exactly. A simplicity about it. A directness. You walk onstage in one of those clubs and you could be Star Trek beaming down on a strange planet. What are those lumps? People or toadstools? Touring it's a whole different trip—they've got one night to see you, bought tickets a month ago, you could shine or suck and all they'll notice is which cuts you do off the album." He took a drag from his cigarette. "But you play for fifty kids who came out to drink beer and get laid—hey, they don't care if the lead break in 'Wonderland' sounds the same as last time. They just care if it rocks."

The glint in his eyes jolted me back to his solo six hours ago on 'Dynamite Wheels.' "It rocked tonight," I said. "Does that count? A couple hundred people and fireworks—not exactly intimate."

Dan laughed. "After a couple thousand, a couple hundred feels pretty damn intimate."

And one person? I almost asked him. How does that feel?

I said, "Will Quasi & Company stick with clubs, then?"

"Can't." He blew out smoke, and added with an impish grin, "If God wanted us to play clubs, He wouldn't have built Madison Square Garden."

I thought he was joking till I noticed that his eyes hadn't changed—deep as Vineyard Sound, glittering like the ring of shark's teeth on Roach's chest—and I remembered The Rind had crashed before they ever reached Madison Square Garden.

"Is that what you want? Back up with the marionettes?"

Dan was still smiling. "Not tonight."

He leaned forward and put his hand on my leg. His fingers were dark as shadows on my white robe, warm as sunshine on my dope-chilled skin.

I blurted out the first question that came to mind. "Will it mess things up if the band gets involved in a police investigation?"

His hand didn't move. "Why do you ask me that?"

I answered silently: Because I've loved you too long from a distance to dare let you come close. Because I don't know what I want, I do know what I want, I promised myself after Larry that I wouldn't let my emotions tangle up my work again and here I am disarmed by the man I'm supposed to be covering. Because it's taken me twenty years to get a shot at the July Fourth cover of Phases, and I'll be damned if I'm going to fuck it up for a rock star.

I said, "I was wondering when I couldn't sleep. How much trouble this might cause."

Dan sat back and folded his arms.

"Or is all publicity good publicity?"

Dan rose abruptly and went to the dresser. He riffled through cassettes; slammed one into the tape deck. Loud music I didn't recognize came blasting from the speakers.

He turned down the volume just enough so I could hear him say, "Publicity? A kid dying during our show?"

I wanted to apologize, to rewind, but the dope had closed in and I couldn't find a way. On the foggy windowpane of my mind only a small clear space was left—just enough for me to see how the faint light was burnishing Dan's shoulders and the ridges of his spine as he stood looking over the tapes.

"No," I shook my head. "No."

Whether that sufficed I couldn't tell. But a few seconds later he shut off the tape.

"Music! Shit." He sat down again on the bed. "Goddam guerrilla warfare."

He reached for his cigarettes. I stood up.

"Thanks," I said. "For the dope and the company."

I walked slowly toward the door. Was he watching me? Would he follow me? I was shivering now, my arms folded tight against my chest. I wanted to turn around, but I couldn't.

"Did it help?"

A shudder. "I don't know yet."

"You can stay here if you want to."

I half turned. He was sitting on the edge of the bed lighting a match.

"You told me that once before," I said.

He looked up at me, mildly surprised. I thought: If you ask me when or where, I swear I'll walk straight out that door.

I pressed my arms tighter under my breasts and waited.

"And did you?" he said.

I shook my head.

"Well, it's up to you."

If I stay, I thought, I'll probably regret it in the morning and for the remaining two days of this trip. If I go, I will certainly regret it in the morning, and possibly for another twenty years.

I walked over and rested my hands on his bare shoulders; kissed the top of his head. He took the hem of my robe in both hands and together we slipped it off over my head.

Chapter 17: Help Me

Sun in my eyes, and the pealing of bells.

As my mind opened, clamlike, it took me a few seconds to grasp where I was. Rumpled sheets, a bare shoulder, the back of a tousled dark head. Dan Quasi's bed in the Hôtel des Fraises.

Well, god damn, I thought. I did it. I spent the night with Dan Quasi.

I shut my eyes and opened them again. Sun, and all those bells. Of course: Sunday morning.

Inching my head around, I could see Dan's gray jacket and black sweater crumpled on the floor. My robe must be down there somewhere—the robe Larry gave me for my birthday last year. Lucky he couldn't see where it and I were right now. *Jesus Christ, Cory, are you out of your mind? A rock musician?*

But instead of cringing I smiled to myself. *Be glad he's not a veep for Revlon.*

The sun was hurting my eyes. I considered getting up to close the shutters, but I didn't want to disturb Dan. Incredible he could sleep so peacefully, when a few hours ago he'd been pressing me into the mattress, twisting his fingers in my hair, exploring my mouth and breasts with his lips, tongue, and teeth till I forgot where we were and who might hear us. Not like making love with Larry. My husband was a thoughtful, careful lover who understood the importance of building to a climax step by step. With Dan it had been the hot hasty passion of dope and rock-&-roll—and for me, too many months without a man.

I'd been terrified at first. Appalled at the abrupt clarity in my head: What am I doing, naked in a hotel room with this stranger? Oh, god, all those Holiday Inns, he must expect, does he want, what if I can't—? I groped for the closeness that had warmed me as we sat talking and couldn't find it. Tried to remember how my blood surged when he spun me around the stage . . . but oh, god, they call it adultery when you're married, with this ring I'm immune, and what if it's true? My fingers fumbling with the button on his jeans: Dan Quasi doesn't wear shorts, that's one fact they'll never read in Phases.

Take it easy, Cory. Not words but Dan's hand hefting my hair, rubbing the back of my neck. His mouth closed over mine, warm and leisurely. *There's no hurry.* And gradually my body accommodated to the shape of his body against me; till my fingers slid inside his jeans, his lips were nibbling my ear, both of us shuddering now, reverberating like plucked strings as we strained to catch each other's rhythm . . . his back taut, chin scraping my cheeks, thighs hard, skin hot . . . and I rose to burst like a firework, our own fête accompli as Dan quickened and erupted like champagne.

He fell asleep just as readily. I lay for a long time with my head nestled into his shoulder, floating in and out of half-dreams, wondering where I'd find myself when morning washed us up like castaways on a public beach.

Now it was morning and I still didn't know. My lover, Dan Quasi. One foot poking out over the end of the bed; his back, hip, and thigh a marble-smooth contour under the sheet. I yearned to touch him but didn't want to wake him up. Maybe he'd feel me watching him and wake up by himself. Smile at me, let me know he was glad to see me. Last night we hadn't taken time to savor each other. I wanted to make love with him now in the open light —get to know him slowly, with my eyes, my fingers, my skin, my tongue. All of him, from his earlobes to his bony toes.

Dan's shoulder shifted and he made a small disturbed groan. My hand moved to stroke his hair—

But what if he turns his head and I can tell he doesn't remember who I am?—or wishes I hadn't stayed?

He muttered something. I pondered. Then I slid my hand over his waist and up into the coarse curly hair on his chest.

Dan rolled toward me, slinging one leg over mine. His eyes opened: not surprised or curious but as if it were perfectly natural I should be here. His fingers stroked my arm, then played an arpeggio up to my neck and drew my head forward till his lips were brushing mine. His tongue flickered around the corner of my mouth.

A syncopated *rat-ta-tat* on the door. Dan pulled away. "Hold on, Terry."

Instantly I was wide awake. I hauled the sheet up to my chin, but that made me feel so much like Doris Day that I threw it off again. Dan was shaking out his jeans, looking for a leg.

I clambered out of bed and grabbed my robe.

It shocked me a little that he didn't ask if I minded before he opened the door. I felt more naked now, waiting to see Terry's reaction, than I had all night.

But Terry only lifted his eyebrows and said, "Hi, Cory."

"What's up?" asked Dan.

"You heard about Bear?"

Dan confirmed it with a nod and a grimace. For a moment they commiserated wordlessly. Then Terry said, "I just found out. Little Sheila called. Did you hear the other bombshell? Hands is kicking us out."

"Fuck!"

"Not officially. She gave me a bunch of crap about electrical problems on the boat—"

"Sure. So we won't sue." Dan flapped a dark blue T-shirt out of the suitcase on the dresser. "What about EuroDisney?"

Terry's answer was a thumbs-down. "She waffled so hard in so many directions, I could tell even she smelled a rat."

For a moment Dan stood with his head and one arm inside the T-shirt. I wished I could see his face—not that I couldn't guess his reaction. When he finally wriggled on through, he said only, "Did you call Marie?"

"Yup. N.A. I left a message."

"François?"

"Not yet. Should I?"

"Yeah. Make sure he's heard; see if he knows anything. And tell him to tell Neil."

"Nobody else is up yet."

"Good. Let 'em sleep."

Terry nodded to both of us and closed the door as he left.

I could see Dan wouldn't be wanting breakfast in bed or a shower for two or any of the other transitions lovers have devised to ease the morning-after split. Still, I refused to walk out like one more chick from the Holiday Inn ice machine.

"Anything I can do?"

He reached for his cigarettes. "No." It was automatic.

I stood for a moment combing my fingers through my hair, unsnarling the tangles his hands had left. I wanted to memorize this scene: the rumpled bed, Dan's jacket and sweater on the floor, the tape deck, the suitcases, the bright slats of the shutters. My personal bootleg tape of Dan Quasi.

I walked over and touched his arm. "See you later."

"Cory." He turned to kiss me goodbye. "Thanks."

As I padded down the stairs to my room, I wondered why it mattered to me to believe his "thanks" hadn't been for spending the night but for asking if I could help.

The desk clerk handed me two messages when I came down for breakfast. One was from John Otis: thanks for your late-night report, talk to you in the morning.

The other was from Marian Thorne.

Oh, hell, I thought, feeling my cheeks redden. Now the hotel staff knows I wasn't in my own room, and Marian knows—

"Cory! Bonjour!" Steve Connelly's jovial voice pinned me from the dining room doorway. "Where've you been?"

"What are you doing here?" I asked him before I thought.

In khakis and a yellow pullover sweater, Steve looked as wholesome as a glass of orange juice. "Looking for you. Judith sent me down to the square to buy pastries and invite you over for breakfast."

He held up a plump white paper bag whose aroma scored a direct hit with my stomach. "Well, thanks, but I'm afraid—"

"Have you heard what's happened with Hands Across the Sea and the band?"

Do I confess? No. "What?"

"They've canceled the rest of their performances."

Mr. Cheerful. Like a TV newscaster announcing a bombing. "Why?"

Steve glanced at the desk clerk and lowered his voice. "Trust me, you really should come for breakfast."

Breaking bread (or cake) with Steve and the Crofts was not how I felt like spending the rest of this morning. But Dan's bitter remark echoed in my head: "Music? Goddam guerrilla warfare."

If this is war, better hit the trenches.

"Let me get a sweater."

We walked through cobbled streets whitewashed with light, past wooden shutters closed to let in the fine June air and shut out the hot sun. Two small boys bicycled unsteadily past us with baguettes in their panniers. I slung my sweater over my shoulder.

"You missed the crowning of the Strawberry Queen," said Steve. "Unless you've been up for a while?"

I smiled evasively. "How was it?"

"Quite the event. The d'Aumonts and the Trévilles were there, upholding the honor of Fraises-des-Bois. The mayor said you came to the police station last night."

A mass of blue and yellow lupines crowded against a wrought-iron fence. "Does it need upholding?"

"After that? Are you kidding?" Steve plucked the head off a lupine that had ventured through the bars. "Or didn't you hear about the lab report?"

My heart sank. "No. What—?"

"Drug overdose. Prescription sleeping pills. A narcotic sold under the brand name Sominol. In that champagne the band had onstage."

"They got the bottle back from that girl?" He nodded. "And ran the tests already?"

"So you know these guys are not fooling around." Steve's fingers shredded the petals into confetti. "They're proud of their town; and I can tell you, they are not happy with Quasi & Company."

"Have they traced the Sominol?"

"Not yet."

"Then why would they think Quasi & Company had anything to do with it?"

"Ha!" As if this was hilarious. "You mean aside from a kid on their crew dropped dead on their stage during their show from a drugged bottle of champagne nobody touched but them? Gosh, Cory, you got me!"

Max and Judith's house was a stucco cube with a steep tiled roof, large wooden-shuttered windows, and a white board fence. Half of its tiny yard was a voluptuous garden: cascades of multicolored roses, peonies the size of soup bowls, towering bluebells and hollyhocks. In my head a sitar whined the intro to "One More Hit to Wonderland," The Rind's psychedelic odyssey. I wished I'd smoked some of Dan's dope before I left the Hôtel des Fraises.

We found Judith in the kitchen measuring out scoops of coffee. She greeted us and handed Steve a tray. I arranged the pastries on a yellow plate. No magic mushrooms here. Just the standard cozy Sunday-morning aromas, sounds, and props: cups and saucers, a crockery pitcher of grapefruit juice, confiture jars with checkered lids, a blue-and-white cow creamer, folded linen napkins.

Max sat out back on the graveled patio, reading a newspaper at a white wrought-iron table. "Good morning." He raised his sleek badger's head. "Lovely day, isn't it?"

We chatted about the fine weather till Judith brought the coffee. I complimented her garden, and she told me they'd bought this house clefs-en-main from a model at a home show—too small for the piano and most of the books, but with the kids out of the nest—

Judith's blonde curls in the sun blended with the stucco wall behind her head. If I were back at the hotel I could find out what Quasi & Company planned to do about getting booted. (From an urban boat cruise and EuroDisney: how wickedly ironic!) Victor Tréville no doubt had woken up Governor Leroy, who might already be on the phone with John Otis . . . Whereas a week from now I'd have all the time in the world for chitchat about equity and hardwood floors over French roast on Newbury Street.

"Max." Steve spooned strawberry jam onto a croissant. "Any news from Monsieur d'Aumont?"

"Oh, for heaven's sake, Steve," said Judith. "Cory doesn't want to hear that while she's eating."

I assured her that indeed I did.

"The police are questioning the band at their hotel," Max told us. "Georges said Dan Quasi made a favorable impression last night."

I dabbed at imaginary crumbs to hide my face.

"No arrests at this point, I shouldn't think. Everyone's anxious to keep it out of the press until they can announce a result."

"They've canceled the rest of Quasi & Company's shows," Steve said.

"Err on the side of caution, eh? Now the drug's identified, it shouldn't take long. Confirm whose it was, legal or illegal, et cetera. Not that there can be any excuse for putting sleeping pills in that bottle. Much less leaving it open on a public stage, where anyone might get it."

"Hold on. You're not—" Start from the beginning, Cory. "Are you saying the police believe Quasi & Company drugged their own champagne?"

Max's eyebrows went up in surprise.

"Not to kill anybody," Judith hastened to reassure me. "Everyone understands that. Don't they, Max? It's different in America."

"But they didn't." I looked back and forth from Judith to Max. "I thought— Didn't Dan Quasi tell Commissaire Guerin last night?"

"Of course." Max nodded. Meaning that although the cops took it for granted the band spiked the kool-ade, they didn't expect them to admit it.

"Are they looking at everyone else who was there? Who danced onstage, or handled the bottle?"

"Who else had a chance?" said Steve. "We're talking about
—what?—five minutes at the most."

"What about Albert Vaux?"

"Why would he put drugs in champagne and then drink it?"
Judith objected.

"Why would the band?"

"Well, to get high! Isn't that what they do? Tune in, turn
on . . . and what's the other one?"

"It's what Albert Vaux did. At least he sure was acting high
before the show. And the other night in Montmartre, too. But for
Quasi & Company, this was a job."

"Oh, come on, Cory." Steve refilled my coffee cup.
"They've been drugging it up ever since the plane landed."

"Not onstage."

"Anyway, nobody in Fraises-des-Bois is into that."

"Into what? Rock-&-roll? Champagne? Sleeping pills?"

Judith pushed the blue-and-white cow toward me. "Cream?"

Max's mouth pursed in mock horror. "About our champagne
we French are very reverent."

"And Quasi & Company are reverent about their music.
That's why they're here."

"Drugs, sex, and rock-&-roll. A time-honored tradition, isn't
it?"

Judith poured me the last drops of coffee. "Back in a jiffy."

Steve leaned across the table. "The point is, Cory, this isn't
just a question of facts. Max was explaining— Will you tell her?"

With a little sigh, Max reached for a tarte aux pommes.
"There's also a question of jurisdiction. In other towns, a suspicious death could be handled by the mayor and the Commissaire
de Police. However, Fraises-des-Bois is in Victor Tréville's *arrondissement* of Brière-Marne. Which is part of Marne-la-Vallée,
where Tréville also holds a government planning position."

"So you're saying— Albert Vaux died on Victor Tréville's
turf?"

"Doubly so. And Georges d'Aumont's and Nestor Guerin's
turf as well."

Merde! That shed a whole new light on Victor's one-man

fireworks display last night.

"Officially it's Guerin's investigation," Max continued before I could rewind. "I think it's safe to say he'd like to reach closure as soon as humanly possible."

"Like today," said Steve. "Before the work week starts and the French government comes charging in, while we're trying to get our ambassadors home to Boston."

"But this only happened, what? Twelve hours ago?"

"Yeah. Not easy. We're dealing with"—Steve ticked them off on his fingers—"high stakes, multiple interests, time pressure, and media pressure. But worth it if we can head off an international incident."

I surmised from that "we" that Steve had appointed himself Hands Across the Sea's point man in Marne-la-Vallée. What did that make me? Dale Evans?

"Our guys overruled Monsieur Tréville about Quasi & Company coming to France. Now we've got to face the consequences. Set aside our biases and find a mutually acceptable solution."

Behind his head the sun was casting stripes down the stucco wall, scalloping a shadow pattern under a hanging vine. Outwardly this was still an ordinary peaceful Sunday morning. A bee nosed around in the lid of a jam jar on the table. Somewhere far away a church bell rang.

While at the Hôtel des Fraises, the flics might be steering Dan, Terry, Roach, Niko, and/or Lacey toward a French jail instead of the plane back to Boston.

"Find a mutually acceptable solution?" I couldn't help myself. "What about conduct an investigation? Collect evidence? Interview witnesses?"

"Sure. That's happening now. Like Max said. It shouldn't take long, with what we already know."

"What do we know, Steve? Albert Vaux took an overdose of sleeping pills. His or someone else's? A residue was found in a champagne bottle he drank from. Put there how? When? Where? By whom?"

"OK, so far it's just circumstantial—"

"Not even circumstantial. He grabbed the bottle from Roach and chugged it. Whose fault is that?"

"Where did Roach get it? He swiped it from Hands Across the Sea."

"Who says it was the same bottle? Were you watching it the whole time? How many other people touched it? Has it been fingerprinted? I saw Roach and Niko drinking champagne onstage. If it was laced with narcotics, why didn't it knock them out?"

"Bravo!" Judith clapped from the doorway. "Cory, you should be a detective."

"Hm. Well." Max took another bite of apple tart.

"Was it the same bottle? Yes," said Steve. "Roach opened it onstage near the end of the show. That narrows the field and the window of opportunity. If it had been sitting up there uncorked for an hour, anyone could have doctored it. As it stands, the Sominol had to be added during those few minutes it was passed around the stage. Why weren't Roach and Niko knocked out? Because they hardly drank any. Interesting, huh? Sneak it out from the trailer, pop the cork, but don't drink it. Give it to a roadie. Albert Vaux, hired by—guess who?—Victor Tréville."

He held out his cup to Judith, who'd returned with fresh coffee.

"And Victor Tréville fits in the picture how?" I asked him.

"He doesn't," said Steve. "Sorry. Tangent. Pass the cream?"

Did that slip mean Steve knew about Roach and Marie? How? From Lacey? Surely not from Victor.

More likely he was alluding to the threatening note that forced Victor Tréville to evacuate his office. Anything John Otis had told me, Jerry Leroy undoubtedly had told his point man in Marne-la-Vallée.

I rose. "I've got to be going."

Judith protested: with the Défilé des Chars coming up, wouldn't I stay and watch the parade with them? Max offered me another croissant. Steve, to my relief, said he'd walk me to the gate.

Inside the house he told me to wait just a second. I stood on the olive-green carpet feeling as if I'd been stranded in a French episode of *The Twilight Zone* until he came back carrying a book.

"I didn't want to show you this in front of Max and Judith."

We strolled down the walk. It wasn't a real book but bound page proofs in a blue paper cover.

"*Inside the Rind*, by Graham Douglas. Go ahead. Open it."

"No thanks. It's still ticking."

"It's set to go off three weeks from now." Under his casual tone Steve's voice was sharp. "Same release date as Unsolved Mysteries. Right before our Phases piece on Quasi & Company's trip to France with Hands Across the Sea."

I opened the cover, but my eyes refused to focus.

"Douglas is full of interesting stories. Like Mickey Ascher's fall into heroin addiction, with a little help from his friends."

The underside of Steve's chin reflected his yellow sweater. Against the backdrop of Judith Croft's hollyhocks and bluebells he looked like a sun-filled TV commercial for one of those essential feminine products too intimate to name.

"And the famous drug bust. Mickey threw a party to celebrate The Rind's new album, but for some reason Dan Quasi never showed up. The cops did, though. Nailed Mickey on enough charges to put him away for life. Douglas says, no question they were tipped off."

"By who?" I folded my arms.

"The same best buddy who disappeared the minute Mickey was behind bars. Turned up again the night he came home. Not for the party but after. Went to Mick's condo, drank champagne with him, and then beat him to death with the empty bottle to stop him taking back control of his band."

"And you believe this crap? Just because it's in a book? Wake up, Steve! Smell the coffee! Any money-grubbing twit can publish the exclusive inside story on a celebrity scandal."

"I checked the facts with the station." Steve's mouth was a tight line. "Everything matches up."

"What facts? Mickey Ascher was a junkie? Dan Quasi missed a party? He left town while Mick was in rehab? So what?"

"So if I was writing a magazine feature on Quasi & Company, I'd think this whole deal was one hell of a strange coincidence."

I stared at him.

"A major musician reuniting a famous band, whether he calls it that or not, with zero publicity? On a bush-league yuppie exchange program? No taping, no cameras—*nothing.* Right? Yet on the other hand"—he lifted it—"who's his best friend? Cory Goodwin of Phases. Sharing the band's limo. Staying at their hotel. Partying with them after the show. Sitting in on rehearsals."

My face felt hot. "You've partied with them more than I have. You rode in their limo, went to their sound check—"

"And every time I've tried to talk to Dan Quasi I get stonewalled."

What could I say? To Steve Connelly, of course it didn't make sense that Dan would open up to a journalist and shut out a radio man. But it wasn't as a journalist I'd gone to his room last night; and it wasn't as a musician he'd asked me to stay.

"Think about it, Cory. That's all I ask. And not just professionally. If half of what Graham Douglas says is true, we're dealing with dangerous people here. Who've made a career out of breaking the rules. I know Dan Quasi is a brilliant guitar player, but as a human being? This is a guy who's never had to compromise. Why shouldn't he act like the messiah, when that's how everybody treats him?"

He paused as if he expected me to answer.

"If he wasn't involved in Mickey Ascher's murder, why disappear? Tell me that. Where's he been hiding for twenty years? Top of the charts, top of his powers—"

I held out the book. "Thanks. Gotta go."

"No, you keep it." Steve's hands went behind his back. "See for yourself."

> *You open up your front door*
> *And he's inside waiting for you!*

The angry beat we'd marched to in D.C. seemed to shimmer off the hot asphalt as I stalked down the street. Mickey Ascher's voice or Niko's? Quasi & Company or The Rind? Did anybody besides me believe it mattered?

Watch out, friend, when you're in the hands
Of the Government Man!

Fuck you! I turned to shout silently at Steve Connelly. Fuck your cloak-and-dagger, fuck your string-pulling, fuck your Graham Douglas, your Jerry Leroy, your radio station, and fuck your goddam speculations! So Dan Quasi's playing messiah if he'll talk to me but not you? So the band must have drugged the champagne that killed Albert Vaux, since they turned Mickey Ascher into a junkie? So it's obvious who was behind the drug bust and murder now that Dougie's pointed the finger? Speaking of the finger—

I wallowed in being pissed off until I reached the main street. Then my mind kicked back in. Good that I had the book. Keep it out of circulation. See exactly what bombs Dougie planned to drop. Check his history of The Rind against Dan's. Maybe even figure out a counterattack.

Slow down, Cory. Journalists' Rule #1: *Banish preconceptions.* Steve was right about that much: my personal biases didn't belong in this picture, any more than Victor Tréville's. I wasn't here to play defense against him or against Graham Douglas.

My job was offense. Take risks and take charge.

Find out who put the Sominol in the champagne, with evidence to prove it.

Facts? Roach opened the bottle onstage. He and Niko both drank from it, and maybe an audience member or two, before Albert Vaux snatched it and chugged the rest. A narrow window of opportunity; a short suspect list.

Even narrower than Steve had said. No one person held onto that bottle for more than twenty or thirty seconds.

Questions: Was Sominol sold in both France and the U.S.? Did anyone in the band use it?

Was it soluble in champagne? Would the pill-popper have to grind up tablets, or empty out capsules, and carry the powder ready for a quick dump? In a vial? A rolling paper?

Who'd be reckless enough to drop drugs in a bottle of champagne on a public stage, in full view of a couple hundred people?

But then, who knew the band would bring a bottle of champagne onstage? Nobody—not even Roach.

There were always drinks for the musicians: a Coke cup on a speaker, a beer beside a guitar case. A well-prepared opportunist could be pretty sure of drugging *somebody*. They just couldn't count on *who*.

Conclusion? If this attack had a target, it wasn't Albert Vaux.

I plucked a daisy from the side of the road. Breakfast chez Croft hadn't been a total loss. After being grilled by the flics all morning, Dan would probably welcome the leads I'd collected. Not that I would let my biases affect my work . . . but didn't my work include stopping the French bureaucracy and Hands Across the Sea from wrecking this exchange program by firing Quasi & Company?

Had he looked for me at breakfast? I twirled the daisy in my fingers. Did he wonder where I'd gone? I plucked a petal: *Il m'aime un peu, il m'aime beaucoup . . .* In France you get better odds, six out of seven. *Il m'aime passionément, il m'aime à la folie . . .*

Up the hill and into the square. All quiet at the Hôtel des Fraises. No truck parked outside, no music floating across the cobblestones. The lobby was empty. In the dining room, Quasi & Company's instruments were set up, but—oh, yes! There was Terry behind the sound board. And next to him, a familiar shoulder in a dark blue T-shirt.

He was fiddling with some piece of equipment, peering, poking, frowning in concentration. For a few seconds I stood in the doorway just savoring the sight of him.

"Hi, Cory," said Terry.

Dan might rather not be interrupted, but I didn't want to wait.

I held out the book.

"Where'd you get that?" Terry asked.

I explained: breakfast, Steve, Max, Mayor d'Aumont—

Was that a nod, or was Dan ignoring me?

"We're sort of busy right now," Terry said kindly. "Can it wait till after the parade?"

"The parade?"

"Gaff," said Dan. Terry handed him a roll of duct tape. Dan tore off a piece and rolled it carefully around a spliced wire.

"Monsieur Qua-see?" It was the desk clerk. "Téléphone."

Dan and Terry exchanged a look: the cops again.

I vetoed my impulse to follow him to the lobby. Not when he was like this. If Terry could take it, slicing the sheathing off wires while the band's future might be unfolding in that phone booth, so could I.

"Cory, give me that gaff, will you?"

I tossed Terry the tape and went after Dan.

He was just coming out of the booth. "Any news?" I asked.

Dan shook his head. I couldn't tell if that meant there wasn't or he didn't want to talk about it. His face was unreadable. I had to remind myself that I'd spent last night curled up against those uncompromising shoulders to keep from backing off.

"You talked to the police?"

"Yeah."

"No arrests, no breakthroughs?"

"Not yet."

"Is Hands still saying there's an electrical problem on the boat?"

"Depends who you talk to. Basically they're saying whatever gets us off the schedule and them off the hook."

"So what's next?"

"The parade." He started toward the front desk. "See you later."

I flushed as if he'd slapped me. Was I so indistinguishable from a groupie chasing him across a hotel lobby?

I caught his arm. "Dan, wait."

The muscles flexed; and I remembered this arm's soft underside against my neck, veined like the back of his hand, and felt a throb of warmth that made it all the more urgent not to let him go. "Look, I know you're busy, but I've just been talking to Steve Connelly, who gave me that book, and Max Croft, who lives here and knows the local power structure, and I thought—"

"I can't do this now, Cory." His blue eyes opaque. "You deal with your magazine and let me deal with the band, OK?"

My hand fell away. Dan walked around the desk and out the back door.

I retraced my steps with my head spinning like the Mad Hatter's Teacups. I've just spent an hour defending you and scouting for you, I spent last night making love with you, and that's all you've got to say?

In the dining room Terry was still snipping and taping. I picked up the book I'd left on the table.

"Did you see it?"

I stared at him without comprehension.

"Did you see the float?"

If acid in the kool-ade is passé, I thought, they'll never prove it by me. I felt as if someone had dropped a tab in my coffee—as if everything around me was gently heaving in and out, changing shape, sparkling with that ultra-vividness which is a sure sign it's not real.

"Open the curtains."

I walked over to the windows along the back of the dining room.

What I expected was M. Vlaemenck's garden, tidy flowerbeds bordering a square of lawn. Instead, in the middle of the lawn sat a flatbed, and on it rose a twelve-foot-high pink-and-blue fairy-tale castle. Children swarmed around with scissors and paste pots. Two mothers with staple guns were draping brown paper over an exposed section of chicken-wire frame. A young father on a ladder fastened a banner to the top of a conical turret. And a stone's throw from my window, Denise the formerly shy waitress was gesturing animatedly to Dan Quasi, who stood with his arm around Lena Michel's shoulders.

Chapter 18: Already Gone

"It's for the parade," Terry explained. "They've got groups all over town making floats. The tractor's coming to pick it up in half an hour. Denise wants musicians on the drawbridge, so we're wiring speakers—"

I watched Denise's hands moving, Dan listening intently, Lena laughing as she tried to translate.

Say, a hundred and fifty days a year on the road. Some of those nights he must have dodged the crowd around the elevator and slept alone. Other nights—who knows?—maybe he took on three or four. Say, a hundred women a year for seven years. And I thought he'd recognize I was different.

Il m'aime un peu. Il m'aime à la folie. Il m'aime pas du tout.

Lacey staggered past the window with a little boy on her shoulders. He was clutching a pot in one hand, a brush in the other, swiping at the castle's conical rooftops, spattering himself and Lacey's hair with blue paint. Niko crouched at the edge of the flatbed, opening the petals of crepe-paper flowers with two teenage girls.

Dan hadn't been surprised by Graham Douglas's book. He must have known months ago that Dougie was preparing an exposé on The Rind. What better counterattack than to bring the band to France with Hands Across the Sea? With no taping, no filming, and no media coverage, all Quasi & Company had to do was keep the customers satisfied—and leave their post-tour publicity to the lady from Phases.

They can't control what I write, I'd reassured myself. But they could control what I saw. I'd sat in on rehearsals, clapped at performances, listened to late-night stories, and wound up like a classic groupie, in bed with the leader of the band. Three days of asking questions and taking notes, and what had I got? Exactly what Dan Quasi wanted. Not a review of the music. Not the inside scoop on why The Rind broke up. Not the key to the unsolved mystery of Mickey Ascher's murder. Just a starry-eyed diary of life in a French hotel with five rock musicians.

A little girl with a pink hair ribbon rammed her tricycle into Lacey's legs. Roach picked her up, bike and all, and set her down outside the flowerbeds.

Was this the real performance? Was I, not Hands Across the Sea, the real audience?

Denise saw me in the window and waved. She had on a Rind T-shirt that must have been Roach's and an equally outsized grin. I forced a smile and waved back.

Lena turned, still laughing at some joke of Dan's. She pressed her hands against the glass and mouthed: "Come help!"

Hah! I thought. But what were my choices? Go call John Otis and hear today's reasons why I should move to the Ritz, or climb back into the saddle?

You're not a spectator, Cory. You're not a pawn. You're a journalist. If this is a performance, review it. And if Dan Quasi can change horses in midstream, damn his shallow self-centered soul, so can you.

So I attached myself to Terry, Mr. Wizard's lovely assistant, and helped him carry out the sound system. Then I got a job from one of the mothers cutting crenelations.

The next half hour rippled by like a hallucination. We pasted and painted, snipped and stapled, till time ran out and the float committee declared the castle finished. All of us together rolled it around the hotel into the square. Denise rode inside with the tape deck. The jubilation on her face when Dan had asked her if she wanted to run sound almost made up for the fist in my stomach when he wiped a streak of paint off Lena's cheek.

Now he was kneeling on the flatbed talking to Denise through the chicken wire. Like a fish in water, Dan Quasi in his band, with an entourage for support and an audience for applause. And all these years I'd imagined he was a loner, trapped behind a microphone with his silver guitar. I hadn't understood how many power amps and effects boxes, wires and speakers, sound engineers, crewmen, and backup musicians it takes to produce a solo.

"Lacey, have you seen yourself?" Niko asked as we stood admiring our work. "You look like one of those blue-haired ladies with the poodles."

"Am I blue?" Lacey sang. "Am I blue?" She pirouetted on the cobblestones, drawing stares from some of the parents.

Terry had left to walk Lena to the bus. Though the others had tried to talk her into staying for the parade, she insisted she needed to turn her Jackson Pollack shirt back into an Armani before lunch with her hosts in Paris.

"Well, *moi* is off to hit the showers," Niko declared. "*Je suis tout en collant!* That's French for 'I'm covered with glue.'"

"Were those chicks teaching you French?" Roach slapped him on the back. "What else did you pick up?"

Niko answered him with an international obscene gesture.

Where Dan had gone I wasn't sure—into the hotel, presumably. I did know I wasn't eager to run into him. Nor, for that matter, to say goodbye to this sunny suburban Sunday morning and hello again to the underworld. So I intercepted Roach at the door; which, as it turned out, was my best move all day.

"Got a minute?"

He shrugged. Taking this for a yes, I followed him inside. Lacey had gone on ahead to grab dibs on the first-floor bath. Roach flopped onto the sofa where Terry and I had shared a pot of cocoa two nights ago. I cringed as his motley jeans hit the upholstery . . . but let M. Vlaemenck worry about wet paint. I had my hands full looking out for his village.

"Roach." I was in no mood to beat around the bush. "Did you put sleeping pills, or anything else, in that champagne?"

His nostrils flared in amusement. "Like I told the cops ten times. No."

"Do you have any idea who did? Or when?"

"Nope." He stretched out his legs. "Not who, not when, not how, not why, not nothin'."

Ask mechanical questions and get mechanical answers. So I switched formats. Could Roach take me through last night step by step, from the moment he decided to liberate a bottle of champagne until Bear collapsed?

His eyebrows went up: Why? I said that however good the French police might be, I remembered enough of the Mickey Ascher investigation that I'd rather not leave this one to an outfit that might be biased against anybody who, shall we say, wasn't local.

Roach grinned, nodded and stretched.

"Especially if the locals think one of their wives may have a soft spot for one of the suspects."

"Ha!" His knuckles cracked approvingly. "No shit! Give 'em a noose and they'd skip the Q and A, huh?" He straightened up. "I guess I am the chief suspect. They spent more time on me than anybody else. More cops, too."

His pride was so patent I had to smile. "What'd you tell them?"

"Nothin'. Like I said, that's what I know."

Yeah, I thought. You and me both. "OK, then. The champagne. You took it onstage . . . ?"

"Yup. Why waste free booze? I stuck it behind that back wall thing where we were waiting. We did the show, and I forgot about it till the fireworks started, on 'I'm the One.' When we hit Dan's lead break, I reached around and there's the bottle, right where I left it. Yank out the cork, aim in the direction of my mouth—"

"Wait." The back of my scalp prickled. "Yank out the cork?"

"Yeah. I've got my bass—"

"Hold on." Goosebumps were skittering down the outside of my calves now. "What about the wire cage on the outside? And the foil?"

"Didn't mess with that shit. Just found a cork and jammed it in there. Figured we'd be drinking—"

I interrupted again. "You jammed a cork in. Meaning the bottle was already open?"

"Sure. All of 'em were. Mostly empty, but not this baby." Roach folded one leg across the other. "I found a wine cork. Champagne ones, they're like mushroom-shaped and you can't get 'em back in. This way, a twist and a yank and out she pops."

Sure, echoed my mind. The French police wouldn't have asked Roach what he meant by "open the bottle." Everyone knew:

one unfoiled, unwired, and uncorked it, and then one drank. Who but an American—a loud-mouthed, bushy-haired Texas hippie— would save an open bottle of champagne?

"Was that all you wanted?" Shifting his weight, ready to leave.

"Almost." Think fast, Cory.

I asked him what the chances were someone could have pulled out the cork, dropped in sleeping pills, and replaced both cork and bottle during the set without his noticing. Easy, he said. If the bubbly really was drugged, that'd be how it went down. But, frog cops, who knows? Bear might've just pigged his brains out on one thing and another, or offed himself, and they didn't want it getting out.

"How high was Bear? Could you tell? Did he act suicidal at all?"

Roach shrugged. "He was for shit as a techie, is all I can tell you. More hangin' out than doing the job. Same as the friggin' cops, man. What the fuck kind of investigation is that? Stuck on The Rind like a broken record—'Government Man,' protest marches, same old crapola—"

"Including your thing with Marie Tréville?"

"Ha!" He guffawed. "Man, did they tippy-toe around that one! You ask me, her old man's got these guys by the balls." He sprawled back against the sofa. "I came this close to tellin' 'em: Yeah, Marie and me, we used to fuck like bunnies! Every chance we got. In the bathtub, on the roof, back seat of the limo— Except, Lacey."

Well, damn! Had I and the flics and Team Leroy all been poking down the wrong rabbit hole? Was it possible the root of this whole briar patch wasn't revenge, ambition, politics, or cover-ups, but plain old sex?

"Is that why— Did you take this gig so you could see Marie again?"

"Wasn't my call." He rose. "Gotta go. Lacey'll kill me if I miss the parade."

He headed for the elevator. I sat right where I was.

Did I believe Roach's double-barreled revelation? Yes. I did.

Could I prove it? Could he? Could anybody?

The flics might be able to. If they searched the trash from the stage area, they should find the wine cork he'd used to stopper the champagne bottle.

What froze me on this sofa was the window of opportunity that had just opened from a few minutes to an hour or more. And with it, a suspect list that had expanded from Roach, Niko, and Albert Vaux to anybody on that stage.

Sneaking past the cops, over the chain, and up the steps wouldn't have been easy, but it wouldn't take a magician.

If you were in the band or the crew? Piece of cake.

Other than having no motive, I was a plausible suspect. So was Dan Quasi.

So, Cory! What are you going to do about it?

I'd seen my dad face this question many times. *Impaled on the horns of a dilemma,* my mom and I call it. Balancing a citizen's obligation to report vital information to the police against using it to solve the problem.

It wasn't a hard decision. No way was I telling the flics that Quasi & Company's bass player was an old lover of Victor Tréville's wife—not with Tréville looming behind them like a puppeteer. And if I withheld that, how could I give them the champagne cork?

In one swift move I rose from the sofa, cut in front of a family meandering toward the elevator, and stepped into the phone booth.

"Allo?"

"Marian, bonjour. Cory ici."

"Chérie," came Marian Thorne's thin voice, "I'm so glad to hear from you. What's this about someone being poisoned at the Fête des Fraises?"

Poisoned. Merde.

I filled her in on last night's events. "But how did you find out?" Thinking: If this has already hit the media—

"Oh, well, I phoned the Trévilles." Marian sounded pleased with herself. "And what a surprise when Victor told me your band sent him a bomb threat!"

"Marian! He told you that? What did he say?"

She explained. It was Marie she'd called, to ask how things were going with Hands Across the Sea; but her husband answered both the phone and the question. "He was quite exercised, even for Victor. Full of dire innuendo. Of course, since he wouldn't tell me what *espèce d'éclat* he thinks they're plotting, I was less than sympathetic."

"He claims Quasi & Company are plotting something? Beyond the sleeping pills in the champagne?"

"Oh, yes. Why else should they turn up in his arrondissement instead of their proper hotel in Paris? And threaten to blow him sky high? I got the impression of . . . well, hardly paranoia, under the circumstances, but certainly an idée fixe."

"But no particulars. Was he being dodgy, or just not sure?"

"Difficult to say. One takes Victor with a grain of salt; still, I couldn't tell if he truly does fear for his safety, or his position, which given French politics is delicate if not precarious, one foot in Brière and one at the far end of Marne-la-Vallée, or if he simply can't think why else your *mecs américains* would play for his wife's little exchange program. I wish I could."

"No. This is very helpful, Marian. I appreciate it."

"Mais bien sur." A moment's hesitation. "But it wasn't about les Tréville or the band I called you, chérie. I wanted to ask when you might come by for a longer visit before you go home."

Immediately I was wary. "I'll have to check." Although I couldn't imagine Larry pressing her from Boston to invite me, this had the sound of a family summons. "Can I get back to you?"

"By all means," she acceded graciously. "I rather hoped you might stop in today for coffee. 'Complacencies of the peignoir,' tu sais."

Her light tone hadn't changed; but that phrase from Wallace Stevens's "Sunday Morning" brought me up short. Yes, it was an acknowledgment of all the Sundays she and Larry and I had measured out in coffee spoons. An invitation to search for lost time, if that's what I wanted. Perhaps for her, too: Marian couldn't have many old friends left in Paris with whom to share the poems we used to recite over Sunday morning coffee. I'd helped her then by endorsing Larry's ties to his past; she'd helped me by endorsing my place in his present.

But that was seven summers ago. Marian wasn't inviting her great-nephew and his girlfriend now. She was inviting *me*. Cory Goodwin.

"Marian," I stammered, "thank you. I'd love to."

"Berthe brings me the papers these days, but she's gone off to her daughter's. I haven't anything to offer you but cheese and fruit, I'm afraid."

"Perfect. I'll pick up some bread on my way to the bus."

"Thank you, chérie."

I hung up the phone and leaned against the cool wall. I felt like Prince Andre opening his eyes after the great battle in *War and Peace* onto empty blue sky.

> *Shall she not find in comforts of the sun,*
> *. . . Things to be cherished like the thought of heaven?*

Why *did* I keep hurling myself into other people's conflicts? Dan Quasi wanted to deal with his band alone? Fine.

Take risks, take charge, and take off!

Chapter 19: Another Park, Another Sunday

The town lay hushed in the midday sun when Paladin stepped into the street. She paused to survey the square. Should anyone be watching her from the hotel windows, which Paladin admitted wasn't likely, he would see from her defiant stance that this was no gunslinger to trifle with.

She strode down the hill with her camera cocked, her notebook and tape recorder loaded and ready in their holsters. Return with us now to those thrilling days of yesteryear! Have pen, will travel!

After changing into a sweater, jacket, and slacks that would see me through the rest of today's events, I'd reviewed my notes. John Otis had left me another phone message which I didn't return: international cooperation, assured by French police, utmost discretion, media blackout, not over there to investigate, hosts, ambassadors, interviews, press releases.

Right. No problem.

Then there was Phases.

I had plenty of material. What I lacked was a story. Specifically, a story newsworthy enough for Rik Green's July 4 cover which I was willing to write.

Find me a fire, he'd said. How about Quasi & Company rising like a phoenix from The Rind's ashes, only for a young crewman to crash and burn on their stage? No question Rik would buy it. But how many ethical lines would I have to cross, how many secrets would I have to betray, to sell it?

It wasn't a fire I needed so much as an angle.

Albert Vaux's death could be viewed as a small-town tragedy or an international hot potato. Either way, it was an unsolved mystery. The wine cork in the champagne bottle might be the clue that would solve it.

I'm a journalist, not a detective, I'd told Rik. Right now I felt pulled in too many directions to know what I was.

When in doubt, find out.

OK. En route to the bus I would cover the Strawberry Parade. In Paris I would pay my family dues by visiting Marian, and ask what else she'd learned from Victor Tréville. On my way to Hands Across the Sea's Seine cruise I would call John Otis. Then I would tell the flics about that cork.

Whatever Fraises-des-Bois's reaction to last night's tragedy, they weren't letting it dampen their Fête des Fraises. I passed walls papered with huge red-and-green strawberry posters, trees festooned with strawberry banners, kids sporting strawberry T-shirts, toddlers licking strawberry-smeared mouths. In front of the bakery stood a cheery concessionaire hawking strawberry ties and baseball caps.

And in place of the bus stop stood a red-and-white canopied reviewing stand with a loudspeaker on top.

Madame la patissière sold me a batard and two strawberry tarts, but where I'd find the bus she couldn't say. I tried the drugstore: closed.

Mesdames et messieurs! announced a blurry amplified voice. *The Défilé des Chars is about to commence! Please welcome the lovely Reine des Fraises and her court!*

There was the mayor clapping at the foot of the steps. The queen beamed at him as she gathered up her white prom skirts and swept back her red velvet cloak to ascend the platform. Between her ladies-in-waiting I glimpsed Steve Connelly's yellow-sweatered arms and shoulders, which I hoped was all of him I'd see today.

And now, if I could find the bus—

Et maintenant, blatted the loudspeaker, *les teuf-teufs!*

Teuf-teufs?

A tiny vintage Alfa sputtered into the square. The driver tipped his motoring cap at the reviewing stand, honked his rubber-bulb horn. Polite applause from the scattered crowd. Five or six other little cars teuf-teuffed along behind him.

Was I the only woman here wearing pants? Also the only one without children. In front of me a pint-sized boy was twisting with impatience for the floats. His mother, no older than Lacey, shifted the baby on her hip and murmured down, "Sois sage!"

As I could be doing right now if . . . Larry and I had meant to have kids. We'd just never managed to reconcile our conflicting schedules, demanding social life, and—let's face it—ambivalence. Here it looked so simple: One year you're the Reine des Fraises, next year a bride, next year a *maman*. While we'd debated romance versus domesticity, day care versus quality time, career ladder versus ticking biological clock, till sometimes I wished the condom would break just to get it over with.

I scanned the square again for clues and spotted Lacey's white poodle jacket. She was climbing onto a tree-stump flowerpot. Her hair was wet but no longer blue. She saw me and waved.

"Cory! Isn't this super?" Lacey's spike-heeled boots teetered over the mouth of the stump, stabbing petunias and geraniums.

"So, no problems with the cops?"

"Nah. The nice one told Niko and me, Go on down and check out the fair. We threw baseballs and knocked the clown in the water, and Niko bought me *barbepapa*. That's French for cotton candy." She pronounced the word with care, as if she expected to need it again.

Niko, lounging by her feet, held up a yellow stuffed dog. "*One* of us knocked the clown in the water. The other one pooped out because she didn't have a prayer of winning this handsome blond pooch." He dangled it at her. "Who I hereby name Steve."

Lacey lunged, but she couldn't reach. Niko dodged behind the stump and fussily set Steve the dog among the flowers.

Mickey and Annette tap-dancing through Fantasyland. "Any more news about tonight?"

She shook her head and swiveled to check on the parade.

Did Lacey ever think about kids? Hard to picture her trading her keyboards for Pampers and strained peas. Or, for that matter, sticking with one man long enough for the question to come up. Last year the vocalist for Magic Fingers, this year Quasi & Company's bass player . . .

Who'd bragged to a trailerful of witnesses that he and Marie Tréville used to be close, and maybe that wasn't over.

Who'd carried an open bottle of champagne onstage, where he left it in reach of anyone with access, a grudge, and Sominol.

Who should have been the first if not only person to drink it.

"Ah, Lacey?" I had to clear my throat. "Where's Roach and everybody?"

"Setting up the club." Lacey jumped down from her stump with a big grin. "Did you hear? We were so hot the other night, Carl really really wanted us back. But we couldn't because of Hands and EuroDisney, but now that's off it's on again, even though François's band always plays there on Sunday nights, but they'd rather open for us anyway because it's an American-style club and we got the biggest crowd they ever had."

"Babble babble!" Niko squeezed her shoulder.

"Are you gonna come hear us?"

"I have to cover Hands Across the Sea."

"Come after that. It'll go late. Get everybody to come! Terry'll give you directions, if he ever gets here." She sighed. "They better not miss this!"

"You're going to miss it if you don't watch," said Niko.

Immediately Lacey craned on tiptoes to make sure the castle hadn't sneaked past her.

My eyes lingered on Niko's hand kneading her shoulder. In the fur of her jacket I could only see his knuckles and the ornate oval of his ring.

Another band member who might have drugged Roach's champagne. Motive? To free Lacey from his sexual tyranny, and the band from his retro musical taste. Means? Easy to pack a dose of Sominol under a stone that opened and shut. And on opportunity, Niko led the pack.

I tried to recall who'd been up front for the last songs, but live music drowned me out. A band was marching into the square, splendid in red-and-white uniforms and tall plumed hats, thumping out (could it be?) "Marching Through Georgia."

Niko scrambled up onto the stump-flowerpot to wave at a

group of girls on ponies.

"Lacey," I knocked on her boot. "The cops at the hotel. Did they let all of you go? Did they act suspicious of anybody?"

A terse nod. "Roach. Because of the champagne."

"Do you think he might have—?"

That spun her around. "No fucking way."

"Then who—?"

"Bear."

"Bear? The crew guy, Albert Vaux?"

"Yup. I don't know if he wanted to kill himself or just get super high. But you can ask anybody, he was wicked weird. I was the only one who got along with him. Even Neil, and Neil's good with everybody. Denise told me when we were building the castle, he's always been like that."

The first float trundled toward us: a unicorn tapestry of colored macaroni. "Like what?"

"Well, like being a pill-head, and being mean. Bullying little kids, harassing girls— Hey, do they have spinach noodles in France, or are those dyed white ones?"

Hold it. Victor Tréville's budding engineer and secret agent, a drug-abusing juvenile delinquent? How did that fit?

"Wow! This one's incredible! Niko, move over!"

Niko pulled Lacey up beside him.

It didn't fit. Weird or not, Albert Vaux couldn't have caused his own death. Even if he'd known there would be an open bottle of champagne onstage (not), and hung onto it long enough to drop in Sominol (not), why would he? Whether his goal was to kill himself or just get super high, he only had to swallow the pills.

Unless . . . Could he have drugged the champagne on Victor Tréville's orders?

That didn't fit either. First, again, neither of them knew Roach would bring it out from the trailer. Second, if Bear's job was to knock out his boss's rival, would he grab the poison away from the target and chug it himself?

And speaking of orders, I had my own job to do here, and it wasn't to second-guess a police investigation.

The next float *was* incredible: a billowing cardboard galleon flying the skull and crossbones. Small pirates swashed across the deck stomping rubber boots, brandishing paper cutlasses, scowling around eye patches, clenching plastic daggers in blacked-out teeth. To cap it off, a row of portholes along the hull shot jets of water into the crowd every few seconds. Already the kids on the ground had made a game of it, daring each other to run up and tag the ship without getting squirted.

"Oh, here comes ours!" Lacey almost fell off her stump. "Cory, quick! Give me your camera."

There it was, our turreted and bannered pink-and-blue castle. In front, Sleeping Beauty beaming and waving in a tulle gown and rhinestone tiara, dodging a juggler and a clown; and in back, on the drawbridge, three junior musicians whamming out lip-synched rock-&-roll. A boy with an eyebrow-pencil mustache banged on a hatbox drum. A taller boy gyrated to the electric wail of his shoebox guitar. Front and center, tossing her long blonde hair, one of Denise's friends pranced around a broomstick microphone.

"Bay-bee, don't waste it!" Her round cheeks were pink with excitement. "Come on and taste it, taste it!"

"Holy cow," Lacey said reverently.

She'd handed my camera to Niko, who'd jumped off the stump to shoot the float from all possible angles without being flattened by the tractor pulling it through the square.

The people of Fraises-des-Bois thought this was marvelous. Some of them looked puzzled, but most were laughing and clapping. Not for the music—who here remembered The Rind? Not for this inspired retaliation by Quasi & Company against EuroDisney for kicking them out. Not for Dan Quasi's shrewdness in using the town's own parade to lobby its honchos. They were clapping for their neighbors who'd built this adorable *hommage* to their region's top commercial attraction, and for the children up there bringing it to life.

While the kids on the ground were still chasing the pirate ship, shrieking when the spray hit them.

Chapter 20: Call on Me

"So what'd you think?"

I swiveled. Dan Quasi stood with his hands in his pockets, his brown leather jacket open over his T-shirt, waiting with a half smile for my answer.

"You're always asking me that." I stuffed my camera into my purse. Lacey and Niko had left after several more bands and floats to go prospecting for beer. "I thought it was brilliant. How about you?"

"If I was a producer I'd sign 'em."

Those flippant blue eyes. As if I needed reminding that if Dan Quasi were a producer, any group would be grateful for a contract offer.

"Looks like you managed the police OK. For somebody who doesn't like interviews."

A pause. Dan regarded me consideringly.

"If you're pissed because I snapped at you before, I'm sorry."

"Sorry you snapped at me or sorry I'm pissed?"

Dan folded his arms. "Look, Cory. It's been a long morning. I'm not up for any more debates right now. I said I'm sorry—take it or leave it."

"Take it or leave it? What am I, a loose end? I'm not asking you for a debate. I haven't asked you for anything at all. Except some ordinary human consideration."

Dan didn't say anything. I couldn't tell whether my salvo had disarmed him, or he was searching his repertoire for human consideration and finding it out of stock.

"Like I said before about your songs." I wanted to touch him now, but I didn't dare. "Taking this macho stance, politics and confrontation and fuck you, baby. Why don't you just act like a *person* sometimes?"

His eyes leveled at me. "You don't think I ever act like a person?"

I could feel myself yielding, ready to reassure him in hopes he'd reassure me. But how could I, when he stood facing me with his arms folded in that leather jacket?

"Never mind," he said finally, and walked away.

I heaved a long sigh as I headed in the opposite direction. Enough parade! Just let me go—to Paris, to Marian's, sanctuary of coffee and poetry. Enough tangled psyche of the rock musician! Give me Wallace Stevens, T. S. Eliot—anybody safely committed to print and immortality.

But there behind the reviewing stand stood Lacey, beckoning vigorously. "Cory! Photo op!"

Across the street a bald grandfather was wheeling a bald infant down the sidewalk. They looked so much alike, even their expressions, that I did take out my camera and snap their picture.

I asked Lacey if she'd seen the Paris bus. She said no, but Dan and Terry had made it here just in time for the float.

"Good," I said. "What about Roach? Did he come too?"

Lacey made a face. "Mr. Snooze! Can you believe, he's *sleeping*. The rest of them are at the café. You want to go eat, or check out the midway?"

"The midway."

We could see most of it from here: a small portable carousel, a handful of rides and games, a barker hustling pinwheels and balloons, quantities of *barbepapa*. I followed Lacey to the carousel. She watched intently as a young mother lifted her small daughter onto a pony, settling her in the saddle with the comfortable ease that had impressed me at the parade. As if they know all the answers, I thought—even if it's only because their kids keep asking questions.

Lacey turned to me with an evil leer. "Isn't she the one who rammed me with her trike? Get me one of those air rifles!" She leaned over the carousel fence. "You better ride fast, kid! I'm gonna shoot the legs off your horse!"

I glanced at the mother in alarm, but either she didn't understand English or she assumed all Americans were harmless lunatics.

"Aren't the women here amazing?" said Lacey as we moved

on down the row. "Did you notice at the parade?"

"Yeah."

"Every single one dyes their hair. *Nobody* in this entire town has gray hair."

Gray hair. Children, mothers, and Thorne Cosmetics.

"Oh, there's the one Roach and me did! I mean, Niko and me." Lacey pointed at a couple of boys throwing baseballs at a target. "Where you knock the clown in the water."

Sure enough, the back of the booth was all yellow stuffed dogs. I pitied the clown, sitting above the target on a plank. His legs dangled, his spotted costume was drooping and dripping, his red-and-white painted face looked patchy as a springtime ski slope. He didn't seem to mind, though. He taunted the boys as they pitched and pelted them with insults when they missed. He waved at Lacey and me as we strolled past.

I said cautiously, "Did you know before you came to France about Roach and Marie Tréville?"

"No." Lacey scowled. "He's such a prick sometimes."

"Imbécile!" shouted the clown. "Cochon! Drug addicte!"

"This whole trip's been so *weird.*" She slapped the fence along the front of the booths. "I've hardly seen him since we left Boston. I look over when we're playing and it's like, hey, there's Roach! I wake up in the morning and he's already gone. I don't know if he's with her or one of his little girls or what. He keeps *shoving* them at me, like I must not care about him unless I'm jealous. Or else he's sleeping, or nostalgia-tripping with Dan and Terry, and I wind up hanging out with Niko."

We'd reached the end of the midway. At the top of the hill a green locomotive chugged by, tooting its whistle.

"Maybe *he's* jealous," I suggested. "You and Niko always look like you're having such a good time."

"What choice have I got?" Lacey leaned on the railing that barred off the street. "It's no good hassling him. If it wasn't for the music—" Her mouth twisted. "The other night we went on and I was feeling down, and I looked over at Terry, grinning how he does, and Roach and Dan poking their guitars at each other, and Niko sending me signals, and all those people out there digging us, and man, what a rush! We came off and I'm still like whooshing through hyperspace. And then, *poof!*—we're back at the hotel, and I just wish I could die till tomorrow when we can do it again."

The same gleam in her eyes as in Dan's last night; the same hungry edge in her voice. I felt a shiver of sympathy for Mickey Ascher, too hooked on flying to notice his wings were melting.

"It's easier for the guys after a show," Lacey went on. "Do a shot, toot a line, grab a chick. You should hear the guys in Magic Fingers talk about girls—like they're part of the furniture, like cold beer in your dressing room. Chug one and chuck out the bottle! I used to give them shit about that." A wry smile. "But Todd, the drummer, goes, 'Don't get on us. Talk to the chicks.'"

I raised my eyebrows, feigning interest. Inside I was curling up.

"Is it the same with this band?"

"Oh . . ." Lacey grasped the tubed metal railing; wriggled her shoulders. "They've been pretty cool so far. I can't tell if it's because you and Steve are writing about them or they're just out of shape. It could be the hotel—this place is for shit as far as partying. No bar, no games, not even an ice machine."

I winced.

"What I want is one of those ritzy hotels with big-time room service and silver buckets of Jack. And some *guy* groupies! Not just to fuck," she qualified as we started up the hill. "Somebody who treats me like a princess. With strong hands, who gives me back rubs and brings me drinks and keeps people from hassling me. Who thinks I'm the most awesome lady he ever met and wants to take care of me."

Take care of me? This from Lacey, the champion scrapper of Quasi & Company?

"Somebody like Dan."

I almost tripped over my foot. "Dan?"

"Oh, you know." Lacey grinned and blushed. "He's so amazing about the band, you can't help but wonder what he'd be like as a guy."

"But that's all he cares about, is the band," I blurted. "Isn't it? I mean, I don't get the idea he puts that same kind of energy into—anything else."

"Oh, well, yeah," Lacey conceded. "I wouldn't actually *seduce* him." She giggled. "Roach said he used to drive the girls crazy in The Rind. He'd be sending out this heavy vibe from the stage, and then they'd all go back to the hotel and Dan would lock himself in his room with a couple other guys and jam all night."

Lacey paused as we reached the summit and had to stop for a passing Alpine village. From the slope of a papier-mâché mountain little girls in ruffled caps and aprons tossed paper flowers to the spectators.

"I guess he's never been good about women. Maybe because there's always so many of 'em. Anyhow, with Dan it's the band first and everything else after. Even his wife."

Right hook to the solar plexus. "His wife?"

"Nicola," Lacey nodded. "She was a model. Now she's in Hollywood making movies."

"But— They got divorced, didn't they? After The Rind broke up?"

"They split up, but they got back together. A bunch of times. She left him once for a director, or was it a cinematographer? And him being on the road so much— Like, Roach said one time they got to Boston for a weekend in the middle of a tour, and Dan went straight to Terry's place in Lincoln and spent the whole time writing songs. Didn't even tell Nicola he was in town."

With an expressive grimace, Lacey turned toward the burgundy-and-blue marching band that was following the Alps across the square.

I gazed at a tuba player and automatically tried to connect that shiny, dented brass funnel with the *boomph, boomph* coming out of it. Married! Well, why not? Just because I'd stopped reading about him in gossip columns, that didn't mean he'd stopped breathing. Or turned to marble before time could tarnish his iconoclastic perfection.

I'd done it. Why not Dan Quasi?

Maybe that was the answer to Steve Connelly's big question. *If he wasn't involved in Mickey Ascher's murder, why disappear?* Because he had dues to pay. Taxes. A mortgage. Home repairs.

Quality time. After too many Holiday Inns, he'd yielded to the pull of that gold noose around his finger.

"So, Lacey," I cleared my throat, "have you, ah, met Nicola? Do you know what she's like?"

Lacey gave me a funny look. "Super gorgeous, Roach says. I've never seen her. Not even a picture. Dan doesn't talk about her."

She turned back to the parade, which I took to mean she assumed my curiosity was professional and therefore not to be encouraged. Good. If Dan hadn't mentioned our affair, or whatever it was, to the rest of the band, then I was free to go on asking all the questions I wanted.

Only right now I didn't want to ask any more questions. I wanted to find my goddam bus and get the hell out of here.

The mirrored foyer of Marian Thorne's apartment smelled richly of fresh coffee and flowers. I'd pressed the bell with such relief that if Larry himself had appeared on the doorstep I'd have shoved him out of my way. Marian greeted me with her customary grace: elegant and fragile, her shoulders so thin in my hands that I feared for an instant I'd break her. She wore a pale silvery gown which rustled as I followed her into the salon, hinting at leisurely summer afternoons of porch swings and parasols. I watched her erect back, her slender arms, and marveled that I'd nearly chosen to stick with Quasi & Company when such a refuge awaited me here.

> *And would it have been worth it, after all,*
> *After the cups, the marmalade, the tea,*
> *Among the porcelain, among some talk of you and me . . .*
> *If one, settling a pillow or throwing off a shawl*
> *And turning toward the window, should say:*
> *"That is not it at all"?*

Paladin left her camera and tape recorder on a table in the foyer. *Mammas, don't let your daughters grow up to be cowboys.*

Marian had arranged chairs for us facing the open french windows. She brought a silver tray out from the kitchen: blue and white miniature cups and saucers at one end, the coffee pot at the other, and in between a platter of sliced pears and apples around chunks of cheese and bread.

I sipped gratefully from my demitasse and thought of the communion services of my childhood. Under our feet the stained-glass patterns of Marian's oriental carpet twinkled and sparkled as the sun shifted through the leaves outside.

"Coffee and oranges in a sunny chair," I murmured.

And Marian smiled, "Mingle to dissipate / The holy hush of ancient sacrifice."

A faint strand of music: Mozart's clarinet concerto. I let my mind rise and fall with the notes.

This was where I belonged: listening to a melody that had lasted for two centuries, longer than any hit Dan Quasi would ever write. So much more to music than rock-&-roll!—and so much more to my life than a weekend assignment with Hands Across the Sea.

"Sunday Morning." Marian leaned up to refill my cup. "I loved that poem the first time I read it. Nothing like the odes and sonnets we got at school." She laughed reminiscently. "My mother was aghast when she found out. The family, tu sais, was High Episcopal."

Indeed I did know. That Gothic gauntlet down which I'd walked in my white wedding dress, ornate and stiff as the cake Larry and I would pose with afterwards.

She dreams a little, and she feels the dark

Encroachment of that old catastrophe . . .

"Did you ever meet Wallace Stevens?" Scrambling for safer ground.

"Ah, no, alas," Marian sighed. "The year he published *Ideas of Order* was the year I left Boston."

That was a story I'd heard more than once: how Marian Thorne cast off her home and family for a room of her own in Paris, carrying only the clothes in her trunk and the poems in her head. Dickinson, Whitman, Eliot, Stevens . . . *things in some procession of the dead, winding across wide water, without sound.* Larry would wink at me when she began reciting lines written before we were born: Quite a memory for an old lady, n'est-ce pas? While Marian wrung music from those dusty lyrics in her prim old-lady's voice.

"Only a few people here had heard of him. But we changed that." Her china-blue eyes twinkled. "My friend Chloe and I threw a party—she was a painter in the Cinquième—and we all read aloud, passing around the book with bottle after bottle of *vin du pays*. Naturally everyone was *étonné* that first night by 'The Idea of Order at Key West'; but after a few weeks we each came to have our own favorites. And then waiting *two years* for the next book! What an event when it finally appeared!"

She chuckled. "That must sound odd to you, now that one can buy all the poems at once and read them in any order one chooses. But what a thrill it was then!—to wait in suspense for each new," she searched for a word, "installment."

"Oh, no. Odd? Au contraire." I smiled back, remembering how Penny and I used to besiege the college bookstore at the first rumor a new Rind album was coming out.

What would Marian say if I told her about Dan Quasi? She'd lived among artists, bohemians. Had she ever opened her eyes after one of those nights of poetry and wine to see a strange man sleeping beside her? Had she ever tried to catch one, like a firefly in a jar, and shriveled up inside when he flew away? Did she ask herself then if it had been worth it, after all, with the past swinging shut across the Atlantic and the future looming like a high windowless wall?

"No, I never met him," Marian continued reflectively, "but I felt as if I had. From his work, tu comprends. I used to imagine he could sense my appreciation, and even perhaps draw strength from all of us wishing him well."

Unwrapping my copy of *Grind*: one last vote of support. Too late for Mickey, murdered before it was issued, or The Rind, killed with him . . .

"But— Didn't he disappear?" I set down my cup. "Am I remembering this right? Wasn't there a long silence after his first success, when nobody knew if he'd ever write another poem?"

"Oh, yes," Marian nodded. "Twice. Seven years of silence after his astonishing debut with 'Sunday Morning,' and twelve more years after *Harmonium*. I've always wondered why—how he could declare himself so irrevocably, and then revoke it. Renounce his *raison d'être*, as it were. Had he so little faith in his gift? Did he fear the form was too limited for his ideas? or his ideas were too limited for the form? Did he feel pressed by other exigencies? I don't suppose we'll ever know, though certainly the experts have theories enough. In any event," she smiled, "enfin he came back."

"The experts!" I leaned forward. "You're the one who recognized him, and followed him, and knows every poem he wrote. What do *you* think?"

Marian considered for a moment. "I like to think that, like Jacob and the angel, he wrestled with his vocation, and in losing, won. That whatever his doubts, he realized that what he could accomplish as a poet was too valuable to waste."

I sat back and raised my demitasse. "Taste it, don't waste it."

"Or as Flaubert wrote to George Sand, 'L'homme c'est rien; l'oeuvre c'est tout.'"

The man is nothing, the work is everything. I felt lightened and comforted, as if the morning's discords had resolved in an unexpected Picardy Third. At this moment, in this calm interlude of coffee, Mozart, and good company, I understood that Dan Quasi was only a mote in a stream. There was nothing he could do to me in five days that would undo what he'd given me over two decades. Oh, bien sur, a few songs I'd never hear the same way again, a gallery of new images to pin up beside the ones I'd hoarded since D.C.; but The Rind would go on, still the sound track of revolution and epiphany, marching in the streets, dancing till dawn, heading in a rented car down highways I knew only from Kerouac, falling asleep in a strange motel bed with my tape recorder beside me.

"L'homme c'est rien; l'oeuvre c'est tout. I'll have to remember that."

"Though of course one wonders if Sand took it more personally than Flaubert intended," said Marian, "given how long she lived with Frederick Chopin."

Of course. Chopin. A keyboard player, wouldn't you know.

"I always meant to check the dates, her writing and his music, for signs of influence from that romance. Aphorisms aside, one does miss things when one looks only at the work. The excitement of watching an artist grow, hearing his voice change from book to book."

Or album to album, I thought. And felt a rush of sympathy for Lacey, asking me questions about the sixties, and for Denise and her friends on the float, miming lyrics off an old tape.

"Not at all the same as discovering him from a collection of greatest hits," I agreed.

A cluster of string chords opened into the sunny afternoon like blossoms.

"Stevens sensed that at the end of his life," Marian continued. "You can see the difference in some of his late poems. Not pushing forward, like the earlier ones, but summing up. Setting the capstone, *on peut dire*."

The capstone. *Grind.* "The End of the Night." No more rallying the students in the streets when your vocalist was burning out on heroin. What must it have been like for Dan that last year, with The Rind sinking downward to darkness on extended wings?

"I sensed such a finality in your last Beaubourg piece," said Marian. "As if you'd reached a limit, come to the end of what you felt you could do. Such a relief to see you back at it, chérie." She smiled. "Those who have such gifts ought not to wrestle with them for too long."

She stood up, to save me the embarrassment of groping for a reply. I heard her go into the kitchen. The acid-trip sensation I'd had earlier flooded my head again, prickled my eyes, shivered through my arms and legs, so that even if I'd felt obliged to ask Marian if she wanted help I couldn't have got either the words out of my mouth or myself out of my chair.

Me, I thought dazedly. She's talking about me. Telling me the doubts she's so graciously refrained from expressing about my marriage to Larry Thorne weren't for his sake, but for mine.

Waves of comprehension and gratitude rolled over me along

with Mozart's strings. I wanted to thank her, to tell her she'd just given me something even more precious than her poems, but I couldn't muster a word.

"I'm afraid the coffee's gone cold," Marian called from the kitchen. "I'll make us some fresh, shall I?"

"Marian." My voice sounded as if it were coming from miles away. "I should be going. I've got a Seine cruise to cover."

"Bien sur." She was pleased.

"But before I leave—may I ask you—?"

"About Victor Tréville?" Her gown whispered across the floor as she came to stand beside me. "Of course."

"You called his position delicate if not precarious. Did you mean generally, or right now?"

"Hm. I meant generally, but after this dreadful business . . . Hands Across the Sea was meant to be Marie's project, you recall. Victor was only a sort of *éminence grise*. But here is your band in his back yard; and now a death."

"Not what he had in mind," I agreed.

"One presumes he's stepped on a toe or two along his way. If he is concerned about grudges, he might take this as someone's chance to throw him to the wolves. And seize his chance to steer the inquiry."

"Onto safe ground. Yes!" I summarized last night's meetings in the trailer and at the police station. "Steer the inquiry toward the expendable Americans, and away from his wife. Toward a fine young man he helped, and away from a troubled kid he exploited, fatally as it turns out."

"Oh, my." Marian pressed her index fingers together and raised them to her lips. "Poor Victor. I begin to see why he was so provoking on the phone."

"About scapegoating Quasi & Company?"

"Mais non, chérie. Campaigning for sympathy. Insisting that he was the one to feel sorry for, rather than the boy who died."

"Him? Why?"

"Well, from what you both have told me, I wonder if Victor must not believe that he was the intended victim when the band poisoned that bottle of champagne in the trailer."

Chapter 21: Same Old Song and Dance

Having left Fraises-des-Bois rejoicing to be off the hook with Quasi & Company, I kicked myself all the way from the Place de l'Opéra to the Pont d'Iéna for not finding out where they were playing tonight.

Some journalist!—so pleased with my clever interrogation of Roach that I'd missed the bigger question: Who did uncork that champagne, and when?

I phoned the Hôtel des Fraises from the Métro station, but I was too late. The band was *parti*, the truck and all the equipment were *parti*, and *non, madame*, they had left no address.

Well, at least they hadn't been arrested. Yet.

From Opéra to Miromesnil I fulminated. By St. Philippe du Roule I'd switched back to practical mode. Was Marian was right? Had Victor Tréville deduced that the lethal bottle was opened in the trailer, not on the stage, and that it was meant for him?

How could he, if he didn't know about Roach's second cork?

He'd told her he'd be on this afternoon's Seine cruise with Hands Across the Sea, so in an hour I could ask him.

Our departure point was a dock near the Pont d'Iéna, the bridge that links the Jardins du Trocadéro with the Eiffel Tower across the river. The ambassadors and hosts had already formed a long line down to the boat when I arrived. Lots of jeans and T-shirts—from here, buses would take everyone to EuroDisney—and lots of dripping ice cream cones from the van up by the Palais de Chaillot. Except for the fishy, tarry smell of the dock, we could have been waiting outside the Brattle Theatre in Cambridge for the latest French film.

I didn't see Victor Tréville nor his wife. Camera cocked, I strolled to the head of the line. This wasn't your standard sight-seeing craft, with glass roof and rows of seats one stayed in while the guide described the passing scenery. This boat was a shallow two-decker: folding chairs scattered around the top tier and the open rear deck below, and presumably a place for the band in the enclosed center.

I devoutly hoped Hands hadn't replaced Quasi & Company with some marshmallow combo. After three and a half days together, the participants finally looked relaxed: happy, excited, photogenic, ready to celebrate our last evening in France with some world-class boogieing. The boat was strung with Japanese lanterns and garlanded with crepe paper. Sun, river, Paris skyline— This was a night for rock-&-roll.

I recapped my camera. Goddam Sominol. Goddam flics. Lacey would have loved this boat.

The line still wasn't moving. I walked toward the gangplank, half expecting to hear Steve Connelly shouting instructions from the upper deck.

Instead, the familiar *thu-du-dum, bump, bump* of drums.

I broke into a jog. Not only drums but a spinet piano on the platform inside the plexiglass windows, and a synthesizer waiting for legs. Quasi & Company must have gotten back on the boat.

The drummer wasn't Terry, though. A bony teenager with hair shaved around his ears and floppy on top . . . Albert Vaux's replacement? The equipment I was sure was theirs. Yes!—voilà Steve the dog on the piano.

In brisk French I explained to the longshoreman guarding the gangplank that I was an American journalist and I had to board this boat right now to cover the cruise for my magazine. He shook his head: not a chance. I waved my tape recorder at him. He glared at me. I told him I was the head of CBS News and we'd sue the personal daylights out of him. This time he heaved a monumental shrug and unclipped the chain.

Under the edge of the roof, twenty feet aft of the instruments, Neil stood at the sound board, his red hair tied back in a horsetail. "OK," he called to the kid behind the drums. "One at a time all the way around." He mimed a circle.

"Neil, where's the band?"

He didn't hear me. His ears were tuned to the *baddla-duddla* coming from the speakers.

Quasi & Company weren't on this level. Running up the

stairs to the top deck I met François coming down, but he hurried past me without even a nod.

Back to Square One. Behind the stage was a wall, beyond that the hall for the restrooms, and forward of that the bar. No bartender or bottles, though, just two ladies setting out platters of cookie-cutter sandwiches. Did they know what had happened with the band? Blank looks. One suggested I go see Mrs. Bailey in the galley.

Around the corner and through a pair of swinging doors. In the galley I found Steve, once again with a bottle of champagne in his hands.

"Cory," he nodded a greeting.

"Quasi & Company," I said breathlessly.

"They let them on after all. Last minute. The crew's still setting up their stuff." Steve poured the champagne into a massive plastic punch bowl, where it mingled fizzily with pink fruit juice and sliced oranges. "They're on their way here now."

"What about Albert Vaux? Did the police find out—?"

"I don't know."

"Are the Trévilles here?"

"Not yet. They should be. Will be. Marie's our tour guide this evening."

"Where's Sheila Bailey?"

"In the loo."

I left Steve popping corks and went back out to try Neil and François again.

Neil was hunched over the board so intently I knew it would be futile to speak to him. "OK up here!" came a distant shout. "Try some piano."

"Piano," called Neil.

The skinny kid stepped out from behind Terry's drums and sat down at the spinet. Between his baggy pants and extra-large U.S. Marines sweatshirt, I wondered how he could maneuver through all those cords and boxes. His hands pranced across the keyboard. From the speakers overhead came a tinny tinkling which rounded out magically into the firm clear notes of Niko's piano.

"More," ordered Neil.

The kid lacked Niko's panache. It was like listening to a jazz student pretending to be Eubie Blake.

So where was the band? In the time it must have taken the crew to load their equipment, truck it here, and set up, Quasi & Company could have driven from the Hôtel des Fraises to the Pont d'Iéna and back.

I looked down at my wrist, but it was empty. Something fluttered in my chest: I'd left my watch on Dan's bedside table.

"Hey, excuse me," Steve called to Neil from the galley door. "Can you hurry that up? We've got to let these people on the boat."

Neil's expression was placid as usual. His answer sounded like a recording. "The band can't play without a sound check, and we can get through it faster without all them in the way." He nodded at the kid at the piano, turned a couple knobs on the board. "Again."

I walked over to Steve. "What do you know about this? Who decided Quasi & Company should play? And when?"

"It must have been right after I left." Steve was still watching Neil. "According to Sheila Bailey, the boat company worked all day on that wiring problem and finally got it straightened out."

"I thought the wiring problem was a myth."

"Not according to Sheila."

I leaned against the white enameled wall beside the galley door. "In other words, not according to Hands Across the Sea."

"Play a song," Neil told the kid on piano. "*Un chanson.*"

"This whole thing has a smell I don't like." Steve looked at me at last. "They better show up."

I was surprised. "Do you think there's a chance they won't?"

Steve raised a wrist, pushed a button on his Rolex. "Six twenty-three and forty-eight seconds. They've got roughly six minutes."

"And what if they aren't here by then?"

"Hold it," called Neil. "What chord are you on? E?"

The sudden quiet as the piano ceased distracted me. Steve said he didn't know what would happen if Quasi & Company missed the boat; but I was listening to a new set of noises. Out on the dock voices were rising. Applause rippled up the line. Evidently the band had arrived, with five and a half minutes to spare.

They thundered up the metal gangplank. I heard Lacey first: "Piano! See? What'd I tell you?" Then her frizzy head popped into view, and her poodle jacket, and the rest of them in leather and jeans, carrying guitar cases.

"Well, shee-it!" Roach lumbered toward the board. "You guys done good! I figured you'd still be setting up."

Dan and Neil immediately began discussing what the crew had done and what the band needed to do next.

Niko said to Lacey, "So we could've finished the tabouli. Shit alors!"

Terry wandered over to the drums, picked up his sticks, gave a cymbal a friendly tap.

Steve started toward the sound board. I could see him preparing to attach himself to Dan like a magnet to a refrigerator. "Steve," I grabbed his arm. "Give them a minute."

Within less than a minute the band members were in place.

"Piano," said Dan. Niko poured out boogie-woogie, long thin fingers skittering like spiders up and down the keyboard.

Ten seconds, then Neil called, "OK." The music halted in mid-stride. "Lacey, let me hear some synth."

"This is a hell of a sound check," said Niko.

Dan said, "We'll have to use the first couple numbers as a sound check."

Roach was slipping his snakeskin strap over his head. He made a gargoyle face. "That sucks."

Lacey played a loud ripple of descending chords.

"We can't leave all those yuppos wilting in the sun," said Terry.

"They don't know it was Hands that fucked up," said Dan. "All they know is the band's late."

Steve beside me made a noise that sounded like surprise. Evidently it hadn't occurred to him musicians were capable of reasoning.

"Keep going, Lacey," said Neil. "Then bass, Roach, OK?"

The kid in the Marines sweatshirt was pulling a foam mitt over a microphone. Niko walked up to peer at the back of the board.

"Dan," called Steve. "How long till we can let everybody on?"

"Neil?"

"Twenty minutes," Neil said into his mic. It reverberated across the deck. I could hear the crowd's disappointed "Oh!" outside.

"Fifteen minutes?" Neil said.

A sprinkle of clapping mixed with groans.

"Steve," said Roach into his mic; but it was dead. He waved at Neil and pointed at it. "Steve!" he tried again, and this time his voice boomed from the speakers. "Give all those folks out there a cold beer! Compliments of Quasi & Company!"

Enthusiastic cheers from the dock.

"Shit," Steve said angrily. He stepped up and shouted to the band, "Hurry it up, will you?" Without amplification it was the voice of a 90-pound weakling. He stalked back into the galley.

Until Victor Tréville arrived, Roach took a break, or Sheila Bailey emerged from the *Dames*, there wasn't much for me to do but spectate. I moved over by the gangplank where I could see the galley doors, the hall, the sound board, and the band.

"OK," Neil said at last. "Give me just the rhythm section, and then everybody, with vocals."

One of the committee ladies held a door open while Steve waddled out carrying the enormous punch bowl. He set it on the bar between rows of plastic cups and paper napkins and platters of sandwiches.

Who would have made the decision to un-ban Quasi & Company? The police? One or both Hands Across the Sea committees? Mayor d'Aumont? Governor Leroy? I didn't know; and I was pretty sure that if Steve knew, he wouldn't have passed up the chance to inform me.

What did this reversal do to the band's club date? Where did it leave tonight's grand finale at EuroDisney?

Roach and Terry were playing together; Neil had left the

board to walk around and listen. "OK," he called, and they cut off in mid-beat. "Try 'Time,' with everybody."

Magic! Out of those disparate sounds came music—

"Hold it," said Neil. The band shuddered to a halt. "Dan, is that you?"

"Sure is," said Dan. "High end."

I had no idea what they meant. It sounded fine to me.

The ladies were setting out more sandwiches. Suddenly I was hungry. I went over to grab some food before the horde arrived—for me and for the crew.

When I handed a piled-up plate to Neil, he stuffed down a chicken salad and grinned as if I'd handed him a bottle of Jack Daniel's. I asked him why things were so rushed. He said they were trying to cram an hour's work into fifteen minutes. "We were halfway through sound check at the club when Hands called and said get your ass over here." He turned back to the platform. "One more time with just the stage. No house."

"Will you still play at the club?"

He nodded, listened, frowned, turned a knob.

"Is EuroDisney still off?"

Another nod; but I couldn't be sure if it was for me or what he was hearing.

No clue from Dan, who stood at the front of the platform with his eyes half closed, swaying a little as his fingers released a cascade of notes. Whatever had been wrong with his guitar, it wasn't now. "Give Me Some Time" sounded terrific.

Oh, here came Sheila, clicking in small high-heeled steps across the deck. She stared frostily, arms folded across her no-wrinkle beige-and-white dress, as Quasi & Company sang the chorus. Even she could see that they wouldn't hear her if she shouted at them. Surely Mrs. Bailey must be a mother—she had that same implacable air of *droit de mère* as the women in Fraises-des-Bois.

"All right, now!" she cried the instant Neil cut off the music. "That's enough practicing! We have to let the hosts and ambassadors on the boat now. We're already late."

"Go ahead," said Neil. "Roach, how's that monitor for you?"

Sheila hesitated. Evidently she'd expected a fight.

"I could use some more of Niko."

I followed her to the gangplank. When I asked her whose heart had changed between nine this morning and six tonight, she gave me that distracted, preoccupied look I recalled from the banquet. One more interruption, when all she wanted was to welcome her guests aboard and get this cruise underway! The wiring problem had been fixed, she replied. Any additional information I'd have to get from Marie Tréville.

I told her I'd be glad to, but where *was* Marie Tréville? Why wasn't she in there mixing punch and cutting sandwiches?

Go ahead, mouthed Sheila to the man on the dock. Marie? Due here any minute. Her husband had been delayed by business. That looked like their car right now.

The chain was unhooked, the queue cheered, and the first passengers charged up the gangplank. I moved to the railing where I could watch the brown Citroën creeping down the dock like a great shiny beetle.

Out of the front seat stepped Marie Tréville. She leaned in to say something to the driver—Victor, presumably—then shut the door.

And for an evening cruise, Madame chooses a sleeveless frock of lemon silk lightly patterned with flowers. Over the arm an ivory shawl whose fringe swished against her leg as she hurried toward the boat. A gardenia in her hair—or was it a camellia? Billie Holiday or Marguerite Gautier?

Either way, she looked appallingly attractive. I wished I could keep her out of Lacey's sight.

But what had she done with her husband? If she'd made him drop her off and go home, I'd kill her. Sent him to park the car? The thumping of the gangplank under all those feet, along with the noise of all those voices, kept me from hearing what she had to say to Sheila Bailey. From her smile, though, I could guess.

I used to have those conversations. *Sorry to be late, but <u>he</u> couldn't get away.* The complacent conspiracy of married women. Drifting together while the men talked football or investments across the room, each of us with a *he* to pepper our remarks. *Oh, I* *meant to watch that, too, but <u>he</u> brought home some people from the office.* As if we bounced through our lives like pinballs, flipping off one event onto another, always rolling toward that pair of outstretched arms that mark the end of the game.

Terry had climbed onto a folding chair to adjust a light. Black cans crouched like a row of toads on a log. Dan, at the board, called something to Lacey about her vocal mic. Neil and François were crawling around the floor taping down wires. Niko sat behind the piano munching the sandwiches I'd left with Neil.

Roach was humming into his mic, whether for Neil or himself I couldn't tell. His beady, bushy-browed eyes inspected each new woman who stepped off the gangplank.

"Rollin'!" he sang suddenly in a husky baritone. A pretty brunette glanced over and smiled. He winked at her. "Rollin' on the ree-vah!"

Damn! It would serve him right if Lacey drugged his champagne. Somebody ought to tell that hippie Casanova—

Not you, Cory. Let Dan deal with the band, OK? You deal with your magazine.

I readied my tape recorder and headed up the stairs. Arriving so late, the Trévilles would have their own version of sound check to do with Mrs. Bailey and the committee. A good time to finish my ambassador interviews.

It was cooler on the top deck, and crowded. The floor jerked under my feet: We were pulling out. I couldn't get near the rail, but I could see the olive-brown river sliding by around us.

There were Rachel and her red-haired friend (Mary Jane? Mary Ann?) and their host families. And Lena Michel, chatting with two men in loafers and polo shirts.

Silly to have been so prickly this morning. I hoped Lena didn't hold it against me. Probably she'd understood from the beginning that Quasi & Company were just one more silhouette in the skyline, one more float in the parade. Maybe someday we could meet for lunch at a Back Bay café and reminisce about our crush on Dan Quasi.

I should go ask questions. *Have you enjoyed this trip? What are the advantages of seeing Paris with Hands Across the Sea? If they offer another Mystery Destination, will you sign up?*

Not yet. For a moment I let myself float between sky and river, taking in the view. Through the faint blue haze that lay over the city I followed streets that shone like silver in the sun: the broad avenue running along the Jardins du Trocadéro, the thinner *rues* of the Right Bank. Beyond what I could see were other places I could easily picture if I tried; but right now I wanted to be only eyes, sweeping like a seagull in a slow circle. Church towers, chimneys, domes, treetops . . .

"Ladies and gentlemen. Mesdames et messieurs." A voice from the speakers cut through the rumble of the boat's motor and the buzz of conversation. Not Quasi & Company. A firm, pleasant contralto.

"Welcome to Hands Across the Sea's cruise on the River Seine. You can see on our right the Eiffel Tower, *la tour Eiffel* . . ."

Our tour guide for the evening: Marie Tréville. Shit alors. Now I wouldn't be able to get near her till the band started.

Which meant that if her husband were here, this was the time to catch him.

I slipped my tape recorder strap around my wrist, swung onto the stairway, and collided with Victor Tréville.

We both grabbed the railing to catch our balance. Reluctance crashed over me like a tsunami: Whatever news he had that I needed, this man meant trouble—threats, drugs, cops, evasions and accusations.

"Cory. I am sorry to upset you." With a smile of official bonhomie he offered a steadying hand. "You work on your story?" The hand, ignored, shifted to indicate my tape recorder.

Acting on impulse, I flipped it into position. Yes, I said. Collecting comments for Hands Across the Sea's press releases. Would he be willing . . .?

Victor's bonhomie brightened. His mouth gravitated toward the microphone as to a lover's lips. Such a fine program, Hands Across the Sea! Such admirable participants! Although his own fond memories of Boston naturally colored his view, he felt safe to say . . . hand of friendship . . . cross-cultural exchange . . . global village . . . technological advances . . .

Why did I let him do this? Had I spent so many hours half-listening to smug men in expensive suits that I'd lost the strength to force the moment to its crisis?

"I was surprised to see Quasi & Company here," I said.

Victor stopped as abruptly as the band at sound check.

"What happened? Why the last-minute change?"

He seemed to fold inward. Not wishing to be fobbed off with wiring problems, I pressed on.

"This morning they were barred from any more Hands Across the Sea functions. An hour ago that decision was reversed. Whose mind changed, and why? Have the police learned anything new about Albert Vaux's death—?"

But Victor was shaking his head. "Ah, but no. Did you yourself not say that this is a matter for caution and discretion?"

I switched off my tape recorder.

He responded with a wan smile. "You are writing a story about this band for a popular American magazine."

Don't argue, Cory. Tune to his key.

"Yes. But my main job is to represent Hands Across the Sea to the Boston media. At the personal request of one of its sponsors —you know John Otis, of the Faneuil Plaza Hotel? He can vouch for my caution and discretion."

Victor thought it over. Or maybe he wondered why his wife's voice had stopped coming from the speakers. A high-pitched screech: evidently Neil hadn't got all the bugs out yet.

"For the media, then, here is what happened." He waited for me to press Record. "Our committee was informed by the charter company that, contrary to our understanding, the electrical system on this boat—"

Silently I fumed.

"—able to change the plans they had too hastily made. And as you see," he gestured at the floor, "here they are."

"Will they be at EuroDisney tonight as well?"

"Unfortunately their plans were not so flexible as that."

Quoi faire? By now the entire phalanx of French and American honchos must be in this loop, trading passive compound complex sentences about every aspect of the situation from illegal use of prescription drugs to international security. Once you get a bunch of guys one-upping each other on that level, forget straight answers.

From the speakers his wife's voice resumed her travelogue.

"Victor, this won't do." I pressed Stop. "I commend your reticence, but I can't respect it. Not when a young man has been poisoned. Not when Quasi & Company are suspected of killing him because he died on their stage."

For a moment I thought he would retort, but he didn't.

"Even press releases require facts. I'll try not to embarrass anyone, or get in anyone's way, but I won't back off. Here are the questions I intend to answer. You can help me—I hope you will. I'll be grateful if you do. Or you can go on trying to block me. But you can't stop me."

Victor's lips pressed together. I could see him readying his reply; but he still didn't speak.

"First: Albert Vaux's death was accidental. Whatever crime was committed, he wasn't the target. So my question is, Did the person who put Sominol in that champagne do it to get high, or to knock someone out, or to murder some other victim?"

By now I didn't really expect him to respond; so after a moment, I went on.

"Second: Quasi & Company got barred from EuroDisney for security reasons." Still no reaction. "Whose security? And are the reasons political or personal?"

Not a flicker. Yet he must know what I was driving at. Damn!—the man was an icicle.

"Third: When was the champagne drugged? The police seem to think it was during those four or five minutes the bottle was open onstage. I don't agree."

"No." As slowly as sunrise, a bleak smile spread over Victor Tréville's face. "Nor do I."

When you finally get it, you want to sneak up on tiptoe, not to startle it away. "May I ask why?"

"Because the chief of the band's crew saw a champagne bottle behind them during the performance, stoppered with a wine cork."

Chapter 22: Don't Ask Me No Questions

Fifteen minutes later I leaned against the wall staring at Quasi & Company, and I didn't hear a note they played.

The police had interviewed Neil and François this morning, Victor Tréville informed me. Since Neil was behind the board all night, he could tell them only that Albert Vaux had appeared intoxicated from the time he arrived. It was François, wandering around checking speakers and lights, keeping an eye out, who'd spotted the champagne.

No, he had not seen anyone go near it. He wouldn't have noticed it, back there in the dark, if Dan hadn't needed a broken guitar string replaced. It stuck in his mind because that was such an odd (read "American") thing to do, to save an opened bottle of champagne—and second-rate champagne, at that, no offense to Hands Across the Sea.

Had Victor heard François's testimony himself? Oh, yes. Yes indeed. He and Mayor d'Aumont had met with Commissaire Guerin at the police station after the crowning of the Reine des Fraises. After François's startling disclosure, they'd conferred with the investigative team and agreed: far more likely the bottle was tampered with after it was uncorked in the trailer than while it sat unnoticed and inaccessible on the stage.

Fortunately, last night after the concert M. d'Aumont—with remarkable presence of mind—had gone back to the trailer and taken the remaining champagne bottles into custody. Three empty, two almost empty. One missing, now recovered.

This morning MM. d'Aumont and Tréville together reviewed the sequence of relevant events for the flics. Minute by minute, as best they could, they worked out when bottles had been opened, where they had been set down, who had poured, passed, and drunk from them.

"The picture is incomplete," Victor finished. "But if our memories are correct, the bottle that was carried outside to the stage, the bottle containing the fatal drug, must have been mine."

His unemphatic delivery gave his point far more force than his theatrics last night. Then I'd felt goaded to argue. Now I shivered.

"Yours?" Wanting and not wanting to hear his explanation.

When Mayor d'Aumont had invited the Trévilles to the trailer, none of them knew the band was still inside. Much less did they expect to find illegal drug use in full swing. In the tension that followed, they backed off. Victor accepted a bottle from Steve —opened, but full—and never returned it. Not that he'd hoarded it, or even kept track of it. He set it on a nearby coffee table and poured from it once or twice. Since neither he nor his wife was a heavy drinker, the bottle remained more than half full when they left.

In my head a young Marie Tréville stood watching The Rind, nursing one glass of wine through the night.

"And you felt no ill effects?"

Victor shook his head. "I drank very little. My wife, however, became very sleepy. A neighbor drove her home."

Neither of them had given it a second thought, with Marie working so hard on Hands Across the Sea. Rising early, staying out late— Not until his meeting at the police station this morning, said Victor, did the first cold breath of suspicion chill his heart. And only when he heard François's testimony did that chill grip him like a bitter frost.

"Is she all right? Have you discussed—?"

Yes, *grace à dieu,* and no. Marie must not know of her brush with death—not now, with a long evening of festivities to get through. In fact she was due to join him here at any moment. They'd arranged to meet Sheila Bailey and some other guests on the upper deck.

"But then . . ." I wished I could tell what he really believed, versus what he wanted me to believe. "Aren't you worried?"

"For my safety? Of course I am worried! Security reasons, you say; what does that mean? To you, an American, a journalist, this band comes to France only to make publicity. Trouble? No! How should that be? Me, I am an official of France. I see threats against my home, my district. Degrading slanders against my wife. I see a young neighbor killed in mistake for myself. I see a deadly shadow who has struck and struck at me and failed. When will he try again?"

"Who? When will who try again?"

He flicked his fingers, dismissing the question.

"If you're so sure it's someone in the band, you must know who."

"Must I? I have a hundred enemies. A thousand. Political opponents I defeated. Students and workers I angered. Farmers and shopkeepers I displaced. Should I know them all? Should I know who are their angry friends and brothers? In the trailer at the Fête des Fraises were ten persons only. Myself and my wife. The mayor. You. Stephen Connelly. And five musicians. Did one of them poison my champagne?" He paused—less for drama than to make sure I got it. "The answer is not for me to guess. It is for Commissaire Guerin and his men to discover and prove."

Victor's fingers were drumming on the rail now, like muffled hoofbeats.

"But you have your suspicions. Given your family history in Boston with The Rind."

"I say again. This is work for the police, not me. They must investigate those ten persons, and every other person who was on the stage or near it. They, not I, must judge the history in Boston of these so-called musicians, these suspected murderers who were never brought to justice."

He flung it at me like a dare. No way, I thought. Not on a wobbly metal staircase in the middle of a river with a man who's been taunting the press since I was a student.

"Why are you here, then?" I said instead. "Cruising the Seine with a potential assassin?"

"I am not so easy to frighten away." Victor's mouth twisted, twitching his mustache. "The police, the laboratory, they are hard at work as we speak. Monsieur le Commissaire assures me that they will labor through the night to find the culprit. Me, I come to support my wife and Hands Across the Sea. On this boat, yes?— the band stays together in one place, lit by the sun, watched by many eyes. This is a risk I am willing to take. But EuroDisney? Pfff!"

Behind him I spotted Sheila Bailey's distinctive blonde curls, and hurried in one last question.

"When do you expect news from Commissaire Guerin?"

"Not tonight, I think. There will be an announcement tomorrow."

He turned away before I could ask what the police chief was likely to announce. Mrs. Bailey gave us a gay little wave. Victor's voice went cheerful: "Sheila, so nice to see you. A fine day, isn't it? We are lucky on our weather."

Pfff! I retreated down the stairs.

Thumps from the speakers suggested Quasi & Company were preparing to play. I shut them out. My brain felt like like a Magic 8-Ball: shake hard, then wait for a revelation.

Lena Michel stood by the rail in a group of ambassadors. Dodge them? No. Time was running out, and interviews I could do on autopilot.

I shook hands with a wiry woman in a pink-and-black striped jersey, a frosted blonde wearing oversized sunglasses, and two men in polo shirts, one yellow and one green, each with an alligator on the left breast. Betsy, Sue, Phil, and— "Sorry, I forget," said Lena.

"Don." He offered me a tanned tennis-player's hand.

Addresses? Occupations? Porter Square, Newton, Belmont, Fresh Pond. Systems analyst, graphic designer, paralegal, assistant D.A. They were loving Paris, making great friends and contacts, looking forward to EuroDisney . . .

Agitation. That's what struck me about Victor Tréville. The fidgety fingers, the twitchy mustache— As if, now that events were finally proving him right, he could drop his mask a little. And the man behind it was torn: defiant, angry, a little scared. How could he not be, watching his dire warnings come true?

Quasi & Company launched into "Sizzle," the fast tune

they'd opened with at the banquet. Mostly instrumental solos. That must be what Dan meant by using the first couple numbers as a sound check.

Oh, hell, this was crazy! My ears straining toward the music like a dog on a leash, my brain obsessively playing solitaire, black king on red queen, while my tape recorder kept rollin' on the ree-vah. High points of this trip? Shopping and the Eiffel Tower (Sue). The Louvre and the Picasso Museum (Betsy). Cafés in the Latin Quarter (the Alligator Brothers). Building a float for the Strawberry Parade with Quasi & Company (Lena).

Did Victor really believe he was the target of a political vendetta, or was he desperate to steer his neighbors, colleagues, and opponents away from his wife's dirty secret?

"Neil?" Dan Quasi stood at the front of the stage shading his eyes. "Is that the house?"

"Yeah," Neil called back.

Dan stepped behind his mic and played a few lines of "Sizzle." The rest of the band kicked in automatically.

Could that be the same secret Albert Vaux had crowed to me about? Had he spied the boss's wife sneaking out for a tryst with her ex-lover?

Could rage and/or fear have goaded Victor into killing the messenger?

A syncopated clap-clap of hands. Quasi & Company finished the chorus: "Come on and have a good time!"

"Op, there it is again," said Neil.

No. Not by drugging a bottle of champagne that neither Victor nor anyone else could guess Bear would drink.

There were too many gaps in my picture. I needed more data.

I needed to talk to the missing vertex in this triangle: Marie Tréville.

"I'll find it." Dan hammered out a strum that fanned into a glissando, a fast survey of every note on his guitar.

"Search and destroy," Neil grinned.

My interviewees were debating whether they'd have time tomorrow morning for a quick visit to the Musée d'Orsay. I said go for it and excused myself. Near the galley doors I found a spot where I could lean against the wall, switch off my tape, and think.

Face it: I didn't have a clue who killed Albert Vaux. How should I? As Victor Tréville, John Otis, and Larry Thorne had all reminded me, crime-solving was a job for the police. I was a journalist, not a detective. My job (thank you, Dan Quasi) was to deal with my magazine.

Dan's impromptu guitar solo was drawing more spectators in from the deck. It did look like a performance: his body curved around his guitar, his head tilted back. One peg of Old Smoky caught the light, blazing like a small sun above his left hand.

"OK," Neil called. "I think we got it."

Dan stopped playing. "Gone," he confirmed.

He looked so single-minded. Head cocked, arm resting on his silver guitar. As if the biggest challenge he faced was getting rid of stray noises. I was jealous: How did Dan Quasi rate such tidy, finite problems?

"I need some more bass," Neil called. "Roach, you're decked out, right?"

Roach, who appeared to be asleep on his feet, opened his eyes.

"Turn it down a little onstage. And, Dan, I want to check your vocals."

Roach nodded, stretched, and reached for a knob.

"Roach." Dan turned. "Do you remember 'Film Noir'?"

"That old acoustic thing of yours?" He considered. "I can fake it."

"Vocals, acoustic guitar, and bass," Dan said to Neil. "How's that?"

"Perfect."

Dan slipped his Stratocaster off over his head; leaned it against a monitor, picked up the wooden Gibson beside it. "This song's for a friend out there who's been asking for it," he squinted into the lights, "though she doesn't know it."

My stomach tightened. Was he looking at me? No. He was nodding at Roach, setting the beat.

Good. I had enough balls to juggle without another curve

from Dan Quasi.

The melody that twined out of the speakers was wry, a tune for a late-night coffeehouse or a rainy afternoon. Oh, well, it seemed to say. Things didn't work out how we planned, did they?

Roach gazed into space. Dan leaned up to his mic.

"He's a movie-maker,
He's got no time for you . . ."

I stiffened.

"He's got things he's got to do . . ."

Some of the ambassadors moved in closer. I could feel my heart in my throat.

"He's got his mind on black-and-white,
No, he don't need your blues."

Dan's foot tapped lightly on the wooden platform. Why don't you write more songs like that? I'd asked him. Why don't you just act like a person?

"And if you show emotion
He will view it in slow motion—
He's got his mind on avant-garde,
No, he don't need your blues."

I glanced at the rest of the band. Terry was eating a sandwich. Lacey was making faces at Niko. Didn't anybody but me care what was happening here?

A movement over by the bar: Lena, coming to watch. She wasn't smiling.

"He fades in, he fades out,
While you pan from doubt to doubt,
Looking for
The frames that he cut out . . ."

I looked at all of him now: the tapping foot that had poked out from our sheet this morning, the hands that had touched places I'd shut away for months, his sweet wide mouth, and those blue, amazingly blue eyes. This was no rock star, flattened by stage lights to a poster. Or a rabble-rouser, or a murder suspect. He was a man who'd been left by a woman he loved, and he'd written this song to ask her to come back.

Lena stared up at Dan as though she'd never heard anything

so beautiful in her life. I wondered if he'd told her about Nicola.

But it's not just for Nicola, I thought; it's for me. He doesn't even know how much it's for me. Walking in slow steps down that endless aisle toward the altar where Larry's and my union would become holy in the eyes of Boston. Holding out my finger for the ring that would weigh down my hand till it couldn't grasp a pen or poise over a keyboard.

"He likes softer focus,
He don't like rougher edges;
He remembers you in dresses,
No, he don't like your rougher edges . . ."

I turned away to keep my swimming eyes from betraying me in front of all these people. I should be writing this down. Rik Green would love it: *Quasi fans stunned by bittersweet indictment of life in the limelight.*

"And you think that maybe time elapsed will fill the gaps . . ."

Past Dan's left shoulder a slim figure in a pale yellow dress slipped in through a door beside the stairs. Marie Tréville.

I would go ask her—whatever it was. I distinctly recalled having some urgent question. I'd remember it and go ask her. Only not right now.

"But still you see where you are—
Film noir."

Chapter 23: Film Noir

"That's good, Dan," Neil called. "I think we got it. You want to do one with the whole band? Maybe 'Time'?"

I blinked. The universe wheeled around my head and settled back into place.

Dan cupped his hand around his mic. "Kirk to Enterprise," he intoned. "All hands to battle stations."

Lacey stood up, shook out her arms, and sat down again. Niko popped a sandwich into his mouth. Terry picked up his drumsticks.

With an effort I focused on my surroundings. Boat. Ambassadors. Quasi & Company. Hands Across the Sea.

Marie Tréville. Where did she go? How had she escaped from her husband and Sheila Bailey?

"Ready when you are," called Neil.

Dan was switching guitars, trading his acoustic for Old Smoky. I'd hoped for contact—a smile, a look— Impossible. Not even if he could see I was here, which in all those lights wasn't likely.

"OK, you guys." Dan addressed the audience. "Are we ready to get *down*? Play some rock-&-*roll*?"

A few whoops. They knew their cues. More people were joining the crowd now, coming downstairs, moving in from the rail to the open floor in front of the band.

"I said, are you *ready?*"

Shouts ran like a wave around the circle. "Yeah! Rock-&-roll!"

I walked over to the board as they slammed into "Give Me Some Time." This was where I came in. I could still hear the bass and drum parts from sound check like a skeleton through the layers of music.

Neil had switched from his main control panel to a cubical blue box with tiny lights winking red and green. "How's it going?"

He shook his head. "Boats!" he said with feeling. "It's all glass and metal in here. We're getting blown away. François says you can't hear shit up top."

I read the hand-lettered tape labels next to his arm: flanger/dub, comp, echo, verb. "They're probably sightseeing up there, anyhow."

Neil's eyebrows lifted, as if anyone who'd pass up a chance to hear Quasi & Company shouldn't be on this boat.

In front of us people were hastily introducing themselves to prospective dance partners. I recalled John Otis's remarks about other Hands Across the Sea bands—that dancing was the key to success. How did Steve Connelly put it? *The girls come for the band, the guys come for the girls.* Was it that simple? Not Peace Corps for the fast track, but a classy alternative to personal ads and singles bars?

And there went Steve leading Lena onto the floor. Across the circle Gary Laporte glanced around anxiously, torn between his syllabus and an unattached Frenchwoman. The deck was throbbing from dozens of feet, rumbling from the boat's engines under us and the din of guitar and piano, organ, bass, and drums pounding from the speakers.

And speaking of sex and rock-&-roll . . .

Marie Tréville was nowhere to be seen. I passed Victor on the rear deck, still lecturing Sheila Bailey's punch-and-munchies brigade: *Chirac, tergiversation, maudit.* Back along the rail to the front . . . Could Marie be upstairs pointing out landmarks?

But as I reached the steps I noticed the door she'd come through earlier. It was stenciled "Passage Interdit"; above this someone had taped a hand-printed "No Entry. Keep Out." That was interesting. "Passage Interdit" literally means "Forbidden to Pass Through"—implying one *could* go through if one ignored the sign.

Once again I had the sensation of jumping down a hole after a white rabbit.

Behind the door was a narrow corridor leading toward the boat's bow and ending with a turn into a triangular area barely wide enough to fit a pair of deck chairs. There weren't any chairs

—the stiff breeze blowing up from the river would have tossed them right over the rail. The sun was fairly warm, but the wind sent me back inside.

What would have brought Marie Tréville out here? Tracking down a missing ambassador? Taking a break from Sheila & Company?

On the upper deck I finally spotted her white gardenia. Marie's hand rested on the rail; the fringe of her shawl fluttered out over the river. Like her husband, she'd gathered an audience. "The name 'Place du Parvis' comes from the Middle Ages, when the people acted out mystery plays in front of the church. The porch represented *paradis*—heaven—which shortened over the years into *parvis*."

Marie upstairs talking of paradise, Victor downstairs consigning France's government to perdition, and in between Quasi & Company tending to the grubby human here-and-now.

They finished their first set as we came up on the Île de la Cité. Apparently this was planned: Marie stepped up with a formal smile to Dan's mic, which he lowered to her height. The band, though, didn't leave. Lacey stretched; Niko folded his hands behind his head. Only Roach and Dan came offstage and sat in chairs to watch, leaning back, their feet sticking out at her in tattered sneakers.

Marie glanced uneasily at the three musicians behind her. On our left, she announced, we could see the Jardin des Tuileries, the garden outside the Louvre, laid out on the site of an old tile works. The bridge we were now passing under was the Pont du Carrousel, named for the Place du Carrousel and the small arch of triumph beside it.

Dan clapped. Roach stood up and strolled back to Neil's vacant stool behind the sound board. He rested his elbows on the board, his chin in his hands.

"In just a moment we will be alongside the Louvre itself, the world's finest art museum—or so we French like to think! The Louvre was built originally as a fortress by King Philippe Auguste in the year 1200—"

Her voice deepened into an echo. It reverberated from the

speakers the way Elvis Presley used to reverberate through my high-school boyfriend's convertible. At the sound board, Roach was now using only one hand to hold up his chin.

Dan looked around in amusement. Marie faltered and then went on resolutely: "Many French monarchs over the years rebuilt and enlarged the Louvre, often using it as a palace. In 1682 the court left for Versailles"—her voice went flat—"and the building was let to tenants. It was Napoleon Bonaparte who expelled the trespassers . . ."

Roach was getting into it. To each change in the French fortunes he gave a change in tone: a full rich steely sound for Napoleon, vibrato for kings, lots of echo for Notre Dame, slightly less for artworks. Marie began by pretending not to notice, but it was clear Roach's game was unnerving her. The funny thing was that the sound shifts were actually helping her speech. I didn't see a soul who wasn't listening.

By the time she came to Sainte-Chapelle, she was losing her composure. She stopped once to wipe her forehead, again when she stammered over a name. That was when Victor strode in and clamped a hand on Roach's shoulder.

Dan was on his feet and halfway to the board before I took it in. Roach turned to knock Victor's hand away, then reached again for the box beside the board. Victor grabbed his arm. If they spoke, I couldn't hear it over Marie's amplified voice. I caught one glimpse of Victor's face in the beam of Neil's tensor lamp: he was furious.

". . . part of the Palais de Justice," his wife echoed helplessly, "on a site used for administrative purposes since the Roman governors."

Dan pulled Roach away from the board—not to stop him but to keep the fight away from the equipment. Victor swung at Roach. Roach swung back. Dan lunged for Victor's arms. Victor hit him with an elbow in the stomach.

". . . the Revolution, when the judicial system was overturned—"

Steve Connelly loped across the deck, with Sheila Bailey trotting frantically behind him. Dan had pinned Victor's arms to his sides. Roach stepped back. Steve charged through the gap and flung himself on Dan. Victor seized his chance and walloped Roach, knocking him into the padded edge of the board. Dan shook off Steve and went for Victor, poised for another punch at Roach. Steve aimed a fist at Dan's back which hit his shoulder and shoved him against Victor.

I didn't know what to do. Marie pressed both hands to her mouth in horror. The audience was starting to realize something was amiss. The people closest to the board had backed off when the fight started, but a couple of them now moved in, glowing with the thrill of battle.

Roach swung around and landed his fist right above Steve's camera. Dan grabbed a double handful of yellow sweater and yanked hard. Victor leapt on Roach from behind.

"Pa-dum pa *dum* dum *dum* dum *dee* ah-dah!"

It was the band: or more precisely, Terry on drums.

"Allons, enfants de la patrie!

Le jour de gloire est arrivé!"

Lacey followed him valiantly, guessing the chords and faking the words. François ran up to vault onstage and assist Niko at the mic. And Hands Across the Sea's two hundred ambassadors from Boston, where *Casablanca* is practically a religious event, joined their hosts in joyful chorus:

"Contre nous de la tyrannie

L'étendard sanglant est levé!"

Marie Tréville gaped at Niko and François. Then she heard the voices singing all over the boat, looked out and saw rank upon rank of faces turned toward the stage, eyes shining with patriotism, fists swinging to the martial beat; and she moved in beside François at the mic.

"L'étendard sanglant est levé!"

Steve straightened up. Victor's head swerved. Dan let go of Steve's sweater. Sheila Bailey goggled. Roach sneaked back to the sound board to mix "La Marseillaise" for drums, synthesizer, and vocals.

I stepped into the light at the edge of the dance floor and waved a V sign of peace at Terry.

But on Victor Tréville's face it was still war. "Get away from there!" he shouted at Roach. "Damn you, get away!"

"Mugir ces feroces soldats!" sang the crowd.

Steve shook Dan's shoulder. "You better stop this!"

"Stop what?" Dan lifted an eyebrow. "The French national anthem?"

"Get him away from that machine! You've got Mr. and Mrs. Tréville very upset!

I looked up. Marie was singing bravely: "Aux armes, citoyens!"

"Don't worry about her," Dan told Steve. "She's cool."

Victor's round face puckered with rage. "That is my *wife!*"

Neil had been hovering at the edge of the vicious circle around his board. Now he elbowed in. "Well, what the fuck you doin,' Roach?" he inquired. "You want to back off my rack and get your ass onstage?"

So that's what that box is, I thought distractedly: a rack.

"She's all yours," said Roach. Meaning the sound system or Marie?

"Qu'un sang impure," roared the chorus in triumph,

"Abbreuve nos sillons!"

A final *pum-pa-dum* on the bass drum; then cheers, applause, shouts and stomping feet. Marie smiled graciously. Roach bowed beside the platform. Lacey and Niko grinned at each other.

But Victor was not mollified. "Insupportable!" he sputtered at Sheila Bailey. "Stop the boat! Throw them off! Throw them off at once!"

Poor Sheila was wilting. I wished I could explain to her about the French penchant for melodrama.

"Monsieur Tréville," Steve intervened, "if I can speak for Hands Across the Sea—"

But Victor railed on. "A disgrace to this program! A disgrace to Boston, Massachusetts! No gratitude, no regard for the hospitality of *la France!* And my poor wife, who planned with such care her exposition—to be so insulted!"

I glanced at the stage. Victor's poor wife was making a quick exit. Dan stopped her at the edge of the platform. I couldn't hear him, but from the way he touched her arm and bent his head toward hers he must have been urging her to stay.

Sheila, meanwhile, verged on tears. Victor had hit full stride: shoulders squared, chin up, eyes and voice crackling with anger. Steve hovered with a smile ready, awaiting his moment to jump in and patch things up.

Shit, I thought, they're not upset. They're enjoying this. Both of them. With poor gullible Sheila as audience.

Not me, boys.

I fled across the half-empty dance floor. Neil didn't seem to hear the tirade behind his back. His eyes were on Dan, his hands resting on the board: rock-&-roll next or a vocal solo? When he reached for a lever I looked at the stage. Marie was walking back out into the spotlight.

"I am deeply touched to see that so many Americans know our French national anthem," came her voice from the speaker over my head.

At the bar Lena poured punch for herself and Betsy. She smiled when she saw me and handed me a plastic cup.

"Boy, they're something, aren't they?"

Betsy interrupted, "What are they doing in Hands Across the Sea? This is so amazing! Lena said you're staying with them? Hanging out at their hotel?"

I glanced back at the sound board. Victor Tréville and Sheila Bailey were shaking hands. Steve's bright yellow back radiated satisfaction.

"It was my hotel first." I wished Betsy would stop staring as if I were a celebrity. Four or five other ambassadors had joined us, full of questions: Was it true Quasi & Company were releasing an album when we got back? With one of Steve's photos on the cover? How about the video? Would they let their Hands Across the Sea fans be in it?

"They're right over there," I said. "Ask them."

"But they're not talking," one of the women objected. "They're getting ready to play."

"Great!" Lena said emphatically. "Let's go hear 'em!"

The dance floor was filling with spectators again. Marie

Tréville must have finished her remarks; François was raising Dan's mic, calling orders to the kid in the Marines sweatshirt across the stage. Dan stood with one foot on a monitor and Old Smoky on his knee, not visibly bothered by the chaos around him, tuning to the orange crescent of a strobe which whirled and slowed into patterns as he set it, plucked a string, watched, and set it again.

Maverick the riverboat gambler, I thought with a surge of affection, spinning the wheel one more time.

Lena nudged me. "So, Cory, how'd you like 'Film Noir'?"

I took in the designer rings on the hand holding her punch cup, her smooth bronze skin under the linked gold medallions inside her half-open shirt, her shining dark curls, and her jungle-fern eyelashes. *Hey, Dan, what happened to your girlfriend?*

"I liked it a lot."

Lena smiled. I drew some comfort from noticing her eye shadow had started to cake.

"And you?"

"Oh!" Lena's lashes wafted up. "I thought it was incredible." She glanced around for a place to put her empty cup, didn't see one, cracked it and dropped it on the floor. "You're a lucky woman, you know that?"

I must have looked startled, because she laughed and said, "Terry told me. Did you know we spent last night together?"

In my head orange crescents spun around and failed to line up. "You—?"

Lena nodded. "Talking." She blushed. "Can you believe? I haven't done that since college! And never with a rock musician. Cory, he's such a sweetie. He showed me pictures of his kids—"

A rapid *thump-pip-pip-pip* of drums and a splash of guitar drowned her out. Lena grinned expressively and turned to watch the band.

My eyes shifted, but the tableau onstage didn't stop the tumult in my brain. Lacey was up front singing. Dan stood nearby with Old Smoky, his eyes half shut, the backs of his knees reflected in the transparent skin of Terry's bass drum, twitching with the beat.

He's a sweetie. Not Dan—Terry. Walking her to the bus after we built the float. Sharing cocoa and sandwiches when they came back from Paris last night.

"I looked him in the eye," sang Lacey,

"I said, You know how I feel!"

And all this time I thought—

"O-o-o-oh,

'Bout the dynamite wheels!" sang Quasi & Company.

"Dynamite wheels!" shouted the ambassadors.

Terry's sticks flickered from snare to tom to hi-hat. I turned to Lena, but she was running onto the dance floor with one of the Alligator Brothers.

For a few more bars my brain went on attempting to arrange data in a meaningful order; but the screen kept dissolving in images. A football spiraling across a quad. Bare feet running over new grass after a frisbee. Hot sun, cold beer, charcoal-grilled burgers . . . and Mickey Ascher's voice blasting from the windows, luring me out of my stifled dorm room into the first car headed for a party.

Through waving arms in half-light I saw Gary Laporte watching the band through his wire-rims. Betsy stood by the bar with a sandwich in her hand and a big grin on her face. Here and there all over the deck old Rind fans were listening as if we'd never heard "Dynamite Wheels" before—which in a way we hadn't.

At the end, the final crash of guitar and cymbals, we clapped so hard that Lacey bowed, smiled, then waved, and then shot a puzzled look at Dan. Terry had raised his sticks for the next song, but when the applause kept on coming he laid them down again.

"I'm the One!" somebody shouted. People were yelling from everywhere: "Government Man!" "Wonderland!" "Tear It Up!"

"Thank you!" said Dan, and signaled to Terry, who signaled to Niko. Apparently all this enthusiasm was causing a change of plans.

"OK!" Dan held up both hands. "Thanks!"

He nodded to the band. A rumble of drums. From the audience, shrieks of approval.

Steve Connelly jumped down from the chair he'd been standing on to shoot photos.

I scanned the crowd, the bar, the sound board, the rail; and I didn't see the Trévilles.

Niko leaned up to his mic with an evil smile.

"You're smokin' down the highway,

With your baby there beside you,

Better empty out that ashtray,

'Cause he's comin' up behind you!"

Were the faces on the dance floor leering back at him, or was it this eerie light?

"He's the government man!" they sang gleefully.

Steve's yellow sweater pushed through the crowd toward the rear deck. I went after him.

"Watch out, friend,

when you're in the hands

of the government man!"

Though the sky had an hour to go till dusk, someone had lit the Japanese lanterns around the stern. Victor and Marie Tréville stood under bobbing colored globes chatting with a group of ambassadors.

Well, of course, I realized with relief. What can they do but ignore it?

Steve headed toward them full of apologies and halted as he saw what a faux pas he was about to commit.

I started back inside, but Steve was quicker. "Cory." He caught my arm. "We need to talk."

"Why?" I inquired as he steered me to an empty corner of the afterdeck. "Camera trouble?"

Steve indicated a bench. I shook my head. I didn't mind missing the rest of "Government Man," but in two more minutes I intended to be back inside.

His smile was grim. "It's time you and I were straight with each other."

I gestured at our sweaters, his Gap khakis, my Liz Claiborne slacks. "How much straighter can we get?"

"There's a couple things I haven't told you. Like why I'm

here shooting pictures instead of Wendy Peres."

Off our stern, brown water was churning into white in the V of our wake. It's contagious, I thought. A melodrama epidemic.

"When Hands Across the Sea's plane took off last Wednesday night, the band was this close to not being on it. Governor Leroy agreed to take the risk—The Rind's reputation, the unsolved Ascher murder—on one condition. Somebody directly responsible to him had to keep an eye on them."

"Let me guess," I said.

He waited as if I'd been serious. After a couple seconds I asked, "Why you?"

"The right credentials."

"What, are you running for something in November?"

"I have a strong media background, as you should have noticed by now. I know the sixties music scene and what to expect from these people."

"Oh, right. How could I forget?—you moonlight in radio."

"Thanks to my Rind connection," he snapped.

That surprised me. It surprised Steve, too. Evidently he hadn't meant to be that straight.

"Partly," he amended. "And other bands. The whole—"

"What Rind connection?"

He shook his head, brushing it off. "Tangent. Not important."

"Come on, Steve. After that build-up?"

I could almost see the cogs in his brain turning. His elbow rested on the rail. "Just one of those things." Gazing at the river, his voice light. "Someone I was close to who was close to them."

"A woman." Obviously. "Ex-girlfriend?"

A nod; a rueful smile.

"Yours and who else's?"

"Yes, I do mind you asking." He faced me. "I took on the governor's assignment because I believe in what he's trying to do. This kind of international dialogue. Sharing ideas, technology, culture. It may sound corny to you, but I see Hands Across the Sea as a crucial step toward resolving economic and political instability—building bridges at the grass-roots level."

I reached for my tape recorder. Nobody I'd interviewed all weekend had come up with a line that quotable.

"Off the record." Steve shooed it away. "Anyhow, that's why I'm here. To make sure Dan Quasi and his band don't fuck that up."

Across the water loomed the mountainous peaks and arches of Notre Dame de Paris. Two hundred years it took them to build that cathedral; and another century and a half before Christopher Columbus discovered there was a continent across the Atlantic to have exchange programs with.

"Don't forget taking pictures," I said.

Steve laid his hand flat on the rail. "This isn't a joke, Cory."

"I'm not joking. To you it may be a sideline, but to me it's my job."

"Well, I'm sorry you feel that way. I was hoping you'd appreciate this is more than just a job we're talking about. As a friend of John Otis," he added pointedly.

A streak of anger shot through me, clenching my fists and my jaw. "Friendship is beside the point. I'm a journalist, not a Green Beret."

"There was a saying about that in the sixties. If you're not part of the solution, you're part of the problem."

"What problem?" I turned on him. "The band's back on the boat. You said yourself they were kicked off for suspicion of involvement in Albert Vaux's death. So, what? The police are satisfied, Hands Across the Sea is satisfied, but not you?"

OK, that wasn't totally straight. Did I need Steve Connelly hanging around my neck like a Nikon?

"We have no proof anyone's satisfied," he retorted stiffly. "I asked Sheila Bailey what the story is and she said ask Marie Tréville. I asked Marie and she gave me the same old crap about wiring problems." He slapped the rail. "Nobody around here knows who's making the goddamned decisions!"

It came out louder than he'd intended. He lowered his voice: "The governor's office should have an update by the time we land. Meanwhile, you can tell Quasi & Company: Just because they let you play on this boat, don't think you're home free. EuroDisney's canceled, and it's up to the police and Hands Across the Sea if they'll be on that plane back to Boston tomorrow."

I looked past him at Notre Dame, eight hundred years old and silent as a rock. I wished this were *Mission: Impossible* and Steve Connelly would start to hiss and then gradually disintegrate in a plume of smoke.

"So, whatever rabbit's foot Dan Quasi has in his pocket? Now's the time to use it."

"Rabbit's foot?"

"Mojo, then. John the Conqueroo. Whatever the hell makes him think he can do any goddamn thing he wants and never get busted."

"Right," I said. "I'll be sure to tell him that."

Chapter 24: Government Man

Dan Quasi had his own message to deliver.

After "Government Man" ended, in a long climactic roll of every instrument onstage, he shook his wet hair and croaked into his mic. "We're taking a short break—"

Groans of protest from the dancers who'd staggered to a sweaty halt on the floor, sagging and clapping.

"But first an announcement." He wiped his forehead on his forearm. "You might have heard we got axed from EuroDisney tonight."

From their surprised frowns and murmurs, they hadn't.

"The preview of our new multimedia show *Mickey Rat*."

Louder murmurs of sympathy. Even people who hadn't been dancing had moved in to listen.

"It's OK. It's still on. Only instead of a big outdoor stage, you can hear *Mickey Rat* up close in a French nightclub. The Club Souris."

A lone spectator clapped wildly and yelled: "Mouse Club! Hurray!"

Laughter and a few cheers. Dan nodded, grinning. I scanned the rest of the band for reactions and saw only that they were hot and tired, ready for punch and sandwiches.

"François has directions. Where's François?" He peered into the darkness. "Back there by the board. What? OK! François says you can see the Club Souris from Sleeping Beauty's Castle."

A flash as Steve Connelly shot a picture. Yes, this was a moment worth recording. How much chance the band had cleared their invitation with Hands Across the Sea? About as much as that Victor Tréville would dash in from the afterdeck to thank them for solving an awkward problem.

Dan stepped off the platform, followed by Terry, Lacey, and Roach, followed by a swarm of fans. I crossed the empty deck to Niko, standing alone in the lights. He'd opened the lid of his spinet piano and was fishing inside with a long-stemmed tool and a flashlight.

Neil's voice floated over from the darkness. "Talk."

Niko sat behind his vocal mic. "Check, one, two. Sound check. Rain check. Hat check."

I took out my notebook, though I had nothing to write. "Problems?"

"Double check." Niko tossed me a smile. "Truck check. Boat check."

Steve the dog had migrated from the piano to Lacey's organ. I picked it up, whopped its yellow stuffed head, and dropped it back on the keyboard.

Niko's eyebrows lifted. "Checkmate."

"Check you." That was Terry, returning with a double fistful of sandwiches.

"Check you. Chekhov. Czechoslovakia."

Terry held out a full hand. I shook my head. "The Club Souris, huh?"

"Yup." He bit off half a sandwich. "Oh, good, chicken. I keep getting"—he chewed, swallowed—"the ones with leaves. What is that stuff?"

"Watercress." Recalling tea at the Plaza Court. Where just a week ago (was it possible?) I'd met John Otis in the Grand Ballroom to toast his exchange program, dodge personal questions, and find out if Hands Across the Sea's Mystery Band was a scoop or a crock.

"Un checking believable!" Niko boomed.

"Was Major Strasser giving you a hard time?"

I blinked back to the present.

"Your photographer," said Terry. "I saw you getting the third degree out there."

I had to smile. "He was trying." A chuckle from Terry at the pun. "I meant to ask: did you know him before? During The Rind?"

"Not that I remember. But, so many people, such a long time ago— Why?"

"Terry?" The disembodied voice of Neil. "I need your riding

tom."

He waved an OK.

"He mentioned a connection with The Rind. Through a woman. His girlfriend."

"That would be Mickey." Terry flashed me a bacchanalian grin. "Mickey was into everybody's girlfriend."

To erratic bursts of drumfire, I searched the boat. Silently I cried to Notre Dame across the churning water: *Sanctuary!*

Sanctuary from the pile of mismatched jobs ahead of me: call John Otis for news, find Marie Tréville for missing pieces, decide if it mattered if Mickey Ascher stole Steve Connelly's girlfriend twenty years ago.

Sanctuary for five minutes alone with Dan Quasi.

He'd given me "Film Noir" and I hadn't had a chance to thank him. Forget words. If there was a patch of privacy on this boat, I'd tell him in the language we used last night.

So, where was he?

Not at the bar. Not near the stage. Not in the galley. A man coming out of *Hommes* assured me he wasn't there, either.

I was about to try the upper deck again when I remembered the door marked "Passage Interdit."

The corridor was darker than before, and chilly. I hugged my arms tight against me for warmth.

Just before the turn onto the bow I heard voices.

I moved cautiously along the cold steel wall, though any noise would be drowned out by the boat's engines and the wind blowing up from the river. Hard to tell what they were saying . . . but I was sure one was Dan.

His voice rose. "So what do you want me to do?"

The answering voice was higher, lighter—a woman's. She sounded upset, as if they'd been arguing about something that mattered intensely to her and he refused to fight over.

"Haven't I seen you every chance I get?" Dan's voice was on edge. "You were the one who walked out. Ever since—"

She interrupted. I couldn't catch the words, but it sounded like she was crying.

"... don't give me such a hard time ..."

"... same thing at all!" Breaking off in a sob.

"... call you at home ... crazy schedule ..."

"... where you were!" she replied hotly. "No message— what could I think but you didn't care?"

A scuffling sound, then a low wail. I had a vivid and painful vision of her head buried in his shoulder, his arms around her, comforting her.

Gritting my teeth, I inched closer.

"You don't know how hard it is!" Her voice was still trembling, broken with sobs. "To set aside so much, make up lies and excuses—and then, last night, to say, All right! Yes! Even this I will do for him!"

"I know," Dan soothed. "It's OK. You're OK. Come on, now." Still gently, but with a trace of impatience. "You don't ... with your face all ... do you? Anyhow, we can't get this straight now."

Straight. Everything straight. As if this weekend were a bent coat hanger that everyone here felt obliged to wrench back into shape.

"But what other chance will we have?" she cried. "You leave me to make arrangements, and then you are busy! Now ... leaving tomorrow ... no more time ..."

What it was they had to get straight I still wasn't sure. I did know who she was, though. I also knew that it was because I'd guessed it in my heart days ago that I'd come out here looking for him. Them.

"She's got nothing to do with it." Dan's voice was abruptly clear. "You know that. She's totally irrelevant. I told you the other night."

"But what about *me?*"

"What do you mean, what about you?"

"You talk about her, your music, your obligations—"

"I can't get into this again. Not now." A clank of something hitting the deck. "Let's go. All those people in there—"

"Let them wait."

"Come on . . ."

"No! I won't leave it like this! I can't!"

"Suit yourself." Dan's voice was curt. "I've got a gig to finish."

I walked quickly back to the door. I didn't want to run into him. I wanted to prolong this moment before it fully hit me how little I meant to Dan Quasi.

Somehow I wound up by the sound board with a large plastic cup of champagne in my hand. Neil had Roach on the platform now playing bass. Lacey stood in front of her organ, shaking her arms, lolling her head, loosening up. They all looked bright and far away. Then the band was back, and the deck was full of people clapping as Dan walked onto the stage.

"Cory." I turned to see François smiling at me. "Want to dance?"

The sun hung from the edge of the roof like a golden spotlight. Soon it would be *l'heure bleue,* when the sky turned the color of faded denim and the river went dark. When new acquaintances winked on like the streetlamps of Paris.

Paris, city of light, city of magic! Paris, mon amour!

Whirling under Japanese lanterns, I shut my eyes to slits. I wouldn't listen to the band, only the music. Bubbling in my blood like champagne, singing in my head, my arms and legs, my hair swirling across my face as we danced. Drums in my feet; piano chords twinkling through my skin.

The music paused, then started up again. A slow number. My old favorite, "The End of the Night." Would this night ever end? François pulled me against him. I wrapped myself in his arms and drifted on the river of sound flowing over us. His chest was warm, his hands strong, caressing my back.

A voice behind me. Someone loomed over François's shoulder. Curly hair, yellow sweater. Steve Connelly. His lips made the shape of my name.

The music was fading away. No! Wait! I wanted to call out. Don't stop!

"Sorry to interrupt."

François's fingers stayed twined in mine.

"Have either of you seen Marie Tréville?"

We shook our heads.

"Nobody's seen her since the break. Her husband's getting pretty anxious."

"Oh la la!" said François, and made a gesture with his free hand which conveyed concern, sympathy, and a soupçon of amusement.

"Sheila Bailey checked the ladies' room and she isn't there. She doesn't seem to be anywhere on the boat."

"Give her a while," I said.

"She was upset about Roach fucking up her speech, pardon my French. I hope she's not . . ."

"She'll be all right," I said. "She's probably just fixing her face before she comes back out."

"Out of where, though?" said Steve.

The music was starting again: a rattle of drums, a splash of organ. François slid his arm around my waist. "Well, we have not got her!"

And the band sang: "Baby, don't waste it!

Come on and taste it, taste it!"

"Too much champagne," I told François. "I need air."

He must have seen I didn't want company, because he didn't follow me. I edged through the other dancers to the afterdeck. With François pressing me close and slow for the last two fast numbers, my wine-dulled self-protective instincts had finally clicked in.

I stared out at the water, at the Paris skyline across the Seine, and I breathed in the cool musky air rising from the river. Why not François? His Gallic assurance was certainly attractive, and the way he dressed and moved—a refreshing change from the rough-hewn style of Quasi & Company. If he'd noticed I was older than most of the women he'd been flirting with this weekend, it didn't appear to bother him. Frenchmen had a better perspective on that sort of thing than Americans. He obviously either didn't know of my brief fling with Dan or didn't care. So why not? I could tell from the way he danced that he'd be good in bed. And after tomorrow I'd never see him again. Wasn't that how it worked on the road?

Dan Quasi and Marie Tréville.

Just one flash, one quick lifting of the curtain, and my insides clenched in pain. This was no good. Better to go back inside and dance. Submerge myself in the beat—let my body do the thinking. Keep my head out of it. Stupid to stand on an empty deck turning over incidents like puzzle pieces and wincing when they matched up.

That first night at the banquet, for instance. She wasn't frightened for her husband's safety; she was impatient for Dan's answer to the note she'd sent him in the dressing room. And when it came, she ran out to a phone: Don't wait up, chéri. I'll stay in town with my cousin.

She must have been furious when she found out Quasi & Company had canceled the Eiffel Tower gig. No wonder Dan dodged her call at the hotel. After all her maneuvering to get them over here, now she had to make excuses to the committee—and Victor. When Dan wouldn't speak to her, she'd badgered Terry and insisted he give Dan the message.

Wrong move, Marie. You should have known he hates being hassled about his band.

I chafed my hands together. No warmth out here under the cold sun. Only the muffled throb of boat engines, drums, and bass.

Bass. Wait. If Marie had been Roach's girlfriend, how could Dan—committed as he was to The Rind—

But that wouldn't work. If I'd learned anything about him this weekend, it was that Dan Quasi didn't play those games by other people's rules. Why should he? Other people were his audience: star-crazed fans who sent him drugs, horoscopes, love letters, room keys. What could we tell him about normal?

The rhythm of the engines slowed. I realized the song must have ended when half a dozen dancers came running out to the stern. One woman lifting her heavy blonde hair off her neck, panting gratefully as she leaned over the rail; another couple laughing, flapping their arms to cool off.

Nowhere to go on this damned finite boat that wasn't full of happy faces high on rock-&-roll. And still the grand finale to get through.

Well, only one more day, thank god. Tomorrow night I'd be standing in my own sublet living room, staring out at the Charles instead of the Seine. Familiar, boring Boston and its dirty water. Where Dan Quasi would shrink back into a name in my notebook, and—with luck—my passport to the July 4 cover of Phases.

Several hours later, or it might have been twenty minutes, our boat bumped gently against the dock beside the Pont d'Iéna. My head was still muzzy with champagne and depression, but I was so glad to see terra firma I hardly cared. I elbowed through the crowd around the band, lined up for the exit, and hoped nobody would talk to me.

François and his crew were unscrewing microphones, nesting the heads in boxes and stacking the stands. Only Lacey remained onstage. Slumped over her keyboard with her fingers to her temples—a headache? meditating? Not like Lacey to deflate after a set.

The line hadn't moved. I gauged the distance between Lacey and François and concluded I could reach her without running into him.

"Lacey?"

She lifted her head: eyes ringed with black, smudged with purple. "Hi, Cory." She forced a smile in case this was official. "What's happenin'?"

"Not much." I was about to pat her shoulder and tell her not to bother acting cheerful; but realized from her expectant look that Lacey had just finished a performance, and I was the only press here, and what she wanted wasn't sympathy but recognition.

"You sounded terrific," I said.

"Yeah?" She clearly thought so too, but she was glad to hear it. "'Wheels' came off better tonight, huh? What'd you think of 'Standard Deviation'? We haven't played that out before. It's a new one of Niko's."

"Which one was that?"

"Fourth number in the third set. Right after 'Taste It.' Like this." She hummed and snapped her fingers.

"Oh, right." That fast one François and I had danced slow to. "I liked it. Not exactly my speed, but—"

Lacey grinned. "You sure looked like you liked it."

I was disconcerted. "You could see me all the way back there?"

"You and François were right under the light. You guys were the only interesting thing out there." Lacey went on blithely, "Niko was calling you Couple Number One. He wanted to give you a prize."

Oh, great. The whole band watching me with François. Still, one corner of my mind was defiantly glad.

"We're playing with them tonight, François's band. You haven't heard him yet, have you? He's really good." Not in the tone of a fellow keyboard player but of a woman praising another woman's lover.

"Lacey, I'm not getting into a thing with François."

Her eyebrows went up; but I was more surprised than she was.

"Well, you still should come. He's got a brand-new Kurzweil," she sighed. "I can't wait!"

They were letting people off the boat now. I told Lacey maybe I'd see her later and walked around to the bar as if for a sandwich, though the last crumbs had vanished an hour ago. At the end of the dock Victor Tréville's brown Citroën sat idling. Up here, Niko stood on the afterdeck talking to Rachel . . . Terry nearby with his arm around Lena . . . Roach flirting over the rail at every woman he could make eye contact with. All present and accounted for but one.

I stationed myself a discreet distance from the door marked "Keep Out." They had to know Victor would be looking for her. They wouldn't stay there long.

The door clicked. I stepped into the shadows.

She came out first: swift steady beat of high heels on the steel deck. Patting at her hair. She looked perfectly composed, like a cat that's just polished off a mouse. A smile for Sheila Bailey at the gangplank; an apologetic nod at the Citroën—sorry I can't stay and help, but *he* has other commitments.

I waited.

In half a minute the door clicked again, and then Dan walked by, tucking his dark blue T-shirt into his jeans.

"Are you driving to EuroDisney?"

"Well—actually—" Steve looked uncomfortable. "I'm going to the Club Souris. With the band. Aren't you?"

"Are you serious?" My voice in my ears sounded remarkably calm. "What about the job? Hands Across the Sea?"

"Well, but what about Phases? I mean—Jesus, Cory!" He pointed down at the dock. "All those people are going to hear Quasi & Company. They made Sheila Bailey reroute one of the buses. Victor Tréville's having a fit and I don't blame him. Half of our ambassadors!"

He was backpedaling so hard that I'd have laughed if I weren't afraid I'd cry.

"Stick with the band. They'll take you in the limo." He clapped my shoulder. "I'm giving rides to everybody who'll fit in Max's car."

Steve wedged himself into the human stream flowing down the gangplank. Inside, a queue still waited alongside the stage. François and his assistant rushed around stripping tape off wires, clipping tops onto speakers, hauling hatboxes full of drums to the edge of the deck where a forklift would carry them to the truck.

I should be able to get on a EuroDisney bus . . .

But no. Steve was right. I'd done my job for Hands Across the Sea. The two loose ends still flapping in the breeze were my promise to John Otis to keep an eye on the band, and my Phases cover story.

This time tomorrow nothing here would be real. I could hang on that long.

Chapter 25: Give Me Some Time

From the train, Marcel Proust described the church of Combray as hovering over the huddled houses and fields like a shepherdess gathering her sheep.

The landscape has changed since 1913.

Quasi & Company's limo whisked us into the Marne river valley on the A4 expressway. In pneumatic silence we glided past farms (some with sheep), cottages, churches, here and there a gas station or convenience store. Once they'd belonged to villages; now they were part of the "new town" of Marne-la-Vallée.

I didn't see the current train, a rapid-transit commuter line from Paris. Our train was a line of cars and buses trailing behind the band's limo like the Main Street choo-choo.

The deal was, we'd all drive together from the boat to the reception center. Then the band group would head for the Club Souris, while the others got greeted, oriented, name-tagged, and packed back into buses for—

EuroDisney. 1,482 acres housing the theme park (29 rides and attractions, 30 restaurants, 36 shops); the Entertainment Center (two dance clubs, a post office, and Buffalo Bill's Wild West Show); Davy Crockett Campground (414 rental trailers, 181 campsites); six hotels, and a golf course. More than 5,000 employees of 180 companies had planted 160,000 trees, carved 21,000 cubic feet of man-made rock for Big Thunder Mountain, attached 900 branches to the trunk for the Swiss Family Robinson Treehouse, and installed 300 artificial cacti and 3 animated coyotes. No Matterhorn—evidently the Europeans were happy with their existing one. Four years to build it; no one knew how long till it made a profit.

Off the A4 onto the D231; and there, rising from the beet fields, loomed a bright blue cone as tall as the Chartres spire. Its white stars and crescent moon glowed pink in the setting sun. A magician's hat, the driver informed us—matter-of-factly, as if cartoon buildings were as common here as cathedrals.

The rest of the reception center appeared as we approached: a ring of gold pillars under the hat, burnished to bronze by the fading light; a yellow wall festooned with blue squiggles and red polka dots . . .

No wonder the farmers ignored our caravan.

To my relief, the band likewise ignored the costumed animals who capered around the car for a photo opportunity. We took off again—narrowly missing a bear—without waiting for the entourage.

The town of Torcy must have ballooned after the forces of Disney bought up the surrounding sugar-beet fields. Past Lacey's head I saw a lot of new-looking steel, concrete, and plate glass. Strings of giant colored beads, like Japanese lanterns, formed construction barriers. Shepherding such drastic change, Victor Tréville might well have made enemies.

The limo pulled into a side street which proved to be the back way into Le Club Souris. The sky was growing dark as we made our entrance: first Dan, Terry, and Roach, then Niko with Lacey on one arm and me on the other.

Down a flight of steps into a basement. The front door was off the tiled central corridor of an underground mall, Lacey explained. Not the intimate French nightclub setting I'd expected from Dan's invitation. Inside, though, the familiar stale reek of cigarette smoke and beer took me straight back to all-night parties in fraternity-house cellars. "That smell!"

"Eau de bar," Niko nodded.

We had to wait outside a swinging door while the bouncer called the bartender, the bartender called the manager, and finally somebody came out to escort Quasi & Company to their dressing room. I hadn't planned to stay with the band, but the fuss with which they were hustled across the floor and out a door by the stage made me realize that once I split off, I might not get back in. So I followed them down a shabby carpeted hall to a room stacked with cardboard cartons and beer kegs, and hoped they'd be too preoccupied to notice.

I needn't have worried. Roach and Niko immediately started

arguing over the set list. Dan listened for five seconds and walked out. Terry opened the guitar case he'd been carrying and strummed loud enough to drown them out.

Lacey nudged me. "Let's hit the john."

Not many people yet in this cavernous space. And no tables, only standing room. On the club walls frolicked a gallery of garishly painted cartoon characters: dressed-up dogs and mice, dancing hippos and ostriches, bunnies, deer, songbirds, fairy-tale heroines, chipmunks, donkeys, animated playing cards, dwarfs, evil queens. None of them looked much like the originals—to avoid lawsuits?—and their poses would have stood Big Walt's hair on end. The mural behind the bar, an underwater scene featuring two buxom and acrobatic mermaids, was aptly labeled "Humpback Whale Moby Dick."

I asked Lacey why the guys were so touchy. She scowled and said Roach was bummed about doing the Rat, Niko was pissed at Dan for not shutting him up, Terry was bummed not to play EuroDisney after they'd come all this way. "And *I'm* pissed at Roach because he's such an asshole."

She sounded alarmingly sincere. "What do you mean?"

Lacey made a face. "Him and his little girls. What about me?"

The john was down a hall near the bar. Except for lacking kegs and cartons, it was as unappetizing as the dressing room: red walls scrawled with magic marker, paint flaking into the sink. And empty; so I asked, "Why doesn't Roach want to do the Rat?"

Lacey entered a stall. "He says, these people want to hear Rind songs, so why fight it? Plus there's no point since EuroDisney fell through. Plus we don't know it that well; plus we shouldn't do it in pieces instead of a whole show. But really he's just not that into it." A pause. "How do you flush this thing?"

"There should be a chain to pull in the back."

Lacey flushed and came out, zipping her jeans. "You know Roach—Mr. Sixties. He'd rather keep the band all natural ingredients," her nose wrinkled, "like granola or something."

"What's unnatural about the Rat?"

"Well, the synthesizers." She looked nonplussed. "The whole

sound. Especially the last part. Didn't I tell you?—Annette and Mickey getting chased through the alley by a gang with chains and knives and shit?"

"Do I want to hear this?"

"No, it's OK. They're a punk band making a video." Lacey dried her hands on her jeans. "They go apeshit over Mickey because he's got that pointy black-and-white face and bizarro ears. And when they find out he did multimedia in L.A.? Awesome! So he's digging being a hot dude instead of a squeaky clown in a tuxedo. And Annette rags on him for selling out. And he sings her 'Mr. Rat.'" Lacey grimaced. "Which I *hope* we're doing tonight."

She pushed open the door. I asked, "'Mr. Rat' is Niko's solo, right? Do you think Roach might be—"

Shouts and waves from the bar. Some of the Hands Across the Sea people had arrived: Rachel, Mary Ann, Betsy, and a couple other familiar faces.

"Come on," murmured Lacey. "I'm not up for them right now, are you?"

So I went with her to the dressing room. In the hall we found François and the club owner in a heated conversation about music. I lingered—better to take my chances with François than run into Dan. Besides, there was something obscurely satisfying about listening to a discussion of Dan Quasi's favorite subject in a language he couldn't understand.

"Cor-ree!" François slung his arm across my shoulder. "You like Le Club Souris? Carl does a nice job to make an American club in France, eh?"

His bare skin was warm against my neck. My impulse to cringe gave way to an instant realization that this wasn't a pass, just a reflex. Anyway, what if Dan did come along? Let him see he wasn't the only attractive man around.

François's arm lifted to fling an exasperated gesture at Carl. I'd lost track of their debate. Still about music, from his insistent tone.

"You think we French know only Jacques Brel and Edith Piaf? If you would study music in America you would learn Saint-Saens and Debussy, yes? Me, I go last year to the University of

Connecticut, and I also study the great artists: Jerry Lee Lewis, Buddy Holly, Chuck Berry."

Carl winked at me. "And steal their chops." They'd shifted to English, apparently for my benefit.

"Not steal. I make tapes, I buy records and CD's, I come back with a big suitcase"—he spread his hands—"and I play everything for Jean-Claude and Paul and Denis, and now we make our own songs."

The dressing-room door was opened by a broad wrist in a flannel cuff: Terry.

"Carl? You got some Jack out there? Lacey needs a fix."

François went with him to find a bottle. My cue to leave? But Carl was telling me how happy he was to have Quasi & Company play here. I wondered if he was one of those emigrés who'd stayed frozen in the America he left behind—noting the battered cowboy boots under his frayed jeans, the grayed and thinning ringlets curling down the collar of his blue work shirt, his belly bulging over a handmade brass buckle he might have bought in Berkeley or Greenwich Village. How did a man like Carl wind up promoting young rock-&-rollers like François in a pod mall outside EuroDisney?

When I asked him, he chuckled and pushed open the door. "Regardez."

The room was three-fourths full. I couldn't see the cartoons on the walls anymore through all the bodies and cigarette smoke.

"You'd never get a crowd like this on Sunday night in Santa Monica. But here? Outta sight, man!"

And he'd found enough American-style bands to make it work? Oh, yeah. No problem. There was a back-to-basics trend everywhere these days. Not as upbeat as the sixties, but kids were after pretty much the same things now as then. Girls, cars, party-party. Rebel against their parents. Get a buzz on—le Coors, le Zhim Bim—and blow off steam before you go back to work Monday.

Somebody waved near the stage. Hands Across the Sea had staked out a section of front-row floor space. The signal was for Steve Connelly and Lena Michel, paying their cover charge at the door. At least, Steve paid; Lena evidently was on the guest list. Good, I thought, she'd convinced Louis and Hélène that the interests of international good will required her to stick with Terry and company.

Carl went out to mingle, and I went with him to observe. The Club Souris was bigger than it looked. Past the bar a few steps led up to another room, smaller than this one, with tables the size of record albums bolted to the floor. Neil and a crew man were up there plugging wires into the sound board, which sat above the end of the bar. On each table a candle flickered in a red glass globe covered with plastic fishnet. Dim light, smoke, the purple glow of the jukebox floating like a jellyfish near the restrooms . . . I could have been back in college, or in hell, or both.

But who was that weird-looking guy stepping onto the stage? Big enough for a linebacker, with hair like somebody had cut it under a bowl and quit halfway. He picked up a guitar. A crewman? His fingers fluttered up the neck; while behind him a shaved head ducked around a cymbal and moved into place among the drums. Then François, transformed by baggy pants and a black sleeveless T-shirt.

Hold it, folks. What happened to the American rock-&-roll?

Fast heavy drums. The bowl-haired guitar player stood rigid except for one twitching knee. Someone else yelped vocals. Not bowl-hair; not François, who was bouncing lightly on the balls of his feet behind a tier of keyboards. By the process of elimination I figured out it was the bass player, though he faced the wall. I watched his back, pale skin under purple fishnet, and wondered if Carl had lived in France so long he'd forgotten what American music looked like.

And sounded like. Their second number was slower, but between the clipped drumming, buzzy bass, and jangling guitar and keyboards, it made me think of a seagull being scraped across a blackboard.

By the fourth or fifth song I gave up and strolled over to the jukebox. Maybe this band was an aberration. Maybe Carl let them play here because of François's connection with Quasi & Company. The kids were still after the same things, he'd said. I ran my finger down the glass, looking for proof—songs like "Government Man" and "Tear It Up" that made you angry and fired you up to do something about it.

Instead, here were "State of Shock," "I Wanna Be Sedated," "Cure for Pain." And the artists—Morphine, Hammer, Beastie Boys— Where had all the flowers gone? I felt like Annette, searching Greenwich Village in vain for hippies.

François's band must have finished their set, because the bartender came over and plugged in the jukebox. The number that popped up was from the Classics section. A low rising hum, then tapped cymbals and drums. The Police. Cops and rock-&-roll? Whose idea of classic was that?

I stepped back, smack into a warm body.

"Want a quarter?"

It was Dan.

"No," I said. "What are you doing out here with the civilians?"

"I like it." He leaned his head over my shoulder and added, "Do you know what a crowd I had to fight through to get over here?"

I hadn't thought of it that way. I couldn't think at all with Dan's breath on my neck.

He nuzzled my ear. "Don't stand! Don't stand so!" he sang softly with the jukebox.

I jerked my head away.

"What's the matter?"

I couldn't answer. I didn't want to turn around and see his face—that face I ached to trust, to let myself care for, and didn't dare.

What do you want from me, Dan Quasi? Why are you following me? Isn't one woman enough for tonight? Or was it too rushed, fucking her on the boat with her husband waiting?

Dan's voice was still teasing. "Hey, anybody home in there?"

He slid his arms around my waist. If he really cared about me he wouldn't be so sure of me. He'd wonder about François. He wouldn't just walk up and surround me like this.

I tried to move away, but I was wedged between Dan and the

jukebox.

"What's the matter?" he asked again.

"Don't stand so close to me." I twisted and faced him. "I'm not—"

Dan removed his hands and stepped back.

My throat was so dry I could hardly swallow. I wished I were over at the bar instead of caught here with Dan Quasi waiting in front of me for an explanation.

"I'm not—" I tried again to swallow. "Used to this. You and —women."

"They come with the territory," he said, not understanding. "I don't go after them."

"You sure don't fight them off, either."

Dan's eyebrows went up. "Why should I?"

I looked at him squarely now. Those damned blue eyes. "Well, I guess I'm not used to that attitude. To being treated like one more—object."

I sidestepped, but he grabbed my arms. "Object, huh? And how are you treating me?"

I stared at him.

"You want to write a story about my band. Fine. We let you hang out with us, ask questions, whatever you want. Nobody asks you questions—that's not the deal. You're a private person with your own private life. Then you come up to my room, you spend the night. Why? Because I'm such a great guy and you'd like to get to know me better?"

Dan let go of my arms. "What do you think it's like, people grabbing onto you every place you go? Do you think I'm so stupid I think it's me they're after? Shit no! They want to fuck a rock star, that's all. They don't care if it's me or Sting or Bono or Neil Sedaka."

A long pause. Finally I said, very quietly, "I would never mistake you for whoever it is or Neil Sedaka."

Dan touched my cheek. He rubbed at the tear that was sneaking down in spite of my most determined intentions. "Hey. Don't get upset about it."

"That's not what I'm upset about." I wiped my cheek and

blew my nose. "I do want to get to know you better. How could I not? I love how you play, how you are with the band, how you talk about music and think about it— Even your coming on this trip, no media, cameras, hoopla, just you guys and the audience. But that's all I ever see! How am I supposed to get to know you when you're always onstage?"

"I'm not always onstage." His arm went around my neck. "I'm not onstage now."

"Don't."

"Why?"

"When we were on the boat," I said, not meeting his eyes, "I thought I'd go see what was behind that door by the stairs marked 'Keep Out.'"

Dan gave a slow nod.

A man in a black-and-yellow shirt came up to put money in the jukebox. "Let's go for a walk," said Dan.

Chapter 26: Taste It

After the club, the air in the alley smelled fresh and sweet. "What about your gig?" I asked.

"We've got a few minutes. Anyway"—Dan shrugged and smiled—"if they want me, they'll have to wait."

We headed toward a neon sign on the corner. I shifted my shoulder bag to the side away from him, just in case, but he didn't touch me. It was a surprisingly quiet neighborhood: a waiter emptying garbage behind the Moroccan restaurant next door in the mall; a long row of silent buildings across the alley that might have been warehouses; and opposite the neon sign, a carved golden horse indicating a butcher shop.

"You're planning on selling what you write about us to Phases."

Not the opening I'd hoped for. "Right," I said cautiously.

"With a band, same as anybody, things happen that you don't want printed in a magazine."

"You said no taping, and I haven't taped you. You said this is a new band, not the Rind, and I've listened to you that way ever since we got here."

Dan was watching the waiter. "But it's your job to write what your audience wants to read, right? Mickey Ascher's murder. French techie OD's onstage. What your editor wants to buy."

"Sure," I said. "Like it's your job to play what your audience wants to hear."

He laughed.

"Don't worry. I've got plenty my editor will want to buy." But I knew that wasn't totally straight, and so did he.

Past the restaurant was a tall iron fence in front of a hedge. A park? A private estate? In the dark I couldn't tell.

"What if I told you some things he'd want to buy for sure, and I asked you not to use them?"

My heart thumped. I could just hear Rik Green: "Promise

him anything, but get the goddam story! We print, he sues, more publicity all around."

"You must know I'd like to go home with as much about Quasi & Company and The Rind as I can. That's what I'm here for."

"*You* must know that if I wanted my secrets published I'd have sold them myself a long time ago. Where does that leave us?"

"I guess I could write up as much as you're willing—"

"None of it."

"Then where does that leave us?" I stopped to look at him.

Dan caught my hand and raised it to his lips. "We can keep on treating each other like objects." He licked the tips of my fingers.

"Or what?" My body was beginning to quiver.

"Or I could tell you an idea for another multimedia piece I might do someday about a sixties rock band, if you'd take it as one hundred percent imaginary and confidential."

"I think I could do that." Though I was so conscious of his hand around mine that I wasn't sure I would hear anything he said.

"I'm serious, Cory." Dan squeezed my hand and dropped it. "Do you promise me you'll never write or tell one word of this to anybody unless you clear it with me first?"

"Yes."

"Do you swear by your—what do you use, a PC?"

I smiled. "I swear by Old Smoky."

"What?"

"Old Smoky. Your guitar."

"Where'd you get that?"

I was startled. "Isn't that what you call it?"

Dan laughed. "Me, call my guitar a dumb name like that?"

He was right. I started laughing with him, it was so ridiculous. "I know I read it somewhere."

"Writers! Jesus!"

"So does that blow my credibility?" Only half joking—I could see he was a little spooked.

"What do you call your computer? Mount Rushmore?"

For half a block I told him every idiotic name I could think of for a computer. Finally, when we'd come to the end of the iron fence, I asked him about his imaginary multimedia piece.

Dan pulled out a pack of Camels. "It starts out like the Wizard of Oz. Black and white into technicolor. You already heard that part." He cupped a match around his cigarette.

"Bye-bye Kansas, hello Hollywood."

"Right. So here's these four guys gaping at a bunch of munchkins holding out albums, recording contracts, bar tabs, and various body parts to get signed, and out of the sky comes a bubble, and inside is the prettiest girl you ever saw."

My face continued to show polite interest. But I knew that tone of voice. Naive and awed—the tone of a man so unused to being impressed by women that he'd lost the habit of guarding how he spoke about them.

"Roach brought her to a gig one night." Dan pinged his finger against a lamppost. "She was about Lacey's age, but she wasn't anything like Lacey. She had an *innocence*—" He paused. "She hadn't been around like American girls. She'd grown up in a convent school in France. She was so scared of us she hardly said a word all night, even though we were falling over each other to loosen her up."

I nodded mechanically. All I could think of was that I didn't want Dan to see how I was shriveling inside, like the witch who was just landed on by a house.

"So, Marie starts coming around with Roach, and Mick and Terry and I are drooling, wondering what's he got that he's landed this amazing chick? Because even after she opened up, she still wasn't like any girl we'd seen before. Usually, the girls who hang around a band, their big thing is to act hip. Show you how cool they are, up for anything."

Dan shook his head. "Marie liked our music, but it was more curiosity than the fame thing. Roach would bring her to some hot-shit party and she'd stand on the side all night watching. She hardly drank at all, never touched drugs, not even cigarettes. We couldn't figure it out. Why did she bother with us?"

I thought of the self-absorbed woman who a little while ago had walked out of her lover's arms and into her husband's car, and

I wondered myself. I said carefully, "You all must have been overwhelming to somebody who'd never met any musicians before."

Dan shrugged. "Anyhow, Roach was head-over-heels about her. She seemed to like him, but she wouldn't let him past first base. Said she was saving herself for her husband. We gave him a hard time about that. Poor old Roach!—it really was kind of comical."

Comical? I thought. Roach reporting his girlfriend's confidences to his buddies, and the four of you chuckling together?

"But Mickey— To Mick it was like a red flag to a bull. At first he just gave Roach an ungodly amount of shit about not being able to stick it to this shy little nowhere secretary. And then"—one last drag on his cigarette—"he moved in on her."

I froze. Not Dan, but Mickey.

"And she—?"

"Fell for him," Dan said flatly. "Her and half the other chicks in the world. Mick made her keep it a secret—supposedly she was still Roach's girl. So we'd be in the studio, and Roach bringing her this funny French tea she liked—"

"Tilleul?"

Dan looked at me, surprised. "Right."

I shook my head: go on.

"Anyhow, Roach waiting on her hand and foot, and Marie's mooning over Mickey. I don't know why Roach didn't see it. Finally I told Mick if he didn't tell Roach, I would. He said I should talk, the way I treated my wife, which was true." Dan grimaced. "And then he said go ahead, tell Roach, and see what happens to the album."

Dan tossed away his cigarette butt and tapped a fresh one out of the pack. This time I took one, too, even though I never smoke Camel nonfilters, especially when they've been mashed in somebody's back pocket. When Dan lit it for me I noticed his hand was trembling ever so slightly.

"Things got somewhat weird after that. I couldn't believe Mick would torpedo *Grind* over this chick, after we put so much into it—we'd already booked the recording studio, and there was a tour as soon as it was done—but then I hadn't realized"—Dan hesitated—"a lot of things. I didn't know what to do." He ran his hand through his hair. "I was so pissed at Mickey I could have killed him. I was living over our studio then, this place in Somerville where we were getting things nailed down for taping, and I figured, best thing is just ignore the whole mess and hope it doesn't blow up till we finish the album. And then one night there's a knock at my door, and it's Marie."

Dan was walking faster now. "So I let her in, and she says Mickey just told her how mad I was about him cutting Roach's grass, and he thinks it's a gas, but she doesn't. She's upset. She wants me to know she's not sleeping with Mickey. Yes, she fell for him, but anybody can see he's crazy, and she's a virgin, and now she's scared because Mickey says The Rind might break up over her. And then she starts crying." Dan shook his head. "I'd been smoking dope, and I gave her some. And next thing I know she's kissing me, or I'm kissing her, and she's crying and telling me she doesn't love Roach, she doesn't love Mickey, it's me she loves. And god damn, I went for it. I couldn't—the band, the album—I mean, these are my best friends, but I couldn't—" He inhaled and blew out smoke. "She wasn't bullshitting, either. She really was a virgin."

He said it with an awe, a protectiveness, that twisted my insides. *I was a virgin, too, that night in D.C. What if I'd said yes to you then? Would it have been me on your mind all these years instead of Marie Tréville?*

"So instead of solving anything, I totally fucked it up. Mickey kind of asked for it, but it was a hell of a thing to do to Roach. Marie and I agreed she had to break off with him. No more hanging around with the band. We'd see each other in secret. And I'd divorce Nicola and we'd get married."

Again Dan shook his head. "Only I didn't want to marry her."

I was shivering. I folded my arms and imagined Dan and Marie, so young, all those years ago.

"Not because of her. I was just crap at being married. It got in the way of the music. And the other way round, if you'd ask Nicola. I'd come home from a tour and she'd have champagne and candlelight, and all I wanted to do was crash for a week.

"So I dodged it. I kept seeing Marie—I couldn't help it, I was hooked—but I dragged my feet on the divorce. We cut the album." He smiled. "It came out better than any of us dared expect. Mickey wanted to throw a party to celebrate. Actually I think that was Gail's idea—his sister—she was worried about him, for good reason. He never even showed up for half the taping sessions. So, great—big bash at Mick's place in honor of *Grind*. And Marie shows up at my door an hour before, and says she's coming with me."

Dan stopped on the sidewalk. "I told her, no way. She tells me if I really loved her I wouldn't treat her— Well, anyhow, it was one hell of a fight. Both of us yelling and screaming, her crying, me saying I wished I'd never touched her, her saying she wished she'd stuck with Mickey—on and on. Finally she said the only way she wasn't going to that party was if I didn't go either. So I said, Fine, I'm staying here. And at six AM Dougie called and told me they'd been busted. The whole band was in jail."

"Oh, no."

"You must have heard some of that." Dan started walking again, stiff-legged, head down. "Our lawyers got everybody sprung but Mickey, whose place it was, and one other guy who was on probation. There were reporters all over the place, and Mick telling them all kinds of drugged-out shit, and Marie still on my ass to marry her, and The Rind's supposed to be going on tour in a week, which we can't with Mick locked up—" Dan lifted his head and hands in frustration. "So, like an idiot, I split. I couldn't handle it. Went to San Francisco. It clears my head to be out there. Didn't tell Marie, Dougie, anybody. And when I came home, Mick was dead, and it was in all the scandal sheets that I'd fucked him over, and meanwhile Marie had panicked and said yes to this asshole she worked for who wanted to marry her, and went back to France."

I let out a long breath. "Oh, Dan."

"I never saw her again until four days ago." He took out his cigarettes. "Want to split the last one?"

I said no thanks. We stood under a street lamp while he lit it.

Odd, noted a remote fragment of my mind, that in this mixed-up crossroads of a town, this jumble of past and future, history and fantasy, they've saved these gorgeous old cast-iron lampposts.

Dan's hair and his raised hands shone silver in the light. I watched the match flare, the round tip brighten and dim, and waited as if my life depended on what came next.

"That was Part One. Part Two started last winter. Marie phoned Terry from Paris and asked him where I was. She said she was coming to Boston with an exchange program and she wanted to see me. Terry told her I wasn't in Boston. I wasn't—I was upstairs in his guest room in Lincoln."

"You were?" You spent last winter ten miles away from me? "Why?"

Dan ticked ashes on the sidewalk and stared down at his hand. "He built us a studio. Out back of the house. In one of the old farm buildings. Ice house?" He sighed. "I guess we always knew we'd get another band together someday, but once we had the place to do it— Like he'd built a mousetrap. And 'Do What You Do' was the cheese." Dan took a drag off his cigarette. "He'd started writing it about a year after we split up. I remember him calling me in Key West and asking how I'd feel about adding keyboards. I told him to go to hell." A bitter laugh. "I was stoned as usual, trying to drown out the noise in my head. Pretty fucked. But it was like nothing I saw made any sense. We'd been fighting for so long to end the war, dump Nixon, stop sending people up for half an ounce of dope— And when it was over—" He frowned. "Guys Mickey and I went to high school with, coming back from Nam ready to shoot the pinko hippies who made America lose the war. Guys I'd played with since Monterey going under left and right. Bands breaking up, people breaking up— Like it was the fighting that held us together, and once we won, we fell apart."

"Yeah." I thought of Larry, asking me what kind of fool he'd have to be to keep struggling with a novel when Thorne Cosmetics had offered him a six-figure vice presidency. "I know what you mean."

"So I split. Went to Mexico, the Greek islands, anyplace where nobody knew who I was. Got in with some people who had a boat and sailed around the world. Learned to juggle." He attempted a smile. "That's about all you can do on a boat besides play guitar and read. I lived in a teepee near Vancouver for a while, no electricity, no music but what we made ourselves. Spent some time in New Zealand, on a sheep ranch. Sheep are greasy, did you know that?"

"No," I said, touched by this barrage of random information.

"And then one day, I was back in Canada, up on the Squamish River, and a guy comes driving out of the woods in a jeep and throws me a package. From Terry Morrissey in Lincoln, Massachusetts. A tape."

Dan sang:
"Nobody knows when it all comes down,
You make your plans and they turn out wrong.
I don't mind growin' old,
That's just the way things go.
Good men just go with their heart
When it all comes down—"

He glanced up the street at the club, looking automatically for his band. "When I heard that, it was like full circle. I rolled up my sleeping bag, hitched down to Vancouver, sent Terry a telegram to call Roach and put out the word for a keyboard player, and I caught the next plane back to Boston."

He put his arm around my shoulders. I slid out from under it. No, Dan. I can't. Not with Nicola waiting for you across the Atlantic and Marie Tréville hanging like the Sword of Damocles over our heads.

"So what happened when you got to Terry's?" I asked him.

I could see he knew why I'd pulled away, and that what he said next might decide whether he ever touched me like that again, and that to a man who was only at home with words when they came with music this was not a comfortable situation. "Well," he said, "when Marie told Terry about her exchange program, he told her we were starting a new band. A couple weeks later the governor's office called and invited us to go to France with Hands Across the Sea."

My hands felt clammy. "You knew she'd set it up."

"Oh, sure. I didn't know what she wanted, though." He hesitated. "It didn't really matter. It was one of those things that just," he shrugged, "felt right."

"Even though Roach—?"

"We weren't doing it because of Marie. We were doing it for us. Roach as much as anybody. He took it hardest that The Rind broke up."

"Did you ever tell him about her?"

Dan shook his head. "Bad enough I'd folded the band. I wasn't about to tell him I'd fucked him over with Marie, too."

We started walking toward the club. I could feel Dan ready to be out of this surreal conversation back onto the familiar solid ground of rock-&-roll.

So much he'd handed me in one block . . . and so much more I needed to know. *How do you feel about her now? What about Nicola? What about us?*

But the only question I could ask—had to ask—was the one he'd already fended off a hundred times. "What about Mickey?"

"What about Mickey?" He patted his pockets. "He was my best friend. He'd just made it through rehab. I thought, finally, we were OK."

"You have no idea—?"

"Who killed him? Fuck no." Dan was shaking his head. "You think I could have let that go?"

I looked away from him, trying to be objective, to set my own biases aside and judge his. What I saw was two reflections sliding across the butcher shop window. A pale woman's face veiled by long hair, and behind her a tall shadow. She looks dizzy, I noticed with detachment. The air here must be thinner than she's used to.

Dan tapped my shoulder. "Ground control to Major Tom."

The face in the window cracked in a smile.

"You got any more cigarettes? What's so funny?"

"I don't think so." I fished in my purse. "Oh, wait." Out came a pack of Merits, straight and orderly in their cellophane wrapping.

Dan shook the pack to pop one out. For a second I thought

he'd squash them.

"So what did Marie want?" I asked lightly as he held out a match.

He didn't answer. His face was hidden by his hands cupped around his cigarette.

"All those people yelling for the old Rind songs," he looked up finally. "I stood on that stage the first night and I felt like they were staring right through me. Like something I did a long time ago mattered more than anything I can do now."

Oh, god, I thought with a surge of hope, if he's telling me that's how it is with her—

"And then Marie and I got together, and at first it was the same kind of thing. Like she was trying to pick up the needle and move it back to 1974. Telling me how she'd set up this whole Hands Across the Sea deal—I couldn't believe it. She'd worked it out for months. Where we'd meet, what story she'd give her husband— She'd even fixed it so he'd stay out of the way. Sent him an anonymous note warning him off."

The clouds parting and dropping down the answer to the bomb threat, and all I could think was: She can't have told him what she said in that note.

"But in a way I was doing the same thing. I should have known she'd be different after twenty years. How could she help it? Married to that asshole— Which wouldn't have happened if I hadn't split. That's all I've ever done when things got complicated, is run."

"Dan, it's not your fault." Blurting in spite of myself; not wanting to argue with him, but not willing for him to believe that spoiled creature on the French committee was any doing of his. "You made your choices and she made hers. You can't take responsibility—"

I stopped, because Dan was only half listening. He was watching a clump of kids up at the corner running across the street toward the mall, tuned as usual to sounds I couldn't hear.

"What did she want?" he repeated at last. "Who knows? A chance to start over, I guess." He tossed his cigarette butt into the street. "Or maybe she just wanted to fuck a rock star."

Behind the tire of a parked car the glowing tip of his cigarette dimmed and died. I couldn't help it. I asked, "And did she?"

"Yeah." Dan answered without looking at me. "She did."

Chapter 27: I'm the One

Le Club Souris had filled up. The crowd looked mostly young, probably local, and all over the map in style. They were pressing toward the stage, moving with the loud music from the jukebox, passing drinks around elbows, shouting to each other. A crew man saw Dan come in the back door and waved. Heads turned to watch us as we pushed through to the dressing room. *Back off!* I wanted to yell at them.

A girl in a vast black sweater and white eye make-up grabbed my arm. "Qui est-ce?"

"Dan?" I called after him. "Are you guys incognito?"

An emphatic shake of his head.

I told her about Quasi & Company. "C'est lui? C'est Qua-see?" she demanded.

"Oui oui!" I assured her.

She poked another girl and pointed at Dan. I felt proud; I felt depressed. Hands reached out to him as ripples of curiosity spread across the club. Most of those flushed faces only wanting to know who the important American was; but some of them excited and insider-smug: "The Rind," I overheard, and "Non, pas mort!"

I didn't go in with him. I had my own job to do out here.

But I couldn't do it. Turn on my tape recorder: *Why did you come here tonight? Have you heard of Quasi & Company? The Rind? Hands Across the Sea?* It wasn't Dan the human being these people wanted. And I wasn't willing yet to switch.

Nor to start pushing around the puzzle pieces he'd given me. Clues, from the police standpoint. Facts relevant to an investigation. Except one could argue that Dan wouldn't have revealed them if that were true, certainly not to Hands Across the Sea's media consultant, even in confidence, which meant that, since he had, I was off the hook. Or (I preferred to think) bound by my promise.

François was walking around the stage tapping mic heads. I

reached in my bag for cigarettes and realized I'd given Dan the pack. Dumb! He could have bummed all he wanted; I'd have to find a vending machine.

Once after a concert I'd seen Mickey Ascher toss away a butt, and an ecstatic girl had pounced and lifted it tenderly from the floor. O to be a Camel between thy lips! Maybe some music critic from *Paris-Soir* would spot Dan smoking one of my Merits backstage tonight, and a new rock-&-roll myth would be born.

But how do you feel about her now? If I'd followed him in there to press it, I'd only have gotten a preoccupied stare. *I don't feel any way about her now. We have a set to play.*

So easy it seemed for men, changing channels. Like Steve Connelly, delivering threats for Jerry Leroy when he wasn't shooting photos for Phases. As if they had a genetic capacity to drop any crisis on demand and pick up the next thing in the In box. Like Larry, deciding he'd done novel-writing long enough and now it was time to be a cosmetics tycoon.

Six hours . . . Late afternoon on the Island. He'd be dusting off his work clothes, pausing for a well-earned martini on the porch. While I stood in a smoky basement pummeled by decibels and beer-chugging kids who looked like sci-fi space invaders, waiting for a man who at this moment didn't exist.

There was a ledge along the wall from the stage door to the upstairs room where people were resting their elbows and drinks and lighting cigarettes from red fishnet-swathed candles. I approached a young Frenchman opening a pack of Marlboros—part of Carl's Americana campaign?—and asked him for one. He lit it for me with a shaky abstracted air that suggested he'd stood here alone drinking for too long. I could tell he was glad to find a woman who'd talk to him. He immediately launched into a long story about throwing his wife out of the house when he came home early on her birthday and found her with another man. Half of it I couldn't follow, but apparently what galled him most was the guy's climbing out the window before he could kill him. His wife was incidental: "So I tell her you faithless bitch get out of my house, and she wa-wa-wa, and I tell her I don't pay your bills anymore, cut your clothes in pieces, and she wa-wa-wa, and I tell her I call your father, say he can have you back . . ."

I could see from his hit-between-the-eyes expression and the mechanical wobble of his head there would be no point asking what his wife had actually said. He was ready to move on: having told me why he was here, what about me? He'd seen me writing in a notebook—was I the girlfriend of someone in the band? I explained about Hands Across the Sea and Phases. He asked again which of them was my boyfriend. I told him more emphatically: none of them. Then he wanted to give me cigarettes, buy me a drink, put his arm around me; and I left feeling I'd been stupid.

Where were Quasi & Company? Why didn't the music start?

I spotted three of them upstairs at a table behind the sound board: Lacey, Niko, and a large bearded man thinly disguised in a leather cap and a blue turtleneck sweater. Lacey cradled a paper bag shaped like Jack Daniel's.

I lowered myself gratefully into their conversation as into a hot tub. Roach was inspecting the speaker over his head—an antique, one of the original Bose, extinct back home. Niko agreed he'd never seen one like it. How old?

"1974." Roach grinned. "Hell of a good year, man."

1974. The year of Mickey Ascher's murder, Marie Tréville, the drug bust, The Rind disbanded, Watergate, the resignation of the president of the United States. But a vintage year for speakers; a benchmark year for rock-&-roll, with "Tear It Up" on every radio station and Grind shooting toward platinum.

Like my summer in Paris seven years ago. In June a three-month overseas assignment; in August a wedding ring. Seven years from now, which would top my memories list?

"When are we playing the Rat?" Lacey glanced at me as she asked Roach. I might have let myself forget I was the resident journalist, but they hadn't.

"End of the set. 'When You,' then 'Mr. Rat,' and we finish with 'Home.'"

"Niko, what are you playing on 'When You'?"

Meaning piano or synthesizer? No: something about his groove. Groove? Cool, man, I can dig it. When they moved on to lines, stops, and spaces, though, I excused myself. Rehearsals I didn't mind not following, but this made me feel like a tourist.

I wanted to go backstage and find Dan, except he'd be too deep in his own groove to indulge my need to connect.

He's a music-maker, he's got no time for you . . .

Odd to write something like that for his wife. Nicola must have spent plenty of long solitary nights during The Rind.

Maybe not. Maybe when your husband trailed an entourage like the Main Street choo-choo, you developed your own traveling friends, your own routine. I'd never felt lonely at Thorne Cosmetics functions until afterward, when the cab dropped Larry and me at home with no one to talk to until Monday but each other.

And of course Nicola knew she was marrying a celebrity, whereas I'd expected my future with Larry to go on just like Paris: two typewriters clattering in counterpoint, two hearts beating together to a different drum. *Aren't you the Cory Goodwin who writes for Phases?* And instead wound up scribbling notes to myself on cocktail napkins while my husband the vice president covered the tablecloth with graphs of next year's lipstick sales.

He fades in, he fades out,
While you pan from doubt to doubt,
Looking for
The frames that he cut out . . .

So far away my life with Larry seemed now. A week ago I'd been obsessed with it, afraid to come back to Paris for fear of haunting the Beaubourg and the Place St. Augustin in a futile search for lost time. I'd vowed then to approach this trip like Proust, as an archeological expedition into the past. Dig, dig! till out of the rubble emerged that other Cory I used to be. Cory the albatross, as I'd begun to think of her . . . no longer a joyful winged creature but a dead weight hanging around my neck.

And you think that maybe time elapsed will fill the gaps . . .

What I hadn't anticipated was that the past doesn't stand still any more than the present. I'd found lost time, all right, only it wasn't mine but Nicola's. Waiting in a bar, chatting with the band, watching the backstage door for Dan Quasi.

Two crew men came out with guitars. Any minute now . . .

There was Terry, at the bar with his arm around Lena. He looked more like an L. L. Bean salesman than a drummer. The girls hovering behind them had picked out François as the rock musician in this line-up. Still in his stage clothes: black drawstring pants and sleeveless T-shirt. He'd slicked back his hair. The girls were giggling, poking each other, hoping he'd turn around and speak to them.

What did I want from Dan Quasi? I didn't know anymore. Not marriage. He'd said himself he was crap at it, and so was I. Two careers clashing, two minds humming on different wavelengths—I'd had enough of that.

The crew men were sliding flat red sensors into the strings under Niko's keyboard. I walked toward the bar. *Nobody knows when it all comes down; You make your plans and they turn out wrong . . .* Terry couldn't have guessed when he kissed his wife and kids goodbye in Lincoln that he'd wind up sharing this weekend with Lena Michel. And Lena—whatever her hopes when she signed up, they couldn't have included a balding married ex-famous drummer.

How come a man do what he do, do what he do?

Maybe the only answer was the one Dan had given me: You never know.

"Sound check to control room," Niko's voice echoed over the speakers. "Got some ivories here that need tickling."

"Play it, Sam!" Terry shouted.

I edged in between Lena and François and ordered a Jack Daniel's.

"Cor-ree! You like my band?" François swung around to kiss me. I cringed: Would Terry think I was playing woman at the vortex, switching off between lead guitar and keyboards? But Terry's smile told me he recognized that François's exuberance wasn't for me, but for having played a good set and being at Le Club Souris with three legends of American rock-&-roll.

I kissed him back. "You were terrific."

"Ah, oui!" François was too elated to be modest. "Les Enchaînés will open for Quasi & Company on their tour, eh? Cory, I give you our press kit. You meet everybody in the band?"

Of course: to him, as to Lacey, Roach, and Niko, my role was to launch this night into the media and into history. "Not yet."

François was all for dragging me straight to the dressing room, but I told him we should wait for my photographer.

The girls behind him were still advancing and retreating like bathers dipping their toes into a chilly ocean. One of them squealed as the others pushed her closer.

"OK," Niko reverberated. "Frrrancois, we'rrre rrready."

François swiveled. Girls he could ignore, but not the sound system.

Lacey and Roach came down the steps as Carl's amplified voice announced Le Club Souris and Les Enchaînés were proud to present some very special guests . . . Terry gave Lena a quick kiss and headed over to join the band.

Lena sighed. "What a sweetie!"

I nodded absently. I was watching the door for Dan.

"I can't believe we're going back to Boston tomorrow, after all this." She gestured around the room. "When the only reason I even came was Jack—my husband—bitching about my midlife crisis!"

My head turned abruptly.

"I said, What midlife crisis? I'm in my prime!" She laughed. "And Jack said, maybe it's not a crisis to you, but if I keep hearing I hate my boss, I hate this house, I hate how I look in these pants, *we're* going to have a crisis."

Lena's smile looked so untroubled I couldn't fit it to what she was saying. I tried to picture her at a kitchen table somewhere in Boston, arguing with this Jack who held such a proprietary interest in her feelings.

"What about you? You had your midlife crisis yet?"

And from her light tone I understood that for Lena this was a serious issue, one she couldn't talk about without that protective smile.

I said I hadn't thought of it that way, but now that she

mentioned it . . . maybe that's why I was here, too. To prove to myself I could still do it—that my life wasn't nailed down too tight to change. And to find out, I heard myself adding, if the life I left was one I wanted to go back to.

"That's it," Lena nodded. "Weird, huh? All those years of who am I, what do I want, who will I marry, where should we live, and—ta-da! Done! And you're going, Wait! Is this it? What happens now?"

Onstage Quasi & Company were nosing around their equipment in the doggy way musicians do: Niko moving a cord and sidling in behind François's keyboards, Terry lowering the mic beside his snare. They'd switched the drums. Evidently a lot had gone on in here while Dan and I were outside grappling with our part of the midlife crisis.

"So you come to France with a rock-&-roll band—" I said.

"Yeah!" She pushed a strand of hair behind her ear. "If we can still wind up in a dive bar listening to rock-&-roll, we're not over the hill, right?"

Lacey was moving up front to a vocal mic. "Dynamite Wheels," I noted automatically. A good opener—get everybody out on the dance floor.

"How do you feel about going back tomorrow?" I asked Lena.

"Oh, well." Her mouth twisted. "It's not like there's a choice. But Terry says, what the hell, we'll always have Paris."

Applause rippled across the room as Dan walked onstage with his silver guitar. Lena clapped, too—as if that were all it took to hold onto the magic, to keep them shining up there in the moment of suspense before the song.

We'll always have Paris. I supposed that was true. But right now it didn't seem like enough.

Steve Connelly found me between the climactic guitar and drum solos in "Dynamite Wheels." He showed up first as a nudge in my side, then a shout in my ear over the music. I mimed that I couldn't hear him. When "Wheels" ended I could feel him watching me, like a retriever with a ball.

I still didn't want to talk to him. But François was slipping through the door by the stage. With half an hour or so before The Rat, this was our best chance to interview Les Enchainés and deal with whatever other gaps needed filling tonight.

Once I argued us past the defensive lineman at the door, Steve stopped in the hall. News first, then Enchainés.

Through the wall I could feel the throbbing of Roach's bass and Terry's drums. Victor Tréville had told me there'd be no news until tomorrow on the Albert Vaux case. What could Steve Connelly have to say that I needed to hear more than Quasi & Company?

He leaned against the flaking paint, arms folded under his camera. He'd run into Victor at the phone booths in the Euro-Disney reception center. "Long story short, no way is the band going home tomorrow. They'll be held here to, quote, assist with the investigation."

"Why?" I only half believed him. "What is this, a hostage situation?"

"The police found the Sominol."

My heart plummeted.

"They searched the band's equipment this afternoon. I would guess that's why the alleged wiring problem. They found a baggie of pills taped under the piano."

A bolt of fear ran from the back of my head to my feet. Would Niko—would anyone in Quasi & Company—have left a lethal weapon in such an obvious place? Not a chance. They'd dumped every drug they had after the first hint Bear might have OD'd.

Except the joint Dan and I smoked in his room . . .

"Victor got the word from Commissaire Guerin. The lab analysis matches the substance that killed Albert Vaux."

"Fingerprints?"

"The baggie was clean. Nothing on the pills."

No way. Nobody in this band would risk their future over a handful of sleeping pills. After six months of rehearsals? After twenty years of exile?

Who would?

Somebody who didn't mind if the stash was found. Or who meant it to be found. Or planted it during the police search for the purpose of being found.

Better empty out that ashtray

'Cause he's comin' up behind you . . .

"Yes," Steve nodded as if I'd asked him a question. "It's that bad. If the whole band ever does get back to the U.S., which I wouldn't bet money on, they're finished. Kaput."

"Oh, but—"

"I talked to Governor Leroy. Over his dead body will they ever play in Boston, or anywhere else he can pull a string. Call John Otis; he'll tell you. Call Rik Green. Your *Phases* story? My radio piece? Down the toilet. No mention of Quasi & Company in Hands Across the Sea's press releases, no photos, *nothing.*"

Pressure rising in my chest. "Really? Does Dan Quasi know about this?"

"Dan Quasi doesn't talk to me." Steve's voice compressed with scorn. "He gets his information direct from God."

"And who does Jerry Leroy get his information from? The ghost of J. Edgar Hoover?"

"The Governor of Massachusetts has every right and responsibility to bar suspected felons from privileged access to the media."

"Oh, bullshit. If you've ever met Rik Green, you know he won't pull this story for Jerry Leroy or anybody. Your governor won't get a publicity blackout, he'll get his face on *Phases'* cover."

Steve was screwing on a lens. "Don't count on it."

"If he even *tries* to blackball Quasi & Company, there won't be an arena in Boston big enough for the crowd they'll draw."

"Won't do them much good behind bars."

"Speaking of bands and bars," I breathed in a lungful of cigarette smoke and beer fumes, "I came here to do an interview."

I pushed past him toward the dressing room. Steve's voice followed me down the hall.

"Make sure you get enough material for a story without Quasi & Company."

Chapter 28: Do What You Do

Les Enchainés were overjoyed to see us. Denis, the bass player, shooed out the girls who'd been keeping them company and gave Steve and me their folding chairs. Jean-Claude, the bowl-haired guitarist, thrust a beer at Steve. I accepted a press kit from François and set my tape recorder on my knee.

But I couldn't focus. Not with Quasi & Company outside grafting new branches onto the roots of rock-&-roll while the Fraises-des-Bois police sprayed the leaves with paraquat and Jerry Leroy hacked at the trunk.

This was a melodrama epidemic run amok. Politicians didn't gag the press and trump up arrests anymore. That went out with Watergate.

According to Steve, Victor Tréville got the lab results from Commissaire Guerin after our boat docked. That meant the pills under the piano must have been discovered hours earlier. Before we set sail. Before the alleged wiring problem was solved and the band unbanned. Before Victor told me, or Marian Thorne, that someone in Quasi & Company had tried to poison his champagne in the trailer.

"Francois," I interrupted. "After the show last night at the Strawberry Festival. What happened to the equipment?"

"We're not talking about that," said Steve warningly.

"How long did it stay on the stage?"

Since I was the one with the tape recorder, Francois answered me. The crew (minus Albert Vaux) had moved everything as usual, off the stage and into the truck, as soon as the crowd made way. Speakers, amps, instruments, all of it was locked inside within an hour.

"And then?"

"You don't have to answer," Steve said in his man-to-man voice. "It's your band we want to hear about. Denis, you were saying. Your CD?"

I switched to French. François shot a puzzled look at Steve and followed me.

The truck spent the night parked outside the police station. That enabled Hands Across the Sea not to hire a guard. The back gate had a separate lock from the cab door. Two keys; two copies. One kept by François, one left with the police.

Steve was focusing his camera, hoping evidently to trump words with pictures. The other Enchainés struck poses and started talking again: Denis outlining their CD plans, Jean-Claude asking Steve if his radio station had connections in France, Paul the drummer staring at the ceiling and reciting the American musicians he despised most.

They should know better. I'd never be able to transcribe this tape.

I couldn't help thinking of Dan and Mickey in D.C.—their approach so opposite to this, brotherhood with other musicians and disdain for interviews. Hard to believe they were younger then than these kids, with three years on the road and three successful albums already behind them. Dan slamming the U.S. government, not the entertainment industry; while Mickey babbled about peace and love, not fame and fortune.

We've had more people buy our records and come to our concerts than Richard Nixon got votes. What did it do to you to be able to say that at twenty-two?

Steve waved Denis and Jean-Claude closer together so he could shoot all four of them. Choppy haircuts and black Chinese slippers, smirking at the camera . . . while Mickey Ascher was dead, a finished body of work before he hit thirty, and Dan Quasi stood outside playing dance tunes on the guitar that once mobilized thousands of protesters. Lines around the famous blue eyes now; twenty years of regrets to cloud The Rind's day in the limelight.

And in Fraises-des-Bois, a new generation of police waiting to take him down.

François! Paul! Jean-Claude! Denis! Don't you know what a Faustian bargain you're signing up for?

When I asked them, they looked blank. The price of success?

Bien sur, we're ready to pay it. Drugs? Booze? Cops? Groupies? No problem. But what about all the others before you who said the same thing and then crashed in flames? What about Jim Morrison, buried at Montparnasse? What about Brian Jones, Jimi Hendrix, Janis Joplin, Keith Moon, Elvis Presley? What about Mad Mick, murdered in his penthouse with his last and best album on the turntable? Les Enchaînés shrugged: It won't happen to us.

I walked outside feeling old. Onstage Quasi & Company shimmered through smoke and red light. It took a moment for the noise from the speakers to match up with the noise in my head.

We're takin' to the street now
And they're comin' with the gas masks . . .

The crowd was into it, but not to hold the line against the pigs. They were jerking as if some invisible puppeteer controlled their legs and arms—high on Zhim Bim and Marlboros, sex and rock-&-roll, one last night to blow off steam before work tomorrow. Their faces glowing like coals; their profiles rimmed in crimson.

Everybody on your feet now!
Link your arms for the last gasp!

Did they get the words? or only the beat?

The rows of glasses hanging over the bar flickered. I ordered ginger ale. Dan's guitar solo was starting: not cries of anguish like the old days but a wild strum that jangled into jittery piano chords.

I should have told him. Forced it. Taking care of my magazine means I have to take care of Quasi & Company, too. How can you not recognize that?

He's the government man—

Distant as a star. The authorities ready to drop a net over his head, and Dan stood there at the helm of his band as steadfast and oblivious as the captain of the Titanic.

Watch out, friend,
When you're in the hands
Of the government man!

I didn't want to watch, or listen. I wanted him to break a string, call up Jean-Claude to sit in, come down here and wrap his arms around me.

"Thank you!" Shaking his already sweat-curled hair. "Niko Marx on piano and vocals. 'Government Man.'"

And would it have been worth it, after all?

A strange twinkling sound from the speakers. The stage lights turned blue. Only Lacey's hands were moving up and down her keys. Then a *bssshh* of cymbals . . . a faint thrum of bass . . .

That must be François's new Kurzweil, those long rising and descending notes. But this was an old sound: a slow song meant for gauzy skirts and orchids, white dinner jackets, punch cups, heads resting dreamily on shoulders.

On the dance floor couples smiled and drifted closer.

A soft back-up *ooh-ooh* in three-part harmony. Lacey nodded to Niko.

"When you wish, upon a star,
Makes no dif-frence who you are . . ."

A few giggles from the dancers. *Qu'ils sont bizarres, ces américains!*

"Anything your heart desires
Will come . . . to . . . you . . ."

Under their duet, a low humming that gradually coalesced into a beat. The voices a shade faster . . . and faster . . . and the rhythm rose till I could see a miniature train chugging up Main Street, carrying a pair of outcasts toward the gate.

When you, when you, when you, when you . . .

Goodbye, Mousecartoon Time! Guest Star Day, farewell! No one tonight to promise, "See you real soon!" All the righteous in a circle behind them—ducks, dogs, dwarfs, queens—fingers pointing, frowns accusing, while two voices went on resolutely:

"When you—wish uh—pon a—star—"

When you! When you! rumbled the wheels.

Till they reached the gate, and Terry's drums beat a triumphant *rat-ta-ta tat-ta-ta,* and the song exploded:

"When you, when you, when you wish upon a star,
It don't matter where you're at, it don't matter who you are!
When you, when you, when you wish upon a star,

You're gonna have a dream come true!"

The dance floor erupted into chaos: waving palms, flapping elbows, clapping hands and stomping feet. The stage pulsed with lights: red and purple, green, blue, gold, bouncing off cymbals and mic stands, spouting from the ceiling like puffs of colored smoke.

"Come on!" Lena tugged at my arm.

And though I hadn't danced with a girl since high school, I plunged with her into that mass of bobbing shoulders and gleaming sweaty faces.

"When you, when you, when you give it all your soul,

They can't shut the music off, they can't stop the rock-&-roll!

When you, when you, when you give it all your soul,

You're gonna make a dream come true!"

Yes! I thought jubilantly, and flung back my hair. In my heart I was a ticket-taker sprung from my booth to welcome Annette and Mickey to the brave new outside world. I linked arms with Lena and we started dancing sideways, a kick line, extending as another arm hooked mine—Rachel, followed by François and Mary Ann, then Jean-Claude and a French girl, till a whole chain of us were snaking across the floor, weaving through couples, drinkers, barstools, clapping spectators.

"Dream, the whole night through!

Dream, and it'll come to you!

When you, when you, when you wish upon a star,

You're gonna make your dream come true!"

Our line was splitting apart. Lena spun off in the arms of Gary Laporte. I wiped my forehead on my sleeve and moved close to the stage. Hard to listen and not dance—but impossible to dance and really listen. That baritone line Roach was booming under the chorus: "Keep—on—dream—ing the whole night through!" And Niko's piano, so gleeful I suspected he was laughing behind his hot spot. Lacey must be in hog heaven pulling trumpets and French horns out of François's synthesizer. It was Terry, though, who gave this number its soul, kept it pumping down the track like a steam engine. And Dan up front at the throttle.

His T-shirt was plastered to his chest, his face slick with

sweat. He looked so happy in his white spotlight I wanted to hug him. *Would* hug him as soon as he walked off that stage. I'd made my own wish last night when I went up to his room, and it had nothing to do with journalism. How could I pass up a dream come true?

When Terry bashed his drums at the end of the song, I clapped as hard as any kid who's ever believed in fairies. For all of them, grinning at each other and mopping their dripping faces; but for Dan most, because I loved him and his music and right now this was the only way to say it.

"Thank you!" The confident nod of a man loved by five hundred people. "Lacey Sky, Niko Marx, 'When You Wish Upon a Star.'"

Enthusiastic shouts from the Hands Across the Sea section. Hey, Steve! Hear that?

"Here's another new one from our soon-to-be-a-major-extravaganza *Mickey Rat.*"

I scanned for a waitress, didn't see one, and opted to stay thirsty rather than lose my floor space. Dan was gulping something from a glass with limes in it. At the other end of the stage Lena waved and started wedging toward me, pulling Phil Alligator behind her. I glanced up again, but Terry's eyes were on Dan.

He set down his glass, slipped off his guitar and handed it to Niko. Lacey crossed to the piano. Dan took Lacey's place at François's stacked keyboards.

"So, Cory!" Phil gave me a friendly hug. "How's it going?"

"Just a second," I said.

Dan pushed buttons, adjusted Lacey's gooseneck mic, nodded to Terry at the drums and Niko up front.

"What's he doing?" asked Lena.

"I don't know."

Phil said, "Playing keyboards?"

Obvious, but accurate. Dan Quasi was playing keyboards—a fast bouncy tune that pushed the needle all the way back to the fifties: Brylcreem and saddle shoes, a stack of 45s with metal centers . . . Except that the sound wasn't stompin' and strollin' but steel drums, while Lacey punctuated on piano, Niko threw in guitar twangs, and Roach and Terry snapped out the beat.

Lena shot me a delighted grin. "What *is* this?"

I laughed. I still couldn't believe it—the Alley Cats, ladies and gentlemen, with Mad Mick on guitar and Dan Quasi on keyboards.

"Don't keep tellin' me how to be a man!" Niko snapped.

"Can't you see I do the best I can?

Trapped inside the mouse you made of me—

Now you say that you're afraid of me!"

I could almost see him sprout round ears and a pointed black-and-white nose as he stalked across the stage. The dancers on the floor, who didn't care who played what as long as somebody kept playing something, jitterbugged as if they'd invented it right here in Le Club Souris. Lena poked me and pointed at a skinny jeune fille in spike-heeled boots twirling through the arm of a garçon with a purple-streaked D.A. Boys dancing with girls, girls dancing with girls—it would have looked like a sock hop if anyone had been wearing socks.

"But Mister Right ain't where it's at—"

A steel-drum chortle of agreement from Dan's synthesizer—

"Babe, I'm Mister Rat!"

Mr. D.A. swung Ms. Boots between his legs and flung her into the air. Lena and Phil ran out to join the fray. Steve Connelly, wherever you are, you'd better be shooting this! Blackball be damned—Rik will kill us if we come back with no record—

I reached for my camera and remembered my tape recorder.

Not for Phases. For me. How could Dan object to that? After tomorrow I might never see him again. After tonight Quasi & Company might not even exist. No one would ever hear it but me. How could I forgive myself, live with myself for the next twenty years, knowing I'd heard Dan Quasi play synthesizer in a French bar and hadn't taped it?

Anyway, he couldn't mind if he didn't find out. Or if he understood what it had meant to me to carry him with me on the road all these years—which of course he couldn't, even if I told him, which I wasn't about to.

"Babe, I'm Mister Rat!"

I held my breath, I closed my eyes; I pressed Record.

Instantly the music changed. The bass went hollow, the drums sharper. A low metallic hum came rising up from the synthesizer like a flying saucer.

My hand jerked away from the button. What were they doing? What had I done?

Niko flicked back his guitar cord like a long black tail. So you thought you had me figured? Surprise!

"Face it, girl, the past is over!

Give up and let it die!

Think it over—

I've got a chance to make another start—

Take my hand! Take my heart!

Take it all or stay behind!"

My cheeks felt hot. I craned on tiptoes, but I couldn't see Dan except for a glimpse of his head appearing and disappearing behind Niko's shoulder.

Oh, yes, I told him silently, you know what she wanted! The same thing we all want: to keep you there in the spotlight, just like the old days. Reminding us how glorious we were when we marched on Washington and celebrated till dawn, when we sat smoking dope around candles in straw-covered Chianti bottles and planned the commune we'd start, the boat we'd sail to Paradise. Only we grew up—got jobs, got married, and now instead of marching in the streets we send checks. But not you! You're Dan Quasi, ringleader of the New England protest movement. If you cop out, what have we got left?

"Cause Mister Right ain't where it's at—"

Dan leaned forward. I saw his eyes connect with somebody at the back of the club.

"Call me Mister Rat!"

A flash of white in the lighted doorway. Marie Tréville.

I stiffened. Linking arms in D.C. Making a barrier with our bodies: Would we hold? Would they flatten us?

But this wasn't the sixties. I took a deep breath and pushed through the dancers toward the door.

Watch out, lady! I'm gonna shoot the legs off your horse!

Chapter 29: Mr. Rat

"Bonsoir, Marie."

She'd unpinned her hair, let it fall in loose waves over her white cotton-gauze blouse. Soft pants that matched her lipstick . . . how could her husband have let her out of the Main Street gate like this? Where did he think she'd be going but to wreak havoc?

"Bonsoir." She glanced at me incuriously. "Cory Thorne, yes? Our journalist."

Her eyes were already moving past my face to the band, then back to the crowd on the floor. I could see what she was thinking: Too much flotsam from Hands Across the Sea. Getting to Dan might be harder than she'd hoped.

"Goodwin." I flipped my tangled hair over my shoulders. "Cory Goodwin."

Marie Tréville nodded noncommittally. She scanned the ambassadors' section at the front of the stage like a cat weighing whether to jump onto a crowded mantelpiece: no worries if she broke something, but would she hurt herself?

"You left the party at EuroDisney?"

Her answer was a reflex. "With so many coming here instead, one of our committee needed to go along."

A shower of piano chords drenched us in light. For an instant I almost turned, jealous of her watching the band when I couldn't. But in her face I saw that she couldn't hear what I heard. I breathed in Lacey's trills and flourishes, Roach's bass hopscotching through the beat like a cheerful bullfrog, and my heart thumped with energy. *En garde*, babe, I'm Mister Rat!

"Madame Tréville!"

François stood with his hand out, grinning and breathless.

"You are so nice to come and hear us! Mrs. Bailey, she is here too? And your husband?"

Marie Tréville reached for her breast as if to cross herself. What new demon was this, sprung from the inferno of writhing bodies in red light to bar her way?

I glared at him with equal displeasure. Had Dan put the word out she might show up here? Was the crew under orders to look after her?

She shook his hand reluctantly. "Excuse me. I was just—" She nodded at the ladies' room.

"Mais non!" François didn't let go. "First you must let me buy you a drink. Cory, you too."

Radiating sincerity. At the bar he ordered a Pernod for Madame, a Jack Daniel's for me, and *un demi* for himself. When I slid over a folded ten-franc note he smiled and pushed it away. I was itching to ask him how he'd known she was here and what the hell he was up to . . . but I didn't dare, and not just because I was afraid she'd hear me.

Across the room Dan tipped back his head. The piano faded, then paused.

Marie Tréville tipped back her head and swallowed Pernod. She drank quickly, not in the delicate sips I remembered from the other night but with the restlessness of any woman waiting in a bar for her lover.

That must be a camellia and not a gardenia in her hair. What did this lady know about the blues? She was grand opera— twisting souls, breaking hearts. And if Dan landed in a French prison instead of Boston Garden, why should she care? This time next week, when she'd finished her *recherche du temps perdu,* she'd smile at that flower on her dressing table: another hoard of memories to live on till boredom closed in again. While in the kitchen her balding husband fixed her a pot of tilleul. No, not ill, she'd assure Victor charmingly, just *un peu fatiguée.*

From the speakers, an eerie rumble that spiraled into a chord.

"Cory." François touched my arm. "I must go get ready. You stay here, eh?"

"Why?"

But he only grinned and moved toward the dance floor, as if he and I were allies in a conspiracy whose purpose nobody would let me in on.

Marie Tréville didn't even glance over as he left. To her

François was crew, I was press—supporting cast, not of interest.

All the gin joints in all the towns in all the world, I thought sourly, and she walks into mine.

It must have surprised her to find Dan back there behind the keyboards instead of up front with his guitar. Maybe he'd never told her about the Alley Cats. Nice to think there was something I knew about him and she didn't.

A rapid-fire tremolo wrenched my mind back into my ears. Dan was easing away from rock-&-roll into a solo flight, a space odyssey toward worlds beyond the stars. Some of the kids on the dance floor slowed to a tentative bounce, turning away from their partners to watch him.

Why should I stay here? I was press—I could pull out my notebook and walk right up to the stage—

No. If she can stand it, so can I.

I closed my eyes. He was in full swing now, the earth far behind, shooting past the sun, past comets and galaxies. Spiraling, falling, rising, twinkling out a fragment of tune and abandoning it, swerving higher, swooping back again to scoop it up . . . till Terry soft-shoed in to join him, and Roach, and the whole band was dancing into one more verse.

A flurry of applause. I clapped too—how could I not? Marie Tréville signaled to the bartender for another Pernod. Her eyes surveyed the club as if to confirm that her lover had given a worthy performance.

I felt like shaking her. Cripes, lady, don't you realize how lucky you are to know a man who can play like that? How can you stand there taking him in and not want to give him something back?

"Marie," I said. "You don't care for rock-&-roll?"

Her smile was faintly amused. "It is not so much a music for adults."

"Your ambassadors are enjoying it."

She lifted an eyebrow.

"You were brilliant to pick Quasi & Company for the Mystery Band. I hope losing your young friend Albert Vaux hasn't spoiled that for you."

Her head went slowly back and forth. Was she answering or tuning me out? The milky oval of her Pernod shifted between her fingers: half gone already. Pernod looks like lemonade and tastes like licorice, but it'll blow off the top of your head. And this was the girl who used to make one glass of wine last all evening.

"This François." She turned just far enough to indicate she was speaking to me. "He is a friend of yours?"

"Cause Mister Right ain't where it's at!" Niko snapped.

"He's a friend of all of ours."

"Babe, I'm Mister Rat!"

Rat-ta-ta-crash! Marie Tréville and I swiveled in unison toward the stage.

Terry tossed a drumstick into the air. Niko set down his guitar, winked at Lacey, bowed and grinned at the applause. Dan was coming up front. He looked exhausted and joyful—blue T-shirt soaked, sweat oiling his skin under the lights. I thought: You'd want shoulders like that if you played for two hours a night. And then: Who could watch him play for two hours and not want those shoulders?

All across the club women were gazing up at him. *Thousands of faces in the dark; eyes that glitter like sparks . . .* each following the curve of Dan Quasi's arm as he reached for his guitar.

Marie Tréville's lips were slightly parted. As if by sheer force of will she could set her seal on him till he was safely off that stage. It wasn't me she was worried about. For her, every girl in this room was the other woman.

While Dan looked around at the only people who mattered right now: Lacey reclaiming her keyboards, Roach handing Terry a beer, Niko settling in again behind the piano.

The applause had faded to the clatter of a typewriter. Paladin drew her pistol.

"So how do you think Dan's doing without Mickey Ascher?" No response.

"Has he changed a lot?"

Her head didn't turn. "How should I know that?"

"You may be the only person here besides Roach and Terry

who knew him in The Rind."

"Oh, when one is young—" She swirled the remains of her drink, still watching Dan.

"Things were different? Simpler?"

"It was a game then, the messages in the songs."

Talking mostly to herself. I took a long shot. "You mean like Dan's thing with the third number?"

She didn't even look startled; just nodded, as if she'd hardly heard me.

"Was that for you?"

Another nod. Her eyes were glazed, reminiscent. "It was a game," she repeated. "What one cannot say, one tells in other ways. On Thursday he plays the song he wrote for me. Tonight on the boat he is annoyed, he tries to hurt me with his cold blonde Nicola. Pfft!" Her fingers puckered in the classic French gesture of tossing away something unpleasant. "What do I care for a little song no one has ever heard? For a woman who has divorced him?"

I gripped my Jack Daniel's and hoped my hand would stop shaking so I could drink it. I needed that rush of warmth to subdue the pounding in my chest.

"For me," she said complacently, "he wrote 'The End of the Night.'"

Confident of my sympathy; never doubting that I, a walk-on in her drama, must be grateful for these intimacies from the star. When I'd have given the July 4 cover of Phases to erase her. Nothing violent—just lift my hand and rub her out. Bar, humping whale, cavorting cartoon animals, red candles, everything could stay the same, only please God, no more Marie Tréville.

From the speaker overhead, legato piano chords. I turned. Niko's shoulders were hunched in white light.

Don't do it! Oh, Dan, you can't play her song, not now—

Then his guitar curled out a harmony, and the sounds shifted into focus. Terry's sticks lightly tapping the rim of his snare; Roach adding the bass part he'd invented on his Sears portable amplifier . . .

Niko leaned forward with a prim smile.

"I hope you get home all right, tonight!"

Some of the couples on the dance floor slid their arms around each other.

"Be sure to walk where there's plenty of light . . ."

They didn't know what lay waiting two verses ahead. A little song no one had ever heard before . . . except me.

"I," sang Niko, "hope you get home all right!"

Marie Tréville held out her empty glass to the bartender.

I felt a sudden urge to smash my fist down on the bar in front of her. And where were you when I sat on the floor watching Dan lift those words off a notebook page into music? Relaxing in your husband's plush suburban *salon*? Lingering over a gourmet dinner? Where were you when I rode with him to gigs, found him a place to stay, translated his questions, helped him build a parade float? Oh, sure, you had him when he was a rock star; but The Rind is over, Marie, as dead and gone as Mickey Ascher. That's *my* song they're playing now, and damned if I'll let you have it!

A burst of light flung colors across the stage. Dan's guitar shrieked down into the bridge.

"Cause Johnny went down in the street last week,

And we lost Angel on the cloverleaf—"

Marie handed the bartender a ten-franc note; slid her glass toward her.

"And nobody knows

What happened to Ro-o-o-salie."

A murmur of organ. Near Dan's feet the thin girl in spike-heeled boots clasped her fingers behind her boyfriend's purple-streaked hair and resumed swaying with the music.

"Well I hope you get home all right," Quasi & Company concluded softly.

Marie counted her change.

Here's a quarter, Dan. Give us another love song. While he stood in the spotlight with his head bowed, his best friend dead, his wife gone, his lover married to another man, fighting ghosts that should have been laid to rest with the sixties. What love song did Dan Quasi have left to offer us but the bitter wish he was singing us now?

I picked up my Jack Daniel's and put down a franc for the

bartender. I didn't need to be here when they finished. I already knew how this one ended.

As I passed the jukebox, tearing cellophane off a pack of Marlboros, light exploded in my face. Through an orange cloud Steve Connelly's voice grinned at me: "Had to get one of our correspondent night-clubbing with Mickey and the gang!"

Matches, I thought. They were here two seconds ago.

"You having fun?" asked Steve.

"Yup," I said. I still couldn't see him. "And you?"

"Oh, sure. Quite the scene, isn't it?" He moved in closer. "I have to say, I'm surprised Marie Tréville showed up here. Leaving the farewell party to keep an eye on—" he nodded at the stage. "You get anything out of her?"

"More than I expected," I said truthfully.

Steve nodded. "I'm going to see if she'll pose for some candids with the ambassadors."

He padded toward the bar, tail wagging. Marie hadn't moved since Quasi & Company had walked offstage. Sitting on a barstool, waiting for the band to come. I gave Steve two minutes at most.

She *had* been awfully forthcoming for a woman who seemed to hope nobody would realize she was here. And optimistic, expecting to pull off a rendezvous with Dan in Le Club Souris. I could appreciate why she hadn't wanted to battle through the girls around the door to catch him backstage; but if I'd changed into my sexiest lounge outfit and shaken off my husband to come meet my lover, I sure wouldn't be hanging around waiting for him to find me. I'd grab the first person who looked trustworthy enough to carry a message—

I stuffed my cigarettes into my purse and ran after Steve. Too late. There went his yellow sweater through the backstage door.

While Marie Tréville sat contemplating the scene over her second Pernod, *la belle dame sans merci.*

Well, let her stay here and see if he showed. *Moi* voted with

Billie Holiday: God bless the child that's got her own.

I elbowed with more vigor than a cosmetics magnate's wife should ever show in public toward a small audience gathering at the other end of the bar. "It's got to be after the boat," Lacey's voice insisted through the hubbub. "They fall down a manhole with the punks chasing them—"

"Boring!" Niko, now neon-blue in his cowboy shirt, broke off a conversation with Rachel and Mary Ann to interrupt. "They meet the punks, and they take them down through a secret entrance under one of those humongo sculptures on Wall Street."

"Blindfolded?" suggested Lena, looking from Lacey to Niko. Tentative but happy—like me three days ago, ready to jump down whatever rabbit hole the band opened up.

"Right." Terry squeezed her shoulder. "The punks want to shoot the alligators in the subways—"

"Shoot them?" Mary Ann was shocked.

"For the video." Niko nudged her to listen.

"—only what they don't know is, the alligators've got razor blades." Terry paused for effect.

"Razor blades?" said Lena.

"Sure! Where do you think they go when you drop 'em down those slots in hotel medicine cabinets?"

"You guys are crazy," murmured Rachel, sidling closer to Niko.

"Speaking of paranoia," Niko kissed her ear, "did anybody see Major Strasser trying to steal my ring off the piano?"

"Cripes! *Why?*" asked Lacey.

"He thinks we poisoned Bear. Like the cops. He's sleuthing for clues."

"What an ambersol!" Lacey was disgusted.

"Are you serious?" asked Lena.

"Who? What?" Rachel asked.

"Steve Connelly," said Niko.

"The kid who OD'd," said Terry.

"Ambersol," said Lacey. "French for *you dumb asshole!*"

So unthreatening they made it all sound. As if the police were just one more late-night phantasm, like alligators in the subway, that would vanish in daylight.

I glanced down the bar. The woman at the vortex was biding her time. Why not? She had nothing to lose either way.

I nodded goodbye to the band. I had a few more questions for Marie Tréville before she drank herself under her stool.

But as I wedged in beside her, a large hirsute man in a leather cap and sunglasses slung his arm around her shoulder. "Hey, babe! Whatcha doin' here? You come to hear the band?"

Marie stared at Roach's hand, then up at his face.

"Is old Veek-tor around or did you lose him?" Roach squeezed her and glared at me, clearly hoping I'd take the hint and leave.

Marie squirmed out from under his arm. She held her glass in front of her as if to ward off both of us. And here came reinforcements—two young fans, in baggy pants and haircuts like Les Enchainés, pressing Roach from behind, tweaking his blue sweater. "Hey, man!" said one. "C'est pas mal!"

Roach glowered at him. "Non sprechenzie French. Bug off."

"Roach! Roach!" the other chanted, and mimed a toke.

"What do they want?" Roach asked Marie. He growled at them: "Get lost, will you?"

"Roach! Roach! Roach!"

Marie was shaking with silent laughter.

He arced a fist at them. "Clear out, you cretins!"

But the scowl that once terrified America was an empty weapon in Le Club Souris. Finally Roach signed a cocktail napkin for each of them. They ran off screaming with satisfaction.

"So what's a nice girl like you doing in a place like this?" He waved at the walls.

Marie spoke into her half-empty glass. "Oh, I thought Sheila Bailey would not like to come here, so I came instead."

"Hah! So you're here to keep an eye on us, huh?" Roach thumped her shoulder. "Don't worry, babe. We're just a bunch of old farts anymore."

In Marie's mind I envisioned the long lithe body of Dan Quasi proving him wrong. The hard curve of his back, his legs; his arms that could lift a woman as easily as a guitar—little changed, I suspected, since the Rind days. But that was something she knew and I didn't.

"So are you still pissed at Dan for bagging the Eiffel Tower?"

Marie and I both started nervously, as if Roach had read our minds.

"Me? No." She touched the flower in her hair. "I know how he is. Only Sheila Bailey was angry, and the committee. They are not so used to men like this."

"You and Dan never did get along much, did you," said Roach. "The other night in the trailer was just like how you two used to go at each other after gigs and shit."

He leaned forward and rested his elbows on the bar. "Not like you got along with Mickey."

The ice clattered in Marie Tréville's glass. "Mickey?"

Roach moved one elbow and turned to face her. "You know what I'm talking about. You think I can't see when a chick's stringing me along?" He took off his sunglasses. "I knew it wasn't me you kept coming around for. Then after you split, Mick filled me in. Told me about it in the detox. How you two had the hots for each other, and that night I passed out in Chicago you went to his room."

Under Roach's casual tone was a threat that alarmed me. Plus I was thoroughly confused. Marie and Mickey?

I heard Marie's voice, but only bits of her reply. "I was frightened," and then, "I thought you might be dead."

"That ain't what Mick told me. He said when the two of you made sure I wasn't going to be waking up, you went on back to his room and spent the night."

"Roach." Marie set down her glass. "I won't tell you you are wrong about Mickey and me because I can see you wouldn't believe me. But I do tell you there is no point to this. I have spent all my nights for twenty years with a man who is not you and not Mickey Ascher. You have your little Lacey now, and a hundred other girls if you want them—"

"You told me you couldn't make it with me because you were a virgin. You told me you were saving it for your husband.

And then you turn around and fuck somebody in my own band? What the fuck kind of move is that?"

"You're wrong, Roach," snapped Marie. "And I don't care to be abused about your imaginary injuries in the past." She slapped a bill on the bar.

Was she going to the dressing room? No: around to where the Hands Across the Sea people were standing. I watched her face re-form in a smile of greeting. The Bostonians were as surprised and delighted as a grade school class whose favorite teacher just turned up at their softball game. Even with a Pernod and a half under her belt, Marie Tréville slipped into the role of committee chair like the politician's wife she was.

Roach, meanwhile, bulldozed a path back to the dressing room like the rock musician he was. I picked up his sunglasses from the bar and dropped them into my purse.

Why on earth would Mickey have made such a confession to Roach? To get back at him for bursting enthusiastically into The Rind just when his own powers were failing? To shore up his ego after Marie threw him over for Dan?

Across from me she stood chatting now with Gary Laporte. He looked earnest as ever, peering at her through wire-rimmed glasses that kept sliding down his nose.

No. It wasn't Marie he was staring at. It was the kid who'd just stepped out of the dressing room to ask her to come backstage.

Bang bang! Paladin flinched as pain seared her chest. Then braced herself, clutching the bar. The hero is shot, but she doesn't fall. The fans are expecting her to reappear next week ready to tackle a new set of villains. Meanwhile, how will she get out of this one?

A tap on my shoulder. "Here's looking at you, kid."

I turned. Terry smiled at me over his lifted glass.

"Want to go for a walk?"

"Yes," I said.

Even around the back door the crowd was so dense I wondered if this were a good idea. Luckily most of them hadn't figured out yet that the chunky cheerful American in the flannel shirt was part of tonight's entertainment. What were all these people doing here, anyway? Was Le Club Souris such an in spot that every trend-surfer in Marne-la-Vallée had shined up his or her vinyl jacket and spray-painted her or his hair to drink bourbon and dance to rock-&-roll?

A girl near the bar climbed onto a chair and shouted down to her friends, "Pas la!"

Not just rock-&-roll. Quasi & Company.

I tried to catch Terry's arm, but he was too far ahead of me. I caught up with him outside the swinging door.

"Listen, podner." He pulled me into a corner. "We're never gonna make it past the banditos like this. You got any shades?"

"As a matter of fact—" I fished Roach's sunglasses out of my purse.

Terry put them on. "No good," I told him immediately. "You look like a rock star in disguise."

We pondered. Then a familiar yellow sweater pushed through the door behind us.

"You! Hold it!" commanded Terry. "Hands in the air!"

Steve looked around in bewilderment.

"Reach for the sky!" I seconded.

"Give me your sweater."

It was an order that didn't allow refusal. I held Steve's camera as he pulled his sweater off over his head.

"This ought to do it." Terry wriggled out of his shirt and into the sweater—a tight fit. He looked ridiculous, his arms hanging down like bananas. "What do you think?"

I grinned at him. "All it needs is a camera."

"Now, wait a minute!" Steve protested; but Terry was already looping the strap around his neck.

"Cory, you're my turista girlfriend." Terry took my hand. "Ready? Let's go."

We left Steve gaping in the vestibule in his wrinkled pin-stripes, holding a flannel shirt and a pair of sunglasses.

Chapter 30: When You Wish Upon a Star

"How much do you know about us and Marie Tréville?"

We sat on the railing outside an empty café, on the opposite corner from the neon sign and the line of rock-&-roll fans stretching down the block from the mall entrance. I'd been sure somebody would recognize Terry just from the hunch of his shoulders, but nobody did. Evidently the kids were too intent on getting inside to hear the famous American band to notice a couple of middle-aged tourists.

"Not much." I hesitated. "More than I'd like to."

Terry nodded, as if that told him what he needed to know.

"We go on again in like ten minutes. Dan's talking to her now, but he's not real good at this kind of thing. Also she's kinda drunk."

He stretched his arms inside Steve's sweater to make elbow room. Aha! I noted, attempting not to feel like a bottle that's been chugged and chucked out. There's something I know about Dan and she doesn't. Davy Crockett? Qui est-ce?

I pushed back my hair to get the smell of cigarette smoke out of my face. If I left soon I could wash it tonight instead of waking up tomorrow morning with my pillow reeking of eau de bar.

Or Dan's pillow . . .

"Terry." I looked at him squarely, without disguise. "What does she want? Do you know?"

Terry's fingers drummed thoughtfully on his knee. "Far as I can tell, she wants to go back to Fantasyland."

"And what about Dan?"

He smiled. I could hear the answer coming: "You'll have to ask Dan."

"I tried that." You brought me out here, dammit—don't act like this is an interview. "Now I'm asking you."

"What did he say?"

"A lot about what happened twenty years ago and practically nothing about now."

"Maybe he doesn't know."

"Maybe. But where does that get us? Back to Square One?"

The toe of Terry's sneaker nudged a pebble on the sidewalk. "I doubt it. We've been around the board too many times." He looked up. "Did he tell you about Mickey?"

"Some. The fight over Roach, and how Mickey moved in on Marie."

"Did he tell you Mickey also moved in on Nicola?"

I watched the pebble roll toward a crack in the sidewalk, and Terry stop it with his foot. "No," I said.

"This isn't for the record."

"Hell no," I agreed. And added with a thin smile, "I'm not *always* working."

He patted my hand.

Across the street a couple approaching the mall saw the line for the club and crossed to our side to get around it. Terry waited till they passed us.

"Mickey Ascher was one of those people who can't stand not being the center of things. You've got to understand that about him. It was like he only existed when people were watching him. You know that thing, when a tree falls in a forest? We were all kinda stuck on ourselves back then—that's part of why you *do* rock-&-roll. But with Mickey it was like he really didn't believe he was making a sound unless somebody was there to hear it."

I nodded. In my head the story of The Rind was taking on a shape: not the linearity of a narrative, but the gradual massing of a jigsaw puzzle. The corners in place now: Graham Douglas, Mickey Ascher, Dan Quasi, Marie Tréville. And the picture growing inward from the edges.

"So when Roach started bringing Marie around, raving about she's the true and only love of his life, Mickey couldn't resist. Women were a weak spot for him—or strong spot, how he saw it. That's part of why he moved from rhythm guitar to vocals. He didn't want to be a sideman. He wanted all the little girls to think Mickey Ascher *was* The Rind." Terry kicked the pebble into the street. "Which they did."

The central piece of the puzzle, I thought, and Terry tosses it out like a chunk of sky.

"Things would have blown up sooner except that Mickey and Dan had been friends so long. When Turbo told us he was splitting if Mickey didn't put more juice into the band, it was like, too bad, but those are the breaks. Dan tended to blame Mickey's messes mostly on Dougie, especially the drugs. Dougie was into getting high like he was into the parties and the limos—wearing a coke spoon around his neck, carrying a little gold monogrammed pillbox . . . And whatever Dougie did, Mickey did sooner or later. Dick Field at Optimum used to say there's two kinds of people in the music business—innovators and imitators. At the beginning it worked out great, Dan having weird ideas and Mickey figuring out how to package them. But once we got established, they were pulling against each other. I could see it. Dougie could see it, and he used it. But Dan never saw it till Mickey went after Marie."

Terry's fingers tapped a rapid flutter on the railing. "When Dan found out about that, the whole house of cards collapsed. He was really pissed. All this time he'd been busting his ass to hold it together— He was married to Nicola then, but it wasn't working. Half the time we were touring, and the other half we were either in the studio or Dan was holed up writing. And here's Mickey not just missing rehearsals, pumping The Rind for everything he could get out of it, but snaking Roach's girlfriend purely for spite. Finally Dan blew up—told Mickey to clean up his act or get his ass out of the band. And that's when he found out his best friend was also screwing his wife."

"Oh, Terry."

"Which even Dan could see was totally fucked," Terry agreed. "Mickey didn't need Nicola, either. She was just his way of telling Dan that Roach wasn't the only one he was out to get."

I couldn't help glancing across the street, as if Dan might be standing under the neon sign on the corner lighting a cigarette, waiting for me to come running over and apologize for not knowing, not understanding— But what I saw was an empty alley, and a line of kids inching toward the awning that marked the entrance to Le Club Souris.

The Rind is over. Mickey Ascher is dead. All this happened so long ago that if I did tell Dan how sorry I am, he wouldn't know what I was talking about.

"We finished *Grind*," said Terry, "I'm still not sure how, and then came the famous Saturday night massacre. The lawyers got us all sprung in a couple days except Mickey. So naturally Dan and I went to see him." Terry sighed. "They had him in detox. He looked like a fucking corpse. And he starts telling Dan he knows he stayed away from the party on purpose, set him up, called the cops—it was so sick, so crazy, I wanted to puke. Dan was so bummed he drove straight to the airport and didn't even call in for two weeks."

I could see half a dozen more holes in my puzzle, but only one I had to fill right now. "Did you know then about Dan and Marie?"

"Yeah." Terry sounded glum. "If it was up to me, I'd have taken that girl out back and shot her. But Dan still thought she was his angel sent personally from heaven to save him from all the other crap. No kinks! he'd say. No hidden motives! It was so long by then since he felt like anybody was being straight with him—" Terry shook his head. "Poor sucker, I don't think he ever realized she'd have stuck with Mickey, the one up front in the spotlight, except he was so close to going under."

"That sure isn't how she talks about it now," I said tartly. "According to her, she and Dan had the all-time great cosmic romance."

Terry stretched out his legs and examined the tips of his sneakers. "Easy to see it that way when you've had twenty years to buff up your memories."

A bubble of hope rose in my chest. *Then do you think there's a chance—?*

But that wasn't a question for Terry.

"I thought about the whole thing a lot while Dan was away," he continued. "He'd planned to confess to Mickey about Marie, but he bagged it as soon as we saw him. You could tell from one look at his face, Mick knew he'd lost The Rind. I mean, here he was at this farm for washouts, no champagne, no coke, no screaming fans, *nothing*. That alone probably would've killed him, except for all the media swarming around. And they weren't asking him about his band. They just wanted the dirt on the drug bust.

"But one thing he said rang a bell to me, and that was how somebody must have set it up. It was one of those things you hate to think but you can't get it out of your head. And I kept coming back to, Why did Marie pick that particular night to stage a fight with Dan? I couldn't believe she'd called the cops—she wasn't the type. But it sure was one hell of a coincidence."

He leaned back and gazed across the street. "Well?" I asked. "Did she?"

"I don't know. Things happened so fast, I never found out. Dougie got Mickey out of rehab while Dan was gone. Took him home, called him, no answer, went over to check—well, you know. Listening to *Grind* from up there in angel-land. After that . . ."

"Dan was in San Francisco?" The kaleidoscope in my head rotating, shifting bits of information, refracting them in new arrangements.

"Yeah."

"Can he prove it?"

Terry's eyebrow went up. "To who?"

"The Fraises-des-Bois police? The Governor of Massachusetts?"

Both Terry's eyebrows were up. I told him what I knew, what I'd heard. Hoping—almost expecting—Terry would laugh, or grimace, and chuck the whole can of worms back in the sewer with the alligators. No such luck. His frown said that not only could he offer no reassurance, but this picture looked grimly familiar. *Band on the Run II. The Musical Mystery Tour is dying to take you away.*

"Arrested in France and banned in Boston," he said, shooting for humor and not quite hitting it. "Damn! If I didn't know better, I'd think somebody doesn't like us."

"Does any of this add up to you?" I asked him. "I feel like

I've got a big box of puzzle pieces that don't match. Marie's threatening note, the drugged champagne, Sominol in the piano, Mickey Ascher, The Rind bust—"

Terry nodded. "Like there's a couple different puzzles mixed in together."

But one face, I almost said, appears in all of them. One person with outstanding motive, means, and opportunity for cropping both Victor Tréville and Mickey Ascher out of the picture.

If Terry recognized it (how could he not?) he wasn't going to say so. Neither was I; my biases were too visible. But I couldn't just let it go. Not with so much at stake.

Should I, after tea and cakes and ices, Have the strength to force the moment to its crisis?

"Terry." My heart pounding in my throat. "Who killed Mickey Ascher? Who could have? You must—I mean, of course, the cops, but— Don't you have at least a suspicion?"

His hands were braced on the railing, one on either side. Now his fingers began to tap again, a complicated alternating rhythm, as if for Terry this was the only way to think.

"Who could have?" he said finally. "All of us." His eyes met mine. "Dan, obviously."

I was about to back off, shift to Albert Vaux, when he went on. "All of us. That was the problem. Mickey Ascher double-crossed everybody he knew one way or another. I told the cops: You should be asking who *didn't* have a reason to kill him. Wise-ass, right? But what I really meant was: Does it matter?"

"*Does* it *matter?*"

"Well, yeah." Terry's shoulders went up and down as if he were embarrassed. "We were living in fuckin' Never Never Land! Four kids with no college degrees, no job skills, and there wasn't a damn thing we wanted we couldn't have. Cars, clothes, drugs, women—Smash up a hotel suite, or a Corvette, somebody cleans it up. No consequences. The infinite credit card. That's what Mickey used to say: Put it on the card!" Terry's left hand drummed a tattoo. "Until he got the bill."

I said carefully, "But doesn't it matter to you now, who . . . sent the bill?"

"Sure. Well." He paused. "I always figured, whoever did it has got their own tab to pay. All that shit comes back at you sometime, somehow. But now . . ." A longer pause. "Funny, I never really— Everything was so different then." He frowned. "Off the pigs, don't trust anybody over thirty— And then the *Grind* bust, we're havin' a party, and whammo! Cops smashing down the door, yelling *Freeze, motherfuckers!* Waving guns at us, handcuffs, dragging us into the street— Two weeks later they're back: *Help us find who killed Mickey Ascher.* Oh, so now you're the good guys? Yeah. Right."

What could I say? I understood completely. I also doubted anyone involved in the present investigation would know what Terry meant. Refuse to cooperate? Withhold information? Question authority? Who'd do that but a criminal?

We sat for a minute or two without speaking. Any moment now, I thought, someone will come for him from the club. Our final night here ticking away like a parking meter, and me without a quarter.

"The problem is, this isn't about solving anything." Terry dropped in his own two bits. "It's about don't rock the boat. How can they get their yuppies safe home to Boston without dropping Hands Across the Sea in the shit? Easy. Lump everything together and dump it on Quasi & Company."

"How? Quasi & Company's five people. Six, counting Neil. Even if they could lump it all together, they can't indict a whole band for murder."

I braced for the obvious reply: *No, but they can indict Dan Quasi.*

"That's what I'm saying, Cory. What's a small-town police department going to do with a hot potato that involves a couple hundred high-rollers in two countries? What *can* they do but dump it? They don't need indictments. Or a trial. They need a performance. Show the sponsors and the media that justice has been done. Round up the usual suspects, lock 'em up and throw away the key. Ta da!"

I stared at the street and groped for some other picture that would fit my box of puzzle pieces. A distant corner of my mind noticed that the line to the mall had shortened. It must be time for Quasi & Company to go on again.

Evidently Terry had the same thought. He stood up and held out his hands. When I didn't take them he said, "You want to miss the next set?"

"How can you be so—nonchalant?"

"I'm not. I'm extremely chalant. But we can't do much about it here."

"Can we in there?"

"Maybe." He pulled me to my feet. "Try and keep a lid on Marie, to start with. And show Hands Across the Sea and the rest of them that what Quasi & Company's doing now matters more than a bunch of crap that went down twenty years ago." He squeezed my hands. "How'd you like the Rat?"

"Can't you tell? I've got blisters from clapping."

"Good for you. Always clap for the band and tip your waitress."

"Is that why you brought me out here?" We linked arms and started across the street. "The waitress complained?"

"What do you think?"

I thought of all we'd talked about, and of all we hadn't. I thought of Dan in the dressing room moving his own puzzle pieces around with Marie Tréville.

"I don't know."

Terry stopped in the middle of the road, faced me and clapped a hand over his heart. "Ilsa, I'm no good at being noble, but it all adds up to one thing. She's got to get on that plane with Victor where she belongs."

I couldn't meet his eyes. "That's up to her and Dan, isn't it?"

"Sure." He hooked his arm through mine again. "Like I said, though—she's kinda drunk, and we're going on in a couple minutes. If you could stay close to her till we finish the set—make sure she doesn't go unloading her memories to Major Strasser—you'd be doing us all a favor."

We made our way between parked cars, around a group of kids arguing on the sidewalk, down the alley to the club's back door. At the top of the stairs I stopped.

"Go ahead. I need a cigarette."

Terry kissed my cheek. I knew he knew why I didn't want to show up unannounced with him backstage.

"You're OK, Cory, you know that?"

"For a journalist," I agreed drily. "Break a leg."

"That," Terry grinned, "is my least vulnerable spot."

Chapter 31: I Hope You Get Home All Right

"Excuse me," I told the bouncer. "I'm with the band." For once I was glad I didn't sound French.

Even before I stepped into the club I could see this wasn't going to be an easy job. Keep a lid on Marie? Try finding her! I maneuvered through the Halloween-party bedlam around the bar —bottles clattering, beer spilling, lipsticked mouths screaming over the din of the jukebox, gestures distorted by booze and noise to caricatures as gross as the cartoons behind them. I dodged a shoving match near the cigarette machine; scanned the row of vacant faces along the wall . . . the bodies wriggling like alewives on the dance floor . . .

No Marie Tréville. Bien sur: why fend for herself out here when she had Dan to look after her backstage?

I did see the Hands Across the Sea party, which had moved to the smaller room above the bar. And barricaded behind them, the other three-fifths of Quasi & Company.

"Les Enchaînés are opening," Lacey shouted to me as I threaded toward their table. "Dan's sitting in for the first number, and then me and Niko and François do our wall-of-keyboards blitz."

Niko raised a familiar square bottle—no longer paper-bagged—to toast my arrival. Roach nodded at me and bellowed, "Hey, man! Don't bogart that Jack."

I squeezed into an empty chair between Lacey and Lena. "We couldn't find Terry." Lena looked glad of reinforcements. "Have you seen him?"

An eruption of drunken yells and stomping feet welcomed François, Paul, Denis, and Jean-Claude onstage. "In the dressing room," I shouted back. "Have you seen Marie Tréville?"

"She's back there too." Lena passed me the bottle. "Arguing with Dan, it sounded like. What's going on?"

I shook my head and gulped a hit of Jack. The backstage

door was opening.

The clamor downstairs rose to a roar as Dan walked onto the stage. Blue light threw a triangle of shadow across his cheek, a trapezoid of shadow down his neck. He nodded to Jean-Claude. The crowd subsided. Pile-driving drums and bass . . . He looked ominous among Les Enchainés, in a black T-shirt now and black boots. No hint in those hooded eyes that he'd just come from his lover. This was a man who could walk forty-seven miles of barbed wire, use a cobra snake for a necktie, and dispose of any woman in his path as fast as changing a string. Davy Crockett, King of the Underworld.

Dan is King of Spades, I could hear Penny incant as she laid out her cards beside the tea table. *Terry is clubs, Turbo is diamonds, and Mickey is King of Hearts.*

"Don't know why I love you like I do!" Jean-Claude growled into his mic.

"Hey!" Lacey poked Niko. "That's old Talking Heads!"

Niko chortled. "Al Green wrote that sucker when Byrne was still playing plastic ukelele. What, Roach, '69? '70?"

"Hah!" Roach pounded his fist on the table. "God damn 1974! Lacey, where's the Jack?"

I handed it over—with a flash of riding the bus to D.C., giddily celebrating the future of America with the fifth Penny and I had liberated from a Springfield liquor store.

"To 1974!"

"I'll drink to that," Niko grabbed the bottle.

"Take me to the river!" chorused the band. "Wash me down!"

I glanced at the door again. Then checked the club, hair and arms tossing on the dance floor, backs hunched along the bar. No white camellia.

Niko and Rachel lurched to their feet. "See you guys later," said Rachel with a conspicuous sniff.

"To romance!" Niko hoisted the Jack. "Bless its cloudy head and muddy little feet."

Rachel swiped the bottle. "I'll drink to that!"

"I'll fuck to that!" Roach seconded loudly, and pulled Lacey over for a demonstrative smooch.

Drugs, sex, and rock-&-roll, I added a silent third: cornerstones of our civilization.

A new voice was coming from the speakers overhead. I looked all around the stage before I realized it was Dan.

"I wanna know—oh! Tell me why, should I stay?"

Curving with the lyrics as he never did when he played, pouring his heart into the mic; and the girls in front lapping it up, eager to help him forget her, whoever she was.

"Lacey." I pushed back my chair. "Do you know where—"

She lifted her hand. A guttural cry from the guitar; and as Roach too stopped talking, I saw that Lacey knew Dan would play a solo here and she didn't want to miss it.

My eyes fastened on his bowed silhouette, my ears on the anguished line wailing from the speakers. I thought: this is coming straight from his hands into my head. And into Lacey's, who in one way at least understands him better than either Marie Tréville or I ever will.

In three more minutes she'd have him back. But right now he was mine. So I shut off my brain and opened my mind. Straining to hear what Lacey heard: the synthesizer's eerie chuckle, drums and bass throbbing like a heartbeat; and beckoning between them, the siren song of Dan's guitar.

Somebody nudged me. I ignored it.

"Cory!" A hiss in my ear. "Look!"

I looked. Lena was pointing at the bar.

I stood up so fast I knocked over my chair.

You couldn't miss him, that gray suit slicing through black vinyl and leather like Galahad's sword. His balding head gleamed, the one shiny surface in a forest of bristles and spikes.

What the hell was Victor Tréville doing here?

His clenched face radiated the answer: a crusader come to rescue the Grail from the infidels.

He'd quit the party at EuroDisney. Followed Marie. Why? Not for Hands Across the Sea. To break up her rendezvous with Dan? Drag her out of here by force?

I wrestled free of my tipped chair. Victor's hand was inside his jacket. Reaching for his wallet? His glasses? Maybe. I didn't know. But I did know it's a more serious crime in France to give drugs to a kid than to kill your wife's lover.

Oblivious of the toes I was mashing and drinks I was toppling, I shoved toward the stairs. Never mind that this man was a local bigwig. When it comes to shootouts, Paladin draws first and talks later.

Ten yards below me Victor too pushed forward, eyes fixed on the stage. Fixed on Dan, who stood with his eyes half closed against the spotlights, unaware of anything but music.

"Take me to the river!" shouted the band.

Hell and damnation! Where was Terry? Where was Steve Connelly now that I needed him? I kept losing Victor behind swaying shoulders and bobbing heads. Didn't anybody realize we had to stop him? Were these kids so jaded they couldn't see that a middle-aged bureaucrat had no business in Le Club Souris?

"Till I can't, till I can't take no more!" Jean-Claude howled.

I caught sight of Victor again as he wedged onto the dance floor. I couldn't see his face now—only imagine what emotions must be roiling inside him as he pictured his wife pressed against the damp chest of a rock musician, throbbing with the beat that to him still meant anarchy and revolution.

The kids in my path refused to budge. I waved my arms. Nobody paid any attention except for a young drunk who waved his arms back and then staggered sideways into a table of empty glasses. If I shouted, who'd hear me over Les Enchainés? Anyway, what could I shout to stop a bullet?

"Wash me in the water, the water!"

A long crash of cymbals. Suddenly the band was taking bows.

Dan set down his guitar and slipped out the door.

Victor halted. He looked startled, as if he hadn't noticed till the noise stopped that he'd been dodging dozens of frenetic sweaty dancers. He scanned the stage, the club, the bar. Then he veered toward the restrooms.

I gauged the crowd density in each direction and calculated I was several seconds closer to the backstage door than to Victor

Tréville.

"Niko!" I cried in relief as he and Rachel came flying up the hall. He didn't even pause. Of course—his audience was waiting.

Both bands' dressing rooms were empty. I ran back to the door and ordered the guard not to admit anybody in a suit and tie. Where were Dan and Terry? He shrugged: If not inside, perhaps Madame would find them outside.

I heaved open the heavy fire door at the end of the hall. If only the alarm would go off— No. But there was Dan, sitting alone on the steps smoking a cigarette.

"Hey, Cory." He stood up, smiling.

"Victor Tréville's here," I said breathlessly. "I think he may have a gun."

Bless the male mind with its capacity for assessing parameters. Dan listened with no comment but a raised eyebrow. When I finished he said, "We better find Carl."

"Where's Marie?"

Dan tossed away his cigarette and pounded on the door without answering. The guard let us in. Then a soprano wail from the end of the hall: "Dan!"

My heart sank.

"Get Carl as fast as you can," Dan told the guard.

Marie came running toward us, cheeks flushed, full breasts bouncing under thin cotton. She halted in front of Dan, panting and accusatory. "Where did you go? I was looking for you!"

"Cory and I have business." His arm brushed mine as if for protection.

Marie shot a glance at me, not friendly. "Will you excuse us?"

"No," said Dan. "She won't."

A tremor rippled between them, set them quivering with attraction and repulsion like a pair of magnets. I could no more have left than if I'd been an iron filing.

"Five minutes, Marie. Sorry, but it's urgent."

"It was five minutes when I came here," she retorted heatedly. "Then five minutes while you talked to that boy with no hair. Then five minutes to play your song."

"I told you, I'm busy."

"Busy!" A scornful laugh. "I call to warn you there will be trouble about the Eiffel Tower, and Terry says Sorry, Dan is busy! You were not busy. You were upset because it was not so good for you and me after the banquet."

I turned away in embarrassment. Dan caught my arm.

"But now it's better! Didn't I tell you?—after so long apart, how can one little night bring us back together? Ah, but you think I want only what *they* want, those girls in there. Acting so cold to me at the Fête des Fraises—flirting with your pretty American to make me jealous—"

"Stop it," Dan said curtly.

"I don't care. Let her believe what she likes! Tomorrow we will see if it is her or me at the end of the night."

"Oh, for Christ's sake." Dan ran his hand through his hair. "Everything I do must be a secret message? You think my life revolves around women? Around you?"

"You played me a secret message at the Fête des Fraises," she countered. "Mickey's favorite song to seduce me behind Roach's back; while behind his back you told me, Choose!" She clasped both hands around his wrist and smiled up at him in triumph. "I choose you."

"That was twenty years ago."

"That was tonight. I left a note in the car at EuroDisney: Mon cher Victor, you must make a new life without me. I am going to Boston with Dan Quasi."

"*What?*"

"Don't follow me, because I will never come back!"

"Jesus fucking—" He grabbed her shoulders. "You told him that?"

Her head swung back. "I was wrong to marry you," she shouted at the ceiling, "and now I must do what will make me happy!"

I lunged for fear he'd break her neck. Before I could hit him his hands dropped. He and Marie stared at each other, breathing hard. Her hair was tangled, her eyes wild. I couldn't tell if she was frightened or elated.

"You know I mean it." Her voice low, the growl of a tigress ready to chomp the leg off an antelope.

"I know you're drunk," said Dan in the same key.

"You belong to me. You couldn't stay away, even after twenty years."

"I didn't come here for you."

Marie gave a throaty satisfied laugh.

"I came for the band."

"Always the band!" she taunted.

"Damn right," said Dan. "It was the band then, it's the band now, and it'll be the band in Boston."

"You love your band, but you love me better." She moved closer, compelling him with her eyes, her scent, the heat of her body. "I'll make you happy, Dan. I'll cook you breakfast, I'll make love with you all night—"

"I don't need a wife, Marie" Dan pulled my Merits out of his pocket as if to fend her off with a smokescreen. "And you already have a husband."

"Would you have me go back to Victor?"

"You married him." He glanced at the door. I could feel him seeking a way out, listening for Carl, gauging how long till the keyboard blitz finished.

"Victor is a *canaille!* A coward who won't fight for me, who tries to hold me with threats!"

"He fought for you on the boat."

"Pfft!" Again that gesture of tossing something away. "Was it for Victor you came to France? Was it for my marriage you tried to kill him last night?"

I'd just been thinking I'd better go find Carl, but at that I froze.

Dan's match stopped in midair. "What?"

"Why else did you put pills in his champagne but to win me back?"

"Me? You know I didn't— That was you!"

"How can you say that?" Marie was outraged. "Me, poison my husband? How can you accuse me—?"

The hall went dead.

For an instant I couldn't tell what had changed. Then I heard: no music. Only drums thumping on alone.

Dan was already out the door.

I scanned the club and didn't see him. The stage was full of colored lights, musicians . . . all glancing around perplexedly except Paul, who went on flicking his sticks from tom to floor drum to cymbals as if he hadn't noticed the rest of the band had stopped.

Lights, but no amplification. Not an electrical failure.

Up by the sound board I spotted Neil's red ponytail hanging through the railing. A dark silhouette on the steps—Dan? The shape behind him was clearly Roach, shouting inaudibly at somebody near the board. Everyone else up there was edging away, pushing toward the stairs.

The sound came on. Loud cheers as Niko and Lacey and Les Enchaînés retrieved the beat and the dance floor re-erupted into motion.

The crowd coming down from the upper room was too dense to squeeze through. Why didn't they look concerned? I intercepted one of the Alligator Brothers. Something wrong with the sound system, he explained. They want us out of the way till it's fixed.

All I could see up there was confusion. Broad shoulders— Terry's?—swaying as if to the music. An arm flung into the air— red sleeve, red fingers, red glint of metal or glass. Hands thrust for the arm and missed. *Bang!* Was that a gunshot or drums? A mouth opened as if in a scream. Somebody stumbled down the steps. No —two bodies were grappling, slipping, one hurling the other into the wall. A bald head snapped forward. A bottle arced over the railing and shattered against Neil's effects rack. No sounds—this was a silent movie with wall-of-keyboards accompaniment. And no audience. They were all watching the show onstage.

"Oh, mon dieu! Victor!"

I'd forgotten Marie till I heard her shriek behind me. Two men were hurrying toward us, one with yellow arms half raised, the other—shit alors!—prodding him with a clenched fist.

"Inside," barked Victor Tréville. He jerked his head at Marie and me. "You too."

No! my brain protested. This is ludicrous! You can't— I don't—

A thumb-sized flash of silver. "Man, you're crazy," Terry said sincerely over his shoulder as Victor marched him through the door.

Into Quasi & Company's dressing room. Marie gave a gasp that was half sob, half laugh. Terry looked remarkably calm for a man with a pistol at his back.

My mind was pounding as fast as my heart. Could I grab a beer bottle out of one of those cases? Did anyone here have any kind of a weapon? No room for me to sneak around and jump him . . .

"It was you!" Marie hurled the accusation like a knife. "You, my own husband, who poisoned my champagne!"

"Tais-toi!" snapped Victor.

"Who killed that boy! For no reason but jealousy!"

Merde! Quadruple merde!

Of course: What trick wouldn't Victor have tried to abort his wife's affair? He knew she was a light drinker, so he'd jacked up the dosage—a dosage probably set by Albert Vaux himself, poor stooge, when he tested the Sominol on Lacey in a Montmartre bar.

"You call yourself a man?"

"Silence!"

He roared it so ferociously that Marie flinched. The scuffle had battered Victor Tréville into a tailor's nightmare—one sleeve ripped, his tie askew, his shirt collar bloody from a gash on his jaw. But most frightening was his face: the cold desperate rage of a man who's wriggled so far out on a limb that caution would be pointless.

"Go outside," he commanded her. "Wait for me in the car."

"No!"

Marie moved toward him, but I grabbed her. "For God's sake, don't do anything dumb."

Terry smiled faintly.

"I have come to take you home," Victor's nostrils flared, "and kill your lover."

Marie let out a wail.

"Ah . . . I hope you're not talking about me," said Terry.

"He's talking about me." Dan stood in the doorway. "Back off, Victor. Let him go."

Cool as a riverboat gambler, though he hadn't even got a sleeve to hide an ace in.

"Tell your friends behind you to go away," Victor ordered, "and shut the door."

Marie's mouth was still quivering, but she'd stopped crying. Her hero had arrived. Everything would be all right.

Dan spoke to someone in the hall and closed the door. Not sharing Marie's optimism, I stepped between him and her husband. "Victor. You don't want to do this. You're too smart a man to make such a bad mistake."

"How's Roach?" Terry murmured to Dan.

"Think of your reputation, your constituents, your family!"

"Winged in the leg."

"It's not too late. If you leave now—"

"Not without my wife!"

Marie blew her nose and dabbed furtively at her eyes.

"Did Carl—?"

"Silence!" roared Victor. He glared at Terry, then Dan. "You pigs! You animals! Why should I not shoot both of you? You invade my country, you turn my district upside down, ruin our festival, degrade our children, steal wives from their husbands, and for what? To amuse yourselves?"

A dramatic pause. Nobody moved.

"Ha ha! Look at these fools who waste their money on our bad music! Look at Victor Tréville, what a joke! He marries a young girl to save her from disgrace and she dishonors him! Ha ha!" He gave Terry a shove with his free hand. "I who have lived as a man of honor, a man of peace, am I to watch you spread your evil and not lift my finger?"

"Man, you've got your finger on the wrong trigger," Dan said coldly.

I wished I could see him. Dan must still be realizing it wasn't Marie he'd been protecting since last night. Au contraire. By ignoring her husband's campaign against his band—by trusting her to keep Quasi & Company safe, and their affair secret—he'd shot himself in the foot.

"You are the fool!" Marie declared with scorn. "You can't have me because I am going to Boston with Dan. And if you shoot him, I will tell Georges d'Aumont you put sleeping pills in my champagne, and killed two men," her voice went shrill, "and if you ever escape from prison, I swear by the good God I will cut out your heart with a knife and feed it to the cat."

Shit alors! And he's afraid of rock-&-roll?

"Then I shall kill him first and you afterwards."

"Now, hold on, monsieur. Take it easy." Terry turned his head a cautious half inch. "Can we just talk this over for a minute? What about Cory's idea—"

"Shut up!" Victor jabbed him with the pistol.

"Do that again, motherfucker," Dan stepped out from behind me, "and you're gonna be shitting cartridges."

Victor almost shifted the gun, but he thought he smelled a trap and pointed it quickly back at Terry. "Over your dead body, Monsieur Quasi, I am happy to say."

"Go ahead." Dan walked toward him. "Try it. You saw those people out there. You think they'll let you leave here alive if you fuck with us?"

"Don't come any closer," said Victor, "or you will not live long enough to hear what I have to say to you."

Terry's expression suggested neither he nor Dan thought this would be any great loss; but Dan stopped.

"Before you die, I want you to know how thoroughly I have beaten you." His voice flat as an oil slick. "You tried to take my wife, but I have got her back now. You tried years ago to debauch her, and I beat you then as well. Do you think she will weep when you are dead? Not for long! No longer than she wept for your friend, that filthy rapist pig, who courted his doom with greed and vanity like you, and fell as you now fall to the hand of justice."

I couldn't look at Dan. Didn't need to. Terry's stricken face mirrored his reaction. *Marie maybe we can negotiate; but not Mickey Ascher.*

"Are you crazy?" Terry croaked. "Murdering innocent

people? You call that—"

"Innocent people!" Victor seemed to swell with anger. "My wife was innocent! This was a girl who had never touched a man until that criminal fiend ravished her! In pity she answered his call for help, and he met her with lust, with violence! What could she do but try to defend herself? And when I came to her aid, when I found her battered and weeping beside the brute who had ruined her, what could I do as an honorable man but make certain he should never destroy a woman again!"

I felt sick. I had guessed Marie must have lied to him, but I'd never suspected this. Mickey must have phoned her when he got out of McLean, the night of his welcome-home party. By then Dan had been gone for weeks—leaving her to face alone the dreadful consequences of having given her virginity to a married man. Who else would have her now? The call from Mickey must have seemed like a miracle: still single and rich, sexy as ever, and officially rehabilitated. Only it wasn't marriage Mick had in mind. He'd already seduced Dan's wife in revenge for losing The Rind. Now he would get the girlfriend.

I glanced over, expecting to see a woman cowed with shame. Au contraire. Marie's spine was stiff, her chin up, her lips pursed. If anything, I thought she looked relieved. Her husband still believed her. Maybe, just maybe, she could pull this off.

But Victor wasn't the only one she had to convince. If the man who smashed Mickey Ascher's skull walked out of here in one piece, it would indeed be over Dan Quasi's dead body.

His fists were clenched. "Marie, what the hell?"

"Oh, Dan!" She seemed to melt, though she barely stirred. "How could I ever tell you?—that your dear friend would do so horrible a thing!"

"Did he"—Dan jabbed a thumb—"kill Mickey?"

"I didn't mean him to be hurt! Even after such a—"

"Marie, dammit!"

"Yes! All right."

Victor growled: "Marie . . . !"

"It was an accident!" Her eyes darted anxiously between them. "Mickey attacked me! I hit him—what else could I do? And he fell. I couldn't wake him up. Was he dead? I didn't know! I was fainting from pain and fear. So I called Victor."

"Frightened half to death I found her!" Victor cut in. "Her clothes torn and bloody— That filthy animal had thrown her down on the floor, beaten her, assaulted her! Hardly could she lift the empty bottle! When I saw her, shaking, barely able to move, smeared with her own virgin blood—" His voice cracked. "Death was too kind for that beast!"

This was Mickey Ascher's murderer. This pistol-waving bureaucrat swaying before me in near-hysterics, his suit ripped, his eyes wild, fillets of black hair snaking up from his bare scalp—this was the man who'd eluded the police and the media for twenty years.

"Dan, you understand, yes? How frightened I was? That you would hate me, for being such a fool to go to him, even though it was for you, his friend, gone away, I didn't know where—"

Dan wasn't listening. He must be replaying the nightmare, piecing scenes together as I was: Victor coldly scouring the penthouse, removing every trace of Marie. Carrying Mickey's still-warm body to the polar-bear rug and pounding it to certain death with the bottle he then wiped clean and dumped among the rest. Throwing the other evidence—sheets? rugs? towels? clothing?—down the garbage chute to be incinerated. Hurrying his rescued damsel-in-distress home to France before she could catch her breath. Sealing their complicity with a white wedding. Then keeping their bargain for twenty years . . . until Hands Across the Sea came along to strip the camouflage off her deceit and his violent temper.

"Hey! Open up in there!" Someone pounded on the door. "The police are on their way! Come out with your hands up!"

I glanced at Terry in hope and fear.

Dan dived at the same instant Victor's gun blasted a hole through the muffled beat of Les Enchaínés. Shattering glass—a scream—and then Victor had Terry by the arm, his pistol pressed into the dimple where an earring used to be.

The door rattled violently. Dan scrambled to his feet.

Oh, god, he's OK!—but for how long?

"Send them away!" Victor screeched.

"Keep everybody back, Carl," Terry called unsteadily.

Dan shifted as if preparing to spring. Terry gave a slight but emphatic shake of his head. "And tell François, if we're not out there soon, keep playing."

He gestured with his eyebrows at Dan. I couldn't read the signal, if that's what it was, but I hoped he'd conveyed what I was thinking: We can't win this on Victor's terms. Either we come up with another plan, and damn fast, or we'll all finish this set in angel-land.

Dan's head swiveled almost imperceptibly, taking in the wall without windows, the stacked cartons, empty guitar cases. No exit. Our only weapon was words . . . and that was my department.

No way, you guys! I'm a journalist, not a performer! Dan— you've written a hundred songs, you know how to manipulate a whole arena—you can do it! Talk! Not to him—to her. Talk to Marie!

But from his rigid mouth I saw he hadn't heard the secret message I'd heard. Bien sur—Dan Quasi's forte was squeezing the universe into three and a half minutes. Verse, chorus, and bridge. Whereas mine was listening for someone else's key and tuning to it.

There comes a time when years of shoring up a doomed marriage to a cosmetics heir is the ideal credential. A time when you have to take risks and take charge.

"Marie." I cleared my dry throat. "You said you need a man who'll fight for you. Well, look at your husband! Why do you think he's risking his career, his reputation, everything he cares about, but because he loves you too much to let another man win you?"

Her eyes widened a notch. Evidently I'd hit the right note.

"Think what you'd have to sacrifice for Dan. Are you a woman who can be happy hanging around in cheap bars? Don't you deserve a man who treats you better than that? Who puts you first? Who loves you all the time, not just backstage between sets?"

"Dan could be such a man, if he will let me take care of

him!"

God forbid, I thought with a shudder. "But Victor *is* such a man."

"Victor! That is love like bread. Dan is *champagne,*" she caressed the word.

An unfortunate analogy. Victor's hand twitched dangerously.

"You can live on bread. You can't live on champagne."

"But one needs champagne to truly live."

"And you've had it."

"Ah, yes." Marie sighed, a trace of a smile behind her *tristesse.* "I have had it."

I resisted an impulse to glance at Dan. So far, so good; but now what? How many reasons can I invent why she should trot back into the corral while I'm kicking up my heels outside the fence?

"You're no fool, Marie." Terry came in as smoothly as if we'd rehearsed this. "You know the problems of three little people don't amount to a hill of beans in this crazy world. Can't you tell your husband you made it up about you and Dan? I'm sure he'd understand."

"Made it up?" Marie was outraged. "I made up nothing!"

Dan picked up his cue. "Terry's right, Victor. Marie and I did get together the other night, but it wasn't what you think. You're the one she cares about." He paused. "I knew that, and so did she, but she didn't want to hurt my feelings. She pretended I still meant something to her, and I let her pretend."

As earnest as if he'd written the lines himself. Victor's eyes, shifting from Dan to Terry to Marie, remained bright and hard as marbles.

"Marie, admit it," Terry counseled. "Inside of us we both know you belong with Victor. You're part of his work, the thing that keeps him going. If that plane leaves the ground and you're on it, you'll regret it—maybe not tomorrow, but soon, and for the rest of your life."

Marie goggled, but one corner of her mouth was curling with satisfaction. At last, homage worthy of a woman at the vortex!

"Marie," demanded Victor, his voice and his gun quivering.

"Is this true?"

She looked at him, then back at Dan. You could almost hear the cogs whir: Watch the police haul her husband off to prison for killing her lover? Let the media broadcast her indiscretions, drag her marriage through the mud, track her all over Boston? Give up her children? her house? her designer dresses? her pearls? Citroën? tilleul in the garden? committee sinecures?

"Yes. All right." She faced Victor. "Yes, it is true. You wounded me to the heart when you tried to stop Quasi & Company from coming to France. How could you trust me so little? How could you interfere with my decisions and shame me to my friends? And then to poison my champagne!" She scrutinized him as if comparing this disheveled warrior with her irksome husband. "But I see now that you did it out of love. And out of love, we must forgive each other." A sidelong glance at Terry. "We must all agree that for the past to be ripped open, every old mistake uncovered, can do only harm."

"Absolutely," muttered Terry.

"The poor Mickey Ascher and the poor Albert Vaux are both in God's hands now. They died by accident. This is very sad, but not a crime for us to revenge or expose."

Dan gave a wary nod. With a fleeting vision of Rik Green stabbing me to death with his blue pencil, so did I.

Marie Tréville's hands folded poignantly over her breast. "Dan I will always keep here," she told her husband, "but I belong with you. Victor, chéri, take me home."

She opened her arms. Victor still wasn't completely convinced this wasn't another nasty American joke; but when she swept toward him, he lowered his gun and embraced her.

For five long seconds the rest of us held our breath. Then Marie, with unexpected sangfroid, tossed Victor's pistol into a beer carton.

Terry wiped his forehead on both sleeves. In his face I saw his life rewinding: his wife, kids, the farmhouse in Lincoln, the band's new studio, his cymbals—and Dan, who pulled him into a hug so heartfelt that tears started streaming down my cheeks, and I had to join them to keep my knees from buckling.

At last Dan, with one arm around Terry and one around me, murmured, "Open the door?"

"Right." Terry grinned wanly. "Call off the SWAT team before they scare away the customers."

"Cory, you OK?"

I nodded. "Except I just got somebody awfully wet."

"Me," said Terry. "No problem." He gave my shoulder a reassuring squeeze. "It's Major Strasser's sweater."

Chapter 32: The End of the Night

You'd think the survivors of a brush with death would be ushered to some quiet spot to recover. Fat chance. We came out of the dressing room into a ring of gendarmes demanding the full story on the scene they'd just heard through the door. Luckily Carl convinced them that (A) Dan and Terry had a set to finish, and (B) it was the man in the suit who'd done the shooting.

Also luckily—miraculously, in my view—nobody had tipped off the media. I didn't even want to contemplate the work ahead of me once the news leaked out about Guest Star Night at Le Club Souris. Not only as a journalist and eyewitness. When at last I opened my purse for tissues, there was the red light of my tape recorder, which had been running nonstop since *Mickey Rat*.

How to balance the demands of truth, justice, and our backstage deal was a dilemma that could wait. Right now my priority was to stay vertical. Dry my eyes, blow my nose, and pull myself together. Field questions from the cops. Watch them snap steel bracelets over Victor Tréville's gold cufflinks. I almost might have felt sorry for him if Marie hadn't been hovering nearby with an exalted smile: My hero!

"Et maintenant, mes amis, Le Club Souris est tres heureux de vous presenter enfin . . ."

"What are we opening with?" Terry whispered to Dan. "Do you remember?"

Past their heads the stage glimmered like the midway in a carnival: Denis of the purple fishnet shirt waving a beer bottle at Roach, red cigarette smoke twining up from an ashtray on Niko's piano, a hand pattering on a bongo drum, Lacey fluffing her frizz of golden hair behind her water-spider organ. Nothing's changed, I realized dazedly. It's all exactly the same as before—except for us.

"Rock-&-roll music first." Dan's arm was around my waist. "Then gimme some lovin'." He kissed me on the mouth. "Come back, OK?"

Loud cheers from the crowd as they walked onstage. Terry remembering at the last minute to pull off Steve's sweater; and Dan changing under the lights into a star, dark demigod of women's fantasies and men's dreams, the leader of the band.

I edged along the wall till I found a place to stand. The stale-smoke taste of him was still roaring in my ears. I lit a Marlboro from a candle and tried to grasp that moments ago this man slipping his guitar strap over his neck nearly became a footnote to history.

"Cory!" A tap on my back. "Where have you been? What happened to Dan and Terry? I can't believe they kept all these people waiting—"

I shushed him. It wasn't over yet. François was handing Dan a vocal mic.

"Lena said Victor Tréville's here," Steve shouted over the clapping. "Have you seen him? Great angle for press releases—French diplomat shows support for international exchange—"

"Shh!" I stepped on Steve's toe. "Listen."

"You guys speak English?" Dan asked the audience.

Yells of confirmation.

"Thanks for waiting. We got held up backstage. Some asshole shot our bass player. Thought he was messing around with his wife."

The audience hollered approval. Roach grinned, pointed to his bandaged leg, and gave Lacey an abashed wink.

"What?" Steve poked me again. "Roach got shot? Holy shit! Somebody had a *gun* in here, with the Trévilles—?"

I nodded. Dan nodded to the band.

"Well, let me hear some of that rock-&-rollin' music!"

Vinyl jackets, harem pants, studded leather vests, Fruit-of-the-Loom T-shirts—everybody in Le Club Souris wanted to boogie. They didn't look ominous to me now, these kids jostling each other for dancing room. They looked like us: hot to take over the world their parents fucked up, bursting with energy that needed an outlet before reality reared its cloudy head again tomorrow.

When Phil Alligator beckoned from the melee I ran to join

him. Let Steve chew on the universe. I was voting with my feet—
American journalist shows support for international exchange in
one last fling with Les Quasis Enchainés.

It was a memorable set: "Gimme Some Lovin'," "Stand By
Me," "Jailhouse Rock," "Midnight Hour," and a hard-driving
"Little Sheila" which Roach dedicated with a big grin to Hands
Across the Sea. Some of them sent my head spinning back to high
school; some I'd heard Quasi & Company play: "Slow Down,"
with Dan's wild spiraling guitar riff on the chorus; "Something
About You," where everybody clapped hands in the air to "Sweet
sweet thing, I'm satisfied!" I didn't tape it. I didn't even take
notes. Once when a flashbulb popped my head swerved—but no,
Victor and Marie were gone, scooped up by the long arm of
justice. Paying their tab for years of clinging to what you can only
keep by letting it go.

When the band staggered offstage after "Shake, Rattle &
Roll," I gasped for breath, whooped for an encore, and prayed that
if they played one it would be slow. My feet hurt all the way to my
knees. My blouse was so wet I stuck to the wall. My shoes were I
didn't know where. I couldn't remember ever feeling more tired
and wired in my life.

Two more rowdy grand finales before Carl switched on the
house lights. I gave Dan five minutes and then plowed toward the
backstage door.

He stood in the hall with a towel around his neck, still in his
soaked black T-shirt, pinned between François and Gary Laporte
on one side and two beaming women on the other. The leader of
the band . . . obliging us with an after-show encore we could each
carry home to our own audience: French rock-&-rollers, a
sociology class, envious teenage kids, a husband whose ardor
needed pricking, or the readers of Phases.

"Cor-ree!" François wrapped me in a sweaty hug. "You tell
me! What does it mean, 'I'm like a one-eyed cat peepin' in a
seafood store'?"

I laughed and patted his back. "Go look in a mirror."

Dan's head turned, and his stage persona dissolved into a
personal grin.

"But in terms of thematic content—" insisted Gary Laporte.

I didn't want to interrupt. There were no words that could possibly convey to Dan how full of joy and relief I felt—and how overwhelmed by his boundless capacity to give me more than I asked.

"—retain the rage of popular music from the sixties, but without the commitment to mobilizing—"

Dan held out his arm. I stepped into it; and told him with a long kiss most of what I wanted to say.

"—an inward-turning expression of alienation instead of a rallying cry—"

"Anner name dry me insane." François shook his head. "C'est fou, ça!"

"Hey," returned Dan. "It's rock-&-roll, not T. S. Eliot."

His fingers were making absent-minded ringlets in my hair. If there had been anywhere to drag him off to and expand on that kiss, I would have.

"Exactly! Yes!" Gary Laporte bounced with impatience. "So the concert itself is no longer an affirmation of shared values, but pure spectatorship. No different from a sporting event."

He'd finally got everyone's attention. The two ambassadors were not quite rolling their eyes. François stared at him with a benevolent blankness that placed Professor Laporte in the same category as a rock concert or sporting event.

"As a musician, can you comment on that?"

"Sure." François smiled broadly, happy to comment on anything. "Les Enchaînés write our songs to say what we feel. This is what you ask me? If the people who listen feel the same, then they will come back and hear us again."

"Well, but what *kind* of songs?" persisted Gary Laporte. "Do you share Mr. Quasi's commitment to sociopolitical consciousness raising? A rallying cry to action?"

I could feel Dan opting not to respond. François looked puzzled. "Do I tell people what they should do? No. I am a musician, not a politician."

"Well, you see, that's my point." Gary Laporte shot a glance of triumph at Dan. "The quantum shift in the role of the musician in popular culture—obvious when you listen to the lyrics."

"Ah!" François grinned in comprehension. "You mean, our songs are not the same as 'I'm like a one-eyed cat peepin' in a seafood store.'"

Dan guffawed as if he'd been trying not to laugh but couldn't hold it in any longer. Gary Laporte stared at him over the rims of his glasses, startled and crestfallen.

In spite of myself I sympathized. "What are you snickering at?" I poked Dan in the stomach. "Who wrote 'Tear It Up'? Who wrote 'Government Man'?"

"Right! Leaders of the New England antiwar movement!" Professor Laporte pushed up his glasses. "Theme song of the protest generation!"

"It wasn't a theme song when I wrote it."

A clatter down the hall as somebody knocked over a chair. I saw two bare feet kicking in the air; then Roach charged unsteadily out of the dressing room with Lacey slung over his shoulder, pounding her fists on his back.

The two women exchanged alarmed looks: So the stories are true! What did he do to her? Will she take him to court? Should we get out before we're implicated?

"Well, but it was to rally the protesters in Chicago!" Gary Laporte said accusingly. "I've still got the review from Rolling Stone—'Rind Throws Sand in Daley Machine.'"

"Nah." Dan pulled me out of range of Lacey's flailing feet. "'Government Man' was just me blowing off steam at the Somerville cops for busting some friends of mine."

"You talking about 'Government Man'?" Roach halted. "That hype Dougie put out about flipping Daley the bird?"

"Our manager thought we should have a concept," Dan explained over Lacey's shrieks, giggles, and threats.

"America's answer to the Stones," said Roach, as authoritatively as if he'd been with the band since its founding. "What was the other one? Rock's deadly curse?" He pointed Lacey's feet at the door. "François, you wanna open that? Lacey needs some Jack."

I watched them go, felt Dan's warm chest against my back,

and paged through clippings in my mind: four truculent young men rallying America's students to revolution; Hands Across the Sea clapping for Quasi & Company's medley of protest hits; Victor Tréville, his shirt streaked with blood, railing against these hoodlums who'd invaded France to lure wives from their husbands and overturn civilization.

"Mickey used to say it was like the Star-Spangled Banner," said Dan. "Some dude lifts an old Brit drinking tune, plugs in rockets and shit, and next thing you know it's the national anthem."

"I can't believe that," Professor Laporte said flatly.

"Believe it or not." Dan kissed my hair. "Come on, Carl's closing down the bar."

It was just as well I'd forgotten my watch, because the dawn's early light was infiltrating Le Club Souris by the time we climbed into Quasi & Company's truck. The last hangers-on from Hands Across the Sea had left when the bar closed. By then Dan and Terry and I had repeated our story—the expurgated version, Jealous Husband Shoots Bassist, Threatens Wife and Self—five times by my count. The last two were for the inevitable TV crews which fortunately arrived too late to shoot anything but the alley steps. Lena and Rachel had reluctantly caught a ride back to their host families when Carl booted Steve Connelly out along with the TV people. Then everybody who was left drifted onto the stage, and into a monumental jam, and the next thing we knew it was morning.

I remembered my camera in time for a group snapshot, but I resisted the urge to photograph Niko's beat-up piano, Terry's red-topped stool, the snare drum whose head I'd helped change our first night in France . . . Merde! Once we said goodbye to those drums it was the end of the road.

"OK, Neil!" Niko's voice echoed in the empty truck. "Roll it!"

"Hey, you guys, thanks," Terry called to Les Enchainés as

Neil backed toward the street.

"Look what Carl gave me!" Lacey flourished a nearly full bottle of Jack Daniel's.

It made the rounds as we headed toward the A4. We sat in a circle on the dusty floor, Dan with an acoustic guitar on his lap, drinking, smoking, and singing: On the road again! Past the conical magician's hat we sang, past the distant blue spires of Sleeping Beauty's Castle, across the beet fields of Marne-la-Vallée, into the silent streets of Paris. Mist was rising from the Seine, where only a few hobos were up to hear us welcome in the morning. The Eiffel Tower looked like an erector-set model for a champagne bottle, a silvery skeleton with its top shrouded in clouds. I wondered if that was how I'd remember it when I got home . . . or in sunlight with Lacey spreading her arms and crowing, "France! I love it!"

I didn't feel a bit tired now. I wished we could drive all the way to Boston like this, with a hit of Jack warming my insides, the gray road unrolling behind us, and the whole world asleep.

Sunrise was turning the cobblestones pink when we reached the Hôtel des Fraises. "Bedtime!" announced Niko.

"Oh, Christ." Terry held out a crumpled handful of yellow wool. "I forgot to give Major Strasser his sweater."

In the elevator Dan kissed my ear. "Come up?"

"See you in a minute."

Lacey linked her arm in mine as she and Roach and I walked down the hall. "So you guys worked it out, huh?"

"Yup." I hugged her; and then Roach surprised me by hugging both of us. "G'night."

Dan was sitting on his bed when I came in, still picking out bits of music. His bare shoulders were striped with brand-new daylight from the shutters. Those shoulders hundreds of hands had clapped for in Le Club Souris . . . mine now for the few hours we had left.

I climbed onto the other end of the bed. Thinking: So long since I've known making love to mean this, that you wake up tomorrow with even more love than you had last night.

Dan glanced up and smiled; but his tune went on curling

around me like a cat in search of a lap.

Why do you do this to me, Dan Quasi? Is it so hard to come down after four days of banquets and boats, clubs and floats? Does it feel so strange to leave your friends for a woman you hardly know, and a journalist at that?

He reached out to squeeze my foot. "No tape recorder?"

"Don't need it." I leaned back in the pillows. "I know this one backwards and forwards."

"You said the other day you liked it."

"Before I found out you wrote it for Marie."

Wondering if he'd take the cue and tell me what I still couldn't ask him: *How do you feel about her now? What did it do to your twenty years of regret to find out she and her husband killed Mickey Ascher?*

"I'm not playing it for Marie, though. I'm playing it for you."

Maybe he hadn't heard my question. Or was I the one who hadn't heard his answer?

"Can you do that?"

"Why not?" A pair of chords echoed the words. "Didn't you connect it with somebody else before you met me?"

Images of floating across a dance floor at Harvard, pine-paneled walls dissolving in the music. And of climbing into bed at the Bluebird Motel, my notebook and tape recorder on the night table, Dan Quasi's voice singing me to sleep.

"It was different then," I said inadequately. A lullaby for nights when I was in love or wanted to be, I almost added, when I lay between unfamiliar sheets searching my mind for a place that felt like home, and no words summed up my yearning like yours. "It was mine then, and now it isn't."

"Sure it is. Yours, Marie's, and a lot of other people's." Dan shifted one leg up onto the bed. "Mine, too, don't forget."

"Yours?" I looked at him curiously. "What does it mean to you?"

He was silent for a moment—paging, I suspected, through his own private scrapbook. "Like you said: it's different." He flashed me that half-smile I first met in a doorway in D.C. "I used to get so sick of it, playing it every night, I wished I never wrote it. But sometimes I'd look out and see a girl . . ." His finger tapped thoughtfully on his guitar. "Who reminded me of somebody I used to know, or looked like she needed cheering up, or her boyfriend was a jerk and I wanted to tell her to hold out for better. And I'd catch her eye, and sing it like I meant it."

"Did it work?" I inquired stiffly.

"For the girl?" He grinned. "Usually. For me, every time."

"Which category do I fall into?"

"What? Oh. No. I was just thinking while I was waiting for you, we probably won't play 'The End of the Night' anymore after we get back."

"Because of tonight? Marie and Mickey?"

His eyes met mine. "That doesn't change anything. Not for the band. At least I hope not." His fingers moved again over the strings, as if to gather his thoughts. "For me it does, obviously. Old doors closing, new ones opening. Facing up to things I should've dealt with a long time ago. Although you don't always see that then."

"No." My hands hugged my knee: the left one bare without its eye-catching diamond. "Sometimes you don't even see the door till after you've come through it."

Dan nodded. "It helped, what you said the other day. You asked me why I don't write songs like that now, and I thought, Christ!—that would be like writing 'Government Man' again. It's so far from what I want to do with this band."

I pressed my bare foot against his back. "So this is the final farewell performance?"

"Yup."

Twisting around to face me, he started from the beginning.

"Thousands of faces in the dark,
Eyes that glitter like sparks
Watching the man
Who's clutching his heart in his hands . . ."

I watched him: not his eyes, which gazed past me, but his hands. In my mind I was stretched out on a lumpy bed with my eyes closed, dreaming that Dan Quasi was sitting by my feet playing this song he'd written for me after our almost-fling in D.C.

It didn't sound like a tape, though. Or a performance, as it had the other night when he put it into the set for Marie.

"But it's you

I'll be waiting to find . . ."

No, I thought, he isn't always onstage, though I and she and a lot of other people keep pushing him back up there. Sometimes he's just an ordinary person, except that it's not easy for him to say what he feels unless it's set to music. A man who speaks through his fingers . . . Whose heart is in his hands, held out to me.

"Shining and true," his blue eyes smiled at me,

"My light at the end of the night."

I leaned up and slid my hand across his shoulder and down his back. Dan set his guitar against the bedside table, strings out, as nearly upright as possible, where it would be safe till morning.

About the Author

CJ Verburg is a writer and editor in fiction, science, biography, and international literature, as well as an an award-winning playwright and director. Her first full-length play was the groundbreaking rock-protest musical *We Could Save the World*. *Another Number for the Road* is her fourth mystery novel and her second book in the Cory Goodwin series, after *Silent Night Violent Night*. Like Cory, she spent many years in Boston; like Dan Quasi, she left it for San Francisco. In between she staged plays on Cape Cod with her neighbor and comrade-in-arts Edward Gorey, subject of her print and e-book *Edward Gorey On Stage: Playwright, Director, Designer, Performer: a Multimedia Memoir*, and instigator of her Edgar Rowdey Cape Cod mystery series.
More at http://*cjverburg.net*

Also from CJ Verburg and Boom-Books:

Silent Night Violent Night
A publisher's Christmas party. A blizzard. Rival scientists. Secret romances. Murder. Only the journalist daughter of New York private eye Archie Goodwin can solve this one.

Croaked: an Edgar Rowdey Cape Cod Mystery
Is the charming seaside town of Quansett a sanctuary or a death trap? It takes a village to find out—led by urban refugee Lydia Vivaldi and reclusive artist Edgar Rowdey.

Zapped: an Edgar Rowdey Cape Cod Mystery
If inventor Pam Nash is right about Zappa, she could revolutionize law enforcement. If she's wrong, they'll kill her daughter.

Also from Boom-Books, by Charisse Howard:
Dark Horseman:
Mystery, Adventure, and Romance in Regency Virginia
and the alphabetical *Regency Rakes & Rebels* novellas
Lady Annabelle's Abduction
Lady Barbara & the Buccaneer
Lady Caroline, the Corsair's Captive

Music Links & Credits

Use this QR code to hear the original songs performed in this book by Quasi & Company and live by Big Sixteen.

Film Noir copyright (c) by Jeremy Brown
Do What You Do copyright (c) by Billy Conway
Dynamite Wheels copyright (c) by Joel Gramolini Cage
I Hope You Get Home All Right copyright (c) by Evan Harriman

Intro: Tom Stoppard, *Rosencrantz & Guildenstern Are Dead*, © 1969; published by Fraser & Dunlop (Scripts) Ltd, London; p. 28.

Ch. 1: Joni Mitchell, "Free Man in Paris," © 1973, Crazy Crow Music, released 1974 on *Court and Spark.*

Ch. 5 ff: pp. 55, 67, 69-70, 71, 196, 236, 252, 317, 339: Cory's referring to T.S. Eliot's "The Love Song of J. Alfred Prufrock," published June 1915 in *Poetry* & 1917 in *Prufrock and Other Observations*, Egoist Press, London.

Ch. 7: p. 81: Grace Slick, "White Rabbit," recorded in 1966 by Jefferson Airplane, released in 1967 as a single, then on *Surrealistic Pillow.*
 p. 85: Billie Holiday, "Fine and Mellow," 1939 Commodore single.

Ch. 8 ff: p. 95: "Dancing in the Street," Marvin Gaye, William "Mickey" Stevenson, & Ivy Jo Hunter, first recorded by Martha & the Vandellas, 1964 Gordy Records single.
 "Street Fighting Man," Mick Jagger & Keith Richards, rec. by The Rolling Stones, released 1968 as London Records single & on *Beggars' Banquet.*

Ch. 12: p. 150: "The Ballad of Davy Crockett, music by George Bruns, lyrics by Thomas W. Blackburn, recorded by The Wellingtons for Walt Disney Studios' ABC TV series *Disneyland*, released by Walt Disney Records,1954.

Chs. 18 & 20: pp. 223 ff: Cory and Marian are quoting from "Sunday Morning" by Wallace Stevens, first published November 1915 in *Poetry* magazine in abbreviated form, then complete in Stevens's 1923 collection *Harmonium*, Alfred A. Knopf, NY.

Ch. 28: p. 317 ff: "When You Wish Upon a Star," original lyrics by Ned Washington, recorded with music by Leigh Harline in 1939 for the 1940 Walt Disney film *Pinocchio,* single & album released by Victor and EMI.

Chs. 30-31, pp. 341-342, 357 ff: Cory, Terry, and Dan quote from the 1942 film *Casablanca*, a Hal B. Wallis Production directed by Michael Curtiz, adapted by a series of screenwriters from the unstaged play *Everybody Comes to Rick's* by Murray Burnett & Joan Alison.

Don't miss Cory Goodwin's previous adventure,
Silent Night Violent Night:

As I swung out of Copley Square onto the Mass Pike, the band on my radio swung into "Hernando's Hideaway." Desultory snowflakes were drifting through the orange sky like petals. Half an inch, the weatherman predicted. I'd picked this station because Oxbridge, Connecticut, is a three-hour drive from Boston and the rest were all playing Christmas songs.

My dad taught me "Hernando's Hideaway" longer ago than I care to remember. He'd stand me on his shoes and we'd sing it together as we tangoed across the parquet floor of our Manhattan living room. Dad's a ballroom virtuoso. As my mom says, he'll always have that to fall back on when he irks the State of New York into revoking his detective license.

What I hadn't noticed until now is that Robert Frost wrote "Stopping By Woods on a Snowy Evening" to the same tune:

My lit, -tle horse, must think it queer
To stop, without, a farmhouse near . . .

Try getting that out of your head when your alternatives are "The Little Drummer Boy" and "Jingle Bell Rock."

At Route 128 the projected snowfall rose to an inch. OK, I thought. No problem. Being a media person myself, I'd thrown my heavy boots in the car just in case. I've spent enough nights stranded in airports and motels to take weather forecasts with a bag of salt.

Dinner around seven-thirty, Lilah Darnell—or, rather, Lilah Easton—had told me on the phone. Cocktails whenever you get here. Come early, Cory, OK?—so we can catch up before the horde arrives.

Right. I was still too astonished to grapple with details. Lilah in suburbia? Hostessing a semiformal dinner party? Never mind that this was a fate we'd been groomed for since birth. The core of Lilah's and my friendship was our vow, copied from Jackie Bouvier (later Kennedy, later Onassis): *Never to be a housewife.* And now the notorious Delilah, legend of the Ivy League, was happily married to a textbook publisher? Unthinkable! You might as well imagine Jerry Garcia designing neckties, or Bobby Seale writing a cookbook.

It must be fifteen years since I'd seen her. Not often after we left college, in the wake of the Vietnam war. Lilah was my senior sister when I was a freshman: back then, a vast age gap. Over the years we'd become contemporaries. Sisters again, too, evidently, or why would she ferret through the Old Girl Network to find me?

The other question—why was I driving halfway across New England to see her?—had more than one answer. Curiosity, certainly. I'd picked Lilah Darnell for my role model before that term existed. She was bold, brilliant, and beautiful—just the kind of uncommon woman I planned to become at Mount Holyoke College. My second week on campus she electrified the grapevine by dumping Harvard's class president for a local woodworker. In January she flew to Japan to spend semester break studying calligraphy and the tea ceremony. In March she won a summer apprenticeship at a foundry in Perugia. Her plan after graduation was to become a famous sculptor, start an artists' commune, and launch a series of international affairs.

With this Amazon for my mentor I flourished. When Lilah sold a terra-cotta demon to a New York collector, I caught a bus to Boston and pitched my first story idea to Phases. While she skied the Alps, I covered the D.C. demonstration against President Nixon's bombing of Cambodia. She chiseled, I wrote; she exhibited, I published. Shortly after Phases hired me as a stringer, I received a handmade invitation to her wedding in the East Village. There we sat up half the night promising each other that our love lives would never overshadow our work. Several years later she turned up on my Back Bay doorstep, divorced; praised my series on urban gentrification, bought me a dinner worth a month's rent, and left me a baggie of ganja from her Jamaican lover. That was the last I'd heard from Lilah until her surprise reappearance in Connecticut.